She looked beautiful. That much hadn't changed.

But it was the *only* thing that hadn't changed.

"How's Toby doing?" she asked as she popped the top on a can of Rowdy's favorite soda.

"Sleeping again. He's really cute. Still sucking his fist, even when he's napping."

Angelica handed Rowdy the soda and took Toby into her arms, landing a soft kiss on her baby's cheek before gently placing him in his car seat so she and Rowdy would have their hands free to eat.

"Still your favorite?" she asked, gesturing toward his soda can.

He lifted the can in salute. "I'm surprised you remembered."

Another flash of pain crossed her gaze. "I remember a lot, if truth be told."

So did he.

And he really, *really* wished he didn't. Because with every unexpected glimpse into their past, every unanticipated memory, it became harder and harder to catch a breath.

He hadn't been ready to see her again.

And he wasn't sure he ever would be.

A *Publishers Weekly* bestselling and award-winning author with over 1.5 million books in print, **Deb Kastner** writes stories of faith, family and community in a small-town Western setting. She lives in Colorado with her husband and a pack of miscreant mutts, and is blessed with three daughters and two grandchildren. She enjoys spoiling her grandkids, movies, music (The Texas Tenors!), singing in the church choir and exploring Colorado on horseback.

Jill Lynn pens stories filled with humor, faith and happily-ever-afters. She's an ACFW Carol Award–winning author and has a bachelor's degree in communications from Bethel University. An avid fan of thrift stores, summer and coffee, she lives in Colorado with her husband and two children, who make her laugh on a daily basis. Connect with her at jill-lynn.com.

And Cowboy Makes Three

Deb Kastner

&

The Rancher's Surprise Daughter

Jill Lynn

LOVE INSPIRED

INSPIRATIONAL ROMANCE

LOVE INSPIRED®

INSPIRATIONAL ROMANCE

ISBN-13: 978-1-335-20197-3

Recycling programs
for this product may
not exist in your area.

And Cowboy Makes Three &
The Rancher's Surprise Daughter

For questions and comments about the quality of this book, please contact us at CustomerService@Harlequin.com.

Love Inspired
22 Adelaide St. West, 40th Floor
Toronto, Ontario M5H 4E3, Canada
www.Harlequin.com

Printed in U.S.A.

CONTENTS

AND COWBOY MAKES THREE 7
Deb Kastner

THE RANCHER'S SURPRISE DAUGHTER 219
Jill Lynn

AND COWBOY MAKES THREE

Deb Kastner

To my dear friend Lisa Palmer. We've kept each other sane through the years and I am blessed to call you my friend. You are one of the strongest people I know. Keep fighting the good fight!

But I trusted in thee, O Lord: I said, Thou art my God.
My times are in thy hand.
—*Psalms* 31:14–15

Chapter One

Angelica May Carmichael had been duped.

By her own grandmother.

She looked around and sighed in exasperation. This wasn't a picnic.

Or rather, this wasn't *just* a picnic, though there were brightly colored baskets covered in ribbons dotting the lawn all across the community green.

Not a picnic. *Picnics*.

And this wasn't a quiet, personal outing with Granny's best friend, Jo Spencer, as Angelica had been given to expect, either. Not that an outing with the boisterous old redhead who owned Cup O' Jo's Café could ever be labeled as *quiet*. That woman wouldn't know quiet if it bit her on the nose.

But a private picnic?

Yeah, not so much.

In hindsight, Angelica realized she should have gone with her gut feeling and headed straight to Granny's ranch instead of stopping in at Cup O' Jo's to let Jo know she'd arrived safely. A phone call would have sufficed.

But no. Jo had been adamant she come straight to the

café, sounding a bit *too* enthusiastic about seeing her again. Everything about Jo Spencer was enthusiastic, but her suggestion had been overanimated even for Jo.

She'd even anticipated Angelica's hesitation, telling her to slip through the back door of the café. She'd assured her that she wouldn't be seen by any customers, and that her nephew, Chance, the cook who would no doubt be in the kitchen, would keep their secret. He wasn't much of talker, anyway.

If only she hadn't been in such a hurry to get into town and out again without being seen that she hadn't recognized the signals, the internal alarms blaring in her head.

Their meeting was only supposed to be her and Jo. Having been Granny's best friend, Jo understood Angelica's dilemma at returning to Serendipity at all—or at least Angelica had thought she had.

"Oh, honey, welcome back," Jo had said, hugging her so hard it pressed the breath right out of her lungs. "And let me see sweet Toby."

Jo had exclaimed over the newborn and then had handed her a letter written by her recently deceased granny, addressed with only Angelica's first name and scribbled in Granny's chicken-scratch handwriting.

"Consider it a last request," Jo had suggested.

Directions?

More like a cryptic note.

Picnic With Jo.

It was a strange thing to ask, but Angelica figured it was the least she could do since she hadn't been able to be there for Granny's last days—or even her funeral. If she hadn't followed the instructions out of love for Granny, she would have followed them out of guilt.

Which was why she had found herself smack-dab in

the middle of a full-fledged town event, Toby tucked into a front pack.

Serendipity did their parties up right, and, as usual, nearly everyone in town was present, enjoying every moment of the event. Here in Serendipity, a person could expect to find a lot of love and laughter.

But even as a youth, Angelica had struggled to capture the happy spirit of the town celebrations. And no wonder. For as long as she could remember, she'd been the town pariah, as well as her family's.

And after the catastrophic series of events that sent her fleeing Serendipity on the eve of her own wedding rehearsal, well, she didn't expect *anyone* to forgive her— least of all her ex-fiancé, sheep farmer Rowdy Masterson.

Standing right in the middle of a large crowd of people, most of whom had known her back in the day and had no doubt *not* forgotten her or her mistakes, was exactly the type of situation Angelica had most wished to avoid.

Thankfully, the event in progress was an auction, with Jo as auctioneer. Something about making money for a new senior center. Everyone was busy watching the platform, where one of the young bachelors on the docket was flexing his biceps for a very appreciative crowd.

Just as long as it kept *her* out of the limelight, she was good. She'd come back home to Serendipity on the sly, for one weekend only, with a deliberate and strategic agenda. Since she would be staying at Granny's now abandoned sheep farm, she hadn't expected to see anyone other than Jo Spencer, who had been named the executor of Granny's estate, and Granny's lawyer, Matthew MacPherson, who would guide her in whatever next steps she needed to take to fulfill the terms of Granny's will—and to sell the ranch.

She'd most definitely had no intention of interacting with all the people who'd known her *back then*. People who would stand as judge and jury on the way she'd lived her life—especially since she'd arrived back in town with a baby in tow and no ring on her finger.

She didn't understand what was going on right now. She and Granny had planned to get together this precise weekend, even before Granny's health had taken such a downhill spiral. She had the sinking feeling Granny had something planned for this auction, something that Jo was now tasked with making sure Angelica followed through on.

Angelica might not be able to avoid the crowd today, but she prayed with her whole heart that she'd at least be able to steer clear of Rowdy. She didn't want to be responsible for suddenly triggering thoughts in Rowdy of a painful past he would no doubt rather forget.

She didn't want to hurt him. Not for the world.

Because long ago, in her youth, she had been in love with him, believing they were soul mates who would grow old together, live happily-ever-after.

Until she'd ruined everything.

Anyway, he'd probably moved on with his life. Perhaps he had even married and started a family. She'd been too ashamed to ask Jo how Rowdy was doing. She was grateful that, so far, she hadn't laid eyes on him, and she hoped to keep it that way.

Her stomach churned like a combine across her nerves and it was all she could do not to be sick. Not for the first time that day, she wondered if she ought not leave before someone recognized her.

Her soft pink hoodie was made of a light cotton material, but she felt uncomfortably warm and stifled as she stood near the back of the crowd on the small-town community green, attempting to remain incognito while surreptitiously watching to make sure Rowdy was no-where in the vicinity.

Up to this point, no one had appeared to take much notice of her, as everyone's attention was still completely absorbed in what was taking place upon the wooden plat-form currently serving as an improvised auction site.

Serendipity, Texas's First Annual Bachelors and Bas-kets Auction was already well under way, with many bachelors—and several married men, as well—already lassoed off the stage and into the care of their winning bidders, ladies beaming and cheering in delight over their triumphant purchases.

What had started as a regular bachelor auction had quickly expanded to include married men offering their skills at fixing dilapidated houses or old cars. The la-dies could bid on whatever man had the skills to match their projects.

Several of the cuter bachelors had been purchased not so much for their practical skills as their good looks and the possibility of a date. The single ladies weren't about to pass up such a grand opportunity.

Not to be outdone by the men, the local women had offered to share decorated picnic baskets brimming with good, homemade country cooking with the fellows they won.

Which explained the picnic.

She wished Granny was still around to explain to her what all this was about. Why had Granny wanted her here?

But then, if Granny was still around, Angelica wouldn't be conspicuously standing in the middle of the community green, feeling as if she had a fluorescent sign flashing over her head announcing her return.

Prodigal Daughter's Homecoming.

Out of nowhere, guilt assaulted Angelica, burning her insides. Through no fault of her own, she'd had to miss the end of Granny's life and even her funeral. But that didn't stop her from feeling bad about it.

Regretful.

Too little, too late.

If only Granny had lived long enough to see this weekend with Angelica. How different life would be then.

She held on to her new faith by the tips of her fingers, but there was so much she still didn't understand. God's ways were different than man's, but how could He have let this happen, just when she'd discovered the joy of knowing Christ?

Granny was still supposed to be alive. When she'd suddenly fallen gravely ill, Angelica had wanted to rush to her side, but there had been complications with the pregnancy and she couldn't travel.

Granny had insisted everything would be okay.

But it *hadn't* been okay.

Granny had passed far too soon.

Oh, how she would have loved her namesake, precious Toby Francis Carmichael. Angelica's heart broke every time she thought about it.

They'd intended this weekend to be a special get-together so Granny could meet Toby, but she'd passed away the very day Toby was born.

Since Angelica's travel plans had already been made, she hadn't seen any reason to change or cancel them. She had come home to pay her respects and meet with the lawyer, not attend a party.

Get in and get out. And the less people who knew about it—about *her*—the better.

The whole atmosphere was charged with joy and excitement, but Angelica, with a baseball cap pulled low over her brow and her hoodie over that, wasn't feeling either one of those emotions.

It had been eight long, painful years since the last time she'd attended a Serendipity function.

Her heart clenched and her emotions took a nosedive. She'd never been anything more to this town than the token troublemaker, no matter how hard she'd tried to change people's opinions of her.

Eventually she'd stopped trying.

Despite Angelica's faults—and what she now realized was a defensively bad attitude—Granny had understood her.

And Rowdy had loved her.

Had being the operative word.

Her thoughts were abruptly called back to the present when Toby, tucked reassuringly close to her shoulder, sighed in his sleep and sucked on his fist, momentarily shifting Angelica's attention away from the platform. Toby was such a sweet, beautiful baby, a real blessing in every possible regard.

Granted, as his mother, Angelica knew she was a little bit biased.

"If I can have your attention, please," Jo announced, pounding a gavel against a podium that had been brought over from the town hall. "We still have several fellows lookin' to be bid on here and a senior center still needin' to be built. And who knows? The best guys might be yet to come. You don't want to miss out on your perfect match 'cause you're too busy jawin' with your neighbors."

Since Jo was serving as the auctioneer, she had ditched Angelica with not so much as a second glance, much less an explanation.

It shouldn't bother her to be left alone. She'd been on her own most of her adult life. But it hurt her nonetheless. Maybe because she felt she was underneath an unseen spotlight.

Or maybe because Jo was a friend.

Angelica had been left to the mercy of the throng as it grew tighter toward the platform, pushing her with them. Her anxiety level rose exponentially as she became farther engulfed by the crowd.

So much for a calm, peaceful picnic.

Angelica pulled Toby a little closer, murmuring soft nonsense words in his ear and tucking her head close to his, inhaling his sweet, soothing baby scent. She reassured herself with the thought that, very soon, this would all be over and she could hightail it out of town and back to Denver where she belonged.

Or not *belonged*, really. She didn't fit in anywhere. But at least she wasn't under the constant judgment she felt sure she would find here in Serendipity.

"All right, folks," Jo announced with a boisterous bounce in her step that sent her red curls bobbing. When the crowd didn't immediately quiet, she pounded her gavel on the podium several times until she was certain she had everyone's attention.

"Next up on the docket," she called, her voice overriding the little section of the crowd that was still speaking, "is a Serendipity fan favorite, especially among the ladies. Drumroll, please. Let's hear it for Rowdy Masterson!"

Angelica's breath froze in her lungs as she slowly raised her head.

Rowdy.

At the first sight of him, her heart jolted to life and then dropped like a boulder to the pit of her stomach, where it rumbled around disturbingly.

The crowd roared as Rowdy stepped up onto the makeshift wooden platform, his mouth creased in a friendly grin. Much had changed over the years, but not Rowdy's smile.

A shiver of awareness vibrated through Angelica at her first glimpse of the man she knew so well, and paradoxically, didn't know at all.

Rowdy.

Angelica cringed as he stepped forward, still slightly favoring his left leg when he walked.

So his injury had never completely healed, then. The inside of her head reverberated, her guilt clanging like a gong, and a wave of nausea washed through her.

Rowdy's injury?

That was all on her.

It was enough to shatter her heart all over again.

Yet another prayer left unanswered. She had so wanted Rowdy to be healed completely of his injuries. If it hadn't been for her pressing him to participate in the saddle bronc event he hadn't been prepared for, he wouldn't be limping in the first place.

Other than the way he clearly put additional effort into moving his left leg over his right, time had been good to him. He was as handsome as ever, with thick wavy blond hair and warm blue eyes. Strong planes defined his masculine face, weathered from the sun and shaded with a couple days' growth of beard, giving him a rugged air.

He'd filled out in the years since she'd last seen him. His shoulders were broader and his muscles more defined from ranch work.

Not surprisingly, Rowdy didn't have to entertain the crowd by doing tricks or flexing his muscles to get their attention, as other men before him had done. He merely flashed them his signature toothy grin and gestured with his fingers for his rapt audience to increase their applause. The resulting hoots, catcalls and laughter made Rowdy's grin widen epically, and he tipped his hat in appreciation.

She remembered Rowdy's smile all too well, along with the whispered words of a happy future meant just for the two of them alone to share.

An ugly, dark feeling churned in her gut and she swallowed hard against the bile that burned in her throat.

She counted those days as nothing more than the naïveté of youth, when they still thought they had their whole lives before them and that they could weather any storm life threw at them as long as they were together.

When they'd believed they were invincible.

They hadn't yet comprehended that life could change in a moment.

But they'd learned. Oh, how painfully they'd learned.

It had only taken one second for their whole world to come crashing down around them.

One second.

And some things a person never recovered from—physically, emotionally or spiritually.

"Hush down, now," Jo called, rapping her gavel to regain control of the crowd. "Quiet!"

A group of laughing young women near the front of the crowd immediately started bidding on Rowdy, cheerfully one-upping each other before Jo could officially open the bidding.

"Wait, wait. No bids, please," Jo said, holding her hands up to stop the ladies from continuing.

The noise of the crowd immediately dropped to a hushed whisper.

"We've got a special case here with Rowdy, today," Jo continued. "I'm sorry to disappoint all you single ladies out there, but Rowdy has already been bought and paid for before this auction even began."

People gasped in astonishment.

"That's not fair," came a youngish-sounding female voice from the crowd. "No one else got to do that with any of the other men."

The crowd rumbled in agreement.

Angelica continued to keep her head low but her ears were perfectly attuned to Jo's words. She had a lot of questions that she was certain were echoing through the crowd.

Who had enough wherewithal to convince Jo to bend the rules of the auction?

Maybe a better question would be—*how?*

Jo tended to rule with an iron fist when she was in charge of an event—which she usually was. Between the two of them, Jo and her husband, Frank, the head of the town council, kept Serendipity running smoothly.

The old redhead was as stubborn as the day was long, and most people in town wouldn't even conceive of trying to change her mind once she'd gone and decided what was what. There was no arguing with her. And she was a stickler for rules—at least when it suited her.

Apparently today it suited her to make up her own new set of rules.

Jo snorted and shook her head, laughing at the negative reaction of the townspeople. She didn't even try to explain herself.

Not good old Jo Spencer.

Instead, she gestured for Rowdy to remove his hat, hitched up the rope in her palm—the one waiting for the winning bidder to lasso their catch with—and expertly flicked the noose around Rowdy, tugging the line tight around his shoulders.

Angelica was impressed with Jo's roping skills. The old woman ran a café, not a ranch. Clearly, she'd been practicing, and apparently, Angelica guessed, whatever was happening here with Rowdy was the reason. She'd known beforehand that she would have to trick rope this particular pony.

Without so much as looking back to see if he was following, she snapped the line taut and led him off the platform, the crowd parting before her.

He was being ushered off to who knows where like a lamb to the slaughter, Angelica thought.

Rowdy didn't resist. Why would he?

He had to be at least as curious as the murmuring crowd as to the identity of the woman who'd purchased him. *Someone* had cared an awful lot to go to the trouble, not to mention expense, of buying Rowdy in such an unconventional fashion.

Angelica didn't even want to know. And she absolutely ignored the sting of envy that whipped through her.

She had no right.

Rowdy was in her past, something she would rather not revisit right now.

Or ever.

She had enough on her plate just caring for Toby—and

now trying to figure out how best to put the Carmichael property to market and still honor Granny's last wishes.

She appreciated the money she'd been left along with the land, and she knew Granny had been thinking of Toby when she'd written that part of her will. But Toby was special and would never run a sheep farm—and Angelica certainly couldn't. She was the furthest thing from a rancher as it was possible for her to be.

She was a pastor's kid—and not a very good one— who had grown up to be simple hotel banquet server. Not the best job ever, but it paid the bills. And as a single mother, she couldn't afford to be picky.

The obvious solution was to sell the ranch that had been in the family for generations, and then pocket the money to use on Toby's future—a future that didn't include working with sheep.

Gramps had died young of a heart attack and Granny's only son, Angelica's father, Richard, had chosen the pastorate over sheep farming, leaving Granny Frances to work the land well past the time she ought to have retired.

Angelica would have been able to save the day merely by marrying Rowdy as she'd once intended to do. They'd planned to join their land together, since his family were sheepherders, as well.

But she hadn't.

And they didn't.

Instead, she'd run away and in the process dashed the hopes and dreams of more than one person.

That for even one moment she'd considered being a rancher's wife without the slightest idea of what that meant, how to work with the sheep and tend to the land, was just one of many ways she'd showcased her youthful ignorance.

It had been all about love, as defined by a woman too young to know how to recognize it.

Pie in the sky, a twinkle in her eye and zero common sense.

Whatever love was, that couldn't have been it.

Rowdy probably thanked the Lord every day that she hadn't saddled him with her utter incompetence as a rancher and a life partner, not to mention her bad reputation across town.

No. As bad as it had been, and still was, she had done him a favor, even if he now hated her for it.

She'd cut those ties. Then her parents had virtually disowned her. Granny was all she had left after she'd left town, and for many years, she'd been too ashamed even to reach out to her.

After she'd discovered she was pregnant with Toby, she had made her life right with Christ and she had reached out for Granny, who had welcomed her back with open arms and a loving and forgiving heart. But Angelica had never gotten back home to see her.

Not in time. Granny had passed away when Toby was born. She hadn't known that Toby would have special needs, be preciously different, and that God meant him for other things.

Extraordinary things.

But not sheep farming.

That was one prayer that would never be answered. Not as Granny had wanted it to be, anyway.

Angelica sighed. No matter how she looked at it, nor how much grief she felt at letting Granny Frances down, selling the ranch was the only conceivable answer to her dilemma—the only one that worked in the best interests of both Angelica and Toby. She was sorry not to be able to fulfill Granny's wishes, but that was just how it had to be.

She had to think of Toby first.

She still had no idea why Jo had brought her here to the auction, when she should be at Granny's ranch putting her affairs in order.

As far as she was concerned, it was well past the time for her to leave the community green and the auction behind and return to Granny's ranch house, where she could mull over her problems in private, release the thunder of emotions that had been hovering over her like a huge black storm cloud all morning.

With her decision made, she turned away from the platform and started walking back toward the street where she'd parked her sedan, knowing Frank would give Jo a ride home.

At the moment, the effervescent old redhead had her hands full with the auction—and, more specifically, with a rope full of Rowdy.

"Angelica May. Wait!"

Angelica skidded to a halt at Jo's use of her middle name. The only other person in the world who had called her Angelica May had been Granny, God rest her soul.

Tears sprang unbidden into Angelica's eyes at the many happy memories that instantly flashed through her mind. Granny loved Serendipity get-togethers and would have been bidding up a storm on behalf of the senior center—probably snatching up one of the good-looking young bachelors from right under the nose of a pretty, single woman.

And then, knowing Granny, she'd have him mucking stalls for her just so she could admire his muscular physique. Gramps had always been the only man for Granny and she'd never married again, but that hadn't meant she couldn't enjoy what the good Lord put in front of her eyes. She was old, not blind, she used to say, and then she and Jo Spencer would cackle over their shared joke.

With the well of deep emotion fractured, grief rolled into anger and Angelica stiffened. The scene unfolding in front of her became increasingly obvious with every step Jo took. She was dragging Rowdy right to Angelica's side.

Angelica didn't dash away, even if every nerve in her body was urging her to do so. Question after question pressed her down.

Why was this happening? Jo had to know there was no possible way any variation of this scenario would turn out well.

Angelica mumbled unintelligible words under her breath, quietly venting her frustration with the situation, but her throat closed around her air and it came out sounding like she was choking on carbonated soda.

So much for remaining incognito.

Now the whole town would know she was here. And she knew she wouldn't be welcomed back with open arms.

Especially not after what she'd done to Rowdy.

Even as a teenager, Rowdy had been popular in town. And from what she'd seen today, with everyone cheering and all those young ladies bidding for some time with him, that hadn't changed.

Rowdy was one of Serendipity's favorite sons.

Angelica...*wasn't*.

She hadn't been well liked, nor had she been understood. No one in town other than Granny, Jo and Rowdy had ever given her a fair shot.

Now everyone would think she'd captured Rowdy at

auction in some underhanded fashion that was unfair to the rest of the crowd.

And the fact that she'd shown up in town unmarried and with a baby?

This was *so* not going to work out well for her.

Oh, why had she ever come home to Serendipity at all?

She turned in time to see Rowdy digging in his heels, his cowboy boots raising dust. His brow was deeply furrowed and his lips were set in a hard line.

Yep. Not happy to see her.

Surprise, surprise.

Jo, however, wasn't taking Rowdy's reluctance as an answer. The more he balked like a mule, the harder she pulled. She stopped in front of a gaping Angelica and dropped the rope into her hand, pressing a sealed envelope into her palm at the same time.

"This particular letter is addressed to the both of you," Jo informed them, pointing to Granny's unmistakable script on the front of the envelope.

Angelica and Rowdy.

Angelica folded it in two and shoved it into the back pocket of her jeans without another look. Her mind was turning so fast she was getting dizzy. She couldn't get her head around what all this meant.

Buying Rowdy at auction before the auction even started. Leaving a note for the two of them.

What part did Granny have in all this? Was she the one who'd put out the funds to keep Rowdy off the auction docket? Had she been conspiring with Jo?

It looked like it. But why?

"I had Chance prepare a special meal for you two in the picnic basket in the far corner of the green by the southeast bench," Jo instructed.

Angelica nodded, but not because she'd needed the directions. She already knew where the picnic basket was. She'd been the one *toting* it, for crying out loud. Toby's baby carrier had been left near the basket, as well, and her sedan was parked on the street just beyond the bench.

She should have realized something was off when Jo didn't insist on taking her basket right into the center of the chaos. Jo wasn't the type to live any part of her life on the outskirts. She wanted to dive in and be smack in the middle of everything.

"Talk to each other," Jo suggested in a no-nonsense tone. "Don't let the past eat you up before you figure out where the present is taking you. Work it out. And don't forget to read what is in that envelope."

Then she turned and headed back to the podium without one more word of explanation.

Work *what* out?

Surely Jo should know Rowdy and Ange were far beyond mending fences.

Rowdy growled and yanked at the lasso, pulling it from Ange's hand. He realized only afterward that he'd probably left a rope burn on her palm as he struggled free of the noose, but if Ange noticed she didn't complain or alert him to the fact. It irked him that he felt a moment of remorse for giving her a second's pain.

Not when she'd given him a lifetime's worth.

He stood up to his full six-foot height and straightened his shoulders. He wasn't the tallest man at the auction, but at her five-foot-four-inch frame, he had plenty of height to glower down at her.

His chest burned with fire but his heart incongruously froze solid as anger sluiced through him like an ice storm in Antarctica.

Ange pushed her hoodie back and whipped off her ball cap, shaking her long blond hair out of their confines. Tilting her chin up, she met his gaze head-on.

It wasn't the expression of someone who was sorry for what she'd done. She still maintained the same solitary determination as ever, ready to run roughshod over anyone who stood in her way.

He wouldn't be a sucker twice.

She opened her mouth to speak, but he dug in before she could say a word.

"Ange," he ground out, his low voice sounding like sandpaper as he leaned back and crossed his arms over his chest, steel walls clamping down around his emotions. No way was he letting her in this time.

"Rowdy," she said, testing his name. She held out a hand to touch his arm but he grunted and twisted away.

But not before he realized she had a baby in her arms.

A *baby*.

"Rowdy," she said again.

His frown deepened at the sound of his name on her lips. It had been such a long time. Her voice was so familiar... and yet, then again, not so much.

He lifted the lasso and shook it under her nose.

"What did you just do?"

Rowdy's eyes briefly settled on the tightly swaddled infant in Ange's arms and then he flicked his gaze to her unadorned left hand. He was reeling with shock to see Ange suddenly back in Serendipity after all this time, especially with a baby in her arms.

Why had she come back?

And why *now*?

She hadn't come home once since the day she'd left him alone and brokenhearted at the altar. She hadn't even bothered to attend her own grandmother's funeral.

And yet now, for no reason Rowdy could guess, she was here, standing in the middle of the community green with a town function going on around her.

Home.

With a baby.

And for some inexplicable reason, she'd somehow finagled things with Jo so she could buy him at auction before the event had even started.

What was with that?

And the craziest thing of all was that she looked nearly as startled about this whole situation as he felt. As if she didn't know any more than he did about what was happening.

Which couldn't be true, since she'd set it all in motion in the first place.

Hadn't she?

It only remained to be seen as to why. What motive could Ange possibly have to want to see him again?

Or at all.

"I—er—" Ange stammered, shifting from foot to foot and lightly bouncing the baby she cradled in the sling. "What do you mean, what did I do? I didn't do anything."

He gritted his teeth to keep from snapping back at her. He could still turn and walk away, and not one person in town would blame him.

She'd come home for a reason, and it couldn't be anything good. If it was only about selling Granny's ranch to him, well, he and Ange didn't have to talk face-to-face for that. Their Realtors could handle all the details regarding the transaction and all he would have to do would be to sign the papers and fork over the funds to make it a done deal.

Or was it more complicated than that?

Was Jo somehow involved? Jo had purposefully forced their sure-to-be-stormy reunion into pretty much the most public arena possible, leaving Ange and Rowdy no choice but to speak to one another with practically everyone in Serendipity looking on.

And then there was the mysterious letter Jo had given Ange—the one she'd immediately shoved into the back pocket of her jeans.

What was up with that?

Maybe Jo thought Rowdy and Ange ought to bury the hatchet, so to speak, although maybe that wasn't the best metaphor to use in this particular situation.

As if he'd listen to anything *Ange* had to say. She'd ripped his heart to shreds. A reconciliation between the two of them was never going to happen.

Full stop.

Not a relationship. Not a friendship. Nor even acquaintances, as far as he was concerned.

He didn't think he'd ever be able to completely forgive Ange for what she'd done, but he *had* put it all behind him. He'd made his peace and had moved on with his life.

Why dredge it up now?

To be completely honest, Rowdy hadn't been sure *how* he would feel if he ever saw Ange again—or if he'd feel anything at all.

Well, now he knew.

And he didn't like it.

As his past rose to meet him, anger and indignation waged a war in his chest, like dueling pitchforks, parrying back and forth, jabbing sharp points into his heart.

Then he took a breath and the stabbing pains morphed into an ache so deep it left a gaping hole in its wake.

How could merely seeing Ange again so easily stoke to flame all the emotions he'd thought he'd tucked away long ago?

He was an even-keeled man. Not much threw him off-balance one way or the other.

Except for one thing—one person.

Ange had the singular ability to knock him off-kilter. She'd always been able to do that.

In the past, he'd thought that was a good thing.

Now he knew better.

He remembered his helplessness and hopelessness when he watched her ride off on her horse after their wedding rehearsal—one of the matched set of horses meant for them to depart on after their wedding—leaving him quite literally in the dust.

She hadn't even had the courtesy to look back and wave goodbye.

And now she'd suddenly returned...*why?*

Rowdy was desperately attempting to corral the emotions stampeding through him like a herd of wild buffalo with a pack of wolves on their heels. It took all his effort to keep his voice low so he wouldn't startle the baby.

"What's the deal here, Ange? Why did you buy me at auction?" he whispered, his voice low and raspy.

Her blue eyes widened, her expression sincerely stunned.

Hurt even.

As if she had the right to be.

"Before I answer that question, I think we'd better take Jo's suggestion and head back to where the picnic basket is located. It's not a lot of privacy, but it'll give us a little more than we have standing here. I don't know about you, but I'm not feeling very comfortable right now with everyone's eyes on us and all of them listening to every word we say."

She nodded toward the crowd. True, many had turned back to watch the next bachelor take the stage—the twentysomethings who didn't remember the night Ange had single-handedly ended her tumultuous relationship with Rowdy.

But there were a few furtive glances and murmurs aimed their direction.

Rowdy shrugged. *He* wasn't the one who needed to feel uncomfortable. *He* hadn't done anything wrong. If some of the older townsfolk had long memories, that wasn't on him.

Still, he nodded in agreement and followed her to a bench well out of the main stream of the celebration, where a festive picnic basket bedecked with baby blue pastel ribbons was waiting for hungry picnickers—which Rowdy wasn't. His gut felt like lead.

An infant car seat and a yellow-giraffe-themed diaper bag covered the rest of the bench, marking it out for Rowdy and Ange's use.

Ange picked up the car seat and set it aside on the ground next to the bench, and then did the same thing for the diaper bag, gesturing for him to sit in the space she'd opened.

She remained standing, shifting from foot to foot in a slow, rhythmic rocking motion as she pressed a kiss to the forehead of the infant she was holding in her arms.

"Okay," she said, blowing out a breath. "I have no idea what just happened back there. Though I expect Jo might be able to answer that question, eventually."

"You aren't the one behind this—whatever *this* is? You didn't buy me behind everyone's back?"

"Absolutely not. Why would I do that? I only came to town to settle Granny's estate."

He wasn't sure he believed her, no matter how adamant her refusal. And though he didn't like it, the way she'd worded her statement about not wanting to buy him stung his ego.

"Well, you didn't bother to come to Granny Frances's funeral." He knew it sounded like an accusation, and maybe it was. "So I have to ask myself why you would suddenly show up now."

Pain flashed across her gaze and she shifted her eyes away from him.

"I couldn't come," she murmured.

He waited for more of an explanation, but none appeared to be forthcoming.

"Can you hold the baby for a minute while I set things up?" she asked, pressing the infant into the crook of his arm before waiting for his answer.

"Uh. Yeah. Sure," he said, seconds after the fact.

He shifted uncomfortably. He didn't know how to hold a baby—at least a human infant—and he felt like an awkward giant made of all thumbs. His gut churned.

He was used to bottle-feeding little lambs, and this tiny bundle of humanity lying in the crook of his arm was a whole other thing entirely.

"His name is Toby." Ange's rich alto was warm and filled with pride and wonder when she spoke of her son. "Toby Francis, after Granny."

Rowdy pushed the pastel green receiving blanket off the baby's forehead so he could see his face better, and a jolt of realization slashed through him.

Toby was…

Ange hadn't said…

"Yes," she affirmed in a whisper, reading the recognition in his eyes. "Toby has Down syndrome."

Rowdy's throat tightened. He was even less familiar with Down syndrome than he was with babies in general, but while this little guy was alert he wasn't fussy, and after a moment, Rowdy's heart calmed.

"He's beautiful," he said, and meant it.

Rowdy brushed a finger over Toby's silky white-blond hair, a shade lighter than his mother's. His almond-shaped blue eyes had popped open at the sound of Rowdy's deep voice and were now staring up at him with interest. The little guy's mouth was nearly wide enough to fit his entire tiny fist, and he was loudly sucking on his knuckles.

Ange's eyes widened at Rowdy's compliment, as if she didn't hear kind remarks very often. And maybe she didn't. People were strange when it came to anything or anyone different than they were.

Special needs freaked some people out, but it didn't bother Rowdy. As far as he was concerned, all humans carried the same dignity because they were made in the image of God. Different was beautiful.

She smiled sincerely, apparently satisfied that he meant what he said.

Rowdy *always* meant what he said.

"I know, right?" she whispered after a moment. "He's such a sweetheart. The biggest blessing in my life."

As little as Rowdy knew about babies, his being a perennial bachelor, he knew enough to realize infants were a challenge for any new mama or daddy, even the experienced ones. He'd watched all of his friends get married and have babies, and seen their slow adjustments to the learning curve called parenting.

Rowdy's closest friend, Danny Lockhart, complained nonstop about having to stay up all night with a fussy infant who had her days and nights mixed up—and then in the next breath he'd proudly show her off, forgetting whatever trials he faced at two o'clock in the morning.

So it seemed strange to Rowdy that Ange would choose to return to Serendipity, where she had no real support as a single mother. Her parents had moved away long ago, not that they were ever terribly supportive of her. And he doubted, given the past, that Ange had many friends here, either, as horrible as that was to think.

Was Toby's father in the picture?

If so, where was he? Holding down the fort in Denver while Ange visited Serendipity?

She didn't have a ring on her finger. Rowdy didn't have much use for men who didn't marry the woman they intended to start a family with.

But that was a discussion for another time.

Rowdy had so many questions that he didn't even know where to begin.

As Ange prepared the picnic lunch, Rowdy studied her face. The telltale dark circles under her eyes and the lines of stress creasing her brow suggested her life hadn't been easy on her.

She looked older than her twenty-nine years, but she was nonetheless beautiful enough to make Rowdy's stomach flip as he attempted to rein in the physical attraction he'd always felt toward her.

That much, at least, hadn't changed. He'd always seen the inherent beauty in her that she didn't see when she looked in the mirror.

But it was the *only* thing that hadn't changed. And he had no idea what she saw when she looked in the mirror these days.

"How's Toby doing?" she asked as she popped the top on a can of Rowdy's favorite soda.

"Sleeping again. He's really cute. Still sucking his fist, even when he's napping."

Ange handed Rowdy the soda and took Toby into her arms, landing a soft kiss on his cheek before gently placing him in his car seat so she and Rowdy would have their hands free to eat.

"Still your favorite?" she asked, gesturing toward his soda can.

He lifted the can in salute. "I'm surprised you remembered."

Another flash of pain crossed her gaze. "I remember a lot, if truth be told."

So did he.

And he really, *really* wished he didn't. Because with every unexpected glimpse into their past, every unanticipated memory, it became harder and harder to catch a breath.

He hadn't been ready to see Ange again.

And he wasn't sure he ever would be.

Chapter Two

Angelica settled cross-legged on the bench next to Rowdy and set her plate in her lap.

"It isn't just the soda." He gestured with his fork to incorporate all the food on his plate. "This is my favorite meal—barbecued pork ribs, fried okra and mashed potatoes in a thick brown gravy."

"The meal was my suggestion, but I can't take credit r the cooking. I can't cook a thing. On my own, I sub st on deli chicken and pizza made from spaghetti sauce nd cheese toasted on a slice of bread."

It only now struck her, as she was going on and on about her usual diet—which Rowdy could probably not care less about—that she had unconsciously asked for Rowdy's favorite meal when Jo had asked her what to pack for the picnic today.

Her breath hitched. All these years, and Rowdy's favorites had still come to mind.

"This delicious meal is all straight from Cup O' Jo's. Chance cooked the food and Jo packed and decorated the picnic basket."

"A baby theme? Clever."

"It's cute," she agreed. "Will you please say grace for us before we start the meal?"

His fork clattered to his plate as he gaped at her in astonishment.

Angelica wasn't surprised by his response. She had grown up a PK—a preacher's kid. Back when she and Rowdy were dating, she was as rebellious as the day was long and wanted nothing to do with church.

Or God.

That had all changed the day she found out she was pregnant with Toby. Suddenly God was very real to her. How else could she explain the tiny human being fearfully and wonderfully formed within her womb?

When she'd told Josh, the father of her child, about their baby, he had scoffed at her, called her horrible names and insisted the child wasn't his. When he walked out the door, he had walked out of her life. And good riddance to him.

Josh had known he was the only man in her life, the only man she had been with ever, because she had only given in to him after months of pressure. But he hadn't wanted to accept the responsibility of fatherhood or the effects it would have on his freewheeling lifestyle. He didn't want to be tied down with a family.

So he'd simply denied the truth and disappeared.

In a way, Angelica felt she deserved that rejection and in the long run God had been looking out for her. It was better for her and her baby not to have been permanently locked into what had never been a healthy relationship to begin with.

God alone had been her constant companion after Josh had left her. She had a few work acquaintances from the high-end hotel in which she was a white-gloved banquet server, but by throwing herself into Denver's nightlife she'd never made any real connections, and she'd let those few friendships lapse when she'd started dating Josh.

Angelica pulled her thoughts from the past and focused her attention on Rowdy.

"I know what you're probably thinking. Have I really changed, or am I just trying to unsettle you by asking you to say grace?"

His gaze widened and then his brow furrowed, a frown gathering on his lips. He put his plate aside.

"You said it, not me."

Toby stirred and Ange set her uneaten food aside to scoop him into her arms. She shuffled through the diaper bag until she found a bottle of formula, giving it a good shake to make sure it was well mixed.

"Discovering I was pregnant with Toby changed my world," she said, glancing up at Rowdy. "And I mean all of it. I realize I've made a lot of mistakes in my past. I've hurt people—"

Her gaze dropped to Rowdy's hands. He was clenching the edge of the bench until his knuckles turned white.

She felt bad for him, but unlike with Josh, she had no fear of him losing his temper. Unless time had completely changed him, he wasn't a man who would fly off the handle. He was self-controlled and even tempered, even with the woman who had broken his heart.

"Hurt *you*," she finished, swallowing hard.

His muscles tightened until his shoulders visibly rippled with tension, and her own stress increased.

"Is this some kind of twelve-step program or something? You're here because you have to make amends?"

"What? No. I'm here to pay respects to Granny, since I was having Toby on the day she passed away. That, and to settle the estate. I already know there is nothing I can do or say that would change how you think about me and what I did to you."

Angelica knew her words alone would mean nothing to the man sitting next to her on the bench, the man she'd once loved with all her heart and who had once loved her. He had been prepared to commit his life to her.

He would never know how much she'd sacrificed, and all because she'd loved him.

Toby batted the bottle in her hand, reminding her that she had a hungry boy to feed.

"I'm sorry. There you go, sweetheart," she murmured, pressing the bottle to Toby's lips.

"He's a noisy eater," Rowdy observed, apparently deciding to keep their conversation at a casual level for the time being.

"He sometimes has trouble latching on and getting his lips where they need to be to get good suction."

"Because he has Down syndrome?"

Ange nodded, but she wasn't dismayed by the fact. Toby was just Toby, her son. "Every day is a new adventure with this little guy."

"And your parents? How do they like their new grandson? They must be proud."

"They don't know about him yet," she admitted, her heart clenching and heat rising to her face. "You probably know that they left the parish here in Serendipity for a small town in Wyoming shortly after I left town.

"My dad pretty much disowned me when I acted so awfully to you in such a public way, because in his mind my actions rubbed off on him. And I guess in a way he is right about that. I was the reason he took a new pastorate far away from Serendipity. I've tried reaching out to Mom, but she doesn't dare cross him, not even for my sake."

"So, you don't see them then?"

"No. Not at all."

He shook his head. "That's a shame."

"It is." She shook her head. "It's frustrating, but I take full responsibility for my own actions. I don't like to see my family torn apart, but I can't blame them for distancing themselves from me."

She scoffed. "I thought I was so worldly, leaving Serendipity behind and going off on my own, but in truth, I was way out of my element from the day I got to Denver. A preacher's kid from a small town? I had no idea what I was getting into and was practically swallowed alive. At first, I didn't want to stay at all.

"But of course, there were even more reasons I couldn't come home—er, back to Serendipity—when things in Denver didn't turn out like I'd planned. Not after...well..."

His eyes snapped to hers. She held his gaze but then had to look away for a moment as guilt flooded through her.

With a deep breath, she returned her gaze to his.

"Obviously, I had no intention of seeing you today. But here we are."

"Here we are," he repeated. He narrowed his eyes on her. "So now what?"

Rowdy's emotions were run ragged and frankly, he had had enough. It was all he could do not to bolt from the scene like a skittish lamb.

He lifted his bruised and battered heart to the Lord. *God, help me.*

A short, concise prayer that said it all.

Ange had returned to Serendipity, no longer the pretty girl with a chip on her shoulder who he'd once known and loved, but a striking, mature woman—and a mother with a newborn baby who had seen her share of rough times.

She hadn't said anything about Toby's father, but Rowdy knew better than to make any assumptions.

Right now, he just hurt, a relentless ache that started in his heart and radiated through his limbs.

"The envelope," Ange said, digging into her back pocket. "Maybe that will give us a clue."

He raised his brows. "A clue to what?"

"What we're supposed to be talking about. Jo slipped me an envelope when she handed me the—er—lariat. It's from Granny and addressed to both of us. The first one only had my name on it."

"There are more than one?"

Ange sniffed softly. "Believe me, I wouldn't be wandering around in public if I'd had any choice in the matter."

"I don't understand."

"Yeah, me neither, exactly. I only came to town to pay my respects and get the sale started on Granny's ranch."

"So, you are selling, then?"

Her gaze widened. "Of course. What on earth would I do with a sheep farm?"

"I'm an interested buyer, you know."

She nodded. "I figured. But I also assumed I could take care of the estate and the paperwork without actually having to see you—" Her words skidded. "I mean, any potential buyers. Instead, I'm out and about at a packed town function. Which is exactly where I don't want to be. Especially not making the kind of scene I ended up making. I absolutely didn't have any intention of seeing you again."

"So why are you here, then?"

"The letter in the first envelope had very specific instructions. It was addressed to me from Granny. Jo said that Granny would understand if I wanted to sell the ranch, but that she requested I follow the instructions in the envelope. Kind of like a last wish, I guess."

"And that said…?"

"Picnic With Jo."

"That's it?"

"That's it."

"Wow. That's about as vague as it gets. But Jo knew a lot more about what Granny was asking than you did. And she didn't even hint about what you were walking into?"

"Not one word. She must have been busting up inside not being able to tell me anything."

"So you didn't know anything about the auction being today? Or, most especially, about buying me at auction before the event even got off the ground?"

"No, but Jo certainly did. And so, I think, did Granny. Before she passed on, she requested that I visit her on this particular weekend. I'm wondering if she wanted me to attend this auction all along, even if she'd still been here to come with me."

"You think we've been set up?"

Ange frowned and nodded, looking none too pleased by the thought.

"But why?"

She shrugged. "Your guess is as good as mine. Maybe Granny wanted to make sure the sale of the ranch went smoothly."

"That doesn't feel like enough of an explanation. We didn't have to meet at the auction to work out the details of our real estate transaction. And why go to all the trouble of the cryptic letter? Why not just spell it all out?" he asked.

Ange held up the second envelope, which Rowdy could now clearly see had both of their names scrawled on it.

"I have no idea. Here's hoping this one will tell us exactly where we're supposed to go from here."

Toby worked the bottle from his mouth with a gurgle and Angelica shifted him to her shoulder.

She pushed the envelope in Rowdy's direction. "I guess we won't know until we open it. Why don't you do the honors, since I've got my hands full?"

Rowdy plucked the envelope from her grasp and gingerly opened it, unfolding the single tri-folded sheet of typing paper. He wasn't sure he even wanted to be any part of this, but Granny Frances, as she'd insisted he call her back when he was a teenage boy dating her granddaughter, had been a huge influence in his life. He couldn't let her down now.

She was a stubborn woman who'd continued to manage her ranch for as long as possible, saying it gave her great joy to be with her animals and her pain wasn't going to keep her down.

But eventually, it had become too hard even for one as strong and stoic as Granny Frances.

In her final weeks, when she'd gotten too sick to care for herself, much less her flock, on her own, a palliative care nurse had come to look out for Granny Frances and Rowdy had stepped in and done the ranch work for her.

In reality, at this point he was already running Granny

Frances's ranch as if it was his own. As long as another buyer with deep pockets didn't sweep in, which wasn't likely in a town as small as Serendipity, it was just a matter of signing the papers to make the land his legally as well as practically.

His gaze quickly took in the words on Granny's missive and he shook his head.

If they were expecting answers, this letter didn't contain them.

These words were, in fact, the exact opposite.

"Feed My Sheep."

Three words in Granny Frances's handwriting.

Three lousy words.

"Great," Ange groaned. "Another cryptic note. What do you suppose this one means?"

Rowdy ran a hand across the stubble on his jaw. "It sounds like something out of the Holy Scriptures. You know, when Jesus was speaking to Peter and kept telling him to feed his sheep? You think this is some kind of secret message?"

"I don't know. I'm not even certain Granny was lucid when she wrote this stuff down. Maybe what she really meant to convey didn't quite translate to paper."

Rowdy hoped that was the case, but he sincerely doubted it. Life was never that simple, and he'd been there during Granny Frances's final days. She had been coherent until her very last moments, when she had given her soul up to Jesus.

"No, I don't think so," he said. "Whatever this letter means, she knew what she was doing when she wrote it. I'm sorry you weren't able to be there with her during her last moments, but I was, and I can tell you definitively that she was fully lucid all the way up to the end."

His words weren't quite the accusation they had been earlier. "The last word she breathed was *Jesus*. Her expression was so peaceful. There is absolutely no doubt in my mind her Savior was there waiting with open arms to welcome her into heaven."

Tears sprang to Ange's eyes and she dashed them back with her palm, while her face blotched with red and purple. Rowdy thought she might be having trouble holding herself together. She'd always been a private person and her struggle with grief was real, even if everything else she'd ever told him varied from the truth in some way.

And the worst part was, seeing her tears tore at him, ripping into his chest.

He didn't know how he felt about her expressing her grief. When Ange had left Serendipity, it had been for good. She had not even come to visit Granny Frances.

Not once.

And though he now understood why she had missed Granny's funeral, that didn't make the whole situation any less confusing.

Here she was now, trying to make things right when it was too late for her to do so.

Too late for Granny Frances.

And too late for him.

For *them*.

He swallowed hard, but a smile lingered on his lips despite the fresh wave of grief.

He stammered quickly over his next sentence, returning the conversation to safer grounds.

"J-Jo appeared to know exactly what was going on," he pointed out. "Maybe we should just toss the letter and ask her straight out. I'll bet she has answers."

"Oh, I intend to," Ange assured him.

"Although how much she'll divulge is another thing entirely. If she made a pact with Granny Frances, we are only going to learn what your granny wanted us to know."

"That's right. So I guess we have to play sleuth and see if we can figure it out on our own before we approach Jo on the matter."

"Well, the first note was literal, right?" he asked, trying to make logic out of the cryptic words. *"Picnic With Jo?"*

"Up to a point, it was. Obviously, there was a lot Granny left out. Intentionally, I suspect."

"So, what if this letter is the same? Maybe she really means you should feed her sheep."

"Me? I don't know the first thing about sheep." Her gaze widened and for a moment, she gaped at him. "There aren't any *sheep* at her ranch anymore, are there? She adored her sheep. I remember she used to lovingly refer to them as her woolies. She wouldn't let them starve. I guess I just assumed that since Granny knew she had a terminal disease, she'd have all her affairs in order and sell her stock off before she passed."

He bit on the inside of his cheek, wondering just how much he ought to tell her.

Any way he looked at it, Rowdy didn't like where this was going. The way he saw it, and the only interpretation that made any sense, was that Granny Frances's intention was for him to subtly introduce Ange to the ins and outs of ranch life, possibly hoping she'd decide to keep the land in the family.

But that was unfair, for so many reasons. For one thing, Ange was the furthest thing from a rancher ever, and she'd need a ton of help—assistance Granny Frances assumed would come from Rowdy.

And for another, though Granny Frances knew he had taken over her ranch out of love for her, she also had to have known he needed to expand if he was going to keep making a profit on his land.

They had never spoken about it, but joining their two ranches was the perfect answer to that dilemma. She would have had to have been blind not to recognize the hope he carried in his heart for the joining of the properties, and Granny Frances was as astute a woman as one could find anywhere.

"I've been taking care of her stock," he admitted, his thoughts working frantically.

Ange looked mortified. "You don't really think she wants you to teach me how to care for *sheep*, do you?"

He shrugged.

It crossed his mind that he could sabotage the plans to get Ange on board to keep the ranch, if that was what they were. After all, Ange deciding to do so was the exact opposite of what Rowdy wanted to happen.

But deep down, Rowdy knew he would never be so underhanded as to resort to anything as devious as that. It wasn't in his nature. Nor would God be happy with that kind of thinking—much less acting.

Besides, as far as he knew, Ange still agreed with him about how Granny Frances's estate should be handled—so there should be no conflict despite Granny Frances's note suggesting that Ange needed to learn to feed the sheep.

No. Ange wanted to sell her ranch.

To him.

And he wanted to buy.

It was a win-win, putting enough money in her pocket

to find a good place to live in the city and have some left over for Toby's long-term care.

It wasn't that he was afraid Ange would change her mind and decide to stick around. Ranch work was hard and dusty. If anything, *Feed My Sheep* would convince her that she should sell like nothing else might.

Even one day of herding sheep and mucking around in a smelly barn would be enough to send her running back to Denver faster than she could say "Giddyap." He would put his last nickel on the fact that she didn't even own a pair of mud boots.

And he *had* loved Granny Frances. That fact was cut-and-dried. If teaching Ange to feed Granny's sheep would honor the deceased's memory, then he would cowboy up and do it, even if every second in her presence was torture, plain and simple.

He just had to hold on to the knowledge that it wouldn't last forever. Whatever the outcome of this game Granny Frances was playing with them, it would end eventually.

He would hold fast to the idea that Ange had indicated she wanted to sell him the ranch. The sooner he cooperated with this—whatever *this* was—the sooner she would leave and he could take full ownership of Granny Frances's ranch and incorporate it into his own.

"You don't think—" Ange started, and then her sentence dropped off and her face drained of color. "This is the second envelope. Jo didn't say it was the *last* one. What if there are more letters after this one? More stuff she wants us to do, more riddles we have to figure out? Could this be some kind of outrageous scavenger hunt Granny is sending us on?"

Oh, no, no, no, no, no, no, no.

Rowdy shook his head voraciously as his thoughts denied the possibility.

"I don't think we ought to keep speculating on this bit. We need to go find Jo and clear up the confusion," he said. "There's no question that I want to honor Granny Frances's memory, but…"

"Exactly," she said, even though he hadn't finished his sentence. "Whatever needs doing, needs doing quickly. I absolutely cannot stick around after this weekend. My flight back to Denver leaves tomorrow afternoon. I've got to return to my job on Monday. It's my first day back after my maternity leave. I'll lose my position for sure if I don't show up. My boss is a real stickler about stuff like that."

"What do you do?"

"I work in a five-star hotel as part of the dining staff for large, catered events. I'm one of those white-gloved banquet servers you encounter when you go to large meetings at a hotel. We have a lot of major corporations that come through, as well as conventions that meet there."

"Sounds interesting."

"Not really. It's a lot of standing and people can get really snooty. But it pays the bills, and I can't afford to be picky. I'm not going to have the money to pay anything if I don't get back there on time. Oh, the joys of living from paycheck to paycheck."

Rowdy didn't know about that. He lived from season to season.

"How old is Toby?" Rowdy asked, as what Ange had said earlier suddenly clicked. She had indicated she'd missed Granny Frances's funeral because she was in the hospital having Toby, but that was only three weeks ago.

"Three weeks," Ange confirmed.

"Don't you get maternity leave for twelve weeks?" He had no idea where he'd pulled that information from. A television show, maybe. But it sounded fair enough.

She scoffed softly. "In the best of all worlds. I'm allowed to take twelve weeks, but my checkbook can't handle the money I'd lose. Now I have Toby to support. I can't afford to take off a whole twelve weeks. Three was pushing it."

Rowdy didn't know if Granny Frances had left Ange any money in her will, but it occurred to him that if they could get this deal done with the real estate, that would give Ange something to ease her load.

"Let's talk to Jo and see what we can do. The sooner, the better. It's possible that we will be able to work out some of the details about me buying Granny Frances's ranch, which would in turn save you the trouble of having to come back to Serendipity."

Her face reddened. "Pushy, much?"

He scowled and shook his head. He was trying to be nice and she was taking it all the wrong way.

"That's not what I meant. Am I mistaken? I thought that selling the ranch was what you wanted to do."

She sighed. "It is. I just don't like feeling as if you are corralling me out of town. You don't have to be brash about it. I get the hint."

She shook her head. "Don't worry. We'll just have to set aside the whole *Feed My Sheep* thing and let Jo know that we aren't going to continue. Surely, it can't be so important that we have to drop our entire lives to pursue it."

"Maybe not," he admitted.

"Well, like I said, I have to be on a plane tomorrow

afternoon anyway, so I can't keep playing this peculiar game even if I wanted to."

She smiled, but Rowdy could see the trouble she was having in curling her lips upward. "You'll be happy to know that I'll be out of your life tomorrow—and you'll never have to see me again."

Chapter Three

True to her word, Angelica took Toby and left Serendipity the next day. But by Friday afternoon, she had returned to her hometown without the slightest idea of what she was going to do next.

She had been telling the truth when she'd informed Rowdy that she didn't plan to pop back up in town anytime soon—or ever—but once in Denver she'd found that she couldn't set her time in Serendipity and with Rowdy aside as easily as all that.

In her heart of hearts, she wasn't sure she had done the right thing by returning to the big city and proceeding with selling Granny's ranch.

Not for herself, and not for Toby.

The whole envelope-deliveries-and-cryptic-messages thing felt like unfinished business. She'd left town without fulfilling Granny's request, and that really bothered her.

She hadn't fed any sheep yet.

Instead, she'd run away from the obligation. Just as she'd done before.

When the going got tough, Angelica bolted.

It was her modus operandi.

She hated to think that after all this time and experience, she hadn't changed. Worse yet, what she did affected Toby.

Was Toby really better off in Denver? Or was she just trying to take the easy way out?

No. She couldn't repeat her mistakes.

Not again.

Not even knowing Rowdy wouldn't be thrilled to see her. She'd simply have to explain her reasons for returning and hope he'd understand.

And she didn't even want to think about how the rest of the town would perceive her return, particularly driving a moving van filled with what little furniture she had, with her car hooked up behind.

Maybe that was part of the reason she had to go back. To prove to herself *and* the people of Serendipity that she had changed. That she was no longer the rebellious teenager and young adult, but that the Lord had touched her heart and altered her world. And that becoming a mother to Toby had made a substantial difference, as well.

She was putting Toby's crib together in the guest bedroom, Toby gurgling in the bouncer by her side, when the doorbell rang. She started in surprise.

She wasn't expecting anyone.

"Guess I'd better get that, yeah, little man?"

She moved Toby, bouncer and all, into the living room and opened the door to find a beaming Jo on the other side, her arms laden with a large box of prepared casserole dishes.

"What is all this?" she asked.

"You should have told me you were coming back," Jo chided, weaseling through the door and into the house without waiting for an invitation. "I had to hear it from the three old men that sit in their rockers outside Emerson's Hardware. They said they saw a moving van passing through and I knew it would be you."

Angelica didn't ask how she had known.

"I'm sure you have more than enough to do getting your furniture into Frances's ranch house all on your own. Give me an hour and I can round up some fellows to do the heavy lifting for you."

"Oh, no. That's okay. I've got most of it already done—or at least what I need for now. I had no use for the furniture I was using in my small apartment in Denver, so I sold it off. I've already unloaded everything I need for Toby."

She relieved Jo of the box of food, which was surprisingly heavy, and placed it on the kitchen counter.

"What is all this?"

Jo chuckled with glee.

"I simply mentioned to some of the ladies of the church that you'd been seen entering town with your moving van, and before I knew it, casseroles were coming in right and left."

Tears burned in Angelica's eyes.

"But I—I—" she stammered.

This was the last thing she'd imagined would happen—her neighbors, especially anyone from the church, offering their support.

"I know what you're thinking, dear." Jo wrapped her in a motherly bear hug. "It's going to be okay. Let it go, honey."

Try as she might, Angelica could no longer hold in her grief. This act of charity from people who had every reason to turn their backs on her broke her emotional dam wide. Sorrow for all she had lost, and all the mistakes she had made, flooded out of her. Jo simply patted her back and made quiet, reassuring shushing noises.

At length, she had no tears left to cry. She pulled back and brushed the tears from her eyes with her palms.

"I'm sorry for blubbering all over you," she said with a hiccup.

"That's what I'm here for, dear. Anytime you need a hug, or just to talk, I'm your woman."

"I know."

"So, it looks like you're moving in, then." It wasn't a question. In fact, Jo sounded as if it had been her idea in the first place.

"I am. I decided I needed to finish what I started here. I need some time to figure out what I'm going to do next."

"What about your job in Denver? Are you taking a leave of absence?"

Angelica laughed, but it sounded more like a snort.

"My boss at the hotel was none too crazy to hear I needed to be in Serendipity to work out the wrinkles in Granny's estate. I believe his exact words were, 'Don't expect a reference.'"

"Oh, no, dear. I'm so sorry."

"It's for the best. I had hoped for better, since I gave him the news face-to-face, but I suppose I can't blame him. When I asked for extended leave without notice, I put him short one banquet server, and the hotel was host-ing a dinner for an enormous Fortune 500 company con-ference that was arriving for the weekend."

"He'll live. Sometimes ya just gotta do what ya gotta do."

"Truthfully, I'm relieved to be rid of the high-stress job. Trying to keep the dishes flowing and the diners happy while management constantly looked over my shoulder isn't my idea of a good time, but I managed to get by on the wages I earned, at least until Toby came into my life."

"Babies are expensive," Jo said. "Diapers, clothes, supplement formula. And that's to say nothing of his crib and car seat."

"So true." Angelica had shifted most of her food budget to covering Toby's needs, and there were many days when she only ate one meal. Not ideal for a nursing mother.

But Granny's passing had changed everything, and Angelica knew Granny would be happy she had given her granddaughter a way out of the rat race, even if it wasn't quite what Granny had in mind.

A sheep farmer she was not.

Still—that was that.

Her job in Denver, such that it was, no longer existed. She had severed her last ties to the big city and would be able to make decisions based on what was best for her and Toby, no matter where she decided to live and what she decided to do in the end.

Maybe, with the money Granny had left her along with the sale of the ranch, she could go to school and become—

Well, she didn't know *what* she wanted to become, only that an overglorified waitress wasn't it.

"I'd like to try to figure out my own head and heart in the slower pace of Serendipity while I stay here at Granny's ranch."

"That's exactly what Frances wanted to provide for you," Jo assured her.

Angelica knew she was facing a whole new set of challenges if she was going to follow Granny's directive—how to feed sheep, for one thing.

How a ranch made a profit. Or what she might be able to get by selling the land to Rowdy.

What the messages in the envelopes meant.

And where the paper trail or scavenger hunt or whatever Granny had considered it would end.

"About this *Feed My Sheep* thing," Angelica asked. "Am I supposed to be learning how to feed Granny's sheep, or am I missing the point? And how many envelopes are there, anyway?"

"All I can say is you're on the right track. And you can expect more from Frances when the time is right. These letters are your granny's last wishes to you. It was her fervent prayer that you and Rowdy would follow her instructions."

Angelica didn't know about Rowdy, but she couldn't find it in her heart to deny Granny what she wanted. Not when she had missed Granny's final days and even her funeral.

In good faith, what else could she do?

"I'll get out of your hair, then. You holler if you need anything." Jo patted Angelica's arm and leaned down to kiss Toby on the forehead before letting herself out, disappearing as quickly as she had appeared.

Jo left Angelica with much to think about. It seemed that Granny had known all along that Angelica would need time after becoming a mother to work out what she wanted to do with her life, to see her future with more clarity.

Granny was the one person in Serendipity—well, one of two, if Angelica counted Granny's bosom friend Jo—

who knew how hard Angelica's life had been after leaving town.

Angelica would follow Granny's directives, but she didn't know what good it would do. How would hanging out with a bunch of smelly sheep, not to mention the hodgepodge of other animals Granny raised, give her a better idea of what she should be doing with her life?

The pungent aroma of country living might clear out her nostrils, but it would hardly clear her head.

Still, she *had* experienced a moment of homecoming when she'd taken what little she and Toby owned and moved it into the sprawling ranch home. She had settled into one of the spare bedrooms across from where Granny used to sleep, and had arranged a small nursery in the other.

Granny's one-level ranch house was as country inside as out, with wooden furniture, homemade quilts and the scent of evergreen from the wood-burning stove Granny had used to heat her home.

Living at Granny's, at least, would be peaceful and a happy reminder of the past spent with her favorite relative. Not having to pay rent was a huge boon, as well, since she'd dropped her month-to-month lease apartment in Denver.

But balancing that with the amount of work she would have to do to keep the ranch going tipped the scales the other direction. She was overwhelmed by the mere thought of trying to do all that and care for her special needs son, too.

How was she supposed to take care of the animals? Rowdy had said the sheep were in the far pasture, and she'd seen the coop of chickens on her way in. The hay fields would be ripe for harvesting come fall. She would have to learn how to herd the flock with the two border collies and ascertain just how Granny's Anatolian shepherd guarded the flock at night. At this point she didn't even know their names. Granny had always taken the border collies inside with her at night. Even as unfamiliar as she was with dogs, Angelica couldn't help but think she ought to do the same thing.

She wondered if Granny's old mare was still stabled on the ranch. And then there was shearing the sheep and gathering the chickens' eggs and who knew what other chores awaited her?

She had a new appreciation for Granny, who had done it all herself after Angelica's grandfather had died twenty years ago. Granny brought in a few men to harvest her hay crop, but other than that she was a one-woman talent show.

The sheep, the dogs, the chickens—that was all her.

Angelica didn't feel nearly up to the task. It was all she could do just to learn to be a mama to Toby. It gave her pause once again to wonder if she'd made a mistake coming back here.

She finished setting up the crib and left a message for Rowdy on his answering machine to let him know she was back in town to take care of the whole *Feed My Sheep* business, as dubious as that was. And the longer she waited for him to return her call, the more she wondered what in the world she thought she was doing.

If Rowdy wasn't the man in question, she would suspect he might not call back at all, that he might be avoiding her on purpose. But it *was* Rowdy, and he wasn't the kind of person to be intentionally unkind, even if it was to the woman who held the town record on heartlessness.

Now that she was back in the hometown she'd never

thought to see again, and waiting on the man she'd once left at the altar—it all felt surreal and it made her a little sick to her stomach.

What was she really doing here, anyway?

She folded a basket full of Toby's clothes while she waited for Rowdy to return her message, but instead of phoning he showed up on her doorstep, the second unexpected visitor of the day, covered with a day's worth of dirt and grime and smelling cowboy fresh.

Definitely not the most romantic scent in the world, by any means, but the combination of old leather and outdoor living was inexplicably appealing to Angelica, at least on Rowdy.

And the all-male smell of him tripped memories long hidden, reminding her of old times in a way she'd rather not think about.

When they were happy together.

Before everything had gone south.

"Rowdy," Angelica exclaimed in surprise, shifting Toby to the crook of her arm. "You didn't have to come over. I just wanted to touch base with you and let you know I was back in town."

"No bother. I come over every afternoon to care for Granny Frances's stock, anyway."

Of course he did.

It wasn't just the sheep. Angelica wondered why she hadn't thought of it before. She hadn't toured the ranch yet, but it wasn't falling down around her and all of the animals she'd seen looked healthy.

Animals that couldn't possibly be there unless someone was caring for them.

Duh!

Someone would have had to take over for Granny when she became too ill to work.

Who else but Rowdy, the friendly young rancher next door, and one of the only men in town who knew how to properly care for a sheep farm?

And he'd clearly continued after Granny had passed.

Angelica's heart sank.

She had no idea how to care for sheep—hence, she suspected, the letter from Granny with Rowdy's name on it as well as her own.

Rowdy was the one man who could truly help her. And the man who had the most to gain from continuing to work the stock, assuming she would be selling both the land and animals to him.

The sooner she got the hang of this, the sooner she could send Rowdy on his way—or he could send her on hers. She was so confused and grieving she couldn't see up from down.

At the very least, if Rowdy showed her how to feed Granny's sheep they would both be able to move on to whatever was in the next envelope. Jo hadn't said how many they were to expect, but Angelica had to believe they were near the end of this crazy chase.

She gestured Rowdy inside. Without a word, he hung his hat on a peg near the door and removed his boots, placing them on the mat next to the hat rack, just as Granny had always insisted he do when Rowdy and Angelica were dating as teenagers.

Her throat burned with grief at the memory and she had to blink back the tears that pricked against the backs of her eyes. Rowdy was the same cowboy he'd been back then. The only difference now was time, distance and the slight limp in his left leg.

And Granny was gone.

Her bright personality that always lit up the atmosphere had disappeared, leaving Angelica's heart dim.

She mentally shook herself. Now wasn't the time for her to break down. She'd done that enough with Jo, and besides, Granny wouldn't want her to spend her days crying. She saved her grief—for Granny, for Rowdy and for the way her life had turned out—for the middle of the night when she was nursing Toby. Her sweet little baby was the only person who could soothe her as she offered tears and whispered prayers into the darkness.

Rowdy hesitated until she'd taken a seat on the rocker before he propped himself on the edge of the couch, clutching his hands in front of him and leaning his forearms on his knees, his gaze on the carefully polished hardwood floor.

She wondered if he was trying to gather his thoughts to say something, but when he didn't speak, Angelica jumped in with the first question that came to mind.

"How much has Granny been paying you?"

His head popped up and his gaze widened in astonishment.

"What?"

"You must have been doing all the chores around here for quite some time. I assume Granny gave you something for all the help you've been to her."

He frowned. "You really think I would do a thing like that to Granny Frances? Ask her to pay me something when she was on her deathbed? That would be a horrible way to treat a friend."

The sound that emerged from deep in his chest was very much like a growl.

"Wow. You really have a bad opinion of me, don't you?

It makes me wonder why you ever agreed to marry me in the first place, if you think I'm that kind of man," Rowdy said. "Then again, I guess when push came to shove you weren't much on follow through, now, were you?"

His barbed words and resentful tone caught on to Angelica's tight nerves and yanked at them, but as much as she wanted to, she didn't bite back.

What good would it serve?

And anyway, he was right.

He shrugged. "I did what had to be done. Out here in the country it's called being neighborly. Maybe you forgot about that after all your years in the city."

"No need to be touchy," she said, trying to keep her voice even for Toby's sake. "It's just that taking over all the chores for the entire ranch, despite its small size, is a tremendous thing to ask, even of a man with as much integrity as you have. Especially since you have—" she gestured toward his bad knee "—health issues. I can't imagine it's easy for you."

"Then don't bother yourself about it." He frowned in objection. "My knee rarely hurts anymore. And it doesn't stop me from doing my job. Ever."

She held her hands up in surrender.

He narrowed his eyes on her, taking her measure. She met and held his gaze.

She no doubt came up wanting in his eyes. But that wouldn't be news to Rowdy.

"Granny Frances wanted to pay me," he finally admitted. "I wouldn't let her."

Angelica nodded. That sounded like Granny. Likewise, it sounded just exactly like Rowdy.

"I don't have much to offer. The money Granny left

me is enough for me to live on for a few months, but not enough to pay for a ranch hand to help me."

She shrugged. "Frankly, without you, there's no way I'm going to be able to take care of all these animals. I know I'm not Granny. Not even close. I can't do it all." She paused. "Although maybe that's to your advantage. The sooner I fail, the sooner you get Granny's ranch."

"I'm not going to sit here and tell you I don't want this ranch. You know I do. My own ranch is barely keeping up with the cost of inflation. The extra land and stock will be just the shot in the arm I need."

"I figured."

"But as far as you failing this test, if that's what it is, I don't think that's what Granny Frances had on her mind," he said thoughtfully. "Why was her letter addressed to both of us if she didn't really want me to give you a hand? She even specifically mentioned the sheep. And anyway, if I am going to eventually own this place—and I've already put it all out on the table and admitted that's what I want in the end—I'd rather keep the ranch in shape than have to do extra work getting everything back in order after the land becomes mine."

Angelica brushed a long strand of hair behind her ear and shifted Toby to her other shoulder. "I'm willing to accept your help, for Granny's sake, but I realize this is asking a lot of both of us. There is one obvious factor we haven't really talked about. She is pushing us together for a reason."

He grunted in agreement and threaded his fingers through his thick blond curls.

"Can we really get along well enough to work together after—well, everything? Because to be honest, I'm not sure that can happen no matter how badly I need this to work out for my own peace of mind."

"I want to honor Granny Frances's memory. And if this is what she wants—" He left the rest of his sentence unspoken. His voice was strong and even—everything Angelica wasn't feeling.

She blew out an audible breath. "I know you don't want me to be here. I'm not exactly sure why I came back. Only that I'm here for now."

"You quit your job?"

Her lips quirked. "That's one way of putting it. My boss practically shoved me out the door. Apparently, I was more expendable than I'd believed." She chuckled at her own joke, but there wasn't much mirth to it. "So now it's Granny's ranch or nothing, at least until I can make other arrangements. In the meantime, I feel obligated to try to meet Granny's last wishes as best I can and keep this ranch in working order. For you, or whatever," she finished with a vague gesture of her hand.

His blue eyes met hers and their gazes locked. For a moment, the only thing between them was their breaths, slow, deep and steady, until they were unconsciously breathing in unison.

Her throat closed, choking off her air, and she looked away.

"Okay," he said, his voice low and gruff.

"Okay?"

"We don't have to like it, but I don't see any way around it. Without my help, Granny's ranch will crash and burn and that would be a real shame—especially since I eventually intend to claim the land. I'll consider my work on this property as my investment."

Angelica bristled, although she couldn't imagine why she would have such an odd reaction to his words.

They'd already talked about this. She'd practically promised to sell Granny's ranch to him. Maybe a little later than Rowdy had originally imagined the transaction would take place, but it *would* take place.

Eventually.

That was what they both wanted, wasn't it?

Rowdy stood and excused himself, saying he needed to finish the chores and get back to his own place. Angelica was all too happy to let him leave.

Her head was spinning and her heart was pounding.

Now that she was here, with no job and nowhere else to be, all she had was the land under her feet. With Toby totally reliant on her to take care of him, it frightened her to feel so helpless.

Maybe the reason she'd failed in Denver was she'd lacked vision and resources. She'd never cared much about money except as a way to make ends meet, at least until she got pregnant with Toby. Then she had another life to care for, and he became all that mattered.

She needed to make a new plan for what she and Toby were going to do long term. She had no solid ideas at the moment, but she'd been tossing around a few thoughts—attending a culinary arts school or cosmetology college or something, just to get her out of waiting tables.

Maybe get an associate's degree in accounting, something recession-proof that would make a decent salary for her and Toby to live on.

This way, that way and the other.

Yeah. She had no clue.

She had enough money to live on right now with what Granny had given her, and if she sold the land to Rowdy, she would have new opportunities for the first time in her adult life. She was overwhelmed considering where to go with those choices.

The only plus she could see to all this was that Rowdy would end up with Granny's land. He would do right by it, and by Granny. That was one less thing she had to worry about.

There was another thought poking out from the back of her mind, demanding attention, but it was hardly worth considering. If by some wonder she could pick up sheep farming and take after Granny, the only woman in her life she had looked up to and who had always believed in her, she would be able to provide Toby with a good, stable life.

Country life, granted, but then, had she really done well in the city?

There were a lot of hurdles in her path, to be sure, not the least of which was her bad reputation in a town that had a long memory. Even with the first baby steps in the way the church ladies had reached out to her, it wouldn't be easy to prove to anyone that she had changed, that she was a Christian now and God had made her heart new.

And Rowdy living next door? Could she ever get over the angst she felt every time she thought about him, much less saw him or spoke to him?

Was this what Granny was thinking when she wrote the notes? To make Angelica and Rowdy work together until they could get over themselves?

Confusion washed through her.

Too many questions.

Too many decisions to make.

It had appeared so cut-and-dried when she'd first come back to Serendipity, ready and willing to sell the ranch.

But now?

Who knew?

Maybe only God. This was new to her, living by faith, but she was determined to do her best to follow Him. She could only pray she would figure out what He had in mind for her and, for once, do the right thing.

The next afternoon, Rowdy met Ange to walk around Granny Frances's ranch and explain what went where and all the daily chores for which she'd be responsible.

"Ready to go?" he asked.

She slipped Toby into a sling and grabbed a notebook and pen with which, she explained, she intended to take copious notes.

"As if sheep farming can be boiled down to a list of things to do," she muttered.

Rowdy laughed and nodded in agreement. "It's more like a list of lists that never ends and rolls around in cycles from day to day."

"I'd like to see Patchwork," she said, a tingle of excitement in her tone.

Ange had spent the last eight years in the city, and even as a child living in Serendipity she'd been a preacher's kid, not a rancher's child. She hadn't learned how to ride a horse until she was a teenager, whereas he had been propped in a saddle before he could walk.

He remembered how excited she'd been the first time he'd helped her onto the saddle, so giddy that even the docile mare had picked up on her exhilaration.

Patchwork neighed and tossed her head in greeting when they entered the barn.

"I wish I could ride her," she whispered. Her gaze twinkled and took on a starry-eyed look.

His breath caught. She had always been a dreamer. It was one of the things that had first attracted him to her.

"Well, why don't you? It will give you two the opportunity to get reacquainted and she could use the exercise."

She glanced down at Toby and her expression instantly went from animated to sober.

"Maybe someday. Right now, I have Toby. Horseback riding isn't in my near future."

He almost offered to care for Toby so she could take Patchwork out. Riding always relaxed him, and she certainly looked like she needed a break.

But he knew nothing about babies and wasn't quite comfortable taking on that kind of responsibility, even if it was only for an hour.

If Toby was his baby, everything would be different.

But he wasn't.

His gut churning, Rowdy suggested they finish the tour of the property.

"The hay is over here," he said, pointing to a corner of the barn. "Granny Frances grew hay on a rotating basis every year, but she didn't need much, so she'd sell the rest off, or give it away to ranchers in need."

Ange smiled softly. "That sounds like Granny."

"The rest of the fields are composed of grass, clover and forbs, all perennials. It's important to move the sheep around so the fields don't get overgrazed."

She scribbled frantically in her notebook.

He showed her the chicken coop, but given the way her brow was scrunched, displaying both her concentration and her anxiety, he gave her a pass and told her he would teach her how to care for the chickens another time.

Rowdy sensed that Ange was feeling overwhelmed by it all. Even though he hadn't seen her for eight years and he'd never been great with reading people to begin with, he could tell from her expression how inundated she was feeling.

And who could blame her?

Any sane person would be feeling that way. He'd grown up on his sheep farm and there were still days where there was more to do than there was sunlight to do it in.

Not one thing about this situation was second nature to her, as it was to him.

If he was being sensible about it, he wouldn't care how she felt about ranch living. His heart tugged to see her so overwhelmed and confused, but his head reminded him otherwise and he was the one most conflicted by it all.

Ange was dangerous.

Off-limits.

But the fact that her floundering was to his advantage didn't play well with him. No matter what their past, Ange was going through some major life changes right now, and he couldn't help but want to cut her a break.

More the fool, him.

Throughout the visit to the barn, Angelica had tented a pastel green receiving blanket over her shoulder and the fabric sling in order to protect Toby from the dust hanging in the air in the stable and then again when the sun shone too brightly on his chubby face. When clouds covered the direct sunlight, Ange uncovered him and let him enjoy the fresh country air. He was the cutest little thing, making the occasional mewling coo, sucking noisily on his fist and appearing quite content just riding along with his mama.

"I tried a pacifier but he always preferred his thumb," Ange said with a chuckle.

For reasons unknown to Rowdy, the baby sounds choked him up. He couldn't even put names to the emotions he was feeling—or why he was feeling anything at all.

It wasn't like Toby was *his* baby.

But he could have been.

If Ange hadn't freaked out and bolted before their wedding.

There it was.

The real reason the infant was getting to him. Not that he was cute or cuddly, although he was both.

But because he wasn't Rowdy's.

He tightened the reins on his emotions and focused on the tour he was giving.

Toby slept through most of the walk around the ranch, making the proverb "sleeping like a baby" come to life right before Rowdy's eyes. He had never seen such a peaceful sight as Toby curled onto Angelica's shoulder. Not even a newborn lamb could compare.

Several times the notion that they could have been a family sneaked up on him. And every time it treaded by, it sucker punched him.

Time and again he fought it as all the air left his lungs in a whoosh, recovering as quickly as he could and pushing his emotions back into the recesses of his heart before Ange could read them on his face.

She'd always been good at knowing what he was thinking, guessing how he felt, and that was the last thing he wanted to have happen now.

There had been a time in his life when that trait had reassured him, but not anymore. They were way, *way* past that point in their lives.

He'd moved on.

Kind of.

He had buried what had happened with Angelica just as deep as it could go. He lived alone, but he wasn't lonely most of the time.

So why was he experiencing this sudden sense of panic in her presence?

The answer was obvious.

He'd come to grips with his past, and now he was inviting that very same past into his present situation, rather like aiming a runaway train toward a caved-in bridge and giving it the go-ahead to move forward.

This was crazy.

He was crazy.

But he had to believe it wouldn't always be like this, the way he experienced a twinge in his heart every time he so much as thought of Ange.

Otherwise, he wouldn't be able to function. And he couldn't run a ranch—*two* ranches—without giving it his full mental and physical effort.

The ache would ease eventually, wouldn't it?

He returned his mind to the task at hand with some difficulty. He had moved the flock of sheep—the very subject of Granny's last letter—to the closest field, so they could walk to it. Walking wasn't quite as effortless as he'd let on, but he never let his injury stop him. He wasn't about to let it interfere with his work, so he sucked it up and used a walking stick to help him balance with his bad leg.

"Ready to go?" he asked.

Ange's gaze widened. "There's more?"

He grinned. "I've saved the best for last."

He whistled for the border collies to accompany him

and had them move the sheep forward so he didn't have as far to go.

As the dogs brought the flock to them, nipping on their heels to keep them moving in the right direction, Rowdy turned his attention to Toby.

"He sleeps a lot, doesn't he?" Rowdy asked, keeping his voice low, so as not to disturb the infant's rest. "Or is he one of those babies who have their nights and days mixed up?"

"Toby is the perfect baby," Ange acknowledged, smiling softly at her son. "He does sleep a lot, day and night. More than most babies, I imagine, but he's very responsive when he's awake and rarely fusses at all."

An awkward silence stretched between them, a chasm Rowdy didn't know how to breach or even if he wanted to try.

"What about Toby's father?" he asked. It was none of his business, but he couldn't contain his curiosity. "Is he in the picture?"

Her face turned bright pink, her expression an alarming combination of embarrassment and anger.

"No. Josh is *not* in the picture. I dated him for two years, and I thought our relationship was serious. And I was very foolish with how I conducted myself during that time. He spent more time at my apartment than his own, but we never talked about marriage. That is, until…"

Her words dropped off and she shook her head.

What had she been about to say?

Until she discovered she was pregnant?

Had Josh reevaluated his life and wanted to marry her then? Be a good father to Toby, even if he hadn't been a good man to Ange?

Rowdy had zero respect for a man who didn't put a

ring on the finger of the woman he loved. Shacking up with a woman was the coward's way out.

Even though in Rowdy's own case his relationship with Ange had turned out in heartbreak, he had been ready to fully commit to her, to give her all of his future, his protection, his heart and his life.

"I was incredibly stupid and completely blind where Josh was concerned. I don't know what I was thinking." She sighed. "Yes, I do. I wasn't thinking at all. I met him when I was serving at a corporate function. He was a big shot with lots of money and little small-town me fell for his outward charm and charisma. Even when I realized he wasn't the person I thought him to be, I didn't walk away. I kept waiting and hoping things would get better between us. I learned the hard way that a woman can't change a man's character.

"But it wasn't only that. I wasn't looking in the right place to find peace and acceptance.

"My whole world changed the moment I found out I was pregnant with Toby. For the first time, I genuinely sought God and found forgiveness. The Lord changed my heart and my life.

"But my change of heart didn't change my circumstances. That was all on me and my foolish choices. So now, it's up to me to dig my way out of them and make something of myself, somebody Toby can be proud of."

Rowdy had always known Ange to be a determined woman, but he'd never seen a spark of dedication like the one she now carried in her beautiful blue eyes.

Had her relationship with the Lord really changed her heart and life that much? Her words sounded so genuine. He wanted to believe them. He wanted to believe *her*.

But Rowdy didn't know if he could trust her, and he definitely couldn't trust his heart to figure out what was really happening with Ange.

"Am I ashamed of the way Toby was conceived out of wedlock?" she continued, even though that question wouldn't have been something Rowdy would ever have asked. She didn't quite meet his eyes until she answered her own question.

"Yes," she affirmed. "I'm terribly humiliated every time I think about that part of my life. But keeping my sweet baby? There was never even the smallest hesitation in my mind and heart. Not for one second. Like I said before, Toby is the biggest blessing in my life."

"Surely Toby's father is obligated to pay child support, at least? Even if he doesn't want to be part of Toby's life?"

Rowdy couldn't imagine a man who would abandon his wife—*girlfriend*, he mentally amended—and their child when Ange and Toby needed him most.

It hadn't taken him long to form an opinion about this Josh fellow, and it wasn't a good one.

She scoffed. "Obligated? Perhaps. But it's not something I intend to pursue. Josh adamantly refused to acknowledge that Toby was his child from the get-go. When I told him I was pregnant, he called me a host of bad names I don't care to repeat and insisted Toby wasn't his, even though he knew full well he was the only man I had ever been with.

"And then he walked away. I don't know where Josh is, and I don't want to know. But he was absolutely right about one thing. He is *not* Toby's father. Not in any of the ways that matter. It takes more than biology to make a dad."

Rowdy growled, agreeing wholeheartedly with Ange's statement. This Josh guy wasn't good enough for Ange and Toby, and leaving was probably the best thing that he could have for them.

It sounded as if she would have been miserable living with the dishonorable jerk. And good riddance to him. But Rowdy still thought Josh should be throttled for walking away from his responsibilities.

"I know in the best of all worlds Toby would be raised by both a loving mother *and* father. I wish it was that cut-and-dried, but that simply isn't our reality.

"Toby and I will be okay. I'll do whatever I have to do to raise my baby on my own. I'm not the first woman who has ever found herself a single parent, and I won't be the last. But I'm bound and determined to be the very best mother I can be."

"I believe you," he said, his throat tightening around his words and making them come out in a deep baritone.

Her surprised gaze swept to his, but he didn't want to explain his last statement.

It wasn't admiration. It was a point of fact.

Ange had proven herself resilient.

And she continued to do so. Perhaps Granny Frances had wanted her to test her mettle on the ranch. To remind Ange how strong she was, that she could do more than just survive.

Rowdy felt like he was starting to get it now, to understand Granny Frances's motivations.

That was all well and good. Living a ranching lifestyle for a while would be good for her. He only hoped Granny Frances's little experiment didn't go *too* well. The last thing he wanted was Ange as a permanent next-door neighbor.

What he wanted—*needed*—was her land.

That was the end game.

It occurred to him that he *could* walk away.

Right here.

Right now.

And leave her flailing.

Failing.

Watch her fall.

But Rowdy wasn't that man.

Maybe Granny Frances wasn't just testing Ange. Perhaps the letter was to prove Rowdy's mettle, as well.

He already knew who he was—a man of the land, proud of the work he did. A man of strength and integrity, who helped the frail and the weak, and offered an arm to anyone who needed a hand up.

And at this moment, the person in need of a hand up was Ange.

He stopped at the gate that led to the pasture the sheep were grazing in and turned to Ange, crossing his arms and leaning a hip on the wooden gatepost.

Her gaze spanned the flock and then she wrinkled her nose as the scent of sheep assaulted her nostrils.

He chuckled. The sounds and smells of the ranch were like background noise to him. He didn't even notice them anymore, except for the way they soothed his heart whenever he was working with the animals.

"Well, there you have it." He gestured to the sheep, lazily grazing on the meadow grass.

Her brow furrowed and she shook her head.

"Have what? All I see are sheep."

"Exactly." He nodded, and he couldn't resist the grin that inched up one side of his lips. "Granny Frances's letter, remember."

"Yes. And?"
He made a sweeping gesture.
"Here you go. *Feed My Sheep*."

Chapter Four

Now that she'd been introduced to some of what running a sheep farm entailed, she knew Rowdy was taking it easy on her, covering most of the ranch chores while she dealt with not one, but two major learning curves—one with the ranch and one with Toby.

Surprisingly, while sheep farming was continuing to improve at a snail's pace for her, she was doing well with Toby. As a single mother, everything fell on her shoulders—the feeding, diaper changing, washing the gazillion clothes that one baby seemed to go through. But she didn't mind a bit. Every part of caring for Toby gave her great joy.

Mothering came naturally to her, much more than she'd expected. The love that flooded through her every time she held Toby, rocked him, changed him or bent over the edge of the crib watching him peacefully sleep was immeasurable.

Even though she was perpetually fatigued by all of the recent events and upcoming decisions, she still enjoyed Toby's 2 a.m. feedings and wouldn't have it any other way. It was their personal quiet time together, where Toby nursed and Angelica prayed in the darkness.

"Are you ready to go, little man?" she murmured as she tucked Toby into his infant car seat. She'd found that was the easiest and most comfortable way to tote him around and keep him by her side while she did chores, at least for now. Plus, she could drape a light blanket over the handle to shade Toby from the sun and dust.

"What am I going to do when you grow out of your car seat?" she asked him, laughing when he gurgled back at her. "I suppose I'll deal with that problem when I come to it. Your great-granny had always said, *Let the future take care of itself. The Good Book says we've got enough to deal with right now without borrowing a cup of trouble from tomorrow.* She was a wise woman. I wish you could have met her."

She sighed. At the moment, she had more than her fair share of weighty issues that fell directly into the scope of today's problems.

She was more exhausted than she'd ever felt in her whole life. Every joint and muscle in her body ached and complained with even the smallest of movements.

How had Granny run this ranch all by herself in the twenty years since Gramps had died?

She'd never uttered one word of complaint that Angelica could remember. She'd always been cheerful and upbeat, quick with a quote from the Good Book and always ready to help a neighbor in need.

Maybe, as with Angelica, she'd saved her tears for the middle of the night.

Angelica wondered how she'd maintained her positive attitude, even when the going got tough. She'd always encouraged Angelica to look on the bright side.

There's a silver lining to every trial the Lord sees fit to walk us through, Angelica remembered Granny saying. *It's all for your own good. Every last bit.*

But back then, Angelica hadn't believed God existed. How could she, when bad things like Rowdy's rodeo accident could happen to the best, most faithful man she knew?

She knew the answer to that question. God wasn't responsible for what had happened.

She was.

She'd been the one to pressure Rowdy into riding in the saddle bronc event, something he wasn't skilled in. And all because of her ego, wanting to be able to brag on her fiancé for winning the title at the ranch rodeo.

"We've got a trial today, Toby," she told her son as she picked him up and slid the car seat into the crook of her elbow. "I'm guessing this new day will be loaded with challenges. I wish I could share a quote from the Good Book the way Granny used to do. But I'll get there, buddy. I'll get there. For now, let's go find Rowdy."

She knew he would be somewhere around the Carmichael ranch. He always did the Bar C chores in the late afternoons after the work on his own ranch was finished.

Yesterday, he'd reintroduced her to Granny's pinto quarter horse mare Patchwork. So far, Angelica didn't know or genuinely care much about ranch life, but she did like horses and was excited for the opportunity to eventually take a ride on Patchwork.

"I spent a lot of time here when I was in high school," she told Toby. He stared up at her with his wide blue eyes, as if he understood every word she was saying. "Your grandpa and grandma were very strict and didn't allow me to date. Rowdy and I had to meet on the sly.

Fortunately for us, Granny was a romantic at heart. She understood our secret love for each other and we ended up spending much of our time here at Granny's ranch.

"Sometimes Rowdy would bring over his gelding and Granny would let me borrow one of her horses to go riding with. They were some of my favorite times."

Memories rushed back, but for once they weren't all cloudy and painful. Rowdy had taught her how to ride, how to tack up her horse and how to care for it—everything from brushing and feeding to mucking out the stalls.

Everything had seemed such a sheer joy when she was with Rowdy. He made everything in her life better and more bearable, even when her home life wasn't the best.

Until she'd ruined everything.

And now she felt like she had a second chance. Not for a relationship with Rowdy. That was far too much for her to even consider. She'd burned those bridges. But one day perhaps they could at least be friends.

She found Rowdy carrying a bag of chicken feed slung over one shoulder and a bag of scratch grains on the other, walking from the barn to the coop. The sacks had to be heavy. Angelica judged them to be about fifty pounds each, but he toted them around as if they weighed nothing. The only signs of strain were the bulges in his biceps and the telltale ripples of his chest muscles when he tossed the bag down just outside the chicken coop.

Angelica averted her eyes for a moment and took a deep breath. It would not do to have Rowdy look up and see her gaping at him in appreciation.

And she did appreciate, however covertly.

Could she help it if he was drop-dead gorgeous?

"How's Toby?" he asked, lifting his black cowboy hat

by the crown and dabbing his forehead with his shirt-sleeve.

"He's fine," she said, stifling a yawn. "He decided he wanted an extra meal last night, though, so he should sleep well while we cover today's chores."

"Hmm. Good."

But I'm thoroughly exhausted, thank you for asking.

Which, of course, he didn't.

Why would he?

So she didn't share her snark out loud.

The truth was, Rowdy had barely acknowledged her at all since he'd walked up. Instead, his attention was entirely focused on the baby.

She set the car seat down near enough to the chicken coop for her to be able to see and hear Toby if he cried out to her, but not close enough for him to inhale any dust or ick scratched up by the chickens.

Rowdy crouched before the baby, making high, nonsense noises and wiggling his fingers until Toby caught his thumb.

Rowdy grinned. "He's got a good grip, this one. I'll bet he'll grow up to be a real bruiser."

Angelica's heart warmed. After the wringer she'd been put through with Josh, she appreciated Rowdy's attentiveness to Toby.

She only hoped that someday Toby would have as good a male role model as Rowdy would be. She couldn't think of anyone who would be better at coaching her son into honorable manhood and showing him the things he needed to know to be successful in life.

But there was no point in going down that road, even if it was just in her mind.

She didn't know if she belonged in Serendipity, where

her reputation was shredded, possibly beyond repair. She might not care for city living, either, but at least Toby would have all the advantages life in the city had to offer—the special schools where he could meet kids just like him. Education. Sports. The arts.

She had to keep her head on straight and realize there was an end to the path she was on right now. She and Toby would no doubt be out of here the moment she was certain she'd fulfilled Granny's last wish.

Although come to think of it, how would she know when she had received the last envelope?

She supposed she'd have to rely on Jo to guide her, and hope the woman didn't have any ulterior plans that would hold her up from moving on with her life.

Whatever that life was going to look like. She continued to think about it, and she still didn't know.

But in the meantime, she would do her best to work hard at Granny's ranch as Granny had apparently wanted her to do. Feed her sheep and take care of the rest of her animals.

"He's sleeping," Rowdy whispered, a rasp scraping against his usual smooth baritone. He carefully removed his thumb from Toby's grasp and covered the seat with a thin blue receiving blanket.

Stretching to his full height, he turned to Angelica. "I guess we need to get to work."

She stifled another yawn against the back of her hand.

"Chickens are on the docket for today, aren't they?" she asked hesitantly.

Angelica didn't know whether it was the muted tone of her voice or her anxious expression, but Rowdy narrowed his gaze on her.

Was that concern she saw in his eyes?

"Are you sure you're up to this?" he asked bluntly, though with enough genuine concern that the question didn't come out bristly. "You look like you're going to fall asleep standing up. Maybe we should save this for another day."

She gestured his query away. "I'm a little tired is all. Nothing I can't overcome with a little determination."

"You always were strong willed."

Angelica couldn't tell by his expression or the tone of his voice whether or not he was complimenting her, so she let the comment go.

"I thought I'd introduce you to Granny Frances's hens today." He nodded toward the chicken coop. "Thanks to them, you'll always have plenty of fresh eggs to cook with."

Angelica's gut tightened.

She liked eggs.

Scrambled eggs was one of the few dishes she could cook on her own.

What she didn't like was how she would have to get the eggs. She wasn't a big fan of chickens—or of any type of bird, really. The truth was, with all of their flapping and clawing and clucking, hens frightened her.

She was terrified that if one of them flapped up at her or got next to her face, she was going to make a total fool of herself.

She'd seen one brightly colored rooster roaming around on the lawn outside the coop, and up until now, she'd managed to avoid it completely. She'd meant to ask Rowdy why that chicken moved about freely while the other chickens were confined, but she supposed she'd probably get the answer to that question today.

She'd been happy to studiously avoid both the brightly

colored chicken *and* the rest of them in the coop, but now all that was about to end.

As Rowdy had said, she was strong willed. She could overcome her fear of chickens. She just had to face it down and work through it.

Maybe the best way to power through her phobia would be to stand right in the middle of the coop until she felt comfortable.

Or she keeled over.

Holding her breath.

With her eyes closed.

Her heart hammered but she forced herself to breathe. Rowdy would be right beside her and he would notice if she started acting funny.

Anyway, how bad could it be?

"Ready?" Rowdy unfolded a knife from his pocket and ripped into the feed, then plunged a scooper into the grain and filled a nearby blue bucket with it.

"Here you go," he told her, passing the bucket to her and flashing an encouraging grin.

"What am I supposed to do with this?"

Rowdy pointed to a feeder box and watering tin cleverly using the space under the henhouse. "Food. Water. Right under the henhouse where they roost and sleep. And this," he said, pointing around the fenced enclosure, "is called the run."

"And we go in and shut the gate behind us?"

She already knew the answer to her question, but she was quite literally shaking in her mud boots. She supposed she'd hoped he'd take pity on her and show her how to do it without her actually having to set foot in the coop herself.

If wishes were horses...

Or anything but chickens.

"I know Granny Frances said we were supposed to feed the sheep, and that's a good start for you, but the chickens are by default part of the package while you're living here at the ranch."

"Unfortunately," she mumbled under her breath.

"What was that?" His brow rose in time with one side of his lips.

She didn't answer him, but instead, opened the gate to the chicken run and stepped through, not even looking to see if Rowdy followed.

Either way, this was on her.

I can do this, she told herself.

I can do this with God's help, she mentally amended.

Her adrenaline spiked when she heard the clang of the gate closing behind her.

A few hens in various shades of brown milled around, scratching and pecking at the fresh pine shavings that covered the ground.

"We have to change the pine shavings frequently to keep the run clean, but let's not worry about it today. I usually spread some scratch grain on the ground in the run. It gives the hens something interesting to do. That's what they're looking for."

A few chickens showed a mild interest in Angelica— or rather her feed bucket—but none of them charged at her with wings flapping and beaks pecking as she'd feared they might do.

See?

She was being irrational.

Fear conquered.

"Dump the feed, and afterward we can grab the hose and fill the water bin."

While she followed Rowdy's instructions, he spread the scratch grain across the run and the hens immediately turned to their dinner.

"Next, we find the eggs," Rowdy said.

Angelica froze right where she was. Were there eggs hidden under the pine shavings somewhere? Would her next step crush a fresh egg and then she'd be on cleaning duty?

"What, like an Easter egg hunt or something?" She tried to sound casual, but her laugh sounded as if she was choking on something.

Rowdy snorted. "It's not quite as complicated as all that. While there are occasions where a hen drops an egg in an odd place, it's a pretty good bet that we'll find most of them in the henhouse where they roost."

"Oh." Heat rose to her cheeks. Every time she opened her mouth, she sounded more and more like the uneducated not-a-rancher that she was.

"It's pretty simple, really," Rowdy said, appearing not to notice how flushed her face must look. "You just check all the nests. If a chicken is roosting and doesn't feel like wandering out into the pen, you check underneath her, grab the egg and put it in the bucket."

Angelica watched while he demonstrated, jamming his hand under the nearest roosting hen, causing her to flap her wings and cluck in complaint.

But despite the chicken's fuss, Rowdy came up with a light brown egg, which he brandished in triumph before placing it into the bucket.

"This part, at least, is a little bit like having an Easter egg hunt." He grinned at her. "Easy as pie. Have at it."

She shook her head and crossed her arms.

"What's wrong?"

"There is no possible way you are going to get me to stick my hand under—" she gestured toward the chicken he'd just taken the egg from "—that." Her voice was no more than a croak.

He bent his head toward her, an amused half smile on his lips.

"What's the problem?"

She opened her mouth to speak but no words came forth. How could she explain herself without confiding in him, displaying her vulnerability and embarrassment, neither being emotions she wished to share with Rowdy.

"I don't like...birds." She took a quick gulp of air. "Actually, I have an irrational fear of them," she finally admitted.

"Really?" he asked, surprised. "Did you watch one too many horror movies when you were a kid?"

She snorted and shook her head. If only it was that easy.

"If you must know, I was out camping with some friends last year and a swarm of hummingbirds decided to dive-bomb me. I am *so* not joking. The buzz of their wings and—ugh!"

She swiped in front of her face as if the hummingbirds were still there.

Rowdy's lips twitched and she narrowed her eyes on him. He gave a valiant effort, but eventually he threw back his head and laughed at the picture she'd painted.

"Excuse me," she protested. "I'm serious here. I ran back to the RV and didn't emerge again until nightfall, when the idea of s'mores finally tempted me back out near the campfire."

"There's quite a difference between hummingbirds and chickens."

She rolled her eyes. "Thank you for pointing that out, Captain Obvious. Now tell me something I don't know."

"Chickens are awesome?" he tried, a chuckle following his words.

"No, I don't think so. Try again."

"I think, given this new morsel of information, that I went about today's lesson all wrong. I didn't realize there might be—*issues*—where chickens were concerned."

"Oh, cut it out. I can't possibly be the only one who doesn't like chickens. You don't have problems because you grew up on a ranch. This is all second nature to you. For me, not so much."

"Right." He stroked his stubbled jaw and scanned the chicken run, as if he was looking for something.

"Ah. Here we go," he said, scooping a chicken into his hands and tucking it under his arm, holding it like a running back would hold a football.

"This here is Lucy," he said in the soft Texas drawl that had always melted Angelica's heart. She'd lost much of her own accent after living in Denver for as long as she had.

"What are we going to do with—er—Lucy?" she asked tentatively.

"Just pet her a bit. Get used to her. Don't worry. I've got a good hold on her."

"She won't peck me?"

He chuckled. "No. Lucy is perfectly tame."

"So I just um, pet her like a dog?"

"Mostly, except she has feathers and not fur. Lucy doesn't mind the attention, do you, Luc?"

The chicken didn't so much as cluck, which Angelica took as an affirmative answer, so, holding her breath, she ran her hand along the bird's feathers, which were surprisingly soft.

"How about that?" she murmured. "Are all the hens as mellow as Lucy?"

"For the most part. Once in a while, you'll get one in a dither about something. That's when they'll peck at you a bit. Just show them who's boss. They're really nothing to be afraid of," he added with a grin.

"Says you. Great. Thanks for the encouragement," she said drily.

"Any time."

He passed Lucy to Angelica and showed her how to hold the chicken. For a full minute, she stood as still as a board, afraid to move, with Lucy under her arm.

But she was holding a *chicken*.

That was progress.

Conquer the fear, she coaxed herself. *Embrace it, and then move beyond it.*

Swallowing hard, she set Lucy on the ground and picked up another hen, just as she'd seen Rowdy do.

The second chicken wasn't quite as docile as Lucy had been, but she didn't try to bite. Angelica called that a win.

Setting the second hen down, she made a tour of the run, determined to touch every last chicken and face down her phobia, send her fears flying—no pun intended— hopefully never to return.

She even slid her hand underneath a roosting hen in the henhouse, exclaiming in delight when she withdrew a bluish-green egg.

Easter eggs, indeed.

A couple of the hens balked, clucking and flapping away from her at her sudden triumphant cheer, but she barely noticed. She had an egg in her hand.

Yessss!

Fist pump.

"You got it, girl," Rowdy praised.

Angelica grinned as her heartbeat slowed. One of her daily chores would be caring for these chickens and gathering eggs.

And she could do it.

She might even learn all their names.

She'd still have to continue fighting her phobia. As much as she would like for it to, it wouldn't go away in one fell swoop, but every time she conquered her fear and entered the chicken run it would become less and less of an issue until eventually she wouldn't think about it at all.

Setting the egg in the bucket Rowdy held out to her, she brushed her palms across her blue jeans and headed back through the coop's metal gate.

Toby picked that moment to make his presence known. He was awake and crying softly, the sweet *ah-wah, ah-wah* of an infant.

"We'd better go in and wash up before I pick up Toby with these grimy hands."

"Mind if I join you?" Rowdy asked. "I'd like to hold the little guy for a minute, if that's okay with you."

Angelica's heart flipped in response. Not too many guys would want to hold a baby who wasn't their own flesh and blood, especially one with special needs.

But Rowdy wasn't most guys.

It wasn't that Rowdy was treating Toby special because he had special needs. Rather, it was more like he just accepted Toby the way the Lord had made him with all of the dignity and respect he deserved as one of God's children.

She reached for the car seat but Rowdy beat her to it.

"I'll get him."

Angelica didn't argue. Her arms perpetually ached from lugging the car seat around with her everywhere, although she would suffer no end to aches and pains for the sake of her precious son.

As the three of them walked back toward the house, Angelica spotted, out of the corner of her eye, the multi-colored rooster running loose across the yard.

She wondered why the rooster was so brightly colored in hues of blues, greens, reds and golds, while its fellow chickens were all feathered in shades of drabby browns and tans. And she'd forgotten to ask why the rooster ran loose when the others were cooped up.

She'd touched every chicken on the property except this one. If she was going to face down her fears, she might as well be off and running at a one hundred per-cent success rate.

Without informing Rowdy of her intentions, she turned and strode straight toward the rooster. She half expected it to flap away to freedom since it wasn't cooped up, but instead, this one appeared to be preparing to face her down.

A chill of alarm zipped down her spine as the chicken puffed itself up and raised its wingspan in an attempt to make itself look bigger.

It looked big enough even without the aggressive movements, and plenty scary when it squawked a warn-ing to her.

It's just a chicken, she reminded herself. It was prob-ably acting that way because she'd startled it and caught it off-guard.

No matter.

She was bigger than this rooster and stronger than her fear.

Taking a deep breath for courage, she stalked forward and held out her hand, determined to touch the colorful rooster's back and end her day on a win.

It was only after she'd firmly committed herself and was mere inches away from the chicken that Rowdy's frantic shout cut through the pounding adrenaline.

"No, Ange. Wait! Don't!"

Rowdy had been deep in thought, wrestling with his stray feelings for Ange and Toby, when suddenly Ange had vectored off the path.

At first, he didn't comprehend her direction or realize where she was heading—that is, until the bantam rooster in the yard squawked and ruffled his feathers.

Rowdy's adrenaline spiked and every nerve ending leapt to life.

What did Ange think she was doing?

Facing down her fear, he realized, too little, too late. Just as she had done in the henhouse.

To her inexperienced eye, a chicken was a chicken was a chicken.

This was *so* not going to end well.

As quickly and gently as possible, Rowdy set down the car seat and lunged for Ange.

Her hand was already well within the rooster's strike zone.

"Ouch," she screeched as she snapped her hand back from the angry rooster. She shook out her fingers. "Ow, ow, ow! It bit me. Twice."

"You need to—" Rowdy started, but Ange was already following the instructions he had yet to give.

She twisted away from the ticked-off rooster and bolted the other direction—also, Rowdy noted, well away from where Rowdy had set Toby. Even in her own distress, her first priority was on protecting her baby.

"Help," she called, zigzagging around and looking behind her, only to realize the rooster was gaining on her. Its wingspan and clucking would be intimidating to even the heartiest of country folk, and Ange was afraid of birds to begin with.

The bantam pecked at her jeans-clad legs repeatedly. Rowdy had been around roosters enough to know this encounter would leave bruises.

But the real damage would be internal.

This was Ange's worst nightmare come to life, especially when the rooster started flapping his wings up toward her face.

With the full-on rooster deluge, Ange wasn't watching where she was going and her feet hit on a patch of loose gravel.

Before Rowdy could so much as lunge in her direction, she'd fallen hard onto the earth, tucking her knees into her chest and protecting her head with her arms.

"Rowdy," she screamed.

His heart was beating out of his chest by the time he reached her.

With one well-timed leap, he batted the rooster away with the palm of his hand and then took his place between Ange and Psycho Rooster to carry on the battle.

Taking the rooster's lead, Rowdy drew himself up to his full height, straightening his shoulders and holding his arms out full-length, palms facing outward, making himself look as large and intimidating as possible.

When the rooster squawked at him, he shouted back.

"Shoo. Get out of here."

Still, the rooster attacked, flying at Rowdy's face, his pointed claws extended.

Rowdy grabbed the rooster's legs and then tucked him under his arm and held on tight, ignoring the pecks and scratches on his forearms and the rivulets of blood dripping from his jaw.

He marched the rooster none too gently to the back of the house and released him, pushing him away and hollering after him.

"Shoo, you naughty fellow. Get on out of here."

He followed up by chasing the rooster a few uneven steps for good measure. Rowdy's limp was always more pronounced when his dander was up, and he was good and angry now.

No agitated rooster was going to attack Ange.

Not on his watch.

His heart was thumping loudly in his chest. What if Ange had been holding Toby?

He refused to follow those thoughts to their logical conclusions. Ange and Toby would be gone soon, back to the city. He doubted she'd run into any Psycho Roosters in Denver.

After he was certain the rooster wasn't going to turn back to follow him and continue the fight, Rowdy jogged back to Ange.

She'd rolled to a sitting position, her arms wrapped protectively around her knees while she attempted to catch her breath.

"What was *that*?" she asked with a grimace.

"The meanest rooster in Texas. The only person that ornery bird ever respected was Granny Frances. What possessed you to chase him, anyway?"

Her cheeks flushed a pretty pink.

"I just wanted to touch him the way I had done with all of the other chickens, so I could call my phobia-conquering exercise a complete success. How was I supposed to know it would freak out on me?"

"Quick lesson on chickens. The nondescript brown ones are hens. That colorful guy is a rooster. He struts around with all those fancy feathers to impress the ladies. Hens are by and large friendly creatures. Roosters, not so much. Better you just stay away from that one."

Ange snorted, then stood and brushed off her jeans. "You don't have to tell me *that* twice."

She shook her head and laughed. "Well, I can definitely chalk that one up to a learning experience."

Rowdy was surprised she could laugh about it quite so easily—and so soon after the encounter.

Sure, it was the kind of story that would be passed around the family table during holidays for years to come, but right this second, Rowdy's heart was still beating half out of his chest.

Ange could have been seriously hurt.

"Rowdy," Ange said, touching his jaw and gently turning his head so she could get a better look at the left side of his face. "You're injured."

He shook his head and held his hands up, palms out. "It's nothing."

"It's not nothing. You're bleeding."

She took his hands in hers and turned them over, examining both sides of his arms.

He shrugged. Okay, so he had a few bites and scratches. He'd had worse.

"You are coming in with me," she said in an unyielding tone that reminded him of Granny. All attitude and no-nonsense. "I remember Granny kept a first-aid kit in one of the kitchen cabinets. Hopefully it's still there."

"That's really not necessary," he protested.

At that moment, Toby wailed in earnest, making his presence known as only a tiny baby can do.

"It sounds like you've got your hands full with your son," Rowdy said with a chuckle.

"Those scratches are not nothing, and I'm not taking no for an answer. It was my fault you got hurt. Again." She choked out that last word.

What did she mean, *again*?

At first, he thought she must be referring to some physical incident, but that couldn't be right.

It took him a minute to sort through his memories and realize she must be talking about emotional pain— something far more damaging than any rooster could do.

The wedding.

His heartbreak.

He definitely didn't want to go there.

"Okay. I think you're making way more of this than it is, but lead the way," he conceded, more to get out of the possibility of having to talk about what happened eight years ago than because he really needed bandaging up.

He gestured toward the house, but she didn't go on ahead of him as he'd expected her to do. Rather, she picked up Toby and placed the car seat handle in the crook of one arm and then slipped her other hand under Rowdy's elbow, as if to somehow support him as he walked.

Which was the outside of ridiculous. Yes, he walked with a limp, but he'd had to deal with that for many years since a freak accident at a ranch rodeo and it didn't slow him down much.

Granted, he was pretty scratched up by his wrestling match with Psycho Rooster, but the steady streams of blood made the injuries look much worse than they appeared. A clean scrubbing with soap and water and he would be as good as new.

Still, he humored her, understanding that she needed to feel as if she was doing something useful.

Before long, they had reached Granny Frances's ranch house. They washed their hands and Ange put Toby down for a nap. Then she seated him at the table in the kitchen and carefully peeled off his blue chambray shirt, leaving him in a white T-shirt, his arms bare.

In moments, she had his arms on the tabletop, couched in a soft towel, while she rummaged through the cupboards for the first-aid kit.

She opened the kit on the table and clicked her tongue against her teeth as she rummaged through the contents. She finally settled on several large bandages, rolls of gauze and tape and some antibiotic ointment.

He was going to be as trussed up as a Thanksgiving turkey by the time she was finished with him if she used all that stuff. His vote was still on soap and water.

But then again, if he'd been alone, he never would have been taking on a mad rooster to defend Ange.

Which, despite his injuries, felt pretty good.

The adrenaline spiking through him. The chance to be a hero. He led a secluded lifestyle on his ranch, so he would take what he could get.

Even if it was stupid.

He sucked in a breath through his teeth when she dabbed at a particularly deep scratch along his forearm with the corner of a wet washcloth.

"What is *on* that thing?"

Her gaze widened. "Rubbing alcohol, of course."

The alcohol burned through the open wound and it was all he could do not to leap off his chair.

"Hold still," she said. Her voice was gentle but she had a death grip on his wrist. "I have to make sure the wound is clean before I bandage it."

"By digging to China? Why did you have to go and use rubbing alcohol? A little soap and water would have sufficed just fine."

"You may be the expert in ranch living, but I took a course in first aid before Toby was born and I am Red Cross certified. Who knows what kind of germs those awful claws are carrying? I don't want any of your wounds to become infected. As it is, that one on your jaw may leave a scar."

A scar?

Cool.

Didn't scars make a man look rugged?

The ladies loved them, right?

Somehow, he suspected Ange wouldn't feel the same way if he were to voice his thoughts.

"That chicken really did some damage."

"Rooster," he corrected without thinking.

"Right. Rooster. The one with the bright feathers. I won't make *that* mistake again. Thankfully, they don't have roosters running loose in downtown Denver."

Rowdy assumed such a statement was meant to reassure him, and he guessed in a way it did. She and Toby would be gone before long, and the land would be his.

But there was a part of him that didn't want her to go, at least not yet. They had unfinished business. He had not yet taught her to know and love sheep farming, and maybe catch a glimpse of what might have been if she had not run off on him the night before their wedding.

Maybe—okay, *probably*—it was wrong for him to harbor those kinds of feelings, almost as if he was plotting some sort of emotional revenge on her.

But was it so wrong that he wanted to open her eyes?

That he wanted her to *see*?

He watched her as she tended to his wounds, gently wiping away the blood and dabbing at the gouges. A lock of long light blond hair dropped over her shoulder and he reached out with his free hand to tuck it back behind her ear, barely resisting the urge to take an extra moment to enjoy the silky feel of her locks, to run them through his fingers to see if her hair was as soft as he remembered.

Rowdy concentrated on not moving his arms as she worked, using the sting of the rubbing alcohol to force his mind away from the road his heart wanted to travel.

The baby monitor crackled as Toby woke with a howl that brought a smile to one side of Rowdy's lips.

"That was a short nap," Ange said. "Excuse me a minute while I go grab him."

How could a baby's cry sound so bloomin' cute? That Toby was in distress in some way—hungry or wet or just needing his mama's arms—shouldn't make Rowdy smile, but something about the mewl went straight to his heart and swelled within it.

Melted it.

What was that, anyway?

Joy?

How could a little squeak from a baby that was not only not of his own blood, but was his ex-fiancée's, have any kind of hold on him whatsoever?

Danger zone.

Somehow, the pain of his past was getting muddled with the confusion of the present.

A cloud of panic overshadowed him as he mentally twisted and turned to avoid making contact with those befuddling emotions.

He had better get out now, while the going was good.

He bolted to a standing position, hitting the table with his thigh and nearly upending the first-aid kit.

"Is Toby hungry?" he asked, as if Ange hadn't noticed that the infant hadn't settled down. She'd been making soft, soothing baby talk to him from the moment he'd awoken, promising her full attention just as soon as Rowdy's injuries were taken care of.

"Sit down, Rowdy," she said, placing Toby in the bouncer. "Toby is fine. He can wait one more minute while I finish patching you up. He only sounds like he's going to perish from lack of sustenance."

"Still, I'd better go."

He grabbed his chambray shirt from the back of the chair and threaded his still-stinging arms through it.

There were a few spots where rivulets of blood still dripped from his forearms, but he ignored them.

"You're being stubborn. Not to mention you're bleeding all over your chambray. Come on. Let me help you."

Her voice was as calm and gentle as a mythical siren's song. It was all Rowdy could do not to slump back into his seat and give in to her ministrations.

But that, he knew, would be a major tactical error. His emotions were all over the place after the adrenaline rush when Ange was attacked.

Stupid rooster.

"Look. You just take care of Toby, and I'll clean myself up. See you tomorrow."

He scrambled toward freedom and was out the front door before she could open her mouth to argue.

Whew. Narrow escape.

Chapter Five

Take care of Toby.

What was that supposed to mean?

She'd mulled over his words all through the night but had come up empty.

Was Rowdy judging her as a mother just because she'd been concerned about his injuries and had left Toby to his own devices for the few minutes it would have taken to patch him up?

How fair was that?

It wasn't as if Toby would have starved to death. Angelica knew her son well enough to know he would find his fist and amuse himself until she could get to him.

As she dressed, she again went over and over Rowdy's words in her mind and the strange way he'd left, saying something ridiculous about not wanting to bleed on the baby.

Wasn't the whole point that she was trying to patch him up so he wouldn't bleed on Toby, or anyone else, for that matter? And that was the thanks she got?

She yawned as she readied Toby for the day. Mornings

came early on the ranch, but that was okay with Angelica. Toby was up and at 'em the moment the sun rose, anyway.

The only conclusion she arrived at was that Rowdy was one stubborn man, leaving the house with his wounds raw and bleeding. She expected the scratch on his jaw made from that razor-sharp rooster claw would scar, especially if it wasn't taken care of immediately.

Rowdy had always been stubborn, but now he was being awfully moody, especially considering all she'd been trying to do was be nice and help him.

Well, no. That wasn't the whole truth, now, was it?

The truth was that she was trying to make amends, to make up for her past mistakes.

She snorted.

As if that could ever be done.

Rowdy was right. Those little rooster scratches, deep as they might be, were nothing in comparison to the other ways she had hurt him or that he'd been hurt on her behalf.

This latest incident proved what she'd known all along. It was the reason he had suggested they break it off all those years ago, and ultimately it was why she had left him at the altar.

She wasn't any good for Rowdy. Whenever she was near him, bad things happened to him. He was probably counting the minutes until she would be gone, so he could join Granny Frances's farm to his and live in peace.

Perhaps it was time to put a rush on this whole process. She knew in her heart of hearts that Granny was hoping for a different outcome, that Angelica and Toby would choose to make their home here, that Angelica would find the same delight Granny had working the ranch.

But that was simply not to be. While Angelica had

experienced moments of joy in the past few days, her failures had far outnumbered her triumphs.

And she would not—could not—live next to Rowdy, even if acres of distance separated them.

This morning, rather than using the car seat to tote him, she slid Toby into a front pack. She needed to feel him breathing and close to her heart. Instead of his giant diaper bag, she wrapped a lunch-sack-sized bag filled with essentials over her hip.

She was as ready as she would ever be.

Rowdy had called and instructed her to leave the chickens alone for the time being, at least until he was around to guide her, which was fine by her. Phobia or no phobia, she wasn't in any hurry to step into that coop again.

Instead of feeding the chickens, she headed out to check on the sheep. Many of the late-season ewes were close to delivering, and it was her job to keep an eye out for new lambs and make sure they were all nursing properly with their mamas.

She also thought she would spend some time learning to herd the sheep with the two border collies, Kip and Tucker, and the Anatolian shepherd, Zeus, who guarded the flock at night.

At least with the dogs she could be herself, with little fear of failure. All three dogs appeared to understand that she was Granny's replacement—not that Granny could ever be replaced. But Angelica was her temporary substitute.

No doubt they'd take to Rowdy even better than they did to her after he took over the land. It saddened her to think about what might happen to Granny's dogs once the sale of the land went through. Rowdy had been caring for the dogs in Granny's absence. Surely they had bonded. But he already had working dogs of his own. Hopefully he'd still want to keep Granny's dogs on, for her memory's sake, if for no other reason.

She remained lost in thought until she had reached the barn. She stopped and inhaled deeply. Maybe it was because she was born and raised in Serendipity and had ranching in her blood, skipping one generation notwithstanding, but it was funny how quickly she'd grown fond of the sights and sounds of the country.

Even the sweetly acrid scent of the animals, combined with the smell of fresh-cut hay and rich grain, along with leather tack, brought her mind right back to a time when Granny's house was the only fortress she had against town rumors and gossip.

It still was that stronghold. She'd found a measure of peace here that she hadn't had elsewhere.

Granny's house needed a bit of repair, and the barn needed a new coat of paint, but Rowdy could take care of those types of minor issues sometime in the future when the property officially belonged to him. Or maybe he would knock the buildings down and make more room for the sheep to graze.

Angelica moved from jug to jug in the barn, small, closed-off areas where Rowdy had sorted the ewes he believed were closest to giving birth or that he thought might have trouble with the birthing process.

She was delighted to find that two of the ewes had delivered during the night and the cute little balls of fluff were contentedly nursing with their mamas. She knew there were various inoculations to give and a few odds and ends to take care of with the new lambs, but they could wait until later this afternoon when Rowdy could attend to them. She didn't want Toby too near the ewes or the newborn lambs for health reasons.

She wasn't an expert, but both lambs looked well and she thought Rowdy would be pleased.

Next, she walked to the nearest field, where Rowdy had cut out and herded the rest of the ewes close to delivering.

She was glad for the opportunity to stretch her legs as she weaved through ankle-high grass to look for lambs that might have dropped during the night.

She didn't see anything until she reached the far end of the field in the southernmost corner, right next to the electric netting that kept the ewes safe and predators out.

Zeus was shadowing the area, barking at her as she approached.

Angelica's heartbeat soared in excitement when she saw two wobbly white newborn lambs.

Twins!

Angelica was elated at discovering the two-for-one special.

She knew Rowdy would be pleased, as well. Extra lambs meant extra money.

But as Angelica stopped to observe them for a moment, she was concerned to see that while one lamb had been warmly welcomed by its mother and was contentedly nursing, the ewe was actively butting the other little lamb away from her, denying the poor thing its right to nurse with its twin.

Did sheep sometimes reject their own young? She suddenly wished she knew more about the animals Granny had committed to her care.

Pulse pounding, Angelica slipped her cell phone from the back pocket of her jeans and pressed Rowdy's number, which he had insisted she put on speed dial because she and Toby were living alone and he'd be the closest one to call in the case of an emergency.

Angelica wasn't certain this qualified as an emergency, but frankly, she didn't know who else to call. It was either Rowdy or the town vet, and who knew how long it would take for the vet to get here.

Plus, she knew Rowdy better, and trusted him implicitly.

"What's wrong?" Rowdy asked without so much as saying hello. "Are you okay? Is there something the matter with Toby?"

She was surprised at the depth of concern in his voice, but she quickly put him at ease on both counts.

"Toby and I are fine. But when I was walking in the field this morning looking for newborn lambs, I came upon a ewe that had just delivered twins."

"That's great," he assured her. "Ewes of this breed often have twins. It's nothing to worry about."

"Yes, well in this case, the ewe appears to be favoring one lamb over the other. She's completely rejecting one, actually, and it has me a little worried. Enough that I thought I'd better give you a call."

"You did the right thing," he said.

"Every time the second lamb moves in to try to nurse, the ewe butts it away." Her words came faster and fiercer with every syllable.

"Take a deep breath, Ange. This happens sometimes, especially with twins. We can take care of it. Where are you right now?"

"In the southernmost corner of the lambing field. The ewe is standing just short of the fence line. You'll be able to see—and probably hear—Zeus when you get close enough. He's been hovering. He really knows his job."

"Sit tight. I have to gather a few things together and then I'll be right over."

"Okay." Relief flooded through her. She was way out of her depth here, but Rowdy would know just what to do.

Rowdy had always been that man to her, the guy she could count on, and apparently, some things hadn't changed.

She thought the words, even if they were never anything she would admit to out loud.

Hero to the rescue.

Rowdy arrived with his bucketful of equipment and quickly assessed the situation. Frankly, he was more concerned about the state he'd found Ange in than for the little lamb seemingly rejected by its mother.

She looked worried. That sensitive side of Ange's heart, her vulnerability, was something few had seen. For some reason, she kept her guard up and didn't put her emotions on display. But Rowdy knew—or he'd thought he had known—who she really was. At least, until she'd run off and abandoned him on the eve of their wedding.

But right here, right now, the soft side of her was back in spades. Her heart was breaking for the rejected twin, perhaps recognizing the parallels in her own life. Her parents had, in all the ways that mattered to a young girl, rejected Ange when she was no more than a child.

And Toby, picking up on his mother's current distress, was squirming and wailing in the front pack, flapping his tiny arms and legs. He wasn't usually fussy, so that told Rowdy a lot.

"Finally," Ange said, laying a palm on her throat. "I

feel so bad for this little lamb. How can the mother be so unfeeling to her own baby?"

"Sheep aren't the brightest animals on the planet," he explained, kneeling next to the ewe and the deserted lamb. "This ewe may not realize the second lamb is hers. She may believe she is protecting the first lamb, the one she thinks is hers, from being pushed out by the twin."

"So what do we do now?" She moved closer, but with Toby in a front pack and a diaper bag slung across her hip, there was no way for her to crouch down by the ewe.

He didn't want her getting too close to the sheep, anyway, especially since he didn't know how strong of an immune system Toby had.

But when Ange said *we*, she meant *we*. He could see it was eating her up to have to stand by and watch, unable to do anything to help.

"First, let's try to coax the ewe into feeding the lamb. Just like with a human baby, the ewe's colostrum is best for the lamb, especially for the first day."

Rowdy scooped the rejected lamb into his arm and positioned himself so his shoulder would take the brunt of the ewe's force should she balk and try to butt the lamb away again.

"You can help block the ewe's movements with your legs, if you want, but be careful. I don't want you and Toby to get caught in the cross fire."

Rowdy half expected her to argue with him. Ange was the type of woman who always wanted to be right in the middle of the action.

But she merely nodded in agreement. "Don't worry. I'll be careful."

He tossed a glance up at her and their gazes met and held. Rowdy's throat burned and he swallowed hard.

Becoming a mother had changed Ange—in a good way. She was still the take-charge, independent woman she had always been, but somehow having Toby had softened her around the edges. He'd always known the gentle side of her was there, but she'd always chosen to hide it. Now, with Toby, that side of her personality beamed through.

The way she put Toby first in everything. That tender way she interacted with him, whether feeding him a bottle or changing a diaper.

Rowdy liked what he saw. And for the first time since she'd left him eight years ago, he allowed himself to acknowledge those feelings.

But only for a moment, since his attention needed to be completely focused on the lamb and its mama. For five minutes, Rowdy and Ange tried without success to get the rejected lamb to nurse on the ewe.

It didn't help that Toby was fussing in earnest, growing louder by the minute. Ange was desperately making shushing noises and using her hands to bounce Toby soothingly, but Toby would have none of it.

Ange flashed Rowdy an apologetic glance.

"I think he's picking up on my concern. He usually doesn't make this much noise, and it's startling the ewe."

"No worries. Why don't you go back to the house and take care of Toby and I'll keep working with the lamb? I suspect we're going to have to go with Plan B with this little girl, anyway."

"Plan B?"

"Plan Bottle-feed. I'll get it started, but I think you'll enjoy watching the process, so I'll wait for you in the barn, okay?"

Her expression shaded in disappointment. Rowdy

didn't know whether she was unhappy because she had to miss watching the beginning of the process of bottle-feeding, or because they hadn't been successful in getting the lamb to suckle on its mother.

He attempted to get the lamb to nurse for an additional ten minutes, but to no avail. There was no obvious reason he could see why the ewe would reject the lamb.

It looked healthy enough to his trained eye. It was possible there was a real problem, something he couldn't see, but he wasn't going to borrow trouble. The ewe's rejection didn't necessarily mean there was anything wrong with the lamb—only that the ewe was confused.

He scooped the lamb up in one arm and lifted his bucket of supplies with the other, then trod back over the field and into the barn, whistling as he went. Working with newborn lambs was one of the real perks of ranch living, and he loved it.

He penned the lamb while he went to work giving it the necessary inoculations and cleaning it, then mixed up a bottle of sheep's colostrum.

He didn't realize Ange was back until he heard a chuckle from behind him, startling him and making his heart gallop.

"That looks familiar," Ange said. "I go through almost the exact same process when I prepare supplementary formula for Toby. Except, of course, that the lamb's bottle is much bigger."

"Yeah?" he said, testing out the temperature of the formula on the inside of his arm.

Her chuckle became a downright laugh. "I do that, too."

"Then you should be an expert at feeding. Why don't

I wash up in the barn sink so I can hold Toby and let you have the honor of feeding the lamb?"

"Oh, could I?" Her eyes brightened. For someone who had no intention of sticking around and becoming a rancher, she certainly looked excited.

Then again, all babies were cute, be they humans or lambs. Maybe that was all it was.

Ange transferred Toby into Rowdy's arms and handed him a bottle of the baby's supplemental formula.

His gaze dropped to the sweet infant curled in his arms. Lambs were cute, but the little fellow blinking up at him with those big blue eyes was a whole other kind of wonderful. It got him right in the heart.

He wasn't familiar with feeding a baby, but he held Toby's bottle much as he would do with a lamb. Toby rooted for it a minute and then settled down to nurse, sucking noisily, his lips not quite sealing around the bottle. A tiny rivulet of milk dripped down his chin and Rowdy dabbed it away with the corner of the receiving blanket Toby was swaddled in.

"Same concept with the lamb," he encouraged Ange.

She awkwardly turned over the bottle, which was substantially larger than the one Rowdy was using with Toby, and pressed it to the lamb's lips.

The lamb didn't budge, as if it had no natural instinct to root for the bottle at all.

Ange sighed in frustration. "What am I doing wrong?"

"It's not you," he assured her. "She just needs a little more coaxing to be shown what to do."

Toby shifted and grunted, pushing the now-empty bottle away. The infant had certainly made quick work of *his* meal.

"Don't forget that you need to burp him," Ange reminded him. "Toby tends to swallow a lot of air when he is bottle-fed and those bubbles go deep."

Rowdy hesitated, not quite knowing what to do.

"Put him up against your shoulder and lightly pat his back," she said. "That will coax out the air."

His blank stare must have clued her in that he was walking around in entirely new territory here.

"Oh, and be sure to put a receiving blanket over your shoulder first. Those burps of his are sometimes a bit wet. You don't want to get formula all over your nice shirt."

Rowdy chuckled. He didn't care about the state of his shirt. He had a dozen just like this one, only in varying colors, hanging in his closet.

He was a cowboy. All he needed were a few T-shirts, some chambray and a couple pairs of jeans plus a Sunday service/wedding/funeral suit.

"I can't even get her to take this bottle," Ange said when the lamb continued to balk.

She shook her head and gestured toward the lamb.

"Can I give her a name?"

"A name? You mean like Rover or Charlie?" he teased. He'd always thought of his sheep by the numbers tagged in their ears. Sheep Nine or Lamb Twenty-One or something. Nothing like what Ange was suggesting.

"Well, yes, kind of," she explained. "You said this little lamb is a female, didn't you? I can't keep calling her *it* or *lamb*. It's too confusing."

Rowdy nodded, trying to conceal the smile that crept up one side of his lips as Ange's expression became thoughtful.

"How about Miss Woolsey?"

Miss Woolsey?

She had to be kidding him right now.

She wasn't kidding.

It took every ounce of his self-restraint not to break into laughter. The only thing that stopped him was how seriously Ange appeared to be taking this. She might pop him in the arm if she had any idea what was going through his mind.

Miss Woolsey.

He didn't know if she realized how difficult it was going to be to tell one lamb from another, assuming she wanted to name every one of them, which he suspected she did.

She would have to check the lamb's tag every time she wanted to address one of them by name, *and* she would have to memorize what name went with which tag. She would need a spreadsheet to keep track of it all.

He held back a snort as he imagined her carrying a physical spreadsheet around—or worse yet, an electronic tablet.

There were a lot of little lambs. He'd purposefully stretched the lambing season later for Granny Frances's flock than his own so he'd be able to work both.

"Okay. So how do I get Miss Woolsey here to nurse?" she asked, holding up her gloved hands and the bottle the lamb was stubbornly refusing.

"Put her between your knees and coax her head up with your free hand."

He waited until Ange had maneuvered herself into position before he continued.

"Squeeze the bottle enough to get the milk flowing and wipe the contents all over her snout, especially her lips. When she latches on, stroke her neck to encourage her to swallow."

Ange did as he'd suggested and Miss Woolsey successfully connected with the bottle.

Ange gave a small whoop of joy and then shushed herself, and Rowdy chuckled in earnest. He hadn't had this much fun during lambing season in years. It was amazing what a woman's perspective—especially one who was completely unfamiliar with sheep farming—could do to a man.

"I don't want to frighten Miss Woolsey away now that I have her eating, but it's so exciting to be able to know I had a part in saving this little lamb. I had no idea country living could be so satisfying."

Rowdy's heart warmed. He'd just shared an important part of his world with Ange, and she'd appreciated it.

Maybe even liked it.

"So, I've been thinking," Ange said as Miss Woolsey nursed off her bottle and Rowdy continued to enjoy holding baby Toby, who'd fallen asleep against his shoulder. "It's been nearly a week and we haven't heard a word about another envelope."

The ball of warmth in Rowdy's chest instantly hardened into ice and plunged into the pit of his stomach.

He'd thought they were making progress here as he taught Ange the ins and outs of ranch life, that they were doing exactly what Granny Frances had expected of them. He was even enjoying himself.

So much so that there were moments when he forgot the whole point was to get this—whatever *this* was—over and done with so he could claim Granny Frances's ranch as his own.

But somehow in the process he started to see—*feel*—tiny inroads into putting the past behind them. Like the sensation of Toby in his arms while Ange bottle-fed the lamb.

As it turned out, all Ange was interested in was the next envelope—moving ever forward so she and Toby could leave Serendipity and put country living behind them.

Of course that was what she wanted.

That was what he wanted, too, wasn't it?

So why was he finding it so difficult to remember the truth of why they were here and his own desire to move things forward toward his future?

Nothing had changed.

He was getting careless with his emotions, allowing Toby to sneak his way into his heart along with remnants of what he'd once felt for Ange.

Because it couldn't be more than that. There was nothing in the *present* about what he was feeling for her. Nothing new.

The first time Ange had left, she'd done so abruptly and without an explanation—although in his heart, he'd known why she had gone. It was because she deserved better than to be tied down to a cripple.

This time, she'd laid it all out for him. No surprises. She would fulfill Granny Frances's last wishes, and then she would leave.

Ange had broken his heart once.

He would not let her do so a second time.

Chapter Six

Angelica finished feeding Miss Woolsey, washed the bottle out in the barn sink and scrubbed her arms clean, and then went to relieve Rowdy of Toby, thinking he'd probably had enough of baby duty by now.

Rowdy had become extraordinarily quiet during the last few minutes, and Angelica couldn't read the unusual expression on his face.

This morning had gone well and she would definitely call it a win. They'd probably saved Miss Woolsey's life. Much more satisfying than feeding chickens.

It was exhilarating work, and Angelica's adrenaline was still pulsing through her veins. She'd learned very quickly to appreciate what ranchers spent their life's work on.

Saving a baby lamb? Now that was work worthy of pursuing.

So what was up with Rowdy?

His attitude had gone from day to night with no apparent explanation.

Maybe he just needed to eat something. In her limited experience with men, they tended to get grouchy when their stomachs were rumbling. Josh had always been that way, as had her father.

Rowdy was *nothing* like either of those men, but it was worth a shot. Even if his mood had nothing to do with the fact that he was hungry, he was still probably hungry.

"Why don't we stop by Cup O' Jo's for some lunch?" she suggested brightly. "It's been a long morning and I'm starving. Plus, I'm buying."

If she'd expected a positive reaction, something to the effect of, "Thank you, yes," she would have been disappointed.

She *was* disappointed.

Rowdy didn't even answer. He just sat on the hay bale where he'd parked himself earlier to nurse Toby and frowned down at the baby.

What was Rowdy's problem, anyway?

They'd had a great morning, and she was just trying to be nice. He'd kept Granny's ranch running and her stock healthy when Granny could no longer do the work herself. He'd continued to take care of the stock even after Granny had passed. He'd helped Angelica out a lot during this past week—and he hadn't needed to do any of it.

He could have let her fail. It might even have worked in his favor. He was helping her because of his love for Granny, and because the land would eventually be his.

Buying him a tasty meal was the least she could do to repay him for all he'd done.

That would also give them the opportunity to speak to Jo about when they should be expecting the next envelope.

She realized this whole conversation had been going on in her head and Rowdy hadn't answered her. Did he want to eat or not? She narrowed her gaze on him.

"Is there a problem here?"

"No. No problem."

He met her eyes, his gaze determined and his jaw set.

She recognized that look. He was being stubborn about something. The only question now was what he was getting his back up about.

She decided to ignore his odd behavior for the time being and instead suggested they head for the café.

"Do you want to ride together?" she asked.

He nodded. "I've got a few chores left to finish here afterward, anyway."

"Let's use my SUV, since I've already got the attachment for Toby's car seat on the seat belt."

His short grunt of agreement was apparently all she was going to get.

Rowdy continued to remain silent during the short drive to the café, staring out the passenger-side window with a pensive expression on his face.

She would have given far more than a penny for his thoughts. She considered everything that had happened that morning, trying to figure out what had changed, where Rowdy's attitude had vectored off course.

She came up with a big fat nothing.

That was one thing the years had taken from them— the ability for them to communicate with one another without words. She used to be able to tell what he was thinking, how he was feeling.

But now, nothing.

Unless he was purposefully shutting her out.

To her surprise, Rowdy's demeanor changed the moment he stepped into the café. Smiling, he greeted Jo with a side hug and a big smooch on her wrinkled cheek, then told her they would seat themselves in his regular booth.

So his attitude was just for her benefit, then. The brooding was all about her.

She didn't know why she was surprised, much less disappointed.

After all of the things she had done to him, some of which, like his limp, permanently lingered, it was a wonder that he even spoke to her at all, much less helped her get a handle on temporarily running Granny's ranch.

When Jo approached with her scratch pad, Rowdy ordered his usual, and Angelica blindly ordered the same, not even knowing what Rowdy's standard lunch order was anymore.

He used to like grilled cheese on whole wheat bread with dill pickle spears on the side and bag of barbecue chips, but the last time she'd sat in Cup O' Jo's with Rowdy had been when they were in their early twenties, and his tastes had probably grown and changed as much as he had.

Angelica didn't miss the many furtive glances and hissed whispers directed at her. Apparently, she was still a pariah. No doubt people were wondering why she was sitting with Rowdy—and why he didn't just up and leave.

It was only then that she realized what harm she could be doing, why Rowdy might have been dragging his feet when she'd suggested lunch at the café.

She'd inadvertently put him in the spotlight, in the awkward position of being seen sharing a meal with his ex-fiancée, and not only that, but a woman with a history of being the town's black sheep.

She respected Rowdy too much to have purposefully placed him in such a position, to put him through this embarrassing ordeal, but it was too late to back out now.

What was done was done.

Now all she could hope for was to make the rest of the meal as painless as possible and get out of there as quickly as they could.

She unhooked Toby from the car seat she'd set next to her on the booth and held him against her shoulder, knowing everyone in the café had a good view of her precious son.

She was a single mother, and maybe she was all those things the town accused her of being. They could judge her if they wanted to. She certainly had made more than her fair share of mistakes, and she owned up to them all.

But she was *not* ashamed of Toby. As far as she was concerned, the whole world could take their fill of looking, witnessing firsthand just how very much she loved her son.

Jo returned with their food—grilled cheese on whole wheat bread with dill pickle spears on the side and two bags of barbecue chips.

Apparently, some things really hadn't changed.

Angelica didn't know why that conclusion reassured her, but it did.

"Let me take that sweet baby while y'all enjoy your meal," Jo said, loud enough for every patron in the café to hear her.

It wasn't a suggestion, and Angelica immediately transferred Toby to her arms, knowing her son couldn't be in safer care.

Jo was like a second mother to most of the town, and any babies who entered her café were fair game for loving on and spoiling by the boisterous redhead.

But Jo taking Toby away and walking him around the café left Angelica alone with Rowdy as they ate. That was sure to stir up the buzz in the gossip hive, as if it wasn't enough that they'd made such an unforeseen spectacle of themselves at the auction.

At least people at the auction would have—*rightly*—assumed Rowdy had been taken off-guard and had no connection with Angelica, and that when Jo lassoed him and led him off the stage, only to deliver the rope into a stunned Angelica's hands, it wasn't Rowdy's fault at all.

The two of them sharing lunch together, though, in public and alone—now that was a sheep of a completely different color.

"I'm sorry," she whispered as Rowdy took a bite of his sandwich. "I didn't think."

Rowdy chewed and swallowed, then dabbed at his lips with his napkin.

"I'm not following."

"I understand now why you were dragging your feet in coming to the café with me today. You can't tell me you haven't noticed the way people are staring at us and whispering behind our backs."

"What did you expect, Ange?" His words were blunt but his tone was laced with gentleness. "You show up eight years after running out on me at the altar and you expect everyone to welcome you with open arms, no questions asked?"

"Of course not. I hadn't anticipated making a public appearance in town at *all*. But that ship sailed the moment I arrived at that stupid auction."

"The auction changed a lot of things," Rowdy agreed. "For both of us."

Angelica was just about ready to excuse herself and let Rowdy eat in peace when he did the most unimaginable thing ever.

He reached across the table and took her hand, locking their gazes as he did so.

Flabbergasted, she could do no more than remain captured by his blue eyes. Her heart stopped beating. Her breath stopped flowing.

What was he doing?

"Sometimes, the best way to face down a problem is to walk right through it. People have their opinions, and whether or not they change their minds is up to them."

"Face down your fear and walk right through it," she repeated. He made it sound so easy, when it was anything but. When her fears were even now staring at them and wondering what was happening between the two of them.

A corner of Rowdy's lips quirked up. "Walk right through it," he gently coaxed. "Unless the fear in question is Granny's Psycho Rooster, in which case I'd advise you to turn and run in the opposite direction."

They shared a laugh, but that only brought more attention from those seated around them.

Rowdy clicked his tongue against his teeth. "Sure, you can try to demonstrate all God has done in your life and how much becoming Toby's mother has altered your character for the better, but at the end of the day, folks will still think and feel what they want."

She realized she didn't care what people thought of her. They would change their opinions. Or not. It didn't matter.

But Rowdy? That was a whole other thing, and her heart warmed at his words.

Did *he* sense a change in her—alteration for the better, as he had said?

But this wasn't about her.

"It's not my reputation I'm worried about. Think about what this is doing to you."

She snatched her hand back and clasped her hands under the table.

"It was wrong of me to bring you here. You shouldn't be seen with me."

"It's not like you hog-tied me and dragged me in here with you. I'm my own man, and I make my own decisions."

And he'd decided to be seen with her?

"Despite the fact that people will be talking about you behind your back?" she pressed. "I know what that feels like, and it's not nice. At best they'll believe you're foolish and vulnerable for spending time with me again after all I've done to you."

"We both know what we're doing and why we're doing it, and that is nobody's business but ours. Speaking of which," he said as he shook out the last crumbs of his potato chips into his palm, "here comes Jo with Toby."

He funneled the chips into his mouth, chewed and swallowed before he finished his thought.

"And she's carrying an envelope."

Rowdy swallowed down the flood of panic that rose like molten lava as he read his and Ange's names scribbled on the front of the envelope.

Just like the last time. The message that had resulted in more confusion than he'd ever felt in his life. He was an emotional basket case.

What now?

Oddly, Ange's expression mirrored his, as if she'd swallowed something too large and it had stuck in her throat despite repeated attempts to swallow.

And yet she'd been the one who'd suggested asking Jo for the next envelope—all the better to leave Serendipity in the dust again with, my dear.

And the sooner the better, in her view.

She should be elated.

But now that the envelope rested on the table between them, she didn't look so certain. In fact, she was staring at the thing as if it were a rattlesnake, poised and ready to strike at her.

Ange had given Jo a bottle with which to feed Toby, and the older woman was seated in a chair nearby—far enough away to lend them a semblance of privacy, but then again, not really.

She was close enough to hear their conversation if she wanted to, and Rowdy guessed she did. She obviously knew a lot more about the envelope trail than he did.

Was this it?

The last missive?

At this point, he had no way of knowing. He would have to find a moment to pull Jo aside and ask her straight out. But first, there was the as-yet-unopened envelope to deal with.

Rowdy tested his feelings, gently poking at his myriad emotions and vulnerabilities.

Good memories. Bad memories. The pain of heartbreak.

And then there was what was happening between them now.

Bonding. Laughing. Spending time with Toby.

A friendship?

Or was he kidding himself and wanted more?

Did he still want Ange and Toby to leave? Was there a tiny, well-buried part of him that hoped, however unlikely, that Ange would stay and make Granny's ranch her home?

He shook his head. Why would he even consider such a notion?

They had a long bridge to cross to get anywhere near the closure they both needed.

However long or short she intended to stay, they hadn't yet approached the tender but necessary subject about what had happened to send Ange literally galloping out of his life all those years ago. It was a conversation they needed to have, no matter what kind of choices Ange made for her future.

But first—the envelope.

He took a deep breath and let it out slowly. So far, the missives, however short and vague, had turned out to be fairly straightforward. Hopefully this one was, too.

Granted, teaching Ange about the work Granny Frances had spent her whole life doing was a pretty tall order, but even in the short term, it was doable. To a point.

Sheep. Chickens. Avoiding roosters.

Ange's first letter, merely inviting her to a picnic, had been only the tip of a very large iceberg hovering just beneath the surface. But they'd weathered that one, too.

"Jo is giving us the eye," Ange said in a stage whisper, leaning forward on her elbows.

"You mean the one that is telling us to hurry up already? The one that brooks no argument?"

Ange chuckled and nodded. "That would be the one."

"Guess we'd better get at it, then."

"I suppose so." Ange picked up the envelope and slid her finger under the seal.

Her breath was coming heavy and erratic, nearly as

erratic as Rowdy's pulse, as he opened the single sheet of tri-folded printer paper and shook it out to read.

"Teach My Lambs."

"What is it with Granny Frances and three-word instructions?" he asked, frustration turning his voice into gravel.

Rowdy had hoped for more, something that they could clearly understand, for starters, and not have to guess as to its meaning.

And then, possibly, something that would keep Ange and Toby in town for a little while longer, at least long enough for him to work out his conflicting feelings toward her and her precious son.

"Okay, then," Ange said, letting out a breath. *"Picnic With Jo* was a picnic with Jo—more or less. *Feed My Sheep* was feeding sheep—and avoiding Psycho Rooster. So now we have *Teach My Lambs.* Teach them to do what, do you suppose?"

At a total loss, Rowdy snorted and shook his head.

"I'm a sheep farmer and I obviously have a strong bias toward them. I honestly care for my stock." He chuckled. "That said, sheep really aren't that smart. If I don't have one of my dogs constantly herding them and one sheep wanders off, the rest will dumbly follow. I've had pregnant ewes get confused and claim a lamb as their own when they haven't even given birth yet."

She shook her head. "And then there was the ewe who rejected one of her twin lambs. How can that even be possible? It still blows me away."

"I'll be honest. I can't think of much of anything we could teach the sheep. And this letter doesn't even mention *sheep*. It says *lambs*. That's just nuts."

In his mind, he was picturing trying to coax a lamb

to jump through a ring or roll over or beg. Bank off a hay bale or do flips?

A *lamb*?

So not going to happen.

"I told Frances this note would be too cryptic for you," Jo said, suddenly appearing at their table. Clearly, she'd been waiting for this precise moment to approach and intervene.

"Scooch over, big guy." She used her ample hips to bump Rowdy farther into the booth and take a seat beside him.

Toby was now sleeping silently in Jo's arms, and Ange offered to put him back in his car seat, but Jo would have none of it.

"I don't have nearly enough opportunities to cuddle with such sweetness," she said, pressing a kiss to Toby's forehead. "You're going to have to pry him away from me before you leave. He has the most precious features, doesn't he? Those almond-shaped blue eyes are to die for. I know experts say it's just a reflex at his age, but I am positive he smiled at me earlier. Plumb takes my breath away."

Rowdy couldn't agree more. He might be turning upside down and backward trying to figure out his feelings for Ange, but he had no such problems when it came to Toby. That little fella had Rowdy's heart wrapped tightly around the tiny thumb he was sucking.

Ange beamed at Jo's compliments about her son, but her expression morphed into a combination of confusion and frustration when her gaze returned to the letter in her hand.

She folded it back into thirds and tapped the corner on the tabletop.

"Obviously, this doesn't give us enough to go on. I'm currently working with Granny's sheep, with Rowdy's help, just like the last note suggested. But now she wants me to do what? Teach my newborn lambs how to sing the 'Star Spangled Banner'?"

He was startled at Ange's use of the word *my*.

She'd said *my* lambs, not Granny's. Did that mean she was taking mental ownership of the ranch work she'd been doing?

Jo chuckled. "Singing sheep. Now that's something I'd like to see."

"Rowdy said it won't be easy to teach a lamb any kind of trick," Ange continued. "Sheep apparently aren't as smart as some other farm animals are."

"But Granny Frances knew that," Rowdy inserted. "So why would she even want us to try? It makes no sense."

"Because, my sweet darlings, she isn't talking about your lambs," Jo said. "She had a much smarter type of animal in mind, though no doubt a good bit more unpredictable."

Amusement twinkled in Jo's eyes. She was thoroughly enjoying taking them on this little roller-coaster ride. Rowdy wished she'd just get to the point and tell them what they were supposed to be doing.

Maybe he could at least get a little something from her without all this game playing.

"You'll tell us when we've received the last envelope, right?"

Her gaze widened in surprise. "Why, of course, my dear. I wouldn't even dream of leaving you both hanging indefinitely. That wouldn't be fair to either one of you."

And yet, she was, saying the lambs in the current letter weren't lambs at all, but not giving so much as a hint as to what they were really talking about.

He realized in hindsight that he hadn't asked the right question to clarify the whole shenanigan. He should have asked how many notes were left, got a precise number so they could at least have some clue where they were on the Granny Frances's Last Wishes Continuum.

Too late now. Knowing that this letter wasn't the last—and ignoring that tiny part of him that was leaping for joy that Ange and Toby weren't going away quite yet—would have to be enough.

At the end of the day, no matter how many envelopes were involved, Ange and Toby *would* be going away. No doubt she was already thinking about Toby's future and the many benefits he would have in the big city that Serendipity simply didn't and couldn't offer. And rightly so.

Rowdy returned his thoughts to the present just as Ange prompted Jo with another question.

"So, the *lambs* we are supposed to teach are actually...?"

"People. Teenagers, to be exact," Jo crowed with laughter at the expressions on their faces.

Teenagers?

Rowdy nearly choked on his breath. What on earth did Granny Frances think he'd be able to do with teenagers? That was so far out of his comfort zone—not to mention his skill set—that it might as well be dinosaurs he was being asked to teach.

And the question remained—teach *what*?

Maybe he'd been mistaken and the letter had only been addressed to Ange.

Rowdy turned the envelope over to check out the front side.

Nope.

There it was, in black and white. Rowdy's name scribbled right next to Ange's, followed by three exclamation points for good measure. Granny Frances had definitely not wanted them to be mistaken on this point.

Ange cleared her throat, so Rowdy knew he wasn't the only one at the table having a hard time breathing through this new revelation.

"Which teenagers, exactly, are we talking about? And the note says nothing about what we are supposed to teach them."

Rowdy was glad Ange had picked up the conversation and was ferreting out the details, because he was still stunned to silence.

"Frances was very involved in the youth group at church," Jo explained.

Rowdy already knew that, but he had no idea what she did when she was with them. Led them in Bible studies and service projects, presumably.

Hmm. They could manage to do that, he supposed, especially if Jo pointed the way for them.

Collect clothing for the needy, or help a neighbor harvest early crops in order to give some of the bounty to some of Serendipity's poorer residents. Maybe do some sort of summer missions project.

"Frances was spearheading the annual ranch rodeo for the Fourth of July."

The *ranch rodeo*?

Jo's words were a sucker punch right to Rowdy's gut, robbing him of breath.

His gaze shot to Ange. Her face had drained of color until she was as white as a sheet. Her mouth opened and her lips were quivering, but no words emerged.

"I know it's usually the ranch hands who compete,"

Jo continued, as if she hadn't taken note of their reaction, "but this year it's going to be the teens from church. She did most of the legwork before she got sick, but she wanted you two to make sure the event goes off without a hitch, if you'll pardon my pun."

Rowdy's hands fisted in his lap.

"You must be mistaken," he said through gritted teeth. "Granny Frances would never ask that of us."

"Oh, I'm not mistaken, and she did," Jo affirmed promptly. "And before you ask, she knew exactly what she was doing when she wrote this letter and she was completely in her right mind. So I suggest both of you cowboy up and get used to the idea, because this ranch rodeo isn't going to happen unless you two get it in gear."

Ange was staring at the tabletop as if she hoped it would open up and swallow her whole.

Rowdy shook his head and set his shoulders.

"Then I'm sorry, Jo. You have to know that up until today, Ange and I have done everything required of us in Granny Frances's directives. We love her and we want to honor her last wishes.

"But a ranch rodeo? That's just not going to happen."

Chapter Seven

Rowdy's response didn't surprise Angelica in the least, and she doubted Jo was shocked by it, either. But Granny's note had floored her as effectively as an uppercut to the jaw would have done.

Fortunately, she was already seated, or the lurch her stomach took might have sent her reeling. And she was glad Jo still held on to Toby. Angelica didn't want her sweet son picking up on the maelstrom of emotions sweeping like a hurricane through her chest.

A ranch rodeo?

How could Granny have even considered such a thing? Not for Angelica and Rowdy.

The ranch rodeo was a yearly event in Serendipity, where local ranchers competed in laugh-out-loud-hilarious events like wild cow milking and paint branding as they mimicked the work they did on the ranch.

"You both owe her so much," Jo inserted, as if in response to Angelica's thoughts—and Rowdy's white-faced expression. "I don't have to remind you that these are her last wishes. Ya gotta do what ya gotta do, no matter how painful it gets."

"Yes, but—" Angelica didn't know how to finish her response, so she let it drop. Her eyes flew to Jo, who nodded as if the matter was settled.

Angelica switched her gaze to Rowdy, who appeared even more befuddled than she was—and angry, as well he should be. His whiskered cheeks darkened to a deep cherry and worry lines creased his forehead.

Granny should never have asked this of him.

For once, Angelica could really see his age, and the effects of all the stress he'd had to endure, including the many ways she'd hurt him.

"You know what you have to do," Jo reminded them. "Frances's plans are in the top drawer of her filing cabinet in her home office. The youth group meets on Sunday afternoons, which means you'll only have a couple of sessions between now and the day of the ranch rodeo to sort out who is doing what and when. We've been rotating teachers from the congregation to fill in for their weekly meetings, but now that you're here you can take over.

"Frances won't be the only one you'd be letting down. The kids will be so disappointed if you don't step up and help them make this rodeo a success. And you only have two weeks to plan."

That was one last jab Angelica didn't need.

"Granny Frances couldn't have meant that she wanted us there," Rowdy protested. "She knew I never attended the Fourth of July activities, and I especially avoided the ranch rodeos. Everyone in town knows why."

Angelica's breath left her in a whoosh and her heart felt as if it was being squeezed by an invisible fist.

The fallout of Rowdy's statement, the emotional shrapnel, rained over her.

Picnicking with Jo, even if she had ended up in the

middle of a town crowd she had very much wished to avoid, and even learning how to work a sheep farm—those were doable, if difficult, tasks.

But organizing and overseeing a ranch rodeo?

Now, that was just plain cruel.

Angelica and Rowdy—especially Rowdy—ought to get up and walk away right now.

She hated to disappoint the teens in the youth group, but one year without a rodeo wouldn't be the end of the world for Serendipity and the teenagers would have many more opportunities to compete in future ranch rodeos.

Besides, there were plenty of other activities for townsfolk to enjoy on the Fourth of July—music, a rope obstacle course for the kids, community games and of course fireworks to end the evening with a bang.

"I know this will be difficult—for both of you," she acknowledged. "But I really think it's important. Important enough for Frances to make this request of you."

"Yeah, but to what end?" Rowdy muttered as his eyebrows furrowed.

"What benefit could she possibly foresee?" Angelica asked, pressing further. "To me, the whole suggestion is a recipe for disaster."

"I'm inclined to agree with you," Jo said, although the determined spark in her eyes said otherwise. "When you've finished your meal, go back to Frances's ranch and read through the plans she left you. Maybe they will clue you in as to why she's chosen you to complete this difficult task."

In the next moment, Jo transformed from an attitude of serious concern to that of bubbly enthusiasm.

"Anyone up for some New York cheesecake?" she

asked brightly. "Phoebe's been working on them all morning. She's actually from New York, did you know?"

Phoebe Hawkins was the local pastry chef who'd transplanted from New York City. She'd had a stellar national reputation, and had left everything to marry Chance, the café's cook and Jo's nephew. And she couldn't have been happier.

At any other time, Angelica wouldn't even have considered passing up one of Phoebe's delectable treats, but right now her stomach was in knots and she was feeling a tad nauseated.

Rowdy's eyes met hers and he gave her a nearly imperceptible nod.

"I think we'll pass on dessert today," Rowdy said, speaking for both of them. "It sounds like we have a lot to work out back at Granny Frances's office, and I know we're both anxious to see what's what on this ranch rodeo and make some decisions on where to go from here."

"Of course, dear. Just remember, that envelope Angelica's holding is an important component of Frances's last wishes. Don't let her down."

They got the message already. Angelica didn't think Jo needed to keep rubbing it in.

Angelica collected Toby and locked him in his car seat, then followed Rowdy out to her SUV.

"I'll take *ignoring the guilt card* for five hundred dollars, please," she remarked the moment they were alone in the vehicle together. She couldn't help feeling slightly snarky about it all.

"Jo did pour it on pretty thick," he agreed, then fell silent.

The ride back to Granny's ranch was made in the same uncomfortable quiet as the ride to the café had been—Rowdy staring out the window in brooding silence and Angelica driving with her jaw set and both hands clenched on the steering wheel, trying to breathe through her frustration.

When they reached the ranch, Angelica suggested she put Toby down for his afternoon nap while Rowdy went to the office to see if he could find the file Jo was talking about.

She sensed Rowdy's hesitation well before he spoke.

"Would it be too much to ask for me to be the one who puts Toby down and for you to go find the file?"

Angelica was nearly as reluctant to revisit the past through the contents of Granny's file as Rowdy was.

But she thought it might be better for them to face it *together*.

"Why don't we both put Toby down and then go find the file?" she suggested gently.

What had Granny been thinking?

She'd been asking that question a lot since she'd returned to Serendipity, but instead of finding answers she kept running into more questions.

Not to mention confused feelings.

Thanks to Granny, she had gone from never, *ever* intending to see Rowdy again to working with him on a daily basis. And now, they were standing together in Toby's nursery preparing the baby for his nap, making the area feel oddly intimate.

Rowdy's large figure took up more than just area in the room. He took up emotional space, as well.

Angelica's pulse was pounding as she changed Toby, and she knew by the way the baby's feet and arms flapped that he was picking up on her discomfort. She took a deep breath and tried to calm the frantic beat of her heart.

Rowdy noticed Toby's disquiet, as well.

"Does the little guy need a bottle or something before we lay him down in his crib?"

Angelica shook her head. "He just needs to be rocked for a minute."

Rowdy came up behind her. He wasn't quite touching her, but she could feel his warm presence as tangibly as if he'd put his arms around her and pulled her close to him.

"May I?" His voice was low and scratchy.

Rowdy picked up Toby and laid him against his broad shoulder, then sang a soft lullaby in a rich baritone while shuffling his cowboy boots around the room in an unchoreographed dance.

Angelica hadn't even known Rowdy could sing, and it occurred to her only now that there were probably many things she didn't know about the man Rowdy had become.

The boy she remembered was not the man who now stood before her—and not just physically, either.

Eight years of living had changed and molded him, just as it had done with her.

But as he bent over the crib to put the now-sleeping Toby to bed, lingering there for a moment with a tender, appreciative expression on his face, it wasn't the past or the present Angelica was considering.

It was the future.

Or at least, the future that might have been if she hadn't ruined everything. For one moment, she allowed herself to compare the differences.

Rowdy as her spouse and her soul mate.

Toby as their son.

But those things were not and could not ever be true. She had to close the door on this way of thinking and all of the emotions such imaginings invoked, or she would drive herself crazy.

And she knew exactly how to close the door on the past and the future.

Permanently.

By opening the ranch rodeo file in Granny's office cabinet.

Rowdy was literally dragging his booted feet as Ange lead him into Granny Frances's office.

He had just experienced one of the most incredible, special moments of his life—getting to participate in an important ritual for baby Toby.

With the three of them taking up the majority of the room in the small nursery, which was furnished with only a crib and a changing table, sharing the space together felt intimate in a way he'd never before experienced.

The comparisons between what was and what could have been didn't escape him.

But for possibly the first time since Ange had reentered his life, he didn't run from those thoughts and emotions.

Toby was such a precious little soul, with so much life teeming from those almond-shaped blue eyes and the heart-capturing smile that only a Down baby could make.

When he'd commented on it, Ange had laughed and said that at Toby's age it was only a reflex smile, but Rowdy still couldn't help but believe the baby's grin was just for him.

As for Toby's mama—he wasn't quite ready to confront all his feelings for Ange, much less contemplate what that might mean for them in the future.

Not that there would be a future of *any* kind for the three of them after they'd taken a look at the contents of Granny Frances's file. Neither one of them even wanted to revisit the past, to think about ranch rodeos, never mind plan one. Rowdy, because of his injury, and Ange, who had jilted him because she couldn't handle the thought of living with a man who might always be bound to a wheelchair.

She'd left without knowing he'd be able to walk again.

But then, he'd told her to leave.

There were too many bad memories.

Part of him just wanted to turn around and walk out without knowing what Granny Frances expected of him, but despite realizing how disruptive the file might be, he couldn't walk away.

Would the contents change everything between him and Ange, when they would have to plan a saddle bronc riding event—especially with teenagers as the participants? With the thought that someone might be injured, just as Rowdy had been all those years ago?

Rowdy hadn't attended a ranch rodeo since his injury, but he knew there hadn't been any accidents since. Even his had been a freak calamity that no one could have foreseen.

There was no reason to think this year would be different. And yet a cloud of doubt hovered over him, and he suspected it hung over Ange, as well.

By the end of today, it might not be him walking away from whatever tentative feelings were growing between them.

Ange might take Toby and *run*.

Upon first entering the office, Ange placed the baby monitor she'd taken with her from the nursery on the edge of the desk, so both of them would hear Toby when he woke from his nap.

After wrestling to open the rusty top drawer of the battered metal file cabinet, she immediately drew out a bright yellow accordion file folder stuffed with papers, some with bent corners sticking out of the top.

Granny Frances was many things, but organized wasn't one of them, at least with her paperwork. She hated that part of owning a ranch and avoided it whenever she could.

Rowdy had visited Granny Frances in her office from time to time, and bills and receipts had always littered the desktop with no rhyme or reason that he could see, although Granny Frances had insisted that she had a system that worked for her.

The bills and receipts were gone now. Jo and Granny Frances's lawyer must have been in here as part of settling the estate.

And yet they had left this one file.

"It's the only thing in here," Ange confirmed when he asked. She used two hands to move the awkwardly large file to the center of the desk.

She took a seat in Granny Frances's office chair and he sat on the opposite side of the desk.

Their gazes locked as Ange removed the thick pile of papers and fanned them out across the desk.

Rowdy knew they were both thinking the same thing—the one and only ranch rodeo he'd ever participated in had been the beginning of the end of their relationship.

Ange cleared her throat and riffled through the pages. "Every youth whose family owns a ranch is a team leader. The kids whose parents work in the community or as ranch hands have all been assigned as seconds. From the look of it, we're going to have at least twelve ranches participating, maybe more."

"We? I haven't agreed to anything yet."

"I know." Her lips curled downward.

"Have you found a list of events yet?" he asked.

She shook her head. "It's not anywhere on these first few pages. Let's see."

She continued to rifle through the papers and eventually pulled one from the center of the bunch. "Here it is— although this looks more like Granny was brainstorming than anything that was set in stone. There are doodles all over the page. It appears to be a mind map of sorts."

"So, what have we got?"

He knew he was speaking through gritted teeth and he tried to relax his jaw, but the more he concentrated on relaxing, the more his muscles tightened. His fisted hands were grasping the edge of his chair in a death grip.

"The usual." She was trying to keep her tone light and even, but he could hear her voice shaking and knew she was going to say *those words* before they ever crossed her lips.

"We've got stray gathering, trailer loading, paint branding, wild cow milking and mutton busting." She paused. "That's always a good one to get the crowd laughing."

He didn't buy her upbeat tone for a second.

"And?" he asked, his mouth dry and his voice coarse.

She dropped her gaze from his.

"And saddle bronc riding."

There.

The words had been said and were now hanging in the air between them.

Saddle bronc riding.

The injury he'd sustained competing in that event was the reason he still walked with a limp to this day.

And it was likewise the reason Ange had ultimately chosen to run away from him before their wedding.

Granny Frances had used three words to communicate her wishes in the notes she had left for them.

But these three words weren't anything like Granny Frances's kind, if cryptic, notes.

They were pure poison, damaging Rowdy and Ange in a way no other words could do.

Saddle bronc riding.

Chapter Eight

Angelica's heart nearly split in two as she watched the pain and agony that crossed over Rowdy's expression before his face hardened.

He must be reliving his accident.

All of it.

She wouldn't blame him if he stood up and flipped the desk over before stalking off in a rage, not that Rowdy would ever make such a display of fury.

He wasn't that man.

But he *should* be angry.

As for Angelica, she had a big fat *guilty* stamped on her forehead in permanent black ink.

She waited for Rowdy to speak, but he didn't. He just snapped the page from her grasp and gave it a long perusal, his hand running across the stubble on his jaw.

"We don't have to keep the saddle bronc riding event," she suggested gently. "We don't *have* to be in charge of this rodeo at all."

Rowdy hissed an audible breath through his teeth.

"Surely with Jo's help we can find someone else to pull this together," she continued. "Someone who doesn't have the kind of history with it as we do. I don't care what Jo said earlier. She would understand why we can't do this."

Rowdy remained silent and thoughtful for a moment, then shook his head.

"Granny Frances wanted *us* to do it. And she knew at least as well as anyone did what kind of history she would be digging up with this request."

"I think I'm beginning to understand where at least part of this scavenger hunt, or whatever you want to call it, is coming from."

"Yeah?"

"Granny was the only one from my old life who I kept in touch with at all," she explained. "And that was only near the end of the eight years I was gone, after I discovered I was pregnant with Toby. That was when I finally reached out to her. When I left Serendipity, I left everything and everyone behind, even Granny."

He grunted in response, leaning back in his chair and crossing his arms.

"After I calmed down and realized what I'd done in running away from our wedding, my mindless fear disappeared and guilt readily took its place. Oh, Rowdy, I am so ashamed of my actions, especially the many ways I hurt you. I truly believed you were the love of my life and the man I wanted to marry. I shouldn't have left the way I did. I should have treated our relationship—and you—with more respect."

Rowdy visibly flinched, his face coloring with emotion.

"Do we have to dig all this up again?"

"Yes. I believe we do. It seems to me that all of this—" she made a grand gesture that spanned far beyond just the office and into the entirety of the ranch and beyond

"—was done in order to force us to cooperate, to work out some of our issues."

She waited for his response, her stomach queasy and her face so enflamed it must be at least as red as Rowdy's.

He stood and stalked to the office door, and for a moment she thought he was leaving but then he turned back and walked in her direction. He planted his fists on the desktop and leaned toward her.

"Why would she do that?" His voice was a gravel-sounding mixture of confusion and anger. "Why force the issue?"

"Honestly, I think, at least for me, she was ripping off the bandage to allow my wounds to heal naturally. To heal my heart."

He looked genuinely perplexed.

"Wounds? What wounds? From where I'm standing, you're the one who did all the ripping." He growled in frustration. "You walked out on *me*, remember?"

How could she not?

It had been on her mind every day since the night it happened.

From the time she'd agreed to follow Granny's missives that included spending time with Rowdy, she'd known this conversation was bound to happen. All of this—staying in Serendipity, discovering Granny's intentions and God's had led her here to this moment.

She wanted to flee from the office and avoid a confrontation, but that was her old self.

Her new self, with the Lord's help, would seek to make amends for all of the pain and suffering she'd caused Rowdy, and seek closure for both of them so they could move on with their lives.

"I did walk out on you," she admitted, folding her hands on the desk and tilting her head up until their gazes met. "Rode off, actually."

That last part was her attempt to insert a note of dry humor into the conversation.

Epic fail.

"But I think we need to go back a little bit further than that," Ange said.

Rowdy's brow furrowed. "What's that supposed to mean?"

"Granny never had a mean bone in her body, so it makes no sense that she would ask us to revisit the ranch rodeo and all the painful memories from it unless she truly felt we needed to begin there and move forward."

Rowdy didn't move a muscle, as if he'd turned to ice.

"If I don't miss my guess, the saddle bronc riding is where she wanted us to start. We have to decide whether or not we want to keep the event in our lineup, which by default means we have to face up to what happened eight years ago. We need to talk about it. Perhaps try to find some kind of closure."

She hitched a breath but it stuck in her throat. "Except there is no closure. Not for you. Not with your—"

She couldn't finish the sentence. Tears pricked at the backs of her eyes and it took every ounce of her willpower not to let them go, knowing if she did she wouldn't be able to keep from sobbing in earnest.

"My limp. You can say it, Ange. I've had eight years to get used to the idea. It hardly bothers me anymore, and I don't mind talking about how I got the injury."

"Does it still hurt?" Angelica pulled her bottom lip between her teeth and bit down hard enough to taste the copper of her own blood. The pain distracted her from her shredding heart.

"No. Not really. It aches a little when we have a cold snap or if I crouch one too many times in a day. Nothing that taking an anti-inflammatory can't fix."

"But you walk with a limp."

"I'll never be at one hundred percent. My leg drags a little when I'm not paying attention or I get too tired. But again, I've learned to live with it and it doesn't bother me. Honestly."

He sat down and rolled his shoulders. "My muscles ache more from daily ranch work than from a rodeo injury that happened years ago."

Angelica couldn't help the way her gaze took him in—his broad shoulders sloping to a lean waist. A well-muscled chest and firm biceps carved from a life of picking up hay bales and feed sacks. Strong legs from walking endless fields and riding horses.

He had no need of a gym. His lifestyle was quite enough to keep him in tip-top condition.

He tilted his head and caught her gaze, and she realized she'd been caught staring—and not only that, but caught staring *appreciatively.*

A spark of humor lit his blue eyes and the heat in her face became a bonfire. Her pulse raced, and it wasn't just because she'd been caught, nor that Rowdy had clearly followed the train of her thoughts.

She was reacting to him.

The man sitting just across the desk from her.

Not the boy who'd believed in her when no one else would give her a chance, nor even the one whose life she'd wrecked with her careless words and actions.

Just Rowdy, the cowboy Granny had recently sent her off on an adventure with.

An adventure they were far from having finished.

She hated to douse the spark in his eyes, or bring the stress back when he'd just now started to relax. His body language said it all.

Suddenly, the baby monitor crackled to life as Toby wakened. Angelica excused herself long enough to bring Toby and his bouncer into the office.

By this time, Rowdy was slumped back in his seat with one ankle crossed over the other knee. The muscles in his shoulders had loosened and he'd laced his fingers over his flat stomach.

"We still have to talk about this," she said, avoiding his gaze.

"Yeah. We do."

Of course. Ange had hit the nail right on the head.

Confronting the past. Laying to rest every nightmare that lingered. Not only revisiting it, but closing that chapter so they could both move on with their lives.

Move on.

He with an expanded acreage and an increase in stock. Ange and Toby with enough money to see them settled for at least the immediate future. Maybe Ange could even start a trust fund for Toby's long-term care out of the sale of Granny Frances's ranch.

A win-win for everyone concerned.

So why didn't it feel like a win to him?

"The accident," he said grimly.

When their eyes had met a moment ago, he'd been certain she'd been giving him a flattering once-over, which only served to make his own attraction for her more undeniable as his pulse quickened.

Some of her allure was her pretty face and hourglass figure, but that wasn't everything.

He'd been drawn to her from the moment they entered kindergarten and she'd been sent to the principal's office on the first day of school for fighting.

Rowdy had seen the whole thing and he knew what had really happened. Ange had stepped into the middle of an unfair struggle with a big bully of a girl who had pushed another, smaller girl to the ground at recess and was pulling her hair until the little girl was screaming in pain.

The other girl had gotten away with nothing more than a reprimand. Ange had come out of the escapade with a black eye and detention, despite the little girls she'd rescued coming to her defense. The situation was made worse by the fact that she was the pastor's daughter and consequently held to a higher standard of behavior.

And yet she'd never said a word to defend her own actions.

Ange was a scrappy little thing, defending the defenseless and taking the brunt of the blame with no care for herself.

Whenever good-little-Christian Rowdy stepped in to help, he was praised, whereas Ange, who defied her faith and her parents, was unfairly criticized, all because teachers and staff had labeled her a troublemaker.

By high school, she was understandably rebellious, skipping school and hanging out with a bad crowd, while Rowdy, though he struggled with academics, was a model student who worked his sheep farm alongside his parents rather than participate in extracurricular activities or sports.

It was Granny Frances who had originally set him up with Ange, inviting both of them to her house at the same time and then acting as if it hadn't been planned. And though on paper a relationship between Rowdy and Ange should never have worked, it did.

Or at least, it had.

Until he got injured at that wretched ranch rodeo. He shouldn't have been saddle bronc riding in the first place. But he'd been young and stupid and had believed, as most youth did, that he was invincible.

"You're right," he acknowledged, knowing that Ange had been waiting for his response. "The ranch rodeo changed everything for us."

She flinched and her lips pressed into a thin, straight line. She squeezed her eyes closed and he wondered if she was holding back tears.

His own eyes were burning as he took a deep breath and plunged into the deep.

"You—you were right to call off the wedding."

There.

He'd said it aloud, words that he had never even dared to admit to himself, much less tell another.

It had been so much easier to point the finger at Ange and harbor resentment toward her than to take the responsibility that belonged only to him.

The truth was so much more complicated than casting blame.

"I was wrong to—" Ange started, but then her words skidded to a halt midsentence. "What did you say?"

This time he didn't stutter or falter in his words.

"I said you were right not to marry me."

Hurt and shock crossed her expression.

"What?"

"You only did what I told you to do. I was the one who said we ought to break it off before the wedding."

"And you meant it?"

He shook his head. "No. I was immature and resentful about my injury. I believed I wasn't any good to anyone, especially you. I didn't know if I would ever walk again, and I couldn't ask you to tie yourself to a man in a wheelchair. I couldn't provide for you if I couldn't work the ranch."

"How could you even think that?" she asked, her voice strained. "I was ready to recite vows that included for better or for worse."

"No marriage should start with *worse*."

"What?" she squeaked.

"Didn't you have your doubts?"

"Of course I did. But not about you being in a wheelchair. Like you said, we were both young and immature. I doubted myself, not you."

"If you did, it was because I hadn't offered you the support you needed to believe in yourself. I was focused on myself, on regaining my own strength, and in the process, I shut you out."

"That's not it at all. I'm talking about how you got injured in the first place. Rowdy, I was *responsible* for your accident. You wouldn't have been on that horse at all if it wasn't for me. You got hurt because of me."

He stared at her in confusion, utterly bewildered.

"You don't even remember, do you?" She sounded flabbergasted. "I dared you to do the saddle bronc riding—pressured you into it, even when you told me that saddle bronc riding wasn't really your thing. If it wasn't for me, you wouldn't have participated. You wouldn't have ridden that bronc, and you wouldn't have had that accident."

She scoffed. "Stupid me. Saddle bronc riding is the most dangerous event in ranch rodeo, and I wanted my fiancé to show off and win so that *I* could have bragging rights. I didn't give a second's thought as to what I might be doing to you. Some loving fiancée I was. It still makes me sick just to think about it."

Rowdy frowned. "How many times do I have to tell you this? I am my own man and I always have been. I wouldn't have signed up for that event unless I wanted to."

"Yes, but that's my point. *Why* did you want to ride? It was because I kept bringing it up and encouraging you to sign up. I wouldn't take no for an answer."

He jerked his head in acknowledgment. "That was part of it. I thought I had something to prove to you, something that riding a bronc would do. But I had something to prove to myself, as well.

"I've always lived a fairly isolated life out on my ranch, even when I was a teenager. I never played sports or did any extracurricular activities. I saw the ranch rodeo as something I could do to become more involved with the community, and maybe I had something to prove to the cattle ranchers. The Triple X Ranch needed a saddle bronc rider, and none of their wranglers wanted to tackle it, so I signed up."

"Even though bronc riding wasn't in your skill set. The point of a ranch rodeo is to mimic the work wranglers actually perform on their ranches. Starting and training horses is a big part of the work on some ranches, but not yours. You never rode broncs."

She sighed. "You would have been better served in an event like paint branding or trailer loading. And you might be the best man in town at stray gathering."

"It sounds foolish and not at all well thought through when you put it that way," he admitted. "But I was nearly twenty-one, in prime physical condition, and I was on top of my world. My dreams were coming true. I was about to marry the most wonderful woman I'd ever known and then we were going to settle down and raise a wonderful family on the land I loved. I got cocky, and then I got hurt."

"I still think I'm to blame," Angelica insisted. "I was the one who put the idea in your head in the first place."

"Maybe so, but there is no way you could have foreseen what would happen. It was a freak accident. Everyone said so, including the saddle bronc experts. My horse panicked and hit the wall, crushing my knee. I couldn't have seen it coming, nor could I have responded quickly enough to have avoided the collision, especially since my focus was on getting to the end of those eight seconds any way I could. I didn't know what my horse was going to do."

He scrubbed a hand across his jaw. "At the end of the day, I rode because I wanted to show off for you. But it wasn't your fault I got hurt."

Toby made a mewling sound from his bouncer, which Rowdy now recognized as his precursor to crying.

"What is it, little man? You think you need to be part of this conversation?" Ange lifted Toby into her arms.

"I know I was a jerk to you after the accident," Rowdy said. "In my anger and frustration at being crippled, I pushed you away."

"You did push me away, but I should never have gone.

I understood your exasperation at being confined to a wheelchair. You are a man of the land, and not being able to do your ranch work must have made you feel inadequate.

"Yet no injury of any kind should ever have pulled me from your side."

She paused and ran a hand across her cheek as if to wipe away a tear. "I never told you how much I admired your determination to work through the pain of physical therapy. I know it wasn't easy for you."

"I'm a proud man," he acknowledged. "Too proud, sometimes. I should have let you in, dealt with this crisis together as a couple should, and instead I told you that you didn't want to marry a cripple. The fact that I didn't really mean the words doesn't negate the fact that they were said."

"I wanted to marry *you*, Rowdy. Like I said before. For better or for worse."

"Then why did you run away?"

Angelica stared down at Toby for a moment, as if searching for the right words with which to answer his question.

At last, she hitched in a breath and plunged forward.

"Because I was afraid."

Rowdy's brow furrowed and he scrubbed a hand through his thick hair.

"And I heard you."

"You heard me? You heard me *what*?"

"Laughing. Joking around with your groomsmen after the wedding rehearsal."

"On the day before our wedding? Of course I was laughing. I was elated, over the moon with joy."

Her face flushed a furious red. "You don't under-stand."

"Then enlighten me."

"You'd been so cross and moody since your accident, which was nothing like you. And as I said, I blamed my-self for that.

"I know we were getting along better as our wed-ding day approached, but we were still working out our problems. When I heard you with your groomsmen, you sounded so happy and carefree. Far more than you'd been with me at any time after the accident."

All this time, he had thought Ange had left him be-cause she'd realized he wasn't good enough for her, that he couldn't provide for her. That she didn't want to be saddled with a man who was less than one hundred per-cent.

But now he realized it was far more complicated than he'd could ever have imagined.

Ange had dropped her gaze and was nuzzling Toby's neck, whispering soft reassurances that Rowdy suspected were as much for her benefit as they were for Toby's.

"You heard me laughing," he repeated, his throat tight-ening around the words. "Honey, you should have said something if it bothered you."

"I know that now. But back then, I wasn't strong enough to face you. I wanted you to be happy, truly happy, and I convinced myself I was the last woman in the world who could give you that joy. I had suspected it for a long time and my fear grew until it overwhelmed me. I realized how wrong the two of us were together. Whether I'd meant to or not, I'd hurt you by insisting you ride in that ranch rodeo, and I knew I was bad news for you.

Maybe it would have been something different, but something else would have happened, again and again. I'm no good for you."

Fresh tears welled in her eyes. Toby made a distressed mewl. Even though he was only a few weeks old, Toby could tell something was wrong. He didn't like his mama sad and crying.

Rowdy didn't want that, either. He picked up a stuffed blue bunny from the bouncer and reached for Toby, giving Ange a moment to compose herself.

He hummed a few bars of a Texas two-step and shuffled and danced around the room with Toby, who appeared to love the attention and the rhythm of the song and dance.

"Don't you think I should have been the judge of that?" he asked between beats.

"Yes. I see that now. But back then I was afraid that if I talked to you, you would convince me to stay, and that was the one thing I couldn't do—not when I believed I wasn't the right person for you to share your life with. I wrongly assumed that after I left, you probably thanked God every day that you hadn't been saddled with someone so inherently wrong for you. Someone who would *not* be a good partner to you in your daily work and life."

"But we talked about that, how you would contribute to running the ranch. Though of course things had changed after the accident. I couldn't do my work, and my church friends couldn't keep running my ranch in my absence forever. Is that what it was?" Because that was the only conclusion that made sense to Rowdy, then or now.

"Injured or not, I didn't come from a ranching background. I had been deluding myself to think I could truly be a life mate to you, to contribute in a way that would make you proud. My life has been a series of one mistake after another. Eventually, I would have dragged you down with me."

"I don't believe that," he said, his voice the consistency of gravel.

"I should have trusted in my love for you," Ange said at last. "I let my hurt feelings get in the way of my good judgment. You'll never know how sorry I am."

Rowdy thought he might.

Because he was sorry, too.

Sorry that she'd judged herself and had come up wanting, when she was nothing like the person she saw in the mirror.

Sorry he hadn't lent her the strength and courage to believe in herself, to see what he saw every time he looked at her.

He'd known that underneath the tough exterior she presented to the world, she was soft and vulnerable. And he hadn't protected her enough to let that part of her personality see the light of day.

Ange sighed. "If only things had turned out differently. Maybe there would have been hope for the two of us. But it's too late now. We made our choices and we have to live with them."

Rowdy wasn't sure he agreed with that last bit.

Yes, they had lost each other in the past, but did that necessarily mean there was no chance for them in the future? Not starting over, exactly, nor picking up where they left off. Too much had happened and too many years had passed for that.

But what about tentatively exploring something new between them, a relationship that not only encompassed the two of them, but Toby, as well?

And God.

The Lord had been missing from their equation back then, but He would be at the forefront of any new relationship they built together.

He studied Ange, wondering if he should suggest they make no permanent decisions until they'd had more time to let all of these new revelations sink in, but she had already shut down, her expression stoic and determined.

He'd seen that look before, and there was no getting through it.

"We'd better get to planning if we're going to get this ranch rodeo up and running by the Fourth of July," she said in a patently false tone.

Rowdy's chest felt like it was being squeezed in a vise. Ange was doing what she always did when confronted with something she didn't want to hear—pulling back into herself and blocking everything and everybody else out.

And after that, it wouldn't be long before she ran away, just as she'd done on the night of their wedding rehearsal.

But this time, Rowdy would anticipate her move. He didn't know what the future held for them, but one thing he did know—

He wasn't going to let her skip out of his life again.

Chapter Nine

Early on the third day of July, with Toby comfortably sleeping in his stroller a few feet away, Angelica directed Rowdy as he guided his empty horse trailer into the correct position inside Serendipity's town arena. He parked it close to one wall, since trailer loading was an event that didn't require as much moving space as some of the others.

The goal was for the cowboy or cowgirl two-person teams to get their horses into and out of the trailer in the fastest time. The trick was, the horses provided were barely started and mostly unfamiliar with being loaded into the big trailer.

Many contestants got inventive when the horses balked, as they inevitably did, and the event was always a true crowd-pleaser.

The whole ranch rodeo carried with it much laughter and amusement. And there were no trophies or monetary awards for the winners. The ranch hands entertained the audience only for their pleasure and attempted to win events merely for yearly bragging rights.

But none of this felt *fun* to Angelica.

For a moment, she mentally shook her fist at Granny for putting her in this situation. Angelica knew that what Granny had done, she had done out of love for her and Rowdy, but her plan had backfired. Granny was no longer around, and Angelica was left with the fallout.

She ached. So deeply and profoundly that nothing could come close to matching it, with the possible exception of the night she'd ridden away from Serendipity on a horse that was supposed to be her bridal transportation.

She and Rowdy had worked up a planned list of events from Granny's notes, and now they were setting everything up in the arena for the next day.

After parking the trailer, they moved on to create a "branding" station—paint buckets filled with blue, green and red paints. On a nearby table were branding irons specific to each competing ranch.

"Do you think we've got enough paint, or should we stop by Emerson's Hardware and grab some extra to keep on standby?" she asked.

"Yes," Rowdy said, his mind clearly elsewhere—probably revisiting the past.

"Yes, we have enough paint, or yes, we need more?"

"What?" he asked, his gaze fixing on hers. One side of his lips crept up in a half-smile. "Yes, I think we have enough paint," he said.

He was silent for a full minute as they marked chalk lines the teens would have to keep their cows within as they attempted to "brand" them.

Then he turned to her, swiping off his black cowboy hat and exposing his thick blond curls.

"So that event is ready. And I've corralled the sheep from your ranch that we'll need for the mutton busting."

Angelica's stomach fluttered when she realized the verbal slip he'd made, calling the ranch hers and not Granny's.

Well, it was Granny's ranch, whatever he said, and someday soon it would be his. So much had happened between her and Rowdy that it was getting harder and harder to remember that.

"Let's take a break before we set up the rest of the events. We won't be bringing in any of the stock until tomorrow morning. I'll help you load a few sheep into your trailer for the mutton busting. I'm picking up a couple of wild cows, Nick McKenna has offered some of his cattle for the herding and branding events and his brother Jax and his wife are bringing in some saddle broncs."

She watched his face as he talked about the saddle broncs, noting the momentary glimpse of agony that flashed through his eyes.

"We can still remove saddle bronc riding from the program," she said, as she'd mentioned several times previously.

She wasn't sure *she* could handle the event. She couldn't imagine how Rowdy, who'd sustained a permanent injury from it that changed his whole life, would deal with it.

He met her gaze squarely.

"No." His voice was firm and unwavering. "Saddle bronc riding has been a treasured part of Serendipity's ranch rodeo for as long as I can remember. It's a big draw, not to mention the most adrenaline-fueled event."

"I should think so, since the rest of the events are meant to be more humorous than skilled."

His lips quirked. "Well, it does take some level of skill to milk a wild cow."

She couldn't help but chuckle.

"Tomorrow, we'll need to do a sound check on the system Frank and Jo Spencer will be using to officiate," he said.

He stroked a hand across his jaw, as he often did when he was thinking, leaving multicolored finger streaks of chalk across his cheek.

Angelica couldn't help it. She put a palm over her mouth and giggled.

His eyebrows rose. "Something funny?"

"War paint?"

His gaze was blank for a moment before he realized she was talking about his face.

Laughing, he used the corner of his shirt to wipe the color away.

"Thank you for pointing that out to me. You could have just left me walking around town like that all day."

The mood had lightened so much Angelica wanted to burst out into a song of praise to God, but because she couldn't carry a tune to save her life, she prayed a silent thank-You instead.

Ever since coming back to Serendipity, she'd been on a roller coaster of ups and downs with Rowdy.

She much preferred the ups.

Because she still cared for Rowdy.

Knowing her feelings would show in her eyes, she quickly turned away, making a big deal of picking up Toby as if she'd heard him cry.

Her son was still sound asleep and hadn't made a peep. He was just an excuse for Angelica to keep her attention focused anywhere but at Rowdy.

After all that had happened between them, she hadn't considered that latent feelings for him might ramp up as suddenly and intensely as they had.

Of course, she would always care for him. She had once been ready to tie her life to his in marriage, as youthful and immature as that love might have been.

But this—*these* emotions were a whole other thing. In just a little over one short month, she had gotten to know Rowdy in ways she couldn't even have imagined in her youth.

She understood and truly appreciated the hard work that had turned him from a lanky boy to a well-muscled and weathered cowboy.

And most of all, she finally *got* the honor and integrity that made Rowdy rise far above all of the other men she'd ever known.

She would never share these newfound revelations with him. It was awkward enough to be around him, sometimes even painful, without blabbing out her emotional discovery.

Besides, he expected her to leave. To fulfill Granny's last wishes and then head on back to Denver, selling Granny's ranch to him.

And up until now, that's just what she'd intended to do. Or maybe she'd just blinded herself as to what was really going on in her heart.

"Is everything okay over there? How's Toby?" Rowdy called.

Heat flamed to her face and she kept her head bowed, carefully hiding it from Rowdy's gaze.

"I thought I heard something, but it's nothing."

Except it wasn't nothing.

Because what she'd heard was the call of her heart.

On the morning of the Fourth of July, Rowdy arrived at the public arena early to deliver the wild cows. He'd helped Ange load the sheep onto her trailer earlier, but she hadn't yet arrived and he was glad for a quiet moment to compose himself.

When the subject of the ranch rodeo had first come up at Cup O' Jo's, Rowdy had tried his best not to react.

In truth, every nerve ending in his body had snapped to life. Even the words *ranch rodeo* made him internally cringe as fear rumbled through his gut.

He'd avoided attending the annual ranch rodeo since the year he'd been injured, but if anyone had noticed, they'd been kind enough not to mention it.

But for some reason, he hadn't wanted Ange to know that the saddle bronc riding hadn't just injured his knee but had crushed his self-confidence, as well.

Pride, he supposed.

He'd been telling the truth when he'd told Ange that she hadn't forced him into the competition that fateful day. He wasn't a wrangler and he'd never started a horse in his life, but he could ride as well as the next cowboy, and anyway, it was a ranch rodeo. There were no rules about spurring and raking. All he had to do was somehow manage to stay in the saddle for eight seconds, any way he could.

How hard could that be?

As it turned out, he'd remained in the saddle for longer than eight seconds—or at least his foot had. His boot had caught in the stirrup and he couldn't get it loose. After the horse bashed his knee into the wall, causing him to lose his precarious balance, he'd been dragged along on the ground until he'd nearly passed out from the pain.

As far as he knew, his accident was the only major incident that had ever happened at the annual event, before or since, and it had been a freak accident that would never be repeated, so he shouldn't be worried. But this year it was teenagers competing in the games.

Nearly all of them had grown up doing a semblance of the kind of skills they'd be demonstrating today, but he couldn't help the hoof-in-the-gut feeling that came at odd intervals and caught him off-guard every time.

He didn't want Ange to see him this way. He didn't want *anyone* to see him like this, lacking the courage to face up to his fears. He'd better cowboy up, and quickly, because Ange's SUV and trailer were just now pulling into the arena.

He waved her over to where he was opening the tops of the paint buckets and stirring each color with a paint stick.

She placed Toby nearby, still strapped into his car seat, close enough to keep an eye on him but well away from the paint fumes.

"The teens are going to have a blast with this," she said, and then paused and observed him closely.

"Yeah. It'll be great fun," he agreed in a ridiculously and patently unbelievable tone that didn't belong to him at all. His voice hadn't been that high and squeaky since his own adolescence.

She put her hand on his forearm. Their gazes met and locked, her liquid blue eyes drawing him in. His heart pounded and his lungs forgot they were supposed to function on their own.

"Are you going to be okay?" she whispered. "Really?"

He wasn't even close to okay, except it had nothing to do with the ranch rodeo or saddle bronc riding and everything to do with the woman before him.

The empathy in her gaze nearly undid him, but there

was something else in her eyes, and that was what caused his pulse to launch into the stratosphere.

It was more than her feeling sorry for him, more than the awful way they'd cast blame back and forth about something that was nobody's fault, or even all of the crazy mistakes they'd made between them.

She cared for him—as a woman cared for a man. He could see it. Feel the warmth emanating from her heart. And somewhere in this crazy storm of emotions stampeding through him, he realized that he cared for her, too.

Everything around them faded into the background, and all he could see was Ange, in all of her vibrant, colorful beauty, both inside and out.

Nothing else mattered besides the two of them, the man and the woman they had become.

Here.

Now.

The products of everything that had gone before, yes, but also with the potential of what was to come.

He framed her face with his palms and tipped her chin up with the pad of his thumb.

Then he paused, needing to be completely sure. If he was misreading the signals, if his heart was getting ahead of his head, the result could be disastrous.

"Rowdy." She said his name in her rich dark chocolate alto.

It was all the encouragement he needed, and he removed his hat and tossed it onto the ground. He brushed a long strand of her straight blond hair off her cheek and tucked it behind her ear, all without losing eye contact with her.

Slowly, his mouth came down on hers, starting with

just the gentlest brush of his lips over hers before he kissed her in earnest.

Her lips were as soft and sweet as he remembered, but she had changed since the last time they had kissed, and so their kiss had changed, as well.

Different.

Mature.

Better.

Even though he'd been trying his hardest to keep them at bay, he recognized the emotions he was feeling—that they were sharing.

Rowdy closed his eyes and deepened the kiss, shoving his thoughts aside to make room for his heart to take over.

Chapter Ten

Ange ran her palms up Rowdy's chest and over his shoulders before locking her arms around his neck and pulling him closer.

He'd changed a lot from when they were young. He carried so much more strength and confidence in his frame. And while their kiss felt familiar, it was equally as foreign, and she desperately wanted to explore all that was new.

With Rowdy, she had always felt loved and cherished, but now she had a new appreciation for what was happening between them.

Something fresh.

Something wonderful.

And, perhaps, something that would last this time.

Even after he brushed one last kiss over her lips, he didn't let her go.

Their connection was magnetic as he tucked her close to his chest. She laid a hand over his heart, finding both comfort and exhilaration in how fast it pounded and how quickly his breath was coming.

"Ange," he murmured into her hair, his voice tender. "I don't—"

Whatever he'd been going to say was cut off by a bubbly laugh coming from the announcer's booth.

With the microphone *on*.

"Do you still think Frances made a mistake?" Jo asked with a throaty cackle. Her laugh reverberated through the thankfully still-empty arena. "Seems to me she knew *exactly* what she was doing."

Angelica expected Rowdy to immediately drop his hands from her waist and step away. When he didn't, Angelica took it upon herself to twist out of his arms.

As usual, she hadn't thought her action all the way through to its logical conclusion.

The moment she'd stepped into Rowdy's embrace, all she could do was follow her feelings and never mind her brain telling her to pump the brakes.

Now her emotions had left Rowdy exposed to ridicule. Angelica had no doubt Jo would razz the both of them. She had set herself up as some sort of errant matchmaker, and that was bad enough.

But what if someone else had come in and seen them kissing—one of the local ranchers or the teenagers who'd be competing in the day's events?

Was it a mistake to have followed her heart?

Her gaze tried to capture Rowdy's. Would he engage with Jo and her teasing, or shut her out with some inane explanation that she hadn't actually seen what she'd thought she saw?

He did neither.

He had already turned away and was opening the trailer door to lead the two wild cows to their pens.

As if their kiss had never happened.

Angelica could take a hint.

She could follow his lead.

"Where's Frank?" she called as she picked up Toby, still covered and in his car seat. She made a show of walking around and blatantly surveying the colored chalk lines that would be used in rounding up strays.

"Draggin' his feet and bellowin' up a fuss, as usual, the old goat. He'll get here when he gets here."

As the teenage competitors and the wranglers from the ranches they represented started arriving and unloading their horses and equipment, Angelica continued her last-minute check of the arena.

Anything to keep her mind off what had happened between her and Rowdy.

Had he just been caught up in the moment, or had he felt the same familiar-yet-different spark that she had?

She ended up at the pen holding the sheep she and Rowdy had brought from her ranch. Rowdy liked to tease her about it, but she recognized many of them now, and they each had a name. Every one of her sheep was an individual to her, not just part of a collective.

If saddle bronc riding was the most high-adrenaline, super-exciting event in the lineup, then mutton busting was the cutest, with the younger members of ranching families wearing hard helmets and getting plopped on top of a sheep to hold on for as long as they could.

Every one of those children would earn bragging rights today. They were the future of ranching.

However, this year, a new event might surpass even mutton busting for the cuteness factor. If the mutton busters were the future of ranching, then the Baby Cowboy was the future's future.

Angelica couldn't wait for Rowdy to see Toby's costume, but she was trying to keep it a secret until the actual unveiling happened.

She'd spent a lot of time planning and executing Toby's outfit, and he was absolutely adorable, if she did say so herself.

Which she did, even if she was totally biased.

First, she'd visited the tiny clothing section of Emerson's Hardware and cobbled together an outfit from what she was able to purchase and what she had on hand.

She'd never learned how to sew, so she thought the fact that she'd cut here and sewn there was pretty impressive, and she was proud of herself. Even if Toby didn't win the contest, he was and always would be number one in her heart.

As the stadium filled, Angelica looked around for Rowdy and found him leaning against the back side of one of the bronc riding chutes, his forearms on the fence and one boot propped on the bottom rung.

His gaze was distant, and she wondered if he was reliving the accident in his mind.

How could he not be?

She wandered over to where he was and bumped his shoulder with hers.

"Hey," she whispered.

"Hey." His voice had the texture of gravel, and when he glanced her direction, his eyes were glazed.

Angelica had removed the receiving blanket that she'd had tented over Toby's car seat and had artfully wrapped it around him so his costume was still hidden.

Rowdy's gaze dropped to Toby. He was awake and alert and immediately grabbed on to Rowdy's finger when he offered it.

"I'm really proud of you for staying and helping out

the teenagers, and for getting out in the arena again," she said. "You once told me sometimes the best way to go beyond fear is to go through it. Today is that day for you, Rowdy."

His brow rose and his expression changed, although she couldn't quite discern what it meant.

"What?"

His lips curved up the slightest bit.

"I appreciate the encouragement. But would you believe I wasn't thinking about my accident?"

"No?"

He shook his head. "At least, not in the way I had expected to be haunted by it."

"It can't be easy for you to be here."

"No. It's not. And I'm not sure how I'm going to feel when the saddle bronc riding starts. But just now, I was thinking about *you*."

"Me?"

Yes, they'd shared that amazing kiss earlier, a real game changer as far as Angelica was concerned, but Rowdy had so much more to be thinking about right now. His past was going to rise up to meet him in a major way in just a couple of hours.

"I was thinking about how things might have been different if either one of us had reached out to the other. If we'd supported each other better. It's amazing to me how easily a simple miscommunication broke our relationship. If I hadn't been so caught up in my own issues, I would have been able to see what I was doing to you."

Angelica's throat tightened and tears burned in the back of her eyes.

"We both made mistakes," she said. "In my view, mine were far worse than yours. But we can't go back, and I wouldn't want to. I might have had a miserable eight years away from Serendipity, but now I have Toby and I wouldn't change that for all the world."

Rowdy wiggled the finger Toby was grasping and the baby smiled, his eyes crinkling.

A low rumble came from Rowdy's chest. "Now tell me that wasn't a real smile."

"He always responds to you in a special way, perking up when he hears your voice, smiling when he sees your face."

"Really?" Rowdy's face colored and he stood an inch taller, looking very pleased with himself. And Toby.

Then he looked back at Toby and cleared his throat, his Adam's apple bobbing.

"I know the past is—what it is—but do you think maybe that we could work toward building something new for the future?"

Angelica's heart warmed until she was beaming with sunshine from the inside out.

Rowdy wasn't being unrealistic or suggesting they just try to pick up where they had left off all those years ago. That would be impossible anyway, because Toby was now in the picture.

But maybe, if they took it slow, they could start to build something new. Something better and more mature.

"We aren't the same people we were eight years ago," she started to say, meaning to agree with him, to let him know the tentative feelings he had expressed were reciprocated, that she was more than willing to take the next step, to explore what might be and not just what had been.

But just then, the microphone pitched in high, squeaky feedback that made Angelica and Rowdy flinch and Toby start crying.

"Sorry, folks," Jo said. "Just a small technical difficulty."

"His poor little ears," Angelica said, cringing.

"Don't worry, little dude. You'll be okay." He pressed a kiss to Toby's forehead and brushed a palm over his white-blond hair.

Angelica couldn't keep her eyes off Rowdy, and her heart was skipping beats all over the place.

He was so good with Toby.

He was so good to *her*.

"Toby's going to rock the Baby Cowboy contest," he said.

Angelica chuckled. "You haven't even seen his outfit yet."

Rowdy shrugged. "I don't need to. Your son is the cutest baby in Serendipity, bar none."

"Thank you for that," she said, a little choked up.

"Just telling it like it is."

Her heart swelled.

"I promise I'll be watching you and rooting for you during the saddle bronc riding."

"You know I'm just a pickup man, out there for safety's sake and not actually bronc riding, right?"

"I know. I just wish I could be out there with you." It was a silly thing for her to say. She'd be useless both to Rowdy and the kids riding the broncs. She just wanted to do something to prove she was ready to pursue a relationship with him. Be the partner she hadn't been before.

But Rowdy evidently didn't read between the lines, or else he'd turned his focus completely on the rodeo to come.

"No worries, Ange. I will be just fine without you."

Rowdy's words had a double meaning. It was true that he had every faith he and his stocky black quarter horse gelding Hercules would be able to keep the bronc riding kids from being injured.

But he was also telling Ange that she didn't need to finish her statement.

What she *had* said was more than enough for him to catch the full drift of her meaning.

They were two completely different people now, not the young adults who'd believed in the kind of love that was only in movies, not real life.

Perhaps their kiss had been some kind of test for her, the opportunity to see if there was anything left of what love there had once been between them.

Rowdy felt sick to his stomach as he mounted Hercules and directed the teenagers into their first event, wild cow milking, a hilarious spectacle meant to get the crowd stoked up for the rest of the rodeo.

Why had he kissed her? He should have realized that he was moving too fast, in the wrong place at the wrong time.

Real romantic, Masterson. Way to blow it.

Kissing her in the middle of the rodeo arena right before a major town event, where anyone could have shown up. Thankfully, it had only been Jo, but that was bad enough.

Oh, Granny Frances, I wish you were here to help me sort this out. Was this what you wanted for us? Have I really messed it up?

Jo and Frank were keeping the events moving, and Rowdy had no choice but to turn his attention to the ranch rodeo. The teenagers "branded" cows with paint, showed their prowess at gathering strays and loaded and unloaded horse trailers with barely started horses, sometimes requiring quite a bit of pushing and pulling of both heads and hindquarters.

The noisy crowd was having a blast, cheering on the contestants and laughing up a storm, encouraging the teenagers to do their best.

Mutton busting in particular was a town favorite, with five-to-seven-year-olds, absolutely adorable little cowboys and cowgirls in hard helmets, holding on for dear life on a sheep which, unused to having a person on its back, bolted forward pell-mell.

And then, at last, came the new event, the one he and Ange had added to the lineup specifically for Toby and the one event Rowdy was actually looking *forward* to today.

"It's time for all our Baby Cowboys and Cowgirls to make their way to the front of the arena," Jo announced.

As usual, Jo was ready for the new event, wearing one of her infamous homemade T-shirts. This one read Let's Go, Babies! Which pretty much summed up her feelings on the new event, and apparently, her opinion on what was going to be the highlight of the rodeo.

Rowdy's pulse jumped, thundering as loudly as if he had his own baby in the race.

In a way, he guessed he did. Although he couldn't have explained why, he couldn't feel more emotionally bonded to Toby than if he was his own son.

Maybe it had something to do with how Rowdy was, and always had been, bonded to the baby's mother.

Whatever the cause, Rowdy's heart was thundering when it was time for Toby to make his official Serendipity debut.

Let's Go, Toby.

Chapter Eleven

A dozen mothers and fathers, all decked out in their country best, stood in the arena just before the announcer's platform holding their little stars in their arms for everyone to see.

Babies and toddlers from newborn to age two had been invited to participate, and Angelica was thrilled at the first year's turnout. She suspected this was going to be a new annual event and something the folks in town would look forward to.

Angelica and Toby were in the middle of the row. Not first, not last. She just hoped the focus would be on Toby and not on herself.

At Jo's announcement, parents unwrapped their children from the blankets covering them and revealed adorable cowboy and cowgirl costumes to the cheering audience.

One at a time, each mother and father walked around the perimeter of the arena so everyone could get a good look at the babies. Angelica didn't miss the fact that she was the only single parent in the group, but it was what it was.

Her life belonged to Toby, and that was good enough for her.

It had to be.

The costumes ran from quickly thrown together to more intricate, although nothing near what Angelica had done with Toby. She suspected that most parents were counting on the cuteness factor for *their* baby to win the contest.

And there was some truth to that. In the parents' eyes, their babies were the cutest.

And it hadn't been a stretch for most of the families to come up with Western outfits. Most of the toddlers already owned at least one pair of denim jeans and a tiny pair of cowboy boots or mud boots. Some even had hats in toddler sizes. Kids started learning how to do ranch chores early in Serendipity, accompanying their parents from the time they could walk.

All of the babies were by far the cutest little ranchers she'd ever seen.

The smaller babies' outfits typically leaned another direction—onesies with cute country sayings on them. Some of the baby girls had bows in their hair, and there was one baby boy who was dressed in nothing more than a denim-decorated diaper.

Every one of them was adorable, too.

But then again, so was Toby. And she'd put a lot of thought and effort into his wardrobe. Maybe it was because she'd been the one to think up this extra event, or maybe it was that she was newly returned to the country, but she had been more detailed in planning Toby's costume. She'd tried to see the big picture and not just focus on a particular item of clothing.

He was a chunky monkey and had been able to fit

into toddler blue jeans, with some minor modifications in length and girth. She'd purchased the smallest bright-blue-checked chambray shirt and used safety pins to size it to Toby.

She'd even taken a length of black ribbon to make a belt and had formed a shiny belt buckle out of tin foil, on which she'd glitter-glued the word *COWBOY*. But her pièce de résistance was the cotton-ball sheep with a black eye and red smile that she'd pinned to his shirt.

As a final touch, she'd found a small length of rope that someone had abandoned in a ditch near her ranch. She'd washed it clean and looped it into a lasso, which she pressed into his fist when it was time for them to make their promenade around the arena.

She'd walked about three feet when a shadow fell over her and she realized someone was walking alongside her.

She looked up to see a grinning Rowdy, waving at the crowd and encouraging them to cheer even louder.

"Rowdy," she exclaimed, before lowering her voice. "What are you doing?"

"When you unveiled Toby's outfit, I just knew I had to be there with you guys. I'm proud of my little cowboy. But the sheep on his shirt? Now that's ingenious."

She flashed him a questioning look.

"I know. It doesn't make any sense. But we sheep farmers have to stick together."

Which made sense, she supposed, and it was a nice thing for him to say. She was shocked that Rowdy had joined them, but mostly, she was grateful.

She'd seen how Rowdy had bonded with Toby. With her *prodigal daughter* reputation, Toby was at a natural disadvantage straight out of the gate. Rowdy's presence with them evened out the scales.

If he could get over their negative history together, surely members of the community could overlook her past and possibly allow her to find her future here.

When they returned to their spot in front of the podium and Rowdy propped his cowboy hat on Toby's head, there was no question as to which baby had most captured the audience's hearts. The crowd was roaring for the baby with the glitzy belt buckle.

For once, she had done something right.

"Ladies and gentlemen," Jo announced, her voice crackling over the microphone's feedback. "We've had our share of cute and lots of laughs. Now it's time for a shot of pure adrenaline in our last event and a fan favorite, saddle bronc riding!"

Rowdy shifted in the saddle, his attention glued to the first chute, where a dark-haired girl wearing a white straw cowboy hat was making last-minute adjustments to her balance on the bronc.

"Let's give it up for Erin Smith riding Charlie Horse."

The crowd cheered. Rowdy tensed and his stockiest quarter horse, Hercules, skittered to the side, reacting to his negative energy.

Erin nodded and a ranch hand pulled the chute gate open.

Charlie Horse sprang into action, twisted and turned; his back legs kicked out and his front legs bucked, sometimes at the same time.

Rowdy pressed his knees into Hercules as he laser focused on Erin and Charlie. Mostly his eyes were glued to the horse, watching for signs that he would make a sudden unexpected move, but from time to time Rowdy glanced up to see how Erin was faring.

If her expression was anything to go by, she was reveling in the ride, totally in control, solid in the saddle and calling to Charlie to urge him onto the best ride she could have.

Eight seconds seemed to take forever to Rowdy, who was counting down in milliseconds, but Erin easily rode out her time and dismounted on her own without Rowdy coming alongside her.

He grabbed Charlie's flank strap and the horse immediately calmed down, happy to be herded off the arena grounds.

Rowdy swallowed hard. One down, four to go, and then he would be able to breathe again.

Next up was a much smaller boy named Ryan who didn't look to be as old as his peers. Maybe he was a late bloomer. Rowdy was worried that he wouldn't be able to handle the horse he'd drawn, but another eight seconds went by without incident. The little scrapper held on like a trooper, and though he flipped and flopped a bit, he stayed in the saddle.

Third up was another girl, Jessie, riding a horse named Cricket. Odd name for a ranch horse, Rowdy thought, but he made a decent bronc. Jessie also stayed on the eight seconds and made a smooth dismount with Rowdy's help.

The fourth horse, Rocket, was ridden by a boy named Philip. Unfortunately for Philip, Rocket didn't feel like living up to his name for the event. He barely bucked at all, just throwing his back feet out from time to time as if the flank strap merely annoyed him.

So it was a disappointed boy who ended his eight seconds with Rocket. The horses' movements made up half of the score, with the cowboy's or cowgirl's riding making up the other half. The rules stated that if a cowboy or cowgirl pulled a horse that didn't live up to the half of the score required for the horse, he or she could choose to make a second ride on another horse. But since it was a ranch rodeo and there were no cash or trophies awarded, Rowdy doubted Philip would bother.

The fifth and last teenage cowboy to make his saddle bronc ride was Jace on a horse called Crash. Hercules shifted, alerting Rowdy to the fact that he'd tensed up again. There was no reason to believe the horse was named on his behavior, but Rowdy wouldn't rest easy until the ride was finished.

Crash was a decent bronc, but as with the other teenaged bronc riders, Jace had spent his life on the ranch and bronc riding came naturally to him.

Rowdy's adrenaline sparked at about six seconds in, when Crash went one way and Jace went the other. There was nowhere for that kid to go but down, but at least the horse had tossed him into the middle of the arena.

Thankfully, Jace landed on the padding the good Lord had given him and immediately rolled to his feet, stalked the few yards to grab his brown cowboy hat off the dirt where it had landed and waved it to the riser full of friends and neighbors to let them know he hadn't been hurt. Everyone cheered for him as loudly as they had the others, and he walked out of the arena with a smile on his face.

Rowdy was about to rein Hercules out of the arena so he could go find Ange and they could celebrate their success with the ranch rodeo when the microphone crackled again.

"Don't leave your seats just yet, folks. Rocket wasn't much of a bronc today, and Philip was unable to show off his bronc riding skills, so he has elected to take a second ride, this time on a horse named Shy Boy."

Rowdy groaned.

Couldn't they just be done already?

Hopefully Shy Boy's name *was* indicative of his personality and they could get these eight seconds over with.

Rowdy was *so* done with this ranch rodeo. He wanted to spend the rest of the day out on the neighborhood green, picnicking with Ange and Toby, enjoying the games and fireworks and showing off to friends and neighbors their adorable little winner of the Baby Cowboy contest.

It was high time for the townsfolk to get over what had happened in the past between Ange and Rowdy. After what they'd shared earlier today, opening their hearts to each other, he hoped he could convince her to stay in town long enough for them to truly pursue their relationship.

His attention had been distracted just for that one moment, as he was considering the future, when Philip nodded and Shy Boy sprang into the arena, furiously bucking and kicking and turning in tight circles, determined to get the flank strap off at any cost, never mind the rider on his back.

For the first couple of seconds, Philip looked as if he was off-balance and Rowdy thought he'd probably hit the dirt pretty quickly and end the ride, but then Philip somehow shifted and regained control.

But Shy Boy was having none of it.

One second the horse was in the middle of the arena as he twisted and turned and altogether put on a good show for the spectators, who were yelling and hooting and cheering him on.

The next moment, the crowd went dead silent as Shy Boy charged straight toward the wall.

Rowdy didn't think. He just acted, pressing his heels into Hercules's side and leaning forward, giving Hercules his full head.

Hercules launched into a gallop, sensing his rider's inner torment.

Rowdy's first thought had been to try to herd Shy Boy away from the wall, but he immediately realized that wasn't going to happen.

Shy Boy was going too fast and was too panicked to realize what he was doing. The whites of his eyes were showing and his ears were pinned back as he whipped his head from side to side in a frantic attempt to lose the rider.

Philip was yelling for Shy Boy to stop and clinging on to the saddle for dear life, with one hand twisted into Shy Boy's mane.

But despite everything, Shy Boy put his head down and made straight for the arena wall.

"Jump off," Rowdy hollered. "Philip, jump off."

But Philip either didn't hear or couldn't move. He appeared every bit as spooked as his horse and only clung tighter as Shy Boy continued galloping forward.

Rowdy reined Hercules between Shy Boy and the wall. He had purposefully picked Hercules because of his size and speed, but he could never have imagined that the scene would play out before him the way it did.

All he knew was that he had to slip into the space between Shy Boy and the arena wall.

As the air created by Hercules's gallop drove the hat off Rowdy's head, Rowdy gritted his teeth and prayed that God would keep Philip safe. Hercules safe. Shy Boy.

And him.

A moment later, Shy Boy lit into Hercules's side and both horses reared and made course corrections—Shy Boy to the middle of the arena and Rowdy into the wall, where his entire left side, head to toe, collided with the concrete.

Pain detonated in Rowdy's knee, and his head exploded with fireworks as bright as the ones Serendipity planned for this evening.

Rowdy had picked Hercules in the hope that the larger, stronger horse would help keep the teenagers' horses under control, and he had.

But at what price?

Rowdy's gaze was clouding in pain.

Something was off.

He felt as if he was seeing everything at a great distance, and then his vision blurred and doubled and he tried to blink it back into focus.

He was mindful enough to pull his boots from the stirrups so he wouldn't be dragged around the arena as he had been last time he'd found himself in this position. With his strength greatly failing, he gripped at his saddle horn and plunged one hand into Hercules's mane. The horse slowed, but it wasn't enough for Rowdy to stay in the saddle.

He was going to go down.

His left leg would give out on him the moment he hit the turf and his vision was already gray, but he did everything he could to remain on Hercules for as long as possible.

Before his body gave out, he had to see what was happening with Philip and Shy Boy.

Had he saved them?

Gritting his teeth, he narrowed his gaze on Philip, trying to focus through his double vision and the darkness threatening to overcome him.

He watched as Philip slid safely from Shy Boy and ran toward the arena gate while one of the mounted ranch hands released the flank strap from Shy Boy.

Rowdy had done it.

Philip was safe.

His last thought before slumping over the neck of Hercules and giving in to the darkness was of Ange and Toby.

He hadn't been able to express how he really felt.

Now the game had changed once again.

She might never know that he was in love with her.

Chapter Twelve

"N-o-o-o-o!" Angelica screamed as Rowdy's limp body rolled over Hercules's neck and he slammed to the ground, flat on his back.

"Please, God, let him be okay." She was praying aloud and she didn't care who heard her.

She grabbed Toby, in his car seat, and dashed out of the announcer's booth and onto the arena floor, where Rowdy was surrounded by the ranch hands, who had been pickup men like Rowdy, one on his horse and two on the arena floor, crouched around Rowdy's unmoving form.

Paramedics were on hand and were also running toward Rowdy with their equipment and a stretcher. Angelica wanted to be right beside him, but there were too many people already there and the paramedics needed room to do their work.

Her heart hammered as her gaze took Rowdy in.

His left leg was bent at an odd angle and a large purple bruise and enormous goose egg was already coloring his forehead.

Oh, Lord. Please no.

Was he breathing?

She couldn't tell.

His chest wasn't visibly rising and falling, as it should have been after surviving such a fall.

She wanted to be beside him, to hold him in her arms and tell him all the secrets of her heart that she had tried to hold back.

Oh, why hadn't she just been honest and told him how much she loved him?

Now he might never know.

Jo reached her and restrained her from moving to Rowdy's side with a firm, no-nonsense hug around her shoulders that Angelica, feeling as weak as she ever had in her life, could not break.

Who knew that the old woman was so strong?

"You have to let the paramedics do their job, honey," Jo coaxed. "I know you want to be at Rowdy's side, but right now what he needs is medical help. And our prayers."

Angelica knew Jo was right, but her heart was shattering into pieces as she watched the paramedics kneel before Rowdy and assess his injuries.

"He's not breathing," she sobbed. "Do something!"

Why weren't the paramedics doing CPR?

"He's just had the wind knocked out of him," Frank Spencer said, arriving at his wife's side and awkwardly patting Angelica's shoulder. "He landed flat on his back."

Angelica's tears poured and her breath came in tiny bursts of hiccups. She was hyperventilating, but she couldn't control her breathing as she watched the paramedics put an oxygen mask over Rowdy's mouth and a neck brace to guard against spinal injuries.

What if this accident was worse than the last one? What if Rowdy was paralyzed? He was a fighter, but he was also a rancher. Taking his life's work away from him would kill his spirit.

After the paramedics had stabilized his breathing and his neck, they carefully rolled him onto a backboard and stretcher. Angelica followed them to the ambulance, feeling entirely helpless as they loaded him up and headed off down the road.

"What about his knee?" she asked to no one in particular, her voice nothing more than a dry croak.

"They've stabilized him, which is the most important part," Jo said. "And now they want to get him to the hospital as soon as possible. I'm sure they'll splint his leg on the way."

"The hospital is nearly an hour away. Shouldn't they have their lights and sirens on? Or be using a helicopter?"

"It's their call, sweetie. If the paramedics thought this was a life-or-death situation, you'd better believe they would have called a helicopter to transport him. If they think he can travel in an ambulance, especially without hitting their lights, that's a good thing, right? It means he's stable enough for them to continue care on the way."

"I need to be there with him."

Jo didn't appear surprised at all by her admission.

"Of course you do. What do we need to do to make that happen?"

Toby kicked off his blanket in a not-so-subtle reminder that Angelica had other responsibilities than just Rowdy. She couldn't leave Toby and run off to be with Rowdy, no matter how much she ached to be by his side.

"Toby will have to go with us, as well, of course," Jo said, as if reading her mind. "I'll tell you what. How about if Frank and I rent a couple of rooms at the hotel next door to the hospital—one for us and one for you and Toby. That way I can babysit Toby while you are visiting with Rowdy, but you won't be too far away from your son."

Tears burned her eyes so that she could barely see Jo through the moisture.

"I couldn't ask you to do that."

"Did you hear anybody asking? You just let old Jo take care of everything, okay?"

Angelica felt like she was not all there. Her mind was in a haze and her heart was with Rowdy. She wouldn't have been able to work this out on her own, and was more grateful to Jo than she could have ever expressed.

Barely aware of the crowd of people exiting the bleachers, Angelica allowed Jo to lead her to a place to sit down, then Jo pulled out her cell phone, promising she wouldn't be more than a moment.

"On hold," she told Angelica after she'd dialed. She shook her head and her red curls bobbed. Covering the receiver, she nodded toward her husband. "Frank, honey, pull the truck around."

"Already going," he assured her.

"Yes, hello," Jo said as someone picked up on the other end of the line. "I'm going to need two rooms for an indeterminate amount of time. Please make them adjacent, if possible. We've got someone in the hospital and it will help us tremendously if we can be next to each other. Oh—and can you please add a crib to one of the rooms?"

She nodded. "Good. Fantastic. We will be checking in in a couple of hours. Put everything in my name."

As Jo continued to give the hotel her information, Angelica fed Toby a bottle of formula and tried to pull herself together. She would be no good to Rowdy if she was a blubbering mess, and Toby was picking up on her distress.

She needed to be strong for both their sakes.

Waiting for Jo to finish and Frank to pull around, she watched a couple of Rowdy's friends loading her sheep into a trailer.

"Those are mine," she said as Jo ended her call.

"They know, honey. You and Rowdy planned this gig, but there were more than just the two of you involved in the execution."

"There were?" Angelica wondered why she hadn't noticed. Maybe because she'd been too wrapped up in Rowdy.

"Yes. Don't worry. They'll deliver your sheep back to your property."

"All of my sheep," she squeaked. "And Rowdy's. What am I going to do? I can't just leave. The ranches don't run themselves."

"That's what friends are for," Jo affirmed.

"But I don't have any friends."

Jo shook her head. "I don't think that's true. Maybe when you first came back to town, it might have been. But people have been watching you with Toby. And with Rowdy. They've seen you in church. They may not know quite how to approach you without bringing up your past, but trust me when I tell you they will have your back during this tribulation. That's just how the folks in Serendipity are."

Angelica fought the sobs that threatened to erupt. She simply could not keep crying every time something happened to her, bad or good, or she wouldn't be able to get through this.

Rowdy needed her to be strong.

So did Toby.

No matter how she felt inside, no matter how her stomach churned and her heart ached and worry clouded her mind like a thunderstorm, she had to be strong.

And she would be.

Rowdy groaned. His eyelids felt like hundred-pound weights had been placed on each of them and he couldn't force them open no matter how hard he tried.

Every muscle in his body ached, even ones he hadn't known he had. He focused his mind on attempting to move, but nothing seemed to work. When he finally got his left fingers to wiggle, they sent a shot of white-hot pain up his arm.

Where was he?

He could hear a steady beeping from some kind of machine to the left of him, but not much else. He knew he was in bed, but for some reason he felt pinned down, as if someone had taken away his ability to control his own body.

And there was something else—something so quiet it took a moment for him to identify what it was.

Breathing.

Soft, steady breathing.

As his eyes slowly opened, he blinked heavily to focus his gaze. He tried to lift his head, but a gentle hand on his shoulder eased him back down.

"Take it easy, son. Try not to move."

He knew that voice.

Jo Spencer.

Why would Jo Spencer be…?

Suddenly it all came back to him in a horrifying rush that made him so lightheaded he nearly passed out again.

Shy Boy heading for the wall with a terrified Philip on his back.

Rowdy urging Hercules between them.

And then—nothing.

"H-hospital?" he asked through dry lips.

"That's right." Jo brushed a sliver of ice over his lips and then gently slid it into his mouth. "We're at Mercy Medical Center in San Antonio. You were taken here yesterday by ambulance from the ranch rodeo. You've been pretty out of it since then."

He groaned.

"You've had surgery on your knee and they set your left wrist in a cast. You've got a big ol' purple goose egg on your forehead. Thankfully, you have a hard head." Jo chuckled at her own joke.

"Water?"

With Jo supporting his neck, he lifted his head just enough to be able to take a sip of lukewarm water out of a straw.

It was only then that he realized someone else was in the room with him.

The breathing he'd heard.

It hadn't been Jo.

Ange had dragged a chair to his bedside and had crooked her elbow on the side of his mattress. She was sound asleep with her head in her palm.

Jo chuckled. "That woman won't leave your side. Hasn't budged since the moment we got here. She would have been in surgery with you if they would have let her. As it is, I've been bringing Toby to her here at the hospital so she doesn't have to leave you alone."

"She doesn't need to do that."

Ange had to be really exhausted. She was still slumped

in a dead sleep with her head in her hand, despite Rowdy and Jo having a conversation. That couldn't be comfortable.

He felt guilty that she'd refused to leave even to take care of Toby or get a good night's sleep, but at the same time his heart welled with the thought that she cared enough to stay with him.

Rowdy's right hand was near enough to her arm that he was able, with effort, to stretch his arm out to touch her elbow.

She jumped up as if she'd been zapped with a bolt of electricity.

"What?" she asked, coming immediately alert. "What's wrong?"

Rowdy tried to chuckle, but it sounded like tires on gravel through his dry throat.

"Rowdy." The sound of his name in her rich alto warmed his chest like a cup of hot chocolate on a snowy day. "Are you hurting? Should I get a nurse?"

He chuckled, then cringed at the rippling effect of his sore muscles on his extremities—especially his left wrist and his knee.

He was in pain, all right, but he didn't want Ange to call a nurse. Not just yet.

"What happened at the ranch rodeo?" he croaked.

Jo patted his shoulder and then gave Ange an animated hug.

"I'll just leave the two of you alone for a minute while I check on Toby. His honorary uncle Frank is entertaining him at the moment with his gruffy, growly faces, but I'll bet that sweet baby is ready to be loved on some by Auntie Jo."

"Thanks," Ange said, her voice cracking with emotion.

With a sigh, she straightened her chair and sat down, pulling her knees up and circling them with her arms.

"What's that face for?" he asked, trying to smile for her sake but not sure he got much past a grimace.

She shook her head and tears filled her eyes, but she didn't speak.

Wow. Did he really look all that bad?

He felt awful, but now it was as much because she was distressed and his heart was hurting for her as that he'd clearly sustained some injuries in the ranch rodeo.

"Hey, do you think you could hitch this bed up for me so I can sit up?"

She rose the head of the bed enough for him to view the damage and take stock of why his pain was a six out of ten on the pain scale.

His left knee was in a brace. That bit of news didn't surprise him, but he felt a little discouraged by it. He'd recovered from a knee injury before, and no matter how long it took and how hard he would have to work, he would recover again.

His chest was tightly wrapped and he suspected he might have bruised a rib or two. And as Jo had said, his left wrist was in a cast.

"Well, I can see that my left side took the brunt of whatever happened to me," he said, and then paused, hoping to encourage her to fill in the blanks.

She just stared at him, her bottom lip caught between her teeth.

"I remember Philip rocking out on Shy Boy, and I remember thinking he was going to hit the wall. He didn't, did he?"

Ange shook her head. "No. When you and Hercules

charged in, Shy Boy veered off. Philip was able to dismount without hurting himself, thankfully."

"That's good."

"You're a hero. Everybody thinks so." She reached out and touched his forearm and he slid his hand down to thread his fingers with hers.

"I don't care what everybody thinks, Ange. It only matters to me what you think."

"I think what you did was amazing. And selfless."

He still couldn't remember every detail about what had happened during the ranch rodeo, but anything that garnered that adoration in Ange's eyes and that kind of praise from her lips had been worth it, fractured bones and all.

Because he felt the same way.

He was in love with her.

And he wanted to be her hero.

His heart swelled to bursting as he struggled to find the words to tell her how much he wanted her and Toby in his life, but his mouth was as dry as desert sand and try as he might his emotions remained unspoken.

Could she read his feelings in his eyes?

For a moment, their gazes met and held and he thought he saw a glimpse of his emotions mirrored in her eyes before her gaze flashed with something else.

Doubt? Uncertainty?

She stood and slipped her hand out of his, brushing the tears from her cheeks before she turned her back on him and went to look out the window.

It took her a moment to gather her thoughts before she turned back to him and spoke with a low, gritty determination.

"And once again, after I encouraged you to ride, you're in a hospital with multiple injuries. How long do you think it will take you to recover and walk again this time?"

He tried to straighten his shoulders but his bruised ribs complained.

"I don't know," he said honestly. He hadn't even talked to the doctor yet and his head was swimming with pain. "It doesn't matter." With Ange by his side, he felt as if he could conquer anything. His new physical issues were just another hurdle to overcome.

"But it does," she whispered raggedly. "It proves what I've been saying all along. You should never have trusted me. Even when I think I'm doing the right thing for you, that I'm supporting you, I make the wrong decision and you get hurt. How many times does this have to happen before you realize how bad I am for you?"

He gritted his teeth to speak through the pain. "I thought we worked all that out."

"So did I." Her voice cracked. "But I was wrong. I want you to be happy, Rowdy."

"I am happy—when I'm with you and Toby."

Emotional pain crossed her gaze that rivaled anything Rowdy was feeling physically. "I'm surprised you can say that in your present condition—in the hospital with the kind of injuries you sustained."

"Which has zero—do you hear me, Ange, *zero*—to do with what you may or may not have said to me. It was my idea to ride pickup, not yours."

"But I encouraged you."

"You did. And you know what? That meant more to me than you'll ever know. This injury," he said, jerking his head toward his left side, "is nothing compared to that. I'm not sure I could have gotten out there if it wasn't for you."

"Which just goes to prove my point." She sniffed and pressed her palms to her eyes.

"No, it doesn't. I don't know how to make you understand. You helped me conquer a fear that had been hanging over my head for eight years."

"And in the process, you landed in the hospital."

"Yes. But not from doing something stupid. This time, I'm here because I saved a teenager from what might have been a bad accident. Big difference. And again, not your fault."

Her gaze met his. Did he see a flicker of hope in her eyes?

She blinked, and the spark was extinguished.

"Now the whole town knows you're a hero." Her low alto was rich with meaning.

"The only opinion I'm interested in is yours. Do *you* think I'm a hero, Ange?"

His breath caught in his throat while he waited for his words to sink in. For her to realize what he was really saying.

A knock at the door interrupted them before Ange could say another word.

A nurse came in to check his vitals and ask about his pain on the pain scale.

"It's not too bad," he said through gritted teeth, cringing when the nurse put her hand on his shoulder.

He wasn't fooling anyone.

But he didn't want to drift away, not when he was so close to making everything right in his world.

The nurse added pain medicine to his IV and his head immediately became fuzzy.

"Ange," he said, reaching for her with his right arm, desperate to finish the conversation.

She stepped forward and took his hand.

But before he could speak, another knock sounded and a man in light green scrubs came into the room.

"Sorry to interrupt you," the orderly said. "I'm here to take you down for an MRI."

First the pain medicine, and now this. Rowdy growled with frustration.

The orderly could not have interrupted at a worse time. Before Rowdy knew that Ange had understood his full meaning.

Understood that he loved her and Toby and wanted them to be together always.

His last thought as the orderly pushed him away and he gave himself in to the pain medication was of Ange and Toby, and the family he so desperately wanted them to be.

Chapter Thirteen

With tears in her eyes and her heart in pieces, Angelica packed up the last box, full of the items she would need immediately when she got to their new home, and marked it with a big red X so she would know to unpack it first.

That she didn't know exactly where that home would be was admittedly a problem, but if she had to, she and Toby could stay in a hotel for a couple of weeks while she searched for the perfect place.

It wouldn't be in downtown Denver. That was no longer her scene. Maybe something in the suburbs, where folks settled down and raised their families.

Lakewood, maybe. Or Westminster.

She was no closer to figuring out what she wanted to do with her life than the day she'd moved back to Serendipity. She'd been too caught up in running the ranch. But again, she could buy herself time by working another job for a paycheck—just not necessarily the one she would eventually make a career path of.

Watching Rowdy being wheeled away by the orderly was the most painful moment of her life, and she'd left the hospital soon after. Despite what he'd said, all the arguments he'd made in her defense, seeing him laid up in the hospital, and knowing that, in part at least, she was the one who put him there was more than her heart could handle.

She had encouraged him back into the arena. Granted, she hadn't realized he could get hurt as a pickup man almost as easily as he had on the bronc eight years ago, but she should have known that if he saw a teenager in danger he would put himself out to make sure nothing bad happened.

She sighed and brushed her hair away from her face with the palm of her hand. Angelica's time on Granny's ranch in Serendipity had taught her a lot. When she looked in the mirror, she saw a mature and determined woman looking back at her, a mother who could and would take care of herself and her son, something she hadn't been certain she would be able to do.

Her only regret was having to leave the Bar C behind. And Rowdy.

But the time had come, because despite everything, despite knowing she would leave her heart behind with Rowdy she knew it was time for her to go.

She wanted to be the right woman for him, the one who, along with Toby, would become his family. Someone who could support him, walk beside him and be his partner in life.

Instead, she had floundered through her multiple attempts to be a rancher and by encouraging him to get back out in the rodeo arena had kicked the cane right out from underneath him.

How many times would he have to suffer because of her?

There was the ranch rodeo eight years ago, and then again last week. The Psycho Rooster, who had scratched him all up and had left what she was sure would become a scar on his jaw—and all because he was trying to protect her from her own foolishness.

She'd left him on the night of their wedding rehearsal and had broken his heart.

This time, when she left Serendipity this second—and last—time, she knew for sure that it was *her* heart that was once again breaking. Hopefully, Rowdy would realize she'd done him a favor, kept him from falling all over again.

As hard as it would be, she wouldn't leave without telling him goodbye this time, even though he already knew the reasons she had to go. She planned to visit the hospital later in the day and bring Toby along for their last farewell. She had learned that much from her past mistakes.

She taped up the box she'd been packing and moved it into the living room, stacking it on top of a couple of other similar-sized boxes.

There weren't many. She and Toby traveled light, and she hadn't purchased much. Other than what they'd brought with them, there were a few sentimental items of Granny's that she wanted to take, but nothing that took up much room.

A quilt. Granny's Bible. An old photograph of Granny and Gramps on the day they were married.

Her heart ached with longing. She could never settle for less than what Granny and Gramps had had, a marriage that withstood the test of time, up until the moment Granny lost Gramps to a sudden heart attack.

She would leave going through the rest of Granny's things to Jo, who would know better than she would how to deal with those items. Angelica had already had enough emotional overload to last her a lifetime. Sorting Granny's belongings would only give her more to grieve over.

She stooped and kissed Toby's forehead. Toby's gaze, far less hazy than when he was a newborn, fixed on her mouth. He lifted one fist to her lips and she gently kissed it. No matter what was right or wrong in her world, she had her son.

Three loud raps sounded on her front door, followed by two more, rousing her from her melancholy.

She wasn't expecting anyone. No one even knew she was leaving, and she wanted to keep it that way.

She hated goodbyes. She'd already informed Jo that she was leaving, and to her surprise, Jo hadn't argued. Maybe the old woman knew how hard this was for her. The only goodbye that still needed to be said would be handled later this afternoon.

Maybe Jo was here to make one last-ditch effort to change her mind about leaving.

"Who do you think that is, big guy?" she asked Toby in a singsong voice she wasn't feeling. She swung the door open, her gaze still on her son. "Are you expecting somebody?"

"Just you and Toby," a deep voice replied. "Why? Do you have someone else hiding in there?"

"Rowdy." Her heart jumped into her throat as he let himself in the door, stepping slowly and leaning heavily on his crutches. "When did you get out of the hospital? What are you doing here?"

Propping his crutches in front of him, he reached into the back pocket of his jeans and withdrew an envelope.

It was an achingly familiar sensation, reading *Angelica and Rowdy* scribbled on the outside in Granny's scratchy script.

She'd known there would be more letters, but she'd intended to leave before getting caught up in the next one. Rowdy needed to recuperate, not run all over town doing who knew what.

Attending picnics.

Feeding sheep.

Getting his bad knee smashed up saving a teenager at a ranch rodeo.

"Special delivery," he said with a grin. "They finally cut me loose from the hospital this afternoon. I thought I'd bring this letter out here in person so we can get right on it and solve our mystery once and for all."

"I don't think so, Rowdy." Her traitorous heart pounded so hard she thought perhaps Rowdy could hear it.

He frowned. "I don't get it. What's changed?"

"Me."

"But Granny—"

"Wouldn't want me to get in the way of you living your life to the fullest."

"What's that supposed to mean?"

"I called the local Realtor. He's going to get with my lawyer and work out the details of the sale of the ranch to you."

His jaw tightened. He looked like he was going to say something, but then he stopped and shook his head.

"No," he said at last, his tone brooking no argument.

"No?"

This was exactly why she'd been trying to leave town without a fuss. So that *this* didn't happen. She didn't know if her heart could handle it.

"Not without opening this envelope. Jo said it was the last one. I don't think you should make any permanent plans without finishing the course and fulfilling Granny Frances's last wishes, do you?"

She blew out an audible breath. That was precisely what she'd been about to do, but now that he was here, with the envelope in his palm, she supposed she might as well see this through. It wasn't as if he was going to let it go. And frankly, she wasn't strong enough to send him away.

She'd planned to say goodbye to him at the hospital. But since he was here, she might as well take advantage of his presence and part with him here in the privacy of her own home.

She picked up Toby from where he was cushioned in his bouncer and pulled him close to her shoulder, seeking comfort from the feel of him in her arms. His baby scent and the precious way he sucked on his fist always calmed her, even when she was as distressed as she was feeling right now.

"So open it." She turned away from Rowdy and paced to the other end of the room.

She heard him shake out the paper and clear his throat, then she turned back toward him just as he read the words.

"Find My Treasure."

"What do you think?" Rowdy asked, scratching his jaw. "Something buried in the back yard?"

She shook her head. "Too over-the-top, even for Granny. She would have kept her treasure close to her. In her personal space."

"Her bedroom?"

"If I had to guess."

"Haven't you been in there? Surely you would have noticed a treasure chest."

"I'm not sure we're looking for an actual chest, and I can't even speculate as to what Granny meant. But no, I haven't been in her bedroom. My grief is still too fresh and I couldn't hack going in there on my own. Seeing Granny's stuff. Being overwhelmed by memories."

Rowdy leaned forward on his crutches and reached for her hand and, Lord help her, she didn't pull it away.

"Happy memories, though, right?" he asked, a catch in his voice.

"Yes. So many."

"Me, too." He paused and squeezed her hand. "I think this is exactly what she wanted. For us to do this together. For me to be here with you. You can lean on me anytime you need to. You know that, don't you?"

Tears burned in the back of her eyes as she nodded fiercely.

She knew that, which was why leaving would be so hard.

"Well, maybe not physically lean on me," he joked, "or we both might tip over."

His words brought a soft smile to her lips despite the ache in her heart.

She leaned down and grabbed the baby bouncer and then gestured down the hall toward Granny's room. "Do you mind going in first?"

"Not at all."

She took a deep breath and followed him through the door into Granny's room.

"Whatever we find in here," he said, "we'll deal with together, okay?"

She nodded, unable to speak.

Angelica placed the bouncer on the floor next to Granny's bed and propped Toby in it.

"Where should we start?" he asked.

"I don't know. Where would you keep your treasure?"

"Assuming I had any? In the closet?"

"Works for me."

She had to remind herself to breathe as he set his crutches aside and dug into the closet. They sorted through Granny's clothing, pushing hangers aside so they could investigate the shelves in the back.

The whole closet smelled of Granny, the sweet scent of rose petals that Angelica would forever link with her.

She blinked away tears, but more took their place.

"I don't see anything that looks like a treasure chest," Rowdy said.

Angelica chuckled through her grief.

"Again, not necessarily a treasure chest," she reminded him.

"I know. But if anyone was going to keep their treasure in a chest, it would be Granny Frances, right?"

He was right about that.

But where else should they look?

Toby made a little mewling sound and Angelica glanced over to make sure he was doing well.

As usual, his fist was in his mouth and he was sucking loudly, but then she noticed he was clutching an old piece of ribbon.

"Where did you get that, little man? It probably shouldn't go into your mouth."

She reached out to take the ribbon away from him and realized it was attached to something, a longer ribbon disappearing under the corner of the bed.

"Rowdy?" she said, following the path of the ribbon until her hand closed around a box the size of a shoebox.

"Yeah?" he asked, popping his head out of the closet. He had left his hat on the hat rack at the front door as he always did, and his blond curls were ruffled with static cling from the clothes.

"I think Toby might have found something here."

As Rowdy sat on the edge of the bed, she pulled the box out from underneath it.

It was an old shoe box, decorated with ribbons that were probably older than Granny had been.

"See? She did keep a treasure chest." His voice was full of awe and respect, but then he flashed her a very Rowdy, toothy, I-told-you-so grin. "What do you know, big guy?" he said, addressing Toby. "You found our treasure for us."

Neither of them spoke as she gently pulled off the lid to the box, careful not to mess up any of the decorations.

The very first thing she saw was an envelope—with her and Rowdy's names on it, on top of a layer of tissue paper.

He chuckled. "I thought Jo said we had already seen the last of the envelopes."

"Maybe she didn't know about this one," Angelica suggested in a hushed tone.

"I opened the last one," Rowdy said. "Why don't you do the honors on this one? I suspect it's going to be special."

Angelica did, too. She held her breath as she slid her finger under the seal and pulled out the tri-folded paper.

"It's more than three words," she said. "In fact, it's an honest-to-goodness page-long letter. A story, I think."

Rowdy rested his palms on his thighs and leaned forward. "Something tells me this is going to wrap everything up. As crazy as the last few weeks have been, we could use a little closure. I can't wait to hear it."

A little closure.

Was that what this was? Because even though she'd

intended to stop by the hospital and offer Rowdy a proper goodbye, closure, it would not be.

Dear Angelica and Rowdy,

I hope you've had fun taking part in my little scavenger hunt. I know there must have been some confusing moments and many emotional ones, but I'm hoping there were happy ones, too.

"You can say that again," Rowdy muttered.

Angelica lifted an eyebrow. "Are you done?"

"Sorry. Sorry. No more commentating." He grinned and zipped his lips.

I have a little story to tell you, one about Josiah— your Gramps, Angelica—and me. I don't think I ever told you, but Josiah grew up on a cattle ranch. It was my parents who owned the sheep. Anyway, a little after we got engaged—at age seventeen, just like the two of you did—Josiah was helping a neighbor at a roundup and got caught up trying to herd a couple of stray cattle across a stream.

The cows balked, and then his horse bucked and he fell off and busted his leg pretty bad.

Rowdy groaned. "This is starting to feel a little bit too familiar."

"Will you hush and let me keep reading?" she teased.

We didn't have access to the kind of doctors and medicines y'all have today. No physical therapy like that which helped Rowdy recover. Serendipity was too far out and far too small for us to have that kind of help. Some old quack just set the bone and Josiah let it heal on its own.

So as a result, Josiah couldn't ride anymore and because of that he judged himself to be less of a man. I didn't see it, because I was head over ears in love with the stubborn man.

Can you believe he tried to run me off, telling me I ought to marry someone whole—whatever that means? Lord knows all of us are broken. Anyway, raising sheep on a small ranch doesn't necessarily require riding on horseback, and before long there were other mechanical means of transportation.

I thought about leaving town. I almost did. That's why my heart broke when you left without coming to talk to me first, Angelica. I knew just how you felt, and I could have shared this story with you and saved you and Rowdy both a lot of pain.

But you did come back, didn't you? And if you're reading this, then you've been spending time with Rowdy. It took Josiah and me a while to work out our problems, but in the end we said our *I do*'s and we had a good life together. A great one, actually.

God is good, all the time. I hope the treasure you find in this box will mean something special to you. You are both too stubborn for your own good, just like your Gramps and me. I hope you see why I felt I had to nudge you on a little bit with those tasks I gave you. And I hope you know I've done this in love.

Angelica, I really wish I could have met your son, but you know I already love him with my whole heart.

Enjoy the treasure I've left you, and bask in the gift of each other and your son. Gramps and I are looking down on you three and smiling.
Love,
Granny

Angelica pressed her lips together, not even trying to stem the flood of tears pouring down her cheeks.

She'd made so many mistakes, and yet—

Granny was so certain she could rise above them. She had known the mistakes Angelica had made eight years ago, hers and Rowdy's personalities together and apart, and she'd still believed in both of them.

"I think there's something inside this tissue." Rowdy leaned down and picked up a tissue-wrapped package. "Do you want to open it?"

Unable to speak, she shook her head and gestured for him to do it.

Fold by fold, he unwrapped the gift Granny had gone to such lengths to give them.

Rowdy laughed as he undid the last fold.

"Look here. Blue baby booties. Hand knit by Granny Frances, if I don't miss my guess."

"Oh," Angelica exclaimed, clapping a hand over her mouth as a sob escaped. "She made these for Toby."

"Yep," Rowdy agreed. "Wait, though. There's someth—" He cut off his word midsentence. "Well, what do you know?"

"What?"

"I may be thick, but even I can take a hint as bold as this one."

He held up the baby booties. Tied to each one was a ring.

Wedding rings, Angelica realized. Rings that had once belonged to Granny and Gramps.

It took Rowdy a moment to untie Granny's ring from the bootie, but he wasted no time in taking Angelica by the hand and pulling her to her feet.

"We've been through so much," he said, his voice clogging with emotion. "But there is so much more ahead of us. I love you, Angelica, and I always have. I think Granny Frances would like it very much if I put this ring on your finger. And I know I would. I want you to be my wife, and I would be honored to call Toby my son. Will you marry me?"

Only an hour earlier, she'd thought she was leaving Serendipity forever. And now thanks to Granny she would never have to leave it or Rowdy at all. Her heart was so full it was all she could do to nod and allow him to slip Granny's ring on her finger.

"Are you sure you're not just proposing to me for my land?" she teased, her voice cracking with emotion.

He grinned and shrugged. "A man can light two candles with one flame, can't he?"

"Point taken." She paused and tilted her head, her lips matching his contagious smile. "But only if you promise me that at our wedding, we'll be lighting one candle with two flames."

"And maybe a third one for Toby?"

She nodded, her eyes once again filling with happy tears.

"Three candles, one flame," he whispered as his lips hovered over hers. "That sounds just about perfect to me."

* * * * *

THE RANCHER'S
SURPRISE DAUGHTER

Jill Lynn

To my amazing readers, thank you for encouraging me and being a part of this writing journey. Your support means so much to me.

And a huge thank you to Lost Valley Ranch for your help and inspiration.

Herein is love, not that we loved God, but that he loved us, and sent his Son to be the propitiation for our sins.
—*1 John* 4:10

Chapter One

Nothing like walking into a situation blind.

Lucas Wilder bounded up the lodge steps, the late-July wind that twisted across his sun-scorched arms as dry as aged kindling.

His sister's text that someone was looking for him in the lodge hadn't been helpful in the least. And then she'd gone off radar, not answering his request for more info. Was it an employee? Shouldn't be a ranch guest as last week's were already gone and a new batch didn't arrive until tomorrow.

Luc crossed into the comfortable lobby that guests could relax in after a day of ranch activities, scanning the room for whoever had beckoned as his eyes adjusted to the dim interior lighting.

"Lucas."

The feminine voice slammed into the backs of his knees. He willed his legs not to wobble like a newborn calf's as he faced her.

Catherine Malory. She sat in the club chair stationed to the side of the front window, sunlight streaming over her shoulder, highlighting rich, dark-chocolate hair.

She looked a hint older than the last time he'd seen her. Worried, and yet somehow the addition of a few lines around her eyes and lips only added to her beauty.

Attraction flared to life, the sight of her like oxygen to an ember Luc was certain he'd stomped out years before.

What was she doing here? It had been years since he'd left Denver and their relationship, yet he'd never been able to fully erase Cate from his mind. Luc handled forty-some guests each week plus a slew of employees. Surely he could handle one conversation with a woman he'd once loved.

"Four years." His words quaked out, a cross between teenage boy and wounded animal. Oh, man. He was doing an excellent job of handling it so far.

A crease formed between Cate's slim eyebrows. "I know how long it's been since we've seen each other, Luc. Four years, four months." So like her to have the details exact.

He simply stared, not knowing how long they analyzed each other before he managed to make use of his voice again. "What are you doing here?"

"I—" Her hands clenched together in her lap. "I need to talk to you about something."

Ah. This felt like safe ground. She must need something. Help, he could do. Love? No, ma'am. They'd tried that once. There'd been some immaturity on his part—he could admit that—but mostly he'd loved her, and she hadn't believed him.

"What do you need?" Even after all of this time, after how they'd left things…he wouldn't turn her away. But hopefully once she said what she needed to, she'd leave. Luc refused to ride that kind of emotional roller coaster again. Since Cate, he'd barely dated. It was easier to focus on work. He had a good life running the guest ranch with his sisters. He was fine on his own. Work might be a lonely companion, but it didn't leave him shattered like Cate had.

"You're going to need to sit down." Her voice came out quiet. Beaten.

"That bad, huh?" Sadness and maybe even a little fear poured from her, and his pulse thundered with curiosity. "Come with me."

When she stood, he led her down the hall to his office for some privacy since a staff member could come through at any moment. Cate shuffled along behind him as though he was directing her to an execution instead of a cushioned seat.

The small space housed a desk, two filing cabinets, framed photos of his family and the ranch in various stages over the years, plus the Top Twenty Guest Ranch Award they'd received the past two years running. Luc motioned for Cate to sit on the charcoal futon that took up one corner.

She sank down, eyes glazed, almost as though she was in shock.

For a moment Luc considered sitting next to her, but the air in the room was already on short supply. Unwilling to risk the close proximity, he perched back against the desk instead, stretching long legs out to hold him steady.

Cate wore a navy shirt with white capris and camel-colored sandals. And even though she looked put together—gorgeous, which he was nowhere near willing to admit—something was definitely off. Luc was almost positive moisture shone in her soft chestnut eyes.

The silence tortured him. "Just tell me, whatever it

is." How bad could it be? His mind raced with possibilities. Her parents had been pretty tough on her. Could it be something with them? But what would that have to do with him?

She sucked in a breath, apprehension flitting across her face before she opened her mouth and let loose. "My daughter needs to have surgery." A hand momentarily pressed against her lips as though stemming the flow. "That wasn't how I planned to say that."

"You have a daughter?" Her revelation pierced like a stab wound. Luc would expect that Cate had moved on after him, despite the fact that he'd never accomplished the same himself. But even now, after all of this time, she still felt like his.

But she wasn't. He searched her finger for a wedding ring, but the skin was barren.

Luc shook off the crushing blow. It didn't matter. Their past—her decisions since then—had nothing to do with him. She had a sick daughter. He'd deal with that now. The rest? He'd wait until after she left to process.

"Do you need money?" Where was the father? Why was she coming to him for help?

"No. I need...you."

He had to be missing something. It had been a long time since Cate had needed him. None of this made sense.

"I didn't know until you'd left. I didn't find out until you'd been gone for over a month that I was pregnant, and then I kept waiting for you to contact me, to try to fix things between us. But you didn't."

He resisted a growl. "You told me not to." What she'd said...how she'd said it...he'd never forget it.

"I know what I told you."

His gut bounded for his boots like a loose boulder on

a steep hill as he processed the rest of what she'd said. *I didn't find out until you were gone that I was pregnant.*

"Cate." His voice was low and barely existent, but he managed to spit out the question rattling his mind while shock and disbelief ricocheted through him. "What are you saying?"

Remorse brimmed again, and Luc read the truth in the soulful depths before she spoke.

"I'm saying… I'm sorry I didn't tell you sooner. And that she's yours."

Catherine Malory thought she'd understood humility, but she'd never been brought so low as this moment. Who walked into the life of a man she'd lied to, hid a child from for years, and just blurted out that he was a father?

Luc would hate her. And she deserved it. In the beginning she'd felt vindicated keeping Ruby to herself—especially with the way Luc had left and how Cate had grown up being torn between her selfish parents. The feeling of being unimportant had never left her, like a disease that infiltrated her bones.

She'd been attempting to put Ruby first. To protect her. But Luc would never understand that.

He pushed off from the desk, a long, lean giant in a heather-brown Wilder Ranch T-shirt, faded jeans and boots. "I…have a daughter? You're saying she's *mine*?"

His words ached with a misery that resonated in her own chest. What had she done? "Yes. I'm so sorry. I know an apology isn't enough. I just—"

"Where—" Luc scrubbed a hand through maple hair, though the short cut left little room for mussing. "Where is she?"

"She's here."

His head rolled back as if he'd taken a blow to the jaw.

"We came in, and your sister Emma was headed out to the barn. I remembered her from you talking about her, but of course she didn't know me. She offered to show Ruby the horses after hearing I needed to talk to you. I tried to say no, but Ruby begged to go with her."

And Cate had realized the conversation would be much easier without Ruby present. She hadn't processed through that before she'd gotten in the car and trucked out here. But what would she have done with Ruby anyway? She didn't have family to watch her. A friend would have, but Cate didn't like to be separated from her daughter. Especially with the girl's heart condition.

"Emma's great with kids." Luc's Adam's apple bobbed. "Ru—Ruby will be fine."

Their daughter's name coming from his lips for the first time sent Cate scrambling to keep her careening emotions under control.

"Why are you here now after all of this time? What changed? And how do I know...?" Luc's chest expanded. Cate could imagine his heart beating triple time, because hers felt as though it might explode. His heated hazel eyes held hers. "How do I know she's mine?"

She'd expected it, even planned for it. Still, the sting surprised her. She stated Ruby's birthday at the end of November. Eight months after Luc had hightailed it out of Denver. "When you first left I thought it was stress making me not feel well. Took me a while to figure it out. By then you were long gone."

Every last doubt scrolled across his face.

"Ruby was born with an atrial septal defect."

Luc's hand splayed against his chest where she knew his own scars were. "Same as me."

"As to why now, she needs to have the hole closed. And I couldn't... If something happened to her and you didn't know she'd even existed..." Cate would never have forgiven herself. She already couldn't forgive herself for keeping them apart for the first three years and eight months of Ruby's life.

The familiar rush of fear that came with thinking of Ruby's surgery and anything happening to her precious daughter blurred her vision. "I knew you needed to meet her before her procedure." God had been working on Cate's hard heart, and He'd made that very clear. Almost as though she'd been given a deadline for fessing up.

Since she'd become a Christian about a year ago, Cate had experienced a number of lessons in growing her faith. Trusting God's insistent nudging to tell Luc about Ruby had been the toughest one by far.

Luc scrubbed both hands across his face as though attempting to wake himself from a nightmare.

"We can do a test to prove you're her father. Your name's on her birth certificate."

Arms dropped to his sides like leaded weights. "If you went so far as to do that..." His voice scraped like sandpaper. Worn. Weary. "Why didn't you tell me right away?"

The question she didn't know how to answer. *I didn't want to share* wasn't exactly a mature, adult response.

Luc knew about her childhood—and her parents' divorce—but would he understand how much their actions had messed with her?

"Never mind." The bite in his tone sent guilt skimming across her skin. "It's too late for excuses. Nothing you say is going to matter right now anyway."

"Okay." Cate raised her hands. Whatever he wanted, she'd do.

Luc sank to the other end of the futon, miles of agony stretching between them.

"Does she need open-heart surgery?"

"No. Cardiac catheterization. They'll close the hole with a device."

His shoulders inched lower, his relief evident that Ruby would only need the less invasive procedure that would involve a catheter from her leg into her heart. Already, even with knowing as little as he did about Ruby and possibly not even believing he was her father, he felt for her. Didn't want her to go through the same trauma he had as a child.

That spoke volumes about him.

"Did you tell Emma who the two of you were?"

"No. I think she thought I was a potential guest or that I was applying for a job." Cate had been purposely evasive.

His audible sigh filled the small space. "That's good. At least for now. Does... Ruby know about me?"

"Lately she's been asking questions, and I've started answering them. She knows you exist, but she doesn't know we're here to see you."

Eyes a mixture of fading green and brown leaves seared into her skin. She half expected to see smoke rise and smell scalded flesh. "In case I didn't see her? If she's my daughter, I would never walk away from her. I think you know that, Cate."

Ouch. That truth stung, as did the *if.* Though she couldn't blame him. Even with Ruby having the same heart defect as he did, why should he believe her? She hadn't exactly proved herself trustworthy over the past four-plus years.

"Do you want to take some time? We can come back.

Talk in a few days." If someone had walked into her life and told her news of this magnitude, Cate would be in a puddle on the floor. But not Luc. How was he so calm? Why wasn't he raging at her?

"I'm not sure time is going to change my shock. I want to meet her."

She'd come here for this, but still, her stomach churned. "Are you sure you don't need some time to process?"

He didn't bother to answer. Just raised an eyebrow.

"Okay." If only saying the word out loud would make it true. Cate could tell herself she was okay a million times, but she was afraid the feeling would never follow. "Then let's go."

Luc's boots echoed down the hallway like a death knell on Cate's conscience. Panicked prayers flitted through her mind as she attempted to keep up with his pace. Cate had been praying for Luc and Ruby since she'd figured out this meeting needed to take place, and she could only hope she hadn't ruined either of their lives with her selfishness. Somehow she wanted healing. For all of them.

But today she simply prayed for survival. Good thing she believed in a gracious God. One who forgave her when she didn't deserve His mercy. Because that was the kind of God a girl like her needed.

Luc should probably take some time to process like Cate had suggested, but since nothing made sense right now, he figured, why wait? If he let Cate and Ruby leave, he might never see them again. Cate already seemed so jittery and nervous that he feared losing them both forever. Not that he had them. He wasn't naive. Cate could just as easily disappear from his life again, taking any chance of his knowing Ruby with her. And if she was his daughter, Luc wanted that opportunity.

If she was his daughter. Mind-boggling. How had his life gone from mundane to unrecognizable in a matter of minutes?

They headed down the lodge steps just as Emma exited the barn, a girl who must be Ruby next to her. The distance allowed Luc to study her. Short little thing—course, she'd only be three years and eight months if Cate was telling the truth. Ruby wore bright pink shorts and a multicolored T-shirt, her animated motions and whatever she said causing Emma to laugh.

After spotting Cate, she ran in their direction, his sister following behind.

Intuitively, Luc had known Ruby would be beautiful—how could she come from Cate and not be?—but the sight of her almost brought him to his knees. Her silky caramel hair was a shade or two lighter than her mother's. Closer to his. He had the niggling sensation that if he rummaged for an old photograph, Ruby would look strikingly similar to his twin sister, Mackenzie, at this same age.

Ruby flung her arms around Cate's legs, and Emma stopped in front of them. "Your girl is a spoonful of honey. We had a good time. Thanks for letting us hang." His sister pulled her hair back and held it at the nape of her neck as a gust of wind wrapped around them.

"Come see me again?" She directed the question to Ruby, who answered with an emphatic nod. After a thank-you from Cate, Emma was off, light brown locks once again twisting in the high-powered breeze as she headed back to the barn. His little sister ran the Kids'

Club at the ranch. She was a kid-wrangling, child-whispering rock star.

"Mommy, can we get a horse-y?"

Cate's laugh was strangled. "Our apartment doesn't allow dogs, let alone horses, sweets."

Ruby looked up, noticing him. "Hi." Big brown eyes—just like Cate's—held his.

A rush of emotion clogged his throat, but Luc managed a response. "Hi."

"I'm Ruby. What's your name? Do you live here? Do you have a horse-y?"

Her questions ignited a grin. "Luc." He glanced at Cate, and she shook her head in response to his unspoken question. Ruby must not know his name to be able to create the link to him being her father. Probably a good thing at this point. "And yes, I live here and I have a horse." Or should he say "horse-y"?

He sank to bended knee in front of the girl, partly to be closer to her height, partly because his legs were about to give out.

The blood in his veins thrummed a rhythm that whispered *mine*. As though it knew without a test or proof that Ruby was his daughter.

Why he believed Cate, Luc didn't know. Course, the heart defect seemed a blatant link. When he'd been a child, they hadn't considered it genetic, but in the years since, they'd proved it often was.

Still, he should be careful until he knew for sure.

Yet even with that logical thought backing him up, everything in his body hurt. He wanted so badly to reach out, to hug her, to somehow know everything about her in one instant. He fisted hands at his sides. The idea that

Ruby was his, that he'd missed so much time if Cate was telling the truth, made every muscle tense.

"Any chance you want to ride one of the horses?" Everything was better on a horse. Plus, it would give him a chance to get to know Ruby a little.

Her chocolate eyes lit up with excitement, head bobbing fast and furious. She definitely had a sense of adventure. Must drive Cate crazy. The thought warmed him.

"Luc—"

"She'll be fine." He stood, earning crossed arms and a scowl from Cate. Her thin, dark eyebrows joined together in obvious agitation, somehow only managing to highlight her beauty. Luc had never had a problem being attracted to Cate. It was in the mature, getting-along department that they'd struggled.

Luc waited an extra beat to see if Cate added any additional protest. He didn't want to be careless with Ruby, but most often her condition had very few symptoms and just needed to be fixed.

When silence reigned and Cate's shoulders drooped as if relinquishing control, Luc put a check in the victory column. Missing almost four years of Ruby's life definitely gave him an upper hand at the moment.

The three of them headed for the corral, and Luc directed them to Buster, one of the smaller palomino quarter horses with a calm temperament, who was already saddled and ready to go. He hoisted Ruby up and made sure she felt comfortable. Told her where to hold on. Her face shone with wonder and excitement as she commented about how the color of the horse reminded her of caramel popcorn.

"I'm going to walk with you and lead Buster the whole

time, and anytime you want to stop or get down, you just tell me."

"I can't do it by myself?"

Adventurous little thing. "Not until you've had more experience. We'd have to get you started on a pony—"

Cate's wide eyes cut him off, communicating all kinds of warning signals and flares. Luc tempered his amusement. He'd probably been getting ahead of himself a bit.

"We'll be back in ten minutes," he said to Cate, lips quirking at her squeak of indignation and the fact that she was, most definitely, not invited.

She'd had Ruby to herself for three-plus years. Luc deserved some time with her away from Cate's hawk-like attention.

Chapter Two

Six agonizing days later Luc paced back and forth near the fireplace in the small living room of his cabin. His friend Gage Frasier perched on the arm of the chair flanking the couch, grilling Luc like the lawyer he was with questions that didn't have satisfying answers.

"Any news on the paternity test?"

"Nope." Luc dropped to the sofa, his body no longer functioning with coherent thought or movement.

He hadn't seen Ruby or Cate since last Saturday because he'd decided the most logical course of action was to wait until he knew for sure that she was his daughter. Though Cate hadn't shown any doubt, she'd agreed to his suggestion that they not say anything to Ruby until they had the paternity test results back.

But waiting was as easy as living with a broken toe.

In the short time he'd spent with Ruby on Saturday while she'd ridden Buster, he'd quickly come to the conclusion that his *possible* daughter was captivating. Entertaining. And bubbled with as much energy as her little body could harness.

The only other time Luc had been smitten so fast was

with one other female, who, when he and Ruby had returned to the corral after twenty minutes instead of ten, had been spitting mad.

Luc could admit he had fully enjoyed Cate's disgruntled state. Currently, his guilt meter regarding anything she thought rested solidly at a zero.

Hers should be shooting through the roof.

"What's she like?"

"Ruby's..." How to narrow it down? "Sweet. She talks nonstop. The kind of girl who would make friends with a fly." He'd gathered that because she had, in fact, talked to the fly that had ridden on Buster's saddle horn for part of the ride. And she'd befriended Luc instantly, jabbering the whole time. He'd learned that she had a best friend at day care and that her mom didn't let her do more than an hour of "lectonics" in a day even though some kids got to do bunches more.

That one had made him smile. He'd found himself silently agreeing with Cate.

Ruby had told him her mom read "lots" of books to her every night, announcing it as though she was the most special girl in the world and their reading time only confirmed it.

That information had created an uncomfortable surge of sympathy in Luc, flooding him with images of Cate juggling everything on her own. Ruby and her condition. Work. Bills. How had she managed it all? From what he knew of her parents, he couldn't imagine them stepping in to help when Cate had found out she was pregnant. But he'd quickly stomped out the rush of concern that came with imagining Cate doing everything on her own.

He was *not* going to feel bad for her. Not after the decision she'd made to keep Ruby from him.

Luc had gotten a DNA test done in town first thing Monday morning. They'd sent in his sample, and Cate and Ruby had gone to the testing place in Denver. Now it was ticking toward five on Friday, and he was tormented to think he'd spend the weekend without knowing the results. So much felt undecided. And on top of his questions, Cate had texted him the date of Ruby's procedure. One week from today.

"So Cate didn't explain why she never told you about Ruby?" Gage's dark hair looked as rumpled as Luc's. At least he could count on sympathy and understanding from his friend. Gage had been through a horrible ordeal when his wife left. Sometimes Luc wondered if the man would ever recover.

"Nope. But I really didn't let her. What does it matter? What's done is done." Anger boiled under the surface. Those last two comments were lies. He both wanted to know what Cate had been thinking and felt so wounded and aggravated that he didn't believe any answer she gave would help.

"Luc." Gage's voice snapped with concern, but Luc wasn't sure he could handle any more girl talk—problems that didn't have solutions were his least favorite subject. "Your phone just buzzed." Gage motioned to the coffee table.

Luc snagged it and opened the new email, relief tingling through his limbs when he saw it contained the results. Sawdust coated his mouth, saliva running for the hills. He clicked to read the report, the letters swimming before him. *Not Excluded* was typed across the top of the page in bold print. The testing facility had coached him on what this meant.

He was Ruby's father.

The phone slipped from his grip, bouncing lightly on the sofa cushion.

"I'm a dad."

It was as though he'd taken a horse kick to the chest, the air in his lungs instantly gone. He and Gage stared at each other. Frozen.

Unable to stay still, Luc pushed up from the couch, his strides quickly covering the small cabin's living room. He ended up at the back window that faced open ranchland, seeing the grass-covered hills in a new light. Yesterday it had been land passed down to Luc and his sisters when their parents had moved to a warmer climate in order to accommodate his mom's health. Today a new generation existed. A little girl with silky hair and a nonstop mouth and adorable brown eyes who was his. *His.*

"I have to see her." He crossed the space and rummaged for his keys in the kitchen junk drawer.

Gage followed him. "Don't you think you should wait? Calm down first?"

Why did he have so many scraps of paper in this stupid drawer? Items tumbled over each other as he searched for the simple metal key ring. "I don't see a real possibility of that happening in the very near future."

"Guess not." Gage nudged Luc to the side, then found the truck keys in a much calmer, more methodical manner.

But then again, Gage hadn't just found out he was positively a father.

His friend offered up the keys on the palm of his hand. "Do you want me to go with you?"

Luc appreciated Gage's support, but he needed some time to clear his head. Maybe the drive would help, though he wasn't confident anything would at the moment. "Nah. Thanks, though." He snatched the metal ring that held three keys and proceeded to the front door, snagging his boots.

"What are you going to do? About custody?"

He paused to glance at Gage after yanking on the first boot. "What do you mean? What can I do?"

"File for it."

"I don't know." He couldn't think beyond seeing Ruby right now. Couldn't deal with logistics. "I'm angry, but I'm not sure that's the answer."

"You need to protect yourself. She's already kept Ruby from you for years. Who's to say she won't take off and disappear to another state and you'll never see your child again?"

Red flashed, and Luc pulled on the second boot with heated force. Cate wouldn't…would she? But the same thought had entered his mind. When they'd readied to leave on Saturday, Luc had wondered if he'd ever see them again. Cate had written down her address and phone number, almost as though proving to him she wouldn't do anything of the sort.

Still, how could he trust her after what she'd done?

"Do you want me to look into it? See what your options are? I know someone who deals with these situations. I can ask."

Gage was the only man Luc knew who ranched as a later-in-life choice. He'd been a smarty lawyer at some big firm until he'd inherited a ranch from his uncle. Gage and his wife, Nicole, had moved to the nearby ranch just over a year and a half ago. And then Nicole had decided a different life looked better, and she'd been gone in a blink. Gage had been on his own ever since. He ran the ranch, very quietly helping the church or people in the community out with legal matters when they required it.

Luc just never imagined he'd be in need of that advice.

"I don't know that I have any other choice." A stampede of hooves vibrated inside his skull. "I'm not sure if I have any rights and if she can control letting me see Ruby. So, yeah. Check it out."

"I will."

"Good thing I have you on retainer."

Gage chuckled. "You don't. You couldn't afford me. This friend business really works in your favor."

"True."

Luc grabbed the piece of paper with Cate's address from the kitchen counter. He'd left it there as a reminder to pray for Ruby—not that the trigger had been necessary. The girl and her mother hadn't left his thoughts all week.

He'd need the details if he planned to show up on Cate's doorstep unannounced.

It wasn't very considerate of him to plan to ambush her at their home. But then again, he hadn't expected Cate to show up on his doorstep with a daughter he never knew he had.

Turnabout was fair play.

"Mommy, will you play the cupcake game with me?" Ruby stood before Cate with a well-loved game in her hand that still boasted the reduced thrift-store sticker price.

Before Ruby, Cate had never stepped foot in a secondhand store. She'd never struggled for money growing up. But love and attention? Those had been harder to find.

It wasn't as if her parents had been abusive in any way. She'd just been more…overlooked. They were simply too caught up in themselves to notice anyone around them—including the little girl left in the wake of their selfishness.

Growing up, her parents never saw eye to eye on anything, but on the subject of her pregnancy, they'd instantly been in agreement. They'd advised her that having Ruby would ruin her life. That it would be too hard. That it would crumple any chance of her being successful and she'd have to scramble to make ends meet. They'd told Cate that if she kept the baby, there'd be no help from them. Money or otherwise. Probably hoping to sway her decision. It hadn't worked. But it had left them estranged.

They'd been right. Cate had hustled. Finished school early on an accelerated path. She'd scrounged for work, taking anything and everything she could find. Raising Ruby was the hardest thing she'd ever done in her life.

But her parents had also been so very, very wrong. Because the adorable munchkin standing in front of Cate hopping up and down—game pieces rattling inside the box as though agreeing with her impatience—was by far the best thing she'd ever accomplished. Worth every second of her energy and love.

"Please, Mommy?"

"Okay, Rubes. I'll play." After a couple of games Ruby would have a little more playtime and then Cate would read to her before bed. She still went down early—partly for Cate's sanity and partly because she often worked the evening hours until falling into bed herself.

Removing the charcoal-framed glasses she wore for computer work, Cate set them next to her Mac computer on the desk that occupied one corner of the living room in their tiny, two-bedroom apartment.

The screen in front of her went dark as it fell asleep,

but she knew what lurked behind the curtain of black. A project with a looming deadline. She was close, but she couldn't quite get the branding package for the local cupcake shop just right. And she needed it to be perfect, because she needed the next freelance job after this. Cate loved her career as a graphic designer and the freedom it allowed her to work from home and cart Ruby to and from the small in-home day care she went to.

A majority of Cate's jobs came from a firm in Denver who hired her as a subcontractor, and she filled in the extra income they needed with side work.

They moved over to the sofa, and Ruby set up the game while Cate covered a yawn and considered making a cup of tea. Twenty-four years old and this was what she'd come to on a Friday night. But then, getting pregnant at twenty had put a damper on any wild and adventurous life plans.

Ruby chose a blue base and began building a cupcake. She never really followed the game cards, instead creating whatever combination suited her fancy at the moment.

"Your turn, Mommy."

Cate picked the yellow holder, choosing to add a plastic layer of chocolate, wishing, not for the first time, that this game consisted of real cupcakes and she could inhale the chocolate one in her hand...after adding a layer of buttercream frosting.

Her mouth watered just as a knock sounded at their door, causing her to jump like a popcorn kernel in sizzling oil.

Who would be at their door on a Friday night? Was it her nosy neighbor again? Millie Hintz wasn't the landlord, but she'd appointed herself as the head of the building's nonexistent neighborhood watch program. A spry eighty-year-old with white hair who seemed to be shrinking in height over time, her unexpected pop-overs were unnerving because she always scanned the apartment from the doorway like she was going to catch Cate with a hidden mountain lion or other unapproved item.

But even though Millie considered it her job to know what was happening in everyone's lives, she was kind-hearted. Cate had decided the visits were more about loneliness than anything else. And if anyone understood that, it was her. Talking to Millie wouldn't cost her more than a few minutes of time.

"You go," she told Ruby, pushing up from the sofa and crossing the few steps to the door. Sometimes Millie brought them cookies. The monster ones with M&M's and chocolate chips. Yum.

Cate pressed her face against the peephole, squeaking in surprise when it wasn't shrinking Millie on the other side of the door, but Luc.

What was he doing here?

All week he'd been on her mind, her thoughts zipping into overdrive… Had she done the right thing telling him about Ruby? She hoped so. It had taken all of her strength to share her daughter with him. They'd done the DNA testing earlier this week, and she'd let him know about Ruby's procedure date, but other than that, she hadn't heard from him. What was he thinking showing up at their apartment like this? Didn't the man know how to use a phone?

And more important, did he know she was home and did she have to answer? Her pulse bumped along like her car had on the gravel road that led to the Wilder ranch. And of course she was in old, black, faded-to-gray yoga pants and a yellow V-neck T-shirt, her hair in a disheveled low ponytail.

Quite the package.

Frustration leaked out in a disgruntled huff. "So much for cookies." She'd take Millie over Luc any day.

"I can hear you through the door, Cate."

She jumped to the side as if he had X-ray vision and could also see her through the barrier.

"You really know how to creep a girl out." Cate quickly redid the tie that held her hair and swiped under her eyes for runaway makeup.

"Are you going to open the door or are we going to keep talking through it?"

Ruby appeared next to Cate. "Is that my friend Luc?"

Ever since they'd been to the ranch, Ruby hadn't stopped chattering about "my friend Luc." It was all Cate could do to keep from plugging her ears, because she didn't have a clue what was going on in Luc's head since she'd shown up and royally flipped his life upside down.

She both wanted and didn't want to know what he was thinking.

What he thought of her.

"Yep, it is." Cate undid two locks with shaking fingers—not that the security mattered so much now that she knew how flimsy her door was—and twisted the knob.

Luc practically took up the whole frame. What was it about him that always made her feel like his presence sucked the oxygen out of the room? He wasn't *that* tall. Maybe an inch under six foot.

His eyebrow quirked. "Can I come in?"

Was answering *no* a legitimate option? Ruby nudged

past Cate, latched on to Luc's hand and pulled him inside. The scent of the outdoors came with him.

"Come on. I want to show you my room and my new doll and my ponies and my pink lamp. Me and Mommy were playing a game. You can play with us if you want."

The adoration for Ruby written on Luc's face was enough to make Cate's knees go swirly. Though none of it was directed at her.

An annoyed *meow* sounded from the top of the couch. Princess Prim rose from her favorite resting place and stretched her spine as if their ruckus had woken her and she was *not* pleased about it. Narrowed eyes dissected Luc, naming him an intruder in one fell swoop. *Good kitty.* Cate silently promised her a treat for later.

"I thought you couldn't have pets." Luc's head swung from the feline to Cate.

"We can't have dogs, but Prim is more royalty than pet. She runs the place. Ruby and I are just her lowly servants."

Ruby giggled and gave Luc's hand—which she hadn't let go of—a determined tug. She yanked him across the small apartment living room and past their dining table. But at the threshold to her bedroom, Luc paused.

"You okay if she shows me her room?"

A dried biscuit had somehow gotten lodged in her throat. Considerate of him to ask, but Luc had as much of a right to Ruby as she did.

That was what scared her the most.

Cate managed a nod, and the two of them disappeared inside. She heard Ruby's continuous chatter and Luc's low voice rumbling back questions or answers. The whole thing made her drop to the couch and hold her head in her hands. What had she done?

God, You'd better be right. Protect her. And me. Please. You know I didn't want to do this.

Princess Prim burrowed onto her lap, tilting her head in a way that asked questions. The royalty wanted answers Cate didn't have.

"What are you? The press?" She scrubbed hands into the soft fur behind Prim's ears. "I just don't want her to get hurt. And I'm afraid of losing her." The whisper came out forlorn, and Prim purred in sympathetic response.

What were the two of them doing in there? Moving Prim to the sofa, Cate eased to the edge of Ruby's room, close enough to hear but not be seen.

Prim let out an incriminating meow. She'd followed Cate and now rubbed against her leg. Cate nudged her gently away with her foot and put her finger to her lips in a shushing motion—as if the cat could understand her. The move only caused Prim to meow with interest and sneak between her feet as though they were playing a game. Cate's hiding place wouldn't last long at this rate.

Tea. She could make that cup she'd been craving earlier. It wasn't eavesdropping if the kitchen happened to be almost directly across from Ruby's doorway.

Cate made her way toward the pint-size kitchen as slowly as possible, her lungs constricting at the sound of Luc's booming laughter mingling with Ruby's sweet giggle. She caught sight of Luc perched on the bed and Ruby on the floor, her head bent in concentration as she showed him something.

And then, instead of finding herself in the kitchen, she was standing in the doorway. Both of them looked up as if questioning the reason for her presence.

"Hey, I…" …*wanted to hear what you were saying.*

"Does anyone want something to drink? Luc? I didn't even offer." *When you showed up unannounced at my door.*

Good thing none of these snarky thoughts were actually coming out of her mouth.

"I'm fine, thanks," Luc answered, and Ruby shook her head.

Dismissed without a second thought. Eerily similar to her childhood. The emotion wrapped around Cate like an old, tattered blanket she'd tried to throw out more times than she could count. But somehow every time she opened her closet, there it was.

Cate microwaved water in her favorite Anthropologie monogram mug—a fabulous thrift-store find. At the insistent beeping that the microwave had finished its work, she popped open the door and dunked her finger into the liquid to check the temperature.

Ouch. She snatched her poor skin back out. Scalding.

Ripping open the calming tea bag—like it would make a dent in her current state of mind—Cate bobbed the trapped tea leaves in the cup, her agitation sending ripples across the water.

When she'd first found out she was pregnant with Ruby, Cate had felt vindicated in not contacting Lucas. He'd never tried to fix what had gone wrong between them or answer the accusations she'd questioned him about in the end. Yes, she'd confronted him about cheating on her after a friend had tipped her off. But Cate had just wanted answers. Wanted Luc to tell her he wasn't seeing someone else and confirm the truth she already felt in her bones. He had quickly denied doing anything of the sort...but the more she'd pushed for details, the more he'd shut down.

They'd fought and said so many horrible things to each other.

Cate sipped her tea, leaning back against the countertop, eyes closed against the memory of that night as hot liquid coated her throat. Man, they'd been young. Stubborn. And completely inconsiderate of each other.

Finally, she'd told him to leave. To never contact her again.

The strangest part was, he'd listened. Cate didn't plan to tell the man currently one room away from her that she'd waited for him to fight for her. To love her. She'd wanted to have a calm conversation about what happened—to find out the truth and listen to Luc—not just lob accusations back and forth.

But she hadn't heard from him after that night. Only radio silence.

Cate crumpled the tea package while blinking away unwanted moisture. She tossed it into the garbage and slammed the cupboard door shut. But the askew trash can blocked it from closing, not giving her the pleasure of a loud crash.

She attempted to leave it for all of two seconds, then groaned and opened the door, straightening the wastebasket so that the cabinet shut flush.

After Ruby had been born and the heart defect had been found, Cate had been so focused on her daughter that she'd attempted to put Luc out of her mind.

She'd decided she was right to keep Ruby to herself. That she was protecting her daughter from being subjected to parents who didn't get along—Cate knew too well the kind of wounding that could inflict on a child. Even after they'd grown into an adult.

She'd clung to bitterness and fear, letting them dictate her choices.

Until just over a year ago. Through a little girl and her mom at day care who invited Ruby to attend Sunday school, Cate had found herself on a padded church chair for the first time in her life. She'd met God within those walls, and a piece of her that had always felt forgotten became known.

God had worked on her over the year, slowly convincing her that while she might not be able to trust Luc or even herself, she could trust Him. Ruby needing the procedure had been the last key in getting Cate to tell Lucas the truth.

But she was still afraid.

That Luc would try to take Ruby away from her. That his presence would wreak havoc on the safe life she'd so carefully woven for them. That she'd foolishly be drawn to him all over again.

If Luc decided to be a part of Ruby's life, Cate's focus would remain on their daughter. She wasn't going to entertain any attraction to Luc or let her mind wander regarding how things had gone wrong so quickly between them at the end.

Cate refused to leave a shattered little girl in the wake of any of her own selfish desires.

Which led to the main question throbbing behind her temples with ferocity. Did she even need to worry about Luc being in their lives? Why was he here tonight? Was it to tell her he was in?

Or out?

Chapter Three

The scent of garlic in Cate and Ruby's apartment—a remnant of dinner, Luc would guess—made his stomach growl. In his hurry to get here and see Ruby, he'd forgotten to eat. Not a normal occurrence for him.

He sat on Ruby's bright purple bedspread while she showed him her colorful ponies. He'd already met her collection of dolls.

On his way into Ruby's room, Luc had given the apartment a quick once-over. The size of a matchbox with everything in its place. So Cate was still the neat freak she'd once been. But the pieces and colors she used in the apartment gave it a comfortable feel. Artistic and homey. Even still, Luc felt strangely claustrophobic. He was used to wide open spaces. The building barely had any grass outside with no playground to be seen.

He had the strangest urge to snap Ruby into his arms, barrel out of here and never come back.

"This one's my favorite." Ruby held up a white pony with purple hair.

At times she talked so fast Luc could barely decipher her words. For the most part he'd been drinking her in—

watching the nuances that made her unique—while try-ing not to overdo it with his interest. So far he'd learned she tugged on her earlobe when she was thinking and that she rarely stayed in one position for more than sixty seconds.

See? She needed a ranch for a backyard. But that wasn't Luc's focus in being here. It was to discuss the paternity test results with Cate, and then for the two of them to tell Ruby he was her father. He needed to stay on point.

"It's time to get ready for bed, Rubes." Cate stood in the doorway to the room, her bare toes peeking inside.

Luc glanced at the small clock on Ruby's nightstand, surprised to see how much time had passed since he'd arrived.

"But…" Ruby's brow pinched, her voice escalating to a whine. "But my friend Luc is here."

Her friend Luc. Sweet girl. Little did she know how her life was about to change. Luc prayed it would be for the better and that she'd adjust without the news harm-ing her or causing turmoil.

"I know," Cate answered with patience and a hint of weariness, "but it's getting late and you need your sleep. We can still read a story if you get your pajamas on and brush your teeth." She infused pep into the last part, but it was lost on Ruby.

A storm of opposition continued to brew in the half-pint in front of him. Luc pushed up from the twin bed, the frame creaking under his added weight. "I need to talk to your mom. I'll do that while you get ready and then maybe…" He looked to Cate. "Maybe I can read you a book?"

After a moment of hesitancy evidenced by the thumbnail slipping between Cate's teeth, she nodded.

Luc followed Cate out of the room, shutting the door behind him and stopping in the middle of the living room. If he walked out the space from wall to wall, he'd probably only get in six long strides. Had it shrunk even more while he was with Ruby? Or maybe it was just being near Cate with no daughter as a buffer.

"I got the test results back. Ruby's mine." His throat tightened. How had they gotten here? Anger and confusion and sadness all whipped through him like a gust of Colorado wind. "They sent an email a little bit ago."

No surprise showed on Cate's features at his announcement. But then, he hadn't accused her of cheating on him four years ago. The opposite had happened. And it had been the worst moment of his life when he'd denied doing any such thing…and she hadn't believed him.

Luc couldn't stand it when someone didn't trust him. He'd lived that back in high school and then again with Cate, and he had no desire to repeat the scenario.

Cate motioned to her computer. "I haven't checked my email, so I didn't get it yet, but I also don't need it. I know she's yours." Weighty silence stretched between them. "But I'm glad you have the answers you need."

"So now what?"

"I don't know." Her hands lifted, their slight shaking gunning for his sympathetic side. He quickly slammed the door on that unwarranted response. "I guess that's up to you. How involved you want to be. If you want to see Ruby."

"If?" Heat seared his voice. Was she joking? Didn't she know him better than that? Cate looked as though she was about to dissolve into an emotional flood, and despite his outrage, Luc didn't want that. Especially for Ruby's sake. They didn't need to start out back in the same boxing ring they'd ended in the last time. He made a second attempt to answer her in a calmer tone. "Of course I want to see her."

"Then I guess we figure out a plan. A schedule."

Luc wanted all of Ruby in his life, not a color-coded calendar of planned times. But that was impossible. Even if he did want to transport Ruby out of this place, he couldn't. Cate would never stand for it. He wasn't that much of a fool.

"What about telling her?"

Her eyes momentarily closed, fingertips massaging her temples. "I've been prepping her as much as I could. I asked her if she'd want to meet her father."

"What did she say?"

Ruby scampered into the hallway. "I'm gonna brush my teeth, and then I know what book I want my friend Luc to read. Boo-boo bear picked it out. But, Mommy, I still need you to huggle me."

After that barrage of information, the bathroom door banged shut.

Luc needed a three-year-old translator. "Huggle?"

"Snuggle and hug combined." Cate's face softened, the curved lips that surfaced over Ruby enough to take out a man with less resentment propping him up at the knees. "And in answer to your question, you've met her—what do you think she said? To Ruby, the more, the merrier. She wants to meet her dad. You."

"So we'll tell her tonight?"

The enormousness of his question made filling his lungs an impossible task. It must have affected Cate the same, because her chest stuttered numerous times as it rose and fell.

"Yes." Sorrow lines surrounded liquid brown pools of remorse. "Luc, I really am sorry."

And he really didn't want to hear it right now. One day they'd have to get into the whys. One day he'd have to move toward forgiving her. Today was not that day.

Luc had been talking to God plenty about Ruby and Cate this week, reaching for answers that felt miles away. And while he knew the man upstairs would be nudging him to deal with his ire toward Cate in no time at all, tonight was about telling Ruby the truth.

When he didn't answer her apology, Cate sucked in a breath too big for her small frame, as if gathering courage. "I need—" her eyes found his and held, pleading "—to know you're in. Not with me—I get that I'm not high on your list of favorites right now. But for Ruby's sake, I need to know you're not just going to cut and run when you figure out being a dad is the hardest thing you'll ever do. I have to know she can count on you."

Despite all the wrong that had transpired between them, Cate was right to ask. To protect her daughter— *their* daughter. A smidgen of respect eased back into play. "I don't do anything halfway, Cate. So in answer to your question, I'm not going anywhere. I'm in Ruby's life for good."

Though Luc didn't know how they were going to tell Ruby. How to explain why he hadn't known about her without making Cate look bad. Because no matter what tension ebbed between him and Cate, he wouldn't start out by maligning Ruby's mother. He *would* put their daughter's needs first.

Luc silently fired off prayers for guidance and wisdom.

Cate's eyebrows plunked together like magnets. "What are you thinking?"

"I'm praying." The answer snapped out a little snarly—ironic, considering the statement. Again, Luc dug for civility. "I've never done this before. I don't have a clue what I'm doing. What we're supposed to do now." He shrugged, offering an olive branch. "So I thought I'd ask someone who does."

Disbelief and curiosity warred on her face. "Since when are you a praying man, Lucas Wilder?"

"Since I left…" *You.* "…Denver. Once I moved back to the ranch, I was…" *A mess.* "I started going to church with my family and it was like something clicked. I'd never really wanted a relationship with God when I was younger, but something changed. And so did I." At least he hoped he had. Luc sure hadn't handled things well with Cate back when they'd been together. He'd done a lot of putting himself first. Had he appreciated Cate back then? Doubtful.

His immaturity during their relationship—including the fact that they'd been pretending to be adults when they were anything but—smarted like a hoof to the shin.

"Ruby and I…we go to church, too. I became a Christian about a year ago." A begrudging tilt claimed her lips. "It's the reason you're standing here right now. Otherwise, I'm not sure I would ever have softened." She shrugged, one shoulder lifting the messy ponytail that had loosened to cascade down her back.

Seeing Cate so casual tonight—without the armor of her well-put-together clothes and wearing very little makeup—made Luc flash back to their younger days. She'd been beautiful back then, but now there was something about her… Maybe it was peacefulness. He wasn't sure. But he liked this casual side of her. Cate looked ready to snuggle up on the couch with a blanket and watch a movie. And the traitor side of him thought he should be the one tucked in next to her. She had that effect on him, and he was still furious with her.

What would happen if he actually managed to forgive Cate? Maybe that was part of the reason he didn't want to—because Luc refused to go anywhere near the possibility for that kind of anguish again.

The kind they'd caused each other.

In all of his aggravation at Cate over the past week, Luc had conveniently forgotten one thing…his fault in what had happened. What he'd been like back then. Even before their last fight, he'd often been quick to tussle with her over the smallest things. They'd been so young, their relationship on fast-forward.

Luc had thought he loved Cate then…but now he wondered if he'd ever truly understood the definition of the word.

Since Cate had reappeared in his life, he'd been so focused on the mistakes she'd made in keeping Ruby from him that he hadn't even considered his selfish decisions.

"I was a jerk when we were younger, wasn't I?"

Cate had the grace not to answer him, but Luc knew the truth.

No wonder she hadn't told him about Ruby. If it had been him in her shoes, he wouldn't have contacted himself, either.

Cate had been in too many hard, unforgiving chairs in doctors' offices like the one currently holding her, but today something was different. Luc occupied the seat next to her.

Ruby climbed all over him, the heat from his lanky frame seeping into Cate's personal space. Of course, he hadn't lost his temper once dealing with all of Ruby's pent-up energy while they waited. But then, he'd only been acting as a parent for six days. He'd fail soon enough, and then she'd feel guilty for entertaining this thought process at all.

Cate had read enough about Ruby's condition to know that not every office did nurse consultations before the procedure, but she was thankful theirs did. The more information she had, the better.

"Do they normally run behind?" Luc asked.

"Not too bad. If you have somewhere you need to be, you can go."

His eyes narrowed at her sugar-sweet offer. "Trying to get rid of me?"

Yes. "No."

The grin commandeering his mouth said he knew exactly what she was thinking and doing. Attraction came unbidden, a surprising shimmy in her gut. *Down, girl. Not your candy.*

He leaned closer, and her body sent off warning flares. Jump ship advisories blared. "I already told you that I'm here for Ruby no matter what. That I want to be a part of her life. The question is whether you're going to let me be."

Since when had Luc turned into this wiser, calmer version of the barely adult man she'd once known?

In the living room the other night, before they'd talked to Ruby, he'd even prayed with her. They'd stood three feet apart and been separated by miles of unresolved issues, but the prayer had held more intimacy than she'd expected.

Luc had asked God to show them what to say and what not to say and to give Ruby an open mind.

The prayer had worked.

When they'd told Ruby that Luc was her dad, she'd asked a few questions that they'd done their best to answer, but for the most part, she'd been more focused on the future than the past. Though Cate imagined those tougher questions would come with time and age, and it would be her job to do the explaining.

Then Ruby had asked if she was going to see Luc again.

Cate had pondered the same question many times as she'd contemplated telling Luc about Ruby.

In answer, Luc had held Ruby's hand in his oversize one. He'd told her he would *always* be in her life—that they were a part of each other—and nothing would separate them again. Ruby had listened intently. The next day she'd started referring to him as "my dad" instead of "my friend Luc."

After Luc had gone back to the ranch that night, Ruby had been unable to sleep from her excitement. She'd told Cate all of the things she wanted to do now that she finally had her own dad. As if she'd gone into a store and picked one out from the shelf.

Camping. Fishing. Where had Ruby come up with those ideas? Probably from a kiddo at day care. Riding a horse again. Cate wasn't sure whether to be relieved or irritated at Ruby's immediate acceptance of Luc.

Of course, she *should* feel the first. But the second was just so within reach. All of a sudden, their lives were flipped upside down—like a bug on its back, legs wiggling to find traction in thin air. Ruby felt okay with that, obviously, but Cate didn't. She wanted safety back.

She wanted to be the only one at this visit instead of one half of a parenting duo.

Cate was definitely having a hard time letting Luc into their lives. And the worst part was, he knew it. He knew her too well. She'd made plenty of changes in the years since they'd dated, but there was still a little girl living inside her who struggled with rejection and trust.

Who couldn't forget the lessons her parents had taught her.

She'd been ten when her parents divorced. Some couples fought for custody because one parent was unstable or unsafe. Because they believed a certain home was the better place for their children.

But hers had simply fought to fight. It hadn't been about protecting her, but more that they didn't want to give in to each other. She'd been collateral damage in their war.

A lost girl who knew intrinsically she wasn't significant in the grand scheme of their relationship or divorce.

Cate didn't want that for Ruby. It was part of why she hadn't told Luc about her. Cate was afraid of losing her daughter. Fearful that Luc would fight for custody and then Cate would be just like her parents—focused on a battle instead of on Ruby.

She wanted Ruby to always feel important. Loved beyond a shadow of a doubt. To never experience the tumultuous pieces of childhood Cate had.

Not that Cate could tell Luc all of that. He would never understand why she'd kept Ruby from him. No answer would be good enough, and she had to be okay with that. Just like she had to figure out how to be more Ruby-like about him being in their lives.

The door to the room opened, and the nurse came

in. Diane. They'd had her many times before. She slid a wheeled stool up to Ruby while greeting them, and Cate introduced her to Luc.

"Ruby." Diane held a teddy bear, one that had obviously been used numerous times as an example. "In two days Dr. Thom is going to fix a small hole in your heart, just like fixing Mr. Bear's tear right here." She motioned to the small gap in the brown fur. "You won't feel it. You're going to fall asleep like Sleeping Beauty, take a little nap, and when you wake up it will be all better."

Ruby listened, enraptured by the idea of starring in her own fairy tale. "Okay, Dr. Thom fix it." She went back to playing with the supplies from her activities bag—a small board she could draw on and then erase.

Over the years and appointments, Cate had told Ruby she had an extra-special heart that held lots of love and needed checkup appointments. She'd accepted that news just as easily as this. Of course, she was too young to truly understand the concept of surgery, but they did need to at least give her an idea of what was to come.

Dr. Thom's whole staff was exceptional about knowing what to say and how to say it to make little minds understand.

Now, if only they had something to eliminate Cate's apprehensions.

Cate let Ruby wear headphones and watch a movie on the iPad while Diane outlined the procedure for her and Luc. Diane talked through a few pages of information, including some visuals, then asked if they had any concerns.

"What will her recovery be like?" For some reason Luc's question surprised Cate, but then, he had the right to be involved. He was here, wasn't he? She should be thankful that he was committed to Ruby—that her daughter could depend on him—instead of being so panicked by what his presence meant.

Pull yourself together, Cate. Even if you can't trust him, you can trust God. The mantra that had gotten her to the Wilder ranch in the first place eased a smidgen of uneasiness.

"With cardiac catheterization, the recovery is minimal," Diane answered. "Nothing like open-heart surgery. Rest is needed while the incision site heals, but many children bounce back at a fast rate."

"And will there be a lot of follow-up visits?"

Cate's brow furrowed. What was Luc fishing for? Was he really this interested? Or was something on his mind?

"If things go as planned, we'll do one about a month after and then we won't need to see her for another year."

"So, if she was living forty minutes outside Denver in a quiet place where she could recuperate—no germs being shared at day care—you don't think that would be a problem? She wouldn't be too far from medical care?" Luc's questions came out in a rush, and Cate's jaw lunged for her toes.

What was Luc doing? What was he thinking? *Was* he attempting to take Ruby from her?

Had she said those thoughts out loud earlier? Or had Luc plucked them from her mind? Eerie. It was as if she'd allowed the truth to surface for one moment, and Luc had immediately set about making her nightmares come true. Her throat closed off, and she couldn't speak over the lump of outraged tears she refused to release.

"We'll know more after the procedure, but I don't think Dr. Thom would have any issues with that. Our patients come from all over the place. Not everyone lives in town."

Cate resisted a hiss at her answer. At Luc's audacity.

And one look at Ruby made it all a thousand times worse. Her headphones were looped around her neck, not on her ears. By the way her face perked with interest, she'd heard everything Luc had just asked. Ruby might not know exactly what Luc was saying, but she knew it involved her.

Who did Luc think he was, throwing out preposterous ideas in front of Ruby like he was…like he was her father and had a say in her life? Ruby couldn't just be uprooted. She had a schedule. Day care. Friends. Luc might not see those things—or Cate—as important, but she did.

Ruby bounced with excitement. "What is it, Mommy? Are we going somewhere?"

Red flames had to be shooting out of the top of Cate's head. Her face radiated with heat, now likely the shade of a scarlet crayon.

Cate sought with everything in her to manage a calm tone. "We'll have to discuss it, sweets." Gaze bouncing from Ruby, she raised a menacing eyebrow at Luc. "As a family." Voice wobbling with barely suppressed anger, she focused on breathing as Diane wrapped up the visit and left.

At Cate's direction, Ruby grabbed her small backpack of supplies from the corner of the room.

Gripping Luc's arm, Cate lowered her voice. "What are you thinking? That I won't care if Ruby comes to live with you? She has a life, Lucas. I realize I kept her from you, but trying to take her from me isn't the answer."

Stunned silence came from Luc. His mouth hung open, much like Cate's had only minutes before.

"I got the big hostable door open!" Ruby stood with her back propping open the wide door, pride evident.

They exclaimed what a good job she did, then followed Ruby down the beige hallway, friction wedged between them like a third wheel.

Luc pulled her behind Ruby's pace. Out of earshot. "I'm not..." His head shook as if he was clearing away cobwebs. "You think I'm trying to take her from you?"

What else was she supposed to think?

"I don't want to separate the two of you. Even I know that's out of the question, Cate. What kind of ogre do you think I am?"

Thankfully, he didn't wait for her to answer.

"I've just been thinking that if you and Ruby would be willing to live at the ranch, even for just a few weeks or a month, it would allow me time to get to know her. We have guests six days out of the week during the summer. If you don't, it will be really hard for me to get away and spend time with her. I'll make it work, somehow, but...it was just a thought." His voice lowered. Hardened. "And I am not such an idiot or jerk that I think she'd be coming alone. I do realize that she's young and the two of you are a package. I wouldn't do that to her."

Now it was her turn to fumble for words. Luc caught up with Ruby, leaving Cate a few steps behind. Good. She needed the space to deal with...everything. Luc's absurd suggestion. Her desire to scream *no* at his back. Or maybe throw something at those annoyingly broad shoulders filling out a cornflower blue short-sleeved button-down.

He was wrong, right? She didn't have to truly consider what he was asking for, did she?

Not one part of her wanted to uproot their lives to live at the ranch, even for a short amount of time. But since

Luc was acting so...so *calm* about all of it—even logical, if she wanted to give him credit for that, which she didn't—Cate probably should try to be, too.

Or at least pretend to be. Right before she told him absolutely not.

Chapter Four

The smell of hospital antiseptic assaulted Luc's nostrils. He hated the scent of anything bleached or overly sterilized. Growing up on a ranch with dirt under his fingernails and dust on his boots, he firmly believed that being covered in or even ingesting a little of God's good earth wouldn't harm a person.

Of course, the fact that he was in the hospital waiting for his daughter to get out of surgery could probably explain his current aversion.

Cate had been as quiet as a teapot just under boiling all morning. He kept wondering when she'd blow. Tears. An outburst. Any show of emotion. But so far, not one crack in her shell.

When they'd prepped Ruby for surgery, they'd given her something to make her groggy and almost fall asleep before doing the anesthesia. He and Cate had been allowed to walk her back to the catheterization area, and then the medical staff had taken Ruby from there.

Luc had thought Cate would crumble in that moment. And it had looked like she was about to. Her shoulders had slumped, eyes glazing over with pain and moisture.

He'd been ready to catch her. To comfort her. No matter what had happened between them, he wouldn't hold their history against her at such an agonizing time.

But then Cate had stitched herself together like a desperate woman out on the trail. Bleeding and alone with no other choice.

Even though he'd been standing right next to her.

It had been like watching a storm roll over the mountains, dark and menacing, only to see it morph into white, harmless clouds that floated by without wreaking havoc.

Cate had stridden by him, shoulders back, stubborn chin thrust out. Down the hallway and into the waiting room she'd gone. She'd dropped into a chair and hadn't moved yet. Not even to use the restroom.

Now she sat next to him with her eyes closed in the unforgiving chairs that boasted cushions but didn't offer comfort. He knew she wasn't sleeping. He'd guess she was coping about as well as one of the consistently used children's books Emma had for Kids' Club. Battered. Worn. With the pages barely holding together under the still-intact cover.

The ticking of the plain-Jane white clock with black hands in the corner marked the excruciatingly slow passage of time.

"You okay?" He finally ruptured the silence, questioning Cate.

"No, I'm not okay." Her voice snapped, but then her chestnut eyes flashed open, filled with regret. "I'm sorry." She toyed with the silver ring sporting a cross on her right hand, concentrating on it instead of him. "I'm just worried."

It was the first chink in her armor that he'd witnessed. Capable Cate made raising Ruby on her own look easy.

Like even single parenthood couldn't deflate the wind in her cape.

"I am, too." The dull ache in his gut had been there for days, reminding him of Ruby's impending procedure.

Cate's brow pinched. "Then why do you seem so calm?"

Funny. Didn't she realize how composed she looked and acted? Something about knowing she wasn't—that she'd confided even that small secret to him—twisted his insides.

"I'm not, really. But I'm choosing to believe she's going to be okay. That's what I've been praying non-stop for." He wasn't going to entertain any other options.

Her lips barely managed a curve. "Me, too."

Had Cate slept at all last night? Drifting off had taken him much longer than normal. And then he'd been up before the sun to get here on time. Hints of tired were visible despite Cate's perfectly applied makeup—not too much, not too little. Her clothes—black jeans, flats and a peach sleeveless shirt partially covered by a button-up gray sweater—shouted that she had it all together. Her protective covering was in place, but her weariness was palpable. At least to him.

"I don't know what I'd do without her." Cate's hand pressed against her mouth. Luc wasn't sure if it was to stifle a sob or because she'd realized what she'd said—and that Luc had, because of her, lived without Ruby for the past three-plus years.

He bit down on the *I know what you mean* that begged for escape. Today was not the day for fighting. Things might not be fixed between them, but the seriousness of Ruby's procedure had caused him to mentally call a time-out from his anger.

He was by no means over what Cate had done in keeping Ruby from him, but he was praying that God would help him to be one day. That kind of forgiveness would have to come from above.

But he did have an idea of what might help heal his wounds. And since they were just sitting here, listening to the unbearably slow seconds tick by…

"Cate, I really think you should consider—"

"You're not going to start bugging me about us moving to the ranch again, are you?"

So much for his stealth move in bringing it up. "It just makes sense. We have guests all week right now and it will be tough for me to see Ruby as much as I want to. It will be easier for me to swing it during the off-season." Of course, he would make it work to see Ruby no matter what, but if Cate would just consider the option, it would be a huge help. "You could contact her day care. See if they could give you a credit for the month. It would save money. My sisters are there—Mackenzie is—" determined, stubborn "—all about adventure and Emma's a rock star with kids. You'd have family. Support. It wouldn't be forever. Just enough time for me to get to know Ruby a little bit better."

A groan came from Cate.

"Is that a yes?"

This time a huff escaped, sounding sky-high on the annoyed meter. Guess she hadn't appreciated his attempt at humor.

"It's a no. The same no I've been telling you since we met with the nurse." Her arms crisscrossed her chest, another shield engaged and ready for battle. "And stop sending me pictures. They're not going to change my mind."

He curbed a grin, deciding his amusement definitely

wouldn't be appreciated. Cate had texted him yesterday morning after he'd bugged her plenty about the option of them temporarily moving to the ranch—*please stop talking to me about the ranch.*

So he'd switched to pictures. He hadn't *said* anything, so he hadn't broken any rules. Until today.

Luc had hoped the visuals might stir something in her. He'd sent her a shot of the cabin they could live in. His— but he'd happily give it up for them. It had two bedrooms, a cozy living room with a fireplace, stackable laundry and a tiny kitchen consisting of a row of kitchen cabinets and small appliances. But since the ranch provided all meals, Cate wouldn't need much space for cooking. Not that she had anything much bigger now. And the cabin was certainly better than the apartment she and Ruby currently lived in. At least in his mind.

He'd also sent her pictures of the horses—that one may not have helped—and of the wide open spaces he considered one of the most beautiful places on planet Earth. He didn't think he'd gotten very far since Cate had simply stopped responding to the photos. Stubborn woman.

"If Ruby bugging me hasn't worked, nothing will. And trust me, she's talked about it nonstop since you dropped the idea on us. Thank you very much for that." She shifted in his direction, jutting a finger at his chest. "Parenting 101—don't say anything in front of a child until it's already been decided. You can't just go around spouting ideas like that. She'll never understand why we're not doing it, and I'll be the bad guy. We have a life, Lucas. We can't just uproot it."

Lucas. Why his full name coming from her lips caused a spark in his chest, he didn't want to know.

"But your work is freelance. You can live anywhere."

Cate's eyelids shuttered as if weighted down. "Let's not do this today, okay?"

Regret flared to life. She was right. Not the time.

Luc stretched his jean-clad legs out in front of him but couldn't get comfortable. He'd worn his Ariat boots today. A green button-down shirt. Something about the hospital—or *hostable*, as Ruby would say—made him feel like a kid playing grown-up, and he'd at least attempted to look the part.

"Can I get you anything? Something to eat? Drink?" Why did he feel the need to keep talking? It wasn't like him. If Luc had to guess, he'd imagine he was more apprehensive about Ruby's procedure than he wanted to admit. Taking care of Cate—scratch that—getting something for Cate would occupy his mind and harness his energy. He'd much rather be doing than sitting.

"No. Thanks. I can't imagine eating anything right now." Her hair was in a low bun today, a pair of simple silver earrings in her ears.

She slid a thumbnail between her lips. Luc had only seen her start to bite her nails once since she'd waltzed back into his life almost two weeks ago. That time she'd quit as soon as she'd noticed what she was doing. Her nails looked nice—painted a soft pink. She must make an effort not to engage the old habit.

He snagged her hand to stop her from wrecking what she'd accomplished, but once it was in his grasp, he wasn't sure what to do. Let go? Hold on? He'd only been wanting to help her. Instead, his mind stuttered like an old, rusty engine at her touch. It had been a long, long time since he'd felt Cate's skin against his. Her hand was incredibly soft compared to his, and he caught the faint scent of a lotion or perfume he remembered her using. Something fresh. Reminded him of a field of wildflowers.

She snatched her fingers away from him, and after a glare in his direction, she shifted so that she sat on both of her hands.

All right, then. Guess that answered that question.

"Catherine Malory?" a voice called from the entrance to the waiting room, and both he and Cate bolted from their seats. They reached the surgeon, and at the last second, the hand Cate had just torn away from his found him again. Surprise rippled through him.

He didn't say anything. Just squeezed and held on, wanting to lend Cate support. She probably didn't even realize her actions.

"Is she okay?" Cate asked before the surgeon had time to speak, her question so rushed it reminded Luc of Ruby.

Dr. Thom's reassuring nod had Luc releasing a pent-up breath. "She did great. Everything went well. You can head back to see her in a couple of minutes."

Cate dropped his hand like a rock. It crashed to his side as she palmed her face, relief and tears mingling.

The quick dismissal of his services—of any connection—left Luc scrambling to catch up. Would this be his new role? Needed one moment, held at a ten-mile distance the next? With the second being the much more common scenario.

Would Cate ever truly let him into Ruby's life? And hers? Because he knew the two were intertwined. He wouldn't have a place with Ruby unless Cate admitted him entrance. Right now he was nothing more than a useless horse sent out to pasture. A backup plan. And if his instincts were right, an unwanted one, at that.

* * *

Cate scanned the premade salads in the hospital cafeteria cooler, the choices as jumbled as algebra. Ruby had been out of surgery for about two hours and doing well. She'd been in pain when she'd first woken up. The entry site in her leg plus the general anesthesia had left her disgruntled, but after the nurse had adjusted her medicine, she'd settled down. Cate had been thankful to see her drift back to sleep. Once she had, Cate had left Luc standing guard.

She'd needed a moment. Time to calm her jittery body with deep breaths and prayers of thankfulness for a successful procedure. So far it still hadn't listened.

Her stomach clamored for something to edge out her nervous hunger. It wanted an extra-large piece of chocolate cake, but she planned to ignore that emotional request.

Everything in Cate's oversize brown leather bag was Ruby-oriented. She'd forgotten to bring anything she might want to eat. Forgotten to take care of herself. Forgivable on a day like today.

She grabbed a chicken kale salad and turned to go, then thought better of it and perused the sandwiches. Luc would likely be hungry, too. Did he still eat like he had at nineteen? Back then he'd been able to clean off three plates in one sitting without adding an inch to his lean frame.

She'd certainly fallen fast and hard for Luc. They'd met at a party at a friend's house. After talking for a few hours that night, he'd asked for her number.

They'd had coffee. And then dinner. He'd been so good about getting to know her that by the time she'd figured out she was in love with him, she'd been miles downstream with no chance of swimming back. Not that she'd wanted to. Sure, they'd had their moments of immaturity. Luc had been quick-tempered back then. A verbal fighter. Always wanting to be right. And she'd only been too willing to get in the ring with him. But despite some childish arguments, Luc had made her feel loved in a way no one ever really had before. Adored even. Like she was the best thing that had ever happened to him.

She missed that. Missed what they'd once been.

Cate selected a club sandwich, knowing Luc wasn't picky enough to complain, and headed to the checkout. She paid, cringing at the exorbitant prices, and returned to Ruby's room. She didn't want her girl to wake up and not have her there. Though now that they had Luc—now that Ruby had her father—Cate wasn't the only one carrying the load of responsibility on her shoulders. Ruby had someone else to depend on.

At the door to Ruby's room, Cate paused. Luc was in a chair close to the bed, his elbows propped against the mattress. Shoulders hunched. Head in his hands. It looked like he was praying. Ruby slept peacefully, eyelashes grazing her soft cheeks.

The dam Cate had built strong and tight in order to survive today burst free, one weak little chink at a time. It was obvious that Luc loved Ruby. He didn't hold back with her. Had pursued her diligently since finding out the test results. They talked every night for at least a few minutes, usually as Cate was putting Ruby to bed. So of course she heard them on her phone. They were already crazy about each other.

And Cate had been the one who'd kept them apart. Yes, she'd thought she had the right to do what she did. Even believed she was doing the best thing for Ruby.

But that didn't make the reality of her choices any easier to swallow.

Cate had been scared of losing her daughter or fighting over Ruby like her own parents had over her. But she had to move past that now. Somehow. It wasn't right that her fears had kept the two of them apart.

Even if Luc had started seeing someone else at the end of their relationship, she should have let him be a part of Ruby's life. And Cate didn't even know if that was true. He'd denied any wrongdoing.

Luc deserved time with Ruby. Deserved to know his daughter like Cate did.

Tears of acknowledgment swept down her cheeks. She was going to have to give in to Luc's request about their living at the ranch temporarily.

Cate's head shook, sending more moisture cascading. Why did God always ask her for the toughest things? The ones she couldn't do. At least not without His strength.

Truly, Cate didn't know if it was God or guilt nudging her, but either way, they were both right. She'd already taken enough from Luc. She didn't need to cause more harm.

Retrieving a tissue from her purse, she swiped away the mascara that had surely loosened with her emotions, then stuffed the tissue back inside.

Her footsteps into the room caused Luc to straighten and turn. He rubbed a hand through his hair, eyes blinking as though they'd been closed.

"Brought you something to eat." She tossed him the packaged sandwich, and he caught it.

"Thanks." Surprise was quickly replaced by gratitude.

Cate stopped directly in front of him, and he studied her, faint concern etching his brow. His jean-clad legs and boots were tucked under the chair. The green button-down shirt he wore made the fern in his hazel eyes pop.

"Have you been crying?"

Her eyes rolled at being so easily caught. Frustrating. They always gave her away. She dug up a smile, albeit a wobbly one. "I'm fine. Just releasing some pent-up stress from today."

His mouth stayed in a firm line. He nodded toward Ruby. "She's been asleep the whole time."

"Good." Cate forced herself to speak. "Okay."

Confusion evident, Luc's head cocked to one side. "Okay, what?"

She could do this. She could put on her big-girl britches and do the right thing. "We'll live at the ranch for a few weeks."

His jaw slacked. Suddenly, he was out of the chair, standing way too close for comfort, hands squeezing her upper arms. "Are you serious?" She wanted to tell him to turn his booming voice down a notch but simply nodded instead.

He whooped and scooped her up in a hug. A very unacceptable, he-did-not-have-permission hug. Cate would try to break free, but she wasn't a match for his strength. Plus, when was the last time she'd been held like this? Probably with the man currently rendering her nerves and muscles the consistency of pudding.

He let her down slowly, as if realizing the predicament he'd put them in. Once her feet were firmly back on the ground, his arms dropped to his sides, but neither of them moved from their close proximity.

"Thank you."

He smelled like the outdoors somehow, even within the walls of the hospital. His face was freshly shaved, and for one wild moment she considered sliding her fingers along his smooth jaw. She'd always liked a clean shave on him.

Enough! Cate mentally slapped away her impetuous hand.

Instead of answering him with *you're welcome*, she went with, "I'm sorry."

He nodded once. "I can tell."

Luc might not be forgiving her, but he recognized her remorse. That had to be a good sign.

"Mom? Dad?" Ruby's groggy voice interrupted them. "I want a huggle, too."

Cate's skin heated, but Luc just chuckled and stepped back from her, flashing a magnetizing grin before facing their daughter. He should really be more careful with that thing. Only use it for special occasions. Ruby's first dance. Inheriting a million dollars.

"Guess what, Rube-i-cube?" Elation oozed from him, the nickname he'd coined for Ruby earning a lilting of their daughter's lips. "Your mom has some news to tell you."

Chapter Five

Three days later Cate reached into the open trunk of her car for a box to carry into the cabin, using the few moments alone to shake off the bad attitude that had trailed her along the dusty drive to the ranch.

She might be doing the right thing, but that didn't make it easy.

Scary was a better word.

"We're a lot to handle, aren't we?" Luc's younger sister, Emma, approached Cate, bursting her momentary bubble of solitude.

Dressed in cutoff jean shorts, flip-flops and a Wilder Ranch tank with her hair in a ponytail, everything about Emma reminded Cate of a beauty-product commercial. One with a girl washing her face and then glancing into the mirror, all fresh-skinned and bright-eyed.

In the short time since they'd become acquainted, Cate had come to the swift decision that she liked Emma. Luc's little sister had a cashmere-like demeanor. A sweetness so noticeable it practically radiated from her tiny pores. Unlike his twin sister, Mackenzie, whom Cate had met when they'd arrived today.

Mackenzie had studied Cate like a college art project deserving a failing grade. And it didn't help that the woman was a superhero. Inches taller than Cate, all tanned muscles and an imposing figure in jeans, boots and a fitted gray T-shirt that pronounced to the world that she couldn't care less about fashion but managed to look like an amazon woman anyway. Cate wouldn't be surprised if she'd zip-lined down from the mountains just to help her move in.

Cate wasn't jealous. After all, Mackenzie was Luc's twin sister. But she could classify herself as a bit intimidated.

"I don't know if I'd say that." She finally answered Emma, settling on something diplomatic.

"You don't have to," Emma said, flashing equally commercial-worthy white teeth. "I'll say it for you." She nodded toward the house a short ways down the hill that Mackenzie had just entered. "She'll come around. Mackenzie and Lucas have this weird twin intuition. It'll drive a person nuts, but they'd do anything for each other. She's just protective of him."

Cate hefted the box of Ruby's favorite snack foods out of the trunk. "And I'm to blame because I didn't tell Luc about Ruby." Why had she just said that? This whole situation was uncomfortable enough without her bringing up awkward truths.

Snagging the extra-large duffel bag filled with Cate's clothes, Emma swung it over her shoulder before filling her arms with another bag. "I remember what my brother was like back then. Short on patience. Not always easy to get along with. I imagine for you to go through all of the trouble of raising Ruby yourself, you probably had a pretty good reason."

Cate's eyes pricked with liquid emotion. Emma had thrown her a lifeline, and she wasn't going to be so stubborn as to not take hold. "Thank you."

Luc had told her Emma had just turned twenty-three. Twenty months younger than Luc and Mackenzie and mature well beyond her years.

The two of them headed for the cabin. "So where's Luc staying while we're here?" He hadn't told Cate any details. "Another cabin? Or with you or Mackenzie?"

"With us." She jutted her head toward the house Mackenzie had entered. "He'd probably choose another cabin over us. Jerk. But they're all full."

"Wow." Cate wrestled open the screen door, holding it for Emma as she went through and then following herself. "I'm sorry for forcing him on you two. Taking up your space."

Emma's easy laugh turned into a snort. "Puh-lease! You brought me a niece. No apologies allowed."

God, did You know I'd need this girl? This welcome? Cate sent up a prayer of thanks as her mouth curved to match Emma's. Ruby's new aunt was good for the soul.

They both put their items down, Cate on the counter to be sorted into cupboards if she could find space, and Emma leaving the clothes with a pile of bags, suitcases, boxes and other items Cate and Ruby had deemed necessary for the next few weeks. They planned to head back to Denver the first Sunday in September since Cate had a meeting that Tuesday with the firm she did freelance for. That way they'd have Monday—Labor Day—at home before jumping back into day care and their normal schedule. She and Ruby would be here just shy of a month.

"The guest-ranch business must be doing really well." And Luc must really want them here to give up his place for them. Why did he have to be so kind? Cate should be paying penance for her sins. But no matter how many times she reminded herself that wasn't how God operated, her brain had the hardest time comprehending the concept of grace.

"It is." Emma stretched one arm over her head, then the other. "Luc does a great job keeping us booked up and running well. Mackenzie, too. We've even earned the Top Twenty Guest Ranch Award twice."

Emma made no mention of her own involvement, but Cate knew from their brief encounter at the ranch that she was phenomenal with kids. Ruby had talked quite a bit about her after their visit. She'd referred to her as "that really nice lady that showed me the horsies." Emma had made a big impression on Ruby in a short amount of time.

"I *think* you forgot someone." Cate pointed an accusing finger as she took a cue from Emma and rolled her neck, muscles complaining about the past few days of hurried packing while taking care of Ruby. "Luc says you really have a gift with kids, and I've seen it firsthand with Ruby. She already adores you. You're very sweet with her."

Emma's eyes lit up, a faint rose color dusting her cheeks at the compliment. "How could anyone not instantly fall for Ruby?"

Cate had been afraid to let Luc—and his family—into Ruby's life for years…but she was starting to thaw. To see the advantages of more people loving her little girl.

"Somebody wants a new place to rest." Luc came out of Ruby's room with her in his arms, an unnecessary ride that their daughter had likely instigated. They'd been given very few limitations for Ruby—basically letting the entry site heal—but they planned to have her take it easy for at least a week. Okay, Cate planned to. Just to make sure she was healed and whole.

Dr. Thom had said the surgery went wonderfully, but Cate might need some time to believe it.

"Says she was bored in there. So the couch it is." Luc deposited Ruby on the sofa, rearranging pillows to make her comfortable. "I'll grab your orange thingy."

Her giggle filled the room. "Dad, it's an Apple. A mini iPad."

"Are you sure it's not a banana?"

Another titter from Ruby.

Emma shook her head, one corner of her mouth inching up. "Oy with the dad jokes."

"What's that supposed to mean?" Luc questioned. "What's a dad joke?"

"Anything lame and not that funny. So basically… you."

At Emma's retort, amusement bubbled in Cate from a place long forgotten. It felt good to laugh.

Luc's eyes narrowed. "I don't like the two of you in cahoots." His scowl wobbled, fighting a curve.

Mackenzie reentered the cabin carrying the last thing from Cate's car—a laundry basket of folded clothes. A cold rush of air accompanied her instead of the August heat. She wasn't *exactly* an ice queen. But her protectiveness of Luc could be spotted from miles away.

Cate understood it. She'd probably be the same way in Mackenzie's boots.

Mackenzie set the basket down and knelt in front of Ruby by the couch, handing her a small wooden box that had been perched on top of the clothes. "This was mine when I was a little girl." She removed the flat wooden doll and showed Ruby how the little pieces of doll clothes could be moved and changed to create different looks. "Now it's yours."

"Really?" Ruby lit up like a Christmas tree the day after Thanksgiving.

"Yep." A rarely bestowed smile framed Mackenzie's face. It was like spotting an endangered animal. A beautiful creature that only surfaced at night. Or in search of prey.

In true Ruby fashion, she went in for a hug. At first hesitant, Mackenzie's arms quickly tightened.

Cate's heart turned to crème brûlée, the crisp shell giving way to the soft custard beneath. If there was a way to win her respect, it was by seeing Ruby for the sweet, wonderful girl she was. Tough-as-nails Mackenzie had found the key. And the fact that she wasn't letting her obvious concern over Cate affect her relationship with Ruby meant Cate's regard for her just shot up another ten notches.

"Anything else you need me to get from the car?" Luc entered Cate's personal space as he asked, sending off those pesky alarms again. He wore a simple blue Wilder Ranch T-shirt boasting their *get out in the wild* tagline, jeans and boots. And he managed to make it look photoshoot worthy. How was that possible? And why did she stay attracted to him like a magnet when she'd told herself numerous times to stop already?

Space. Cate needed a few miles of separation between them right about now. Was it too late to hop back into her car and escape?

"I don't think so. Pretty sure Mackenzie got the last of it." She busied herself with a few of Ruby's snacks, tucking them into surprisingly empty cupboards. Luc must depend on the communal meals for most of his nourishment.

He stayed still, watching her. Luc had a habit of noticing her. She wasn't sure what to make of it. It was hard to be next to him and not wonder about them. The "them" that had existed before Ruby. Before that last awful fight. But then, she'd promised herself she wouldn't go anywhere near that kind of thought pattern. Ruby came first, and Cate wasn't about to let herself fall in and out of a relationship with Ruby's father. She knew too well from her parents' example how that ended. Yet another lesson they'd graciously demonstrated.

"Dinner is at six at the lodge." Mackenzie paused by the door before leaving. "I left my cell number for you, but coverage can be spotty. Emma and I are here if you need anything." Serious blue-gray eyes met Cate's—the kind that saw all and dissected before coming to a conclusion—their message clear. Mackenzie might not be ready to forgive Cate for what she'd done to Luc, but Ruby wouldn't suffer because of it. Cate got the impression she could count on Mackenzie for just about anything regarding Ruby and the woman would come through, superhero muscles not even sporting a scratch.

Comforting thought. If Emma was made of love and wispy cotton candy, Mackenzie was built of steely strength. Both were good to have in her corner.

"Thank you." Funny how much they'd just communicated without speaking.

"I'm going, too," Emma piped up. "The afternoon Kids' Club starts in a few minutes." She gave Cate a quick hug, like it was a normal, everyday occurrence and didn't make her breath catch in her throat like it did in Cate's. The simple gesture warmed Cate in a place that had frozen over years before. Around the time when Luc had walked out of her life. Her heart had shattered when she'd told him to leave and never contact her again—and he'd listened. Now it was like a puzzle on the thrift-store shelf with torn edges and missing pieces.

"Thank you for your help," she called after the two women. Her voice quickly faded, leaving only the sounds of the show Ruby watched.

Luc stood still as a statue, glancing between her and Ruby.

"Don't you need to go?"

"Yes. But I can find someone else to cover the shooting range. One of the wranglers can handle it."

And then what? Luc would stay here with her and Ruby? No, thank you.

Cate jutted her chin in Ruby's direction. "She's doing really great, Luc. I'll just let her watch something while I unpack and get my computer set up. You go do your thing and we'll see you for dinner."

That sounded like a date.

"At the lodge," she added. With lots and lots of other people.

His breath rushed out. "Okay. Call me if you need anything. I'll have my cell turned way up, but since they don't always work, I can check in on you girls after—"

"We're fine." Cate infused some Mackenzie-like steel into her voice. "That's only a few hours away. You don't need to check on us this afternoon." She placed her hands on his shoulders, turning him toward the door like a little kid's spin top. Heat met her fingertips through his T-shirt, and she cast her eyes toward the ceiling to avoid concentrating on his shortly cropped hair that begged for her attention. Or touch. "Time to go away now." She shoved lightly, knowing her strength might not propel him physically, but he should get the picture.

A quiet chuckle shook his back, and Luc raised his hands in defeat. After calling out a goodbye to Ruby, he was gone.

Cate indulged in a supersize inhalation that felt like the first in days, releasing it slowly.

Why did his presence make her feel so...jittery? The illusion of safety and yet hopped up on caffeine at the same time. But Luc was nowhere near safe. In the beginning he might have been, but then she'd fallen too hard and loved him too much. That got a person in trouble.

Cate couldn't make decisions based on emotion. Ruby needed her to be logical and steer clear of any thoughts revolving around a relationship with Luc.

"Mom, can I have some juice?"

"Sure." She got out the apple juice and added some to Ruby's cup, topping it with the lid and straw.

After her parents' divorce, there'd been a short time— about a year later—when they'd attempted a reconciliation. Not that they'd told her. But Cate had been eleven and not as oblivious as they imagined. She'd sat on the stairs, hearing their laughter. The clinking of wineglasses. Hope had ignited as she'd slunk back up to bed at her mom's house. Could they really be a family again? It was every kid's dream. But Cate should have known better, even at that age. A few short weeks later it was heated voices that rose and fell. New arguments. And even more tension and viciousness than when the divorce first happened. It had almost been harder for Cate the second time around. Taking any dream of them reuniting that she'd secretly harbored and running it through the paper shredder of life.

Her parents had taught her exactly what happened when feelings led the way. Logic was, by far, the better choice. When Cate had been nineteen and in love with Luc, she'd had all of the first and none of the second. And just look how that had turned out.

She passed the juice to Ruby, running a hand over her forehead and smoothing her hair back. "I'm not going to do that to you, sweets."

Ruby looked up. "What, Mommy?"

"Nothing." Cate managed a shaky smile.

Ruby might not be able to keep her emotional distance from Luc—and she shouldn't—but Cate could. She could protect herself. They might be living at the ranch for Ruby and Luc's sake, but that was the only concession Cate planned to make.

Luc pushed away from his desk. Paperwork. Bills. Bookkeeping. These were his least favorite parts of the job, but they were important. Which was why he forced himself to do them when he'd rather be out leading a trail ride or doing any of the other outdoor activities.

The week since Ruby and Cate had arrived had flown by, and Luc had gotten to spend time with Ruby each day. He popped over to their cabin as much as he could between responsibilities. Ate meals with them every day.

Since he had a few minutes and the numbers in front of him had started swimming, he'd head up to see her now. He wanted to take advantage of Ruby's presence at the ranch. Couldn't help feeling like the time would be over with the snap of his fingers.

His phone beeped with a text as he walked the gravel path that snaked through thirsty grass. His mom.

Praying for you today, hon. Be who God is asking you to be in this situation. He'll give you peace and wisdom.

Luc had told his parents about Ruby after the test came back positive. They'd been shocked, of course. He understood the sentiment well. In the days since, they'd been trying to wrap their minds around the situation and had also been praying for him, Ruby and Cate. It meant a lot to him that they weren't completely freaking out. Not that he knew that for sure. His mom was an interesting mix of calm and protective mama bear. She'd likely be full of more and more questions as time progressed. Ones Luc didn't have answers to. He was flying by the seat of his pants. Or maybe the better way to say it would be, following God blindly.

He knocked quietly on the cabin door in case Ruby was sleeping. Though she hadn't been napping much at all. Cate said before surgery, she got tired a lot faster. But her energy levels had gone up since the procedure. That had to be a good sign.

No one answered the door. Luc eased it open an inch and called out in a loud whisper. "Cate." Still nothing. He edged it farther and heard Cate's voice.

Sounded like she might be on the phone in the bedroom. Luc stepped inside and caught part of her discussion about colors and a vector file—not that he had a clue what that last thing was. Must be work related.

He'd just say hi to Ruby and then be out of here.

She was on the far side of the living room, playing with her colorful ponies under the back window.

"Ruby." He said her name quietly, hoping he wouldn't scare her.

In response, Prim gave a snarly meow from the kitchen

sink, arching her back. The cat had taken to napping—or perhaps just hiding—in the sink. Almost as if she was waiting for Luc to enter the cabin so she could scare the living daylights out of him.

But that couldn't be, could it?

Either way, he definitely had not won over the feline's affections.

Ruby's head swung in his direction, eyes widening with excitement. She crossed the room in a flat-out run to give him a hug, and he swung her into his arms, not sure he'd ever get used to a greeting like that. By far the best part of his day.

"How's my girl?"

"I want to go play with the horsies, but Mommy said I have to stay here while she does her meeting." Her mouth formed a pout. A cute one. Ruby wore jean shorts and a purple T-shirt, her bare toes sporting bright pink nail polish. "I don't want to stay in the cabin anymore."

At first, Cate had wanted Ruby to lie low until the incision site healed. But it definitely had. And despite Cate's lingering worries, Ruby was over being cooped up.

Luc didn't blame her. He'd always been far more comfortable outside than in.

He also didn't blame Cate. She had work to do, and he'd told her they'd be a help not a hindrance. At this point Ruby could be back in day care and Cate would have time to accomplish her projects without interruption. Luc didn't want Cate frustrated and scrambling out of here before their planned departure date. He'd ask Emma if there was room for Ruby in Kids' Club. And Luc could keep her with him for a bit of time each day. That way Cate would have the hours she needed for work and not want to tear out of here before the month was up.

"I think I have a cure for that. Why don't you come with me for a little bit?"

Ruby's head bobbed.

"Or you can go with your aunt Emma and the other kids. I'm sure she'd love to have you."

The nodding increased. "I want to do that."

"Which one?"

"Aunt Emma."

Luc would be more offended that she'd chosen Emma if his sister wasn't so amazing with kids. He'd pick her, too.

"Get your shoes on and we'll go."

He plunked her down, and Ruby disappeared into her room. Luc could still hear Cate on the phone, and he didn't want to interrupt by text or in person, so he scavenged in the junk drawer for a piece of paper and a pen. He wrote a note, then tried to figure out where to put it so she'd see it.

The cabin was immaculate. A vase of wildflowers decorated the kitchen countertop, a marshmallow-scented candle burning next to it. And on the fireplace mantel, she'd displayed a number of small, clear glasses he recognized from the cupboard, filling them with branches and other greenery. Things he never would have put together but that now looked like they should go in an art show.

Cate had been here for one week and she'd already managed to make the cabin into more of a home than he ever had. Luc had kept things tidy, but she made him look like a slob. The counters were gleaming. Even the small toaster had been stored.

He opened a cupboard and spied some crackers. He set the box on the edge of the counter closest to the bedroom and propped the note against it. That would have to do. Surely Cate would see something out of place right when she walked out.

Ruby was back at his side in no time at all wearing pink sandals. Luc wasn't sure that worked for what Emma had on the schedule for today, but it would have to do.

He'd need to get Ruby some boots if she planned to grow up on a ranch. Except…she wasn't going to, was she? Luc was living in a fairy tale his daughter would watch in one of her movies if he thought that was a possibility.

Cate had agreed to stay at the ranch for a few weeks on a temporary basis. Probably out of guilt. The rest of Ruby's life would be torn between two places.

He hated the thought of that.

"I'm ready." Ruby tugged on his hand.

He was nowhere near ready to let go of her. Never would be. Course, Ruby was talking now, and Luc was jumping into the future. She'd just gotten here—the ranch and his life. He needed to take things one day at a time. "Then let's go."

They walked down the path, dust rising under their shoes and joined hands. Ruby chatted at the speed of light while Luc contemplated how to repair something that wasn't anywhere near fixable.

Chapter Six

If money didn't matter so much, Cate would send the client across the screen from her packing. He was demanding. Impatient. And sometimes offensive. But she needed the work—always did—so none of the above mattered. Being a single mother didn't allow her the opportunity to be choosy.

"One more thing." Vincent held up a thick pointer finger that came across the screen as menacing. "I know this is the color scheme I said I wanted, but I don't like it." He motioned to the paper in his hand. "I really need you to rework this. And I need it by tomorrow."

Of course he did. Cate indulged in the fantasy of letting go of a long, loud, overdue scream, but she didn't think that would go over well. Vincent was one of her bigger clients. She didn't have a choice. She'd have to turn this job around. Again. And then hunker down to complete the magazine for the Denver Building Association she had due at the end of this week.

Cate clarified a few points, and then the two of them disconnected. She dropped her head to the small table she was using as a desk in the corner of Luc's room—now temporarily hers. Her brain tumbled like a pebble in the drum of a washing machine. If only she could tell Vincent she didn't want to work for him anymore. The man was her least favorite client. Full of last-minute deadlines and changes. But the money was too good to pass up. And she'd definitely charge him for these. She always made him sign off on changes so that she could add additional fees while proving he'd made the requests. And for some reason, he kept hiring her.

Stretching arms over her head, Cate attempted to release the kinks in her neck and unwind her screaming muscles. Stress of any sort made her twist up like a rubber band.

She removed the long silver necklace that she'd worn over a dressy turquoise tank top for the meeting and placed it on the desk. She'd paired the shirt with black skinny ankle pants, wanting to look professional even over the computer screen.

The time in the corner of her computer made her gasp and pop up from her seat. Ruby would be climbing the walls by now. The girl was too social to survive five minutes by herself. Cate was surprised she hadn't popped in once or twice during her Skype call, but then, she had bribed her with a Popsicle if she could occupy herself for the supposed-to-be-half-hour meeting that had morphed into an hour.

The mark of a good parent—bribery. At least that was what Cate told herself. Survival came in all forms.

"Sorry, Rubes." She opened the slightly ajar bedroom door. "I didn't know the meeting would go so long. I owe you big-time, kiddo."

There was no sign of Ruby in the living room or bathroom. Maybe she'd crawled into her bed and decided to take a nap. Ha! Now Cate really was being delusional.

Crossing to the other bedroom, Cate stepped inside the darkened space. No Ruby in the bed. Or under it. Cate's pulse revved as she walked around the bed just to make sure Ruby wasn't hiding on the other side. She checked the closet. Nothing. There was nowhere else Ruby could be in the bedroom, so Cate took off for the living room again.

She scanned the couch and fireplace. Ruby's ponies were set up on a wooden bench under the window. Prim watched Cate from the fireplace hearth.

"Where's Ruby, Prim? Where'd she go?"

This was where a dog might be a better fit than a cat, because Prim's answer was to squint and lick a paw.

Weakness spread through Cate's limbs. The places Ruby could be hiding were diminishing. Just like her attempt at remaining calm.

She checked the bathroom again, this time flipping on the light and yanking back the shower curtain with shaking hands.

Empty.

Cate ran for the front door and ripped it open. The step was vacant, the dirt path barren. Cate had thought maybe Ruby had wanted to sit outside, but there was no sign of her or any of her toys.

She called for Ruby numerous times, volume heightening with each attempt to locate her daughter. No answer.

A fist closed around her throat. Could Ruby be playing a game of hide-and-seek?

Cate tore back into the house, leaving the front door open in case anyone had heard her calling and offered any help. "Ruby, if you're hiding from me it's not funny anymore. I need you to come out. You're going to get a Popsicle, remember?"

Surely that would do the trick.

But no giggle or small voice answered her. Just an agitated meow from Prim. Cate opened the lower cupboard doors. She couldn't imagine Ruby fitting inside, but it was worth a try. After that she checked the small closet to the side of the front door. The outdoorsy scent of Luc wafted from the coats and sweatshirts that hung in the space. Cate shoved the boots on the floor to the side. No Ruby.

Once again she offered a treat, this time upping the ante to ice cream. But when she didn't receive an answer, her panic shot into the red.

Ruby wasn't here.

The cabin wasn't big enough for her to hide and Cate not to find her. Besides, the girl wasn't that good at hide-and-seek yet. A portion of her body was always visible, sticking out from behind a piece of furniture or shaking with laughter under a blanket.

What should Cate do? Had Ruby wandered out the door? The ranchland was endless. She could be anywhere, surrounded by any number of wild animals. Cate's heart ping-ponged in her chest.

What had Ruby been wearing? Her mind scrounged for the description she'd need to supply to the search-and-rescue crew.

Snagging her phone from her desk, she tried Luc as she walked back into the living room. No answer. Next, she called Mackenzie, impatience mounting with each ring. Maybe she and Emma had seen Ruby or even had her with them.

It *had* to be something simple like that. But while her

mind agreed with that logic, her body was too busy mentally assuming the fetal position.

"Hello?" Mackenzie answered just as Cate spied the note propped against the cracker box on the counter. Luc's writing. She blinked, attempting to focus long enough to read his message.

"Cate? Everything okay?" Funny. Even Mackenzie knew if Cate was calling her, something must be wrong. Only it wasn't.

She scanned the scrap of paper. "No. I mean yes. Everything is okay. False alarm. I—I couldn't find Ruby, but I guess Luc has her."

"Oh, yeah. She's actually with Emma and the other kids at the moment."

Heat engulfed Cate's face, matching the indignation churning inside. "Thanks." She swallowed. Tried to get some moisture back into her mouth. "That helps."

They hung up, and Cate placed her hands against the counter, inhaling long and slow in an attempt to settle her buzzing nervous system.

What had Luc been thinking? Why hadn't he at least popped in and motioned to her or something? Who did he think he was, taking Ruby like he had?

Cate pushed off the counter. She needed to talk to him, and there was no way the conversation could wait until dinner.

"You all set?" Luc questioned Brant, the nineteen-year-old who would lead the afternoon trail ride. The kid had been a godsend when he'd shown up last summer looking for work. He knew more about flowers, birds and anything to do with nature than any of the other leads, and the guests loved him.

"Yeah, dude. Ready to rock."

Dude. Brant was far more snowboarder than cowboy, but he knew these trails in and out. Being a wrangler at the ranch was the perfect fit for him because it meant he had portions of the winter months off and could spend his time on the slopes.

Brant whistled to get the group's attention, then began his short instruction spiel. He tugged on the straps to his backpack while talking, which was loaded with emergency supplies—granola bars and extra water for the guest who forgot theirs. It was important to stay hydrated, as altitude sickness could come on fast and fierce.

"Mr. Wilder, I wanted to ask you about the dance at the end of the week." An older woman with gray hair and squeaky new cowboy boots approached. Those were going to rub some mean blisters into existence by the end of the day.

"Call me Luc… Mrs. Tepa," he finally recalled.

"I don't have any clothes for the dance, not a single dress, and I'm…" She continued talking as Cate stormed down the trail from the cabins, looking like she'd been stung by a bee and was in hot pursuit of blaming…someone.

If he called out *not it*, would she head in another direction and find a different target?

He and Cate had managed to avoid any of the real issues swimming under their bridge this week, but it looked like their raft was about to crash over the falls.

His head shook at the thought.

"So I can't wear casual clothes?" Mrs. Tepa asked.

"Oh, sorry. I wasn't answering you. I— Yes, you can. The dance is casual. Nothing fancy. Boots and jeans make the most sense. That's what everyone wears, ma'am."

The square dance that finished off each week was a highlight for the guests. Luc asked people to fill out a short survey at the end of their stay, and that always ranked as one of the favorite activities. Along with moving the cattle. People loved the thought of doing what had been done in the West for centuries.

"Okay, thank you so much." Mrs. Tepa rejoined the group headed for the corral as Cate zoomed in for a landing. Her narrowed eyes were aimed right at him—no surprise there. Though Luc didn't have a clue what he'd done.

And then she was in front of him, the August sun beating down on them and singeing the back of Luc's neck. He'd forgotten to grab his hat on the way out of the lodge and now regretted it. He could have tipped the brim low to deflect a bit of the self-righteous heat pouring from Cate.

Dressed in fancy work clothes and black sandals, Cate looked like she belonged in a Denver office building instead of kicking up dust on a ranch.

Luc wore a different variation of the same thing every day—boots and jeans. A ranch T-shirt or button-down, depending on the weather. And in the winter, a brown Carhartt coat. What had he ever been thinking, falling crazy in love with this woman? He and Cate had so little in common.

"*What* were you thinking?" Her question mimicked his thoughts. Thankfully, the guests were far enough away that they didn't turn to investigate her snippy, accusatory tone.

"Regarding what?" The two of them had plenty of situations she could be referring to. "Past or present?"

His quip only increased her scowl. "You took my

daughter without telling me. I didn't see your note," she spit out, "until after I'd panicked. I thought maybe she was wandering around outside. I didn't know if she was lost or stuck somewhere. And I didn't have a clue where to start looking. It was awful." Her voice wobbled, and her eyelids fluttered like hummingbird wings. Trying to control her emotions? Too bad. Any empathy he might have mustered had deflated with her choice of words.

"*Your* daughter?" If his voice held a bit of malice, sue him. Anger over the decisions Cate had made bubbled as scalding and fierce as the hot spring that sprang up from God's imagination on Wilder land.

Cate's arms crossed in a huff, eyes jutting to the side as her chin eased forward in defiance. "You know what I mean."

"You're right. I do. You mean Ruby's yours. You might be making a small attempt right now to compromise by staying here, but in a few weeks you're planning to high-tail it out of here so fast there'll be a trail of dust a quarter mile wide behind your car. I'm not a fool, Cate. I see what you're doing. You're trying to retain as much control over Ruby as possible while keeping me out."

"I never said that."

"You didn't have to."

This conversation was oddly reminiscent of a fight they would have had when they were younger. Different verse, same chorus. They'd always been feisty with each other—or at least he'd been with her. But their arguing was one of Luc's biggest regrets. If he'd handled those days better and chosen maturity instead of self-ishness, maybe he and Cate would still be together. And Ruby would be *their* daughter. And then he wouldn't have missed the first three-plus years of her life.

No. He wouldn't go down that road again, no matter how much he wanted to be right in this situation. Getting along with the mother of his child was the better choice.

And he certainly hadn't meant to worry Cate.

"I'm sorry."

Her chin jerked back, eyes widening. "What?"

He almost chuckled at her response. He'd thrown her for a loop not continuing to engage in battle with her. Maybe it could be a first step in showing Cate he wasn't that same kid anymore. She would never believe him if his actions didn't back up what he claimed.

"I didn't mean to scare you, taking Ruby. I thought I was helping. I could hear you talking to someone about work, and she was bored. Part of you being here was for us to help, not for you to be working and taking care of Ruby by yourself." He shrugged. "So I asked Ruby if she wanted to stay with me or go with Emma and the kids, and she chose her aunt. Of course."

"Oh." Some of the wind left Cate's sails, though her eyes were still shooting sparks.

"I left you a note."

"I didn't see it right away." Her quiet answer told him she was starting to back down from her high horse, but he needed her to go another few notches before they could have a calm conversation. One without snapping at each other.

"Come with me." Luc hooked a thumb toward the lodge.

"Why?" The woman could sure pack a lot of distrust into one little syllable.

"Do you have to question everything?"

"Yes."

He half laughed, half sighed. Nodded toward the lodge

again on his second attempt. "Do you want a brownie? They're fresh from the oven."

Her lips pressed together, contemplating. Show-off. She didn't have to draw any attention to the spot. He already had it memorized.

"What does that have to do with anything?" Curiosity joined the edge to her voice.

Only Cate could question the motive behind a brownie. "Just come on." He snagged her arm, directing her. If he waited for her to decide, they'd be here all day. His hand felt right at home against her skin, but he ignored the increased rhythm in his chest at being near her. She smelled like flowers and good pieces of the past.

Luc matched his longer stride to Cate's shorter one. He probably had close to half a foot on her in height, but she made up for it in spunk. Case in point: she shook his hand off her arm like she was dealing with an insect instead of a man. His mouth twitched. As long as she kept walking, he wouldn't fight her.

What was it about Cate that both infuriated him and intrigued him at the same time? Just her presence wreaked havoc on him. He wanted to tuck into her and take a good long breath, as if he'd been holding his for the years during their separation and his lungs could finally function again. But he wasn't allowed those kinds of liberties anymore, and he wouldn't take them if he could.

He and Cate had bigger things to focus on than their wayward relationship. Like their daughter. Which was exactly what he wanted to talk to her about.

"Joe made brownies. I could smell them when I was in my office earlier. They're amazing right out of the oven."

Her sideways glance included more narrowing of those

caramel eyes. "Are you trying to bribe me into a conversation with the promise of a brownie, Lucas Wilder?"

"Yes, ma'am. That's exactly what I'm doing."

Chapter Seven

The empty kitchen's immaculate stainless-steel counter-tops and appliances spoke to the neat freak living inside Cate. White fluorescent lights bounced from the surfaces, and the smell of disinfectant from the last meal's cleanup whispered across her senses along with the sweet smell of still-warm chocolate.

Luc went to an open metal shelf lined with rows of filled baking pans and slid one out, placing it on the counter.

"Have a seat." He nodded toward the countertop.

"Won't I get in trouble for that? Isn't that against the rules or something?"

He snagged two small plates, then some silverware from the round metal canisters. "I know the people who run this place. I think you're in the clear." Humor crinkled his cheeks. "Plus, I'm kind of intimidated by Joe. He's been the chef since I was a kid and has reamed me out for being in here more times than I can count. So I'll definitely clean up any mess I make." He glanced at the wall clock. "We have at least thirty minutes before the kitchen staff comes in to start prepping dinner."

Cate pointed to the section of brownies where he'd just cut two large squares from the corner. "That's not going to be a clue?"

His boyish grin grew, causing an ache to echo in her chest. That easy lift of his lips should be illegal. It was too attractive to resist.

After scooping one man-size portion onto the small plastic plate, he handed it to Cate with a fork perched on the side. She touched the top. Felt the warmth.

Setting the plate down, she scooted backward onto the countertop, then picked it back up. This was exactly the kind of thing the old Luc would have made her do. Not quite breaking the rules but not quite following them, either. Good-looking trouble. That was what he was.

She took a bite, the rage that had propelled her in search of Luc melting with the cocoa tantalizing her tongue. This had been a smart move on his part. Not that she was over and done with what had happened.

"Oh, my." She mumbled over the bite of brownie, not in the least bit proper, then swallowed the fudge-like treat. "Are there chocolate chips in these?"

"Yep."

They were still gooey from the oven, and for the moment Cate decided to concentrate on the brownie instead of Luc. She liked one more than she liked the other right now.

Luc slid backward to sit on the counter, too, then picked up his plate. He dug in, and Cate took another forkful, savoring with her eyes closed.

"I take it you still feel the same way about baked goods as you did at nineteen."

His tease held a hint of intimacy. A dance of remembering back to the time when they'd been inseparable and had known all there was to know about each other.

"Maybe." She went with a light answer, unwilling to engage the deeper feelings simmering under the surface. Cate allowed herself another bite, the sugar easing into her system. "Okay, Wilder. You've got me mellowed out. Now what do you want?"

He speared another bite of brownie but left the loaded fork on his plate. "I really didn't mean to upset you about Ruby. I thought you'd see the note. I even pulled a cracker box out of the cupboard to prop it up. The cabin is so neat I thought you'd notice something out of place right away."

She did like having everything clean and orderly. It made her feel safe. In control. Like she could handle the other burning fires if her home life was organized.

Cate could concede that Luc had tried to communicate with her. "I'm surprised I didn't notice. I got done with my meeting and rushed into the living room, but then I couldn't find her anywhere and I just…freaked."

"I'm sorry for that."

"Okay." She could accept his apology. "Thanks."

"You're not used to anyone but you taking care of Ruby."

She mulled over his statement, then decided on acceptance. After all, Luc had chosen not to continue fighting with her when she'd flown at him in full attack mode. "You're right. I'm not."

"That's what I want to talk to you about."

Where was Luc going with this?

"You're holding me back, Cate." His voice was quiet. Nonconfrontational. But it still stung. "Not necessarily from Ruby, though I would imagine she can sense the turmoil between us. It's funny. You're the one who kept Ruby from me, but it almost feels like..." He set his scraped clean plate down, and it clattered against the metal.

"Like what?" Her voice hitched. She both did and didn't want to know.

"Like you're mad at me."

Oh, boy. A layer of moisture coated her eyes, surprising her. She blinked it away quickly, mind reeling at his statement.

She'd never thought about it before, but he was right.

She *was* mad. About the way it had all ended so horribly. Gutted that he'd left after their fight, no matter what she'd said to him. If he'd been telling her the truth, why hadn't he fought for her? She'd told him to leave, but she'd wanted him to stay and convince her his feelings were true.

"I guess..." Cate set down her empty plate and studied her fingernails, barely resisting the urge to slip her thumbnail between her teeth. She'd been doing so well on breaking that habit. She shoved her hands beneath her legs and glanced to Luc, who was patiently waiting for her to continue. Analyzing her intently in that unnerving way he had. "I suppose you're right. It was easier to be upset with you for what happened at the end—"

Luc growled. "I never so much as laid eyes on another woman, Cate, if that's what you're referring to."

What did he want her to say? *Suddenly, I believe you*? Cate had fallen so hard and fast for Luc when they were young that when the question of trusting him had arisen, she didn't have an answer. How did a person go about choosing to put their faith in someone? How did that work? And what if they made the wrong choice? Cate's trust button was broken, and she didn't know of a repair shop that worked on that kind of issue.

Except for God. But He hadn't healed that gaping wound in her life. At least not yet.

"Let me finish. It was easier to be mad at you for how things ended than it was to be upset at myself for doing what I did to you. Easier to blame you than to admit it was fully my decision to keep Ruby from you. Because if I could focus on what I saw as your part in all of it, I didn't feel as guilty."

Ouch. Cate had never admitted anything of the sort to herself. She'd just been pointing fingers. Deep down, she'd known it was wrong not to tell Luc about Ruby, but she'd been so afraid of losing her daughter that she'd let that keep her from doing the right thing.

What a mess she'd made.

Luc was right. It wasn't just her and Ruby anymore. Luc was part of the picture. And she needed to stop treating him like he was an intruder and start treating him like Ruby's father.

No matter how painful the change.

This was the most truthful Cate had been with him yet. Luc wasn't sure if it was the brownie or the calm conversation that had her defenses down, but he liked this side of her. Then again, maybe it was dangerous to have Cate open up like this, because it flooded him with memories of what they'd had when they were younger.

Before she'd stopped believing him.

When they'd had that last fight—when she'd asked him for the truth—Luc had told her he'd never cheated in any way, shape or form. But when she'd pushed him, needing more information that he didn't have to give, he'd snapped.

Nothing messed with him like when people didn't take him at his word. It had happened in high school. A group of teens had vandalized the school. Yes, his buddies had been involved. No, he hadn't been. Yet, somehow, even his own parents hadn't believed him. Luc had looked them straight in the eyes and told them the truth—that he'd been at home in bed. He could understand the story sounding fake, but it hadn't been. But they'd trusted someone on the school staff—an eyewitness who placed him at the scene of the vandalism—instead of him. And he'd been forced to do community service with the guys who had caused trouble.

Ever since then, not being believed was his greatest aggravation. When Cate had done the same thing to him, despite him telling her nothing but the truth, something in him had hardened. Cracked and bled.

He'd been done. That was why he'd run and never let himself look back, though the temptation had been strong to call Cate the morning after they'd fought. To make everything right again.

But it hadn't been any old argument. Not to him.

Not one part of Luc had wanted to walk away from Cate, but he'd made himself. How could they have continued a relationship when she didn't trust him?

Bruised and limping, he'd gone back to the ranch. Soon after, his parents had needed to move for his mom's health, and he and his sisters had taken over.

And he'd been fine. For the most part. Until Cate had shown up with Ruby.

But now he couldn't avoid Cate's lack of trust. They had Ruby, and they had to deal with each other. The question was, how? Today showed that the way they'd been functioning wasn't working.

Cate hopped down from the kitchen counter that held them both, and Luc's breath hitched. Was she going to take off? End their conversation? Because he wasn't done yet.

She grabbed her plate, then his, heading for the industrial sink.

His shoulders relaxed. "I'll do that."

She waved one hand, her back to him. "Strangely enough, I like washing dishes."

"I'm not going to argue with that." He didn't know if she smiled or not, and curiosity inched along his spine. It was easier when he could read her. If he could manage to.

She pulled down the sprayer and squeezed the handle, the water making a zinging noise as it hit the dishes and stainless-steel sink.

"Cate, we have to figure out how to get along." The water momentarily stopped. "For Ruby's sake." Back visibly unknotting, she went back to cleaning—squirting dish soap and using the sponge resting near the edge of the sink. "I want you to let me into your lives. It doesn't work for our relationship to be just about Ruby. I mean, yes, that's the focus, but we can't hold each other back with steel rods. She'll figure out soon enough that we can't get along. It won't work. Not in the long haul. We have to parent together."

It was almost easier to talk to Cate with her back turned. But at the same time, he'd give good money to see her face. During his speech, she'd continued scrubbing one of the little plates as if it was covered in hardened cement she needed to scrape free. Finally, she put both plates in the metal drying rack to the side of the sink and turned to face him.

"So what are you saying?"

"I'm saying I want in. I want permission to have Ruby, to let her go off with Emma or Mackenzie or me without thinking you're going to come after me with a pitchfork. I want the chance to be her dad and have the responsibility and freedom that comes with it. And I'd like us to be on the same team."

Luc held his breath while Cate processed, letting it out in a gush of air when she outlasted him.

She lifted her thumbnail to her mouth, then ripped it back out. "Okay. I hear you, and you're right. I have been holding you back. So I'll stop, and we'll parent together." A flash of pain crossed her face, followed by a look of determination. "We can manage that, can't we?"

Luc pushed off the counter and stood. "I think we can."

Doubt and concern swirled in her pretty brown eyes, and he resisted the urge to reach out, tuck her into his chest and just hold on. Would it heal something between them if he breached the gap of hurt that separated them?

If only it were that simple.

Cate slid the brownie tray back into its spot on the shelf, and Luc dried their plates and put them away. They faced each other again, both leaning against a counter.

A lock of hair tumbled across Cate's face, and she tucked it behind her ear. "So, does this mean I get to make all of the decisions, and as long as I talk to you about them first, you have to agree?"

"No." Funny girl. "If anything, it should be the other way around."

Her nose wrinkled. "I don't really see that happening."

"I don't, either." A chuckle vibrated his chest. He'd take humor over fighting any day.

They walked through the dining room and into the lobby area of the lodge. Luc had always found it a comforting place. Large, overstuffed leather couches and chairs. A fire burning on cool evenings.

Cate paused by the front door. "I meant to tell you Ruby's day care called, and they're going to refund part of the month. They found someone who needed a temporary spot while they're on a waiting list. I know you said you'd pay for it in order for her to be here, but now you don't have to. It's nice. Between that and the meals being provided, I'm actually saving money." She looked surprised by her own admission.

"Good. I'm glad to hear it." He still didn't know how Cate had scraped by as a single mom. She must have worked incredibly hard to stay afloat. "There's something I've been meaning to tell you, too."

She waited for him to continue, but nerves got tangled up, congregating in his throat. What in the world? It was just Cate he was talking to. Just the mother of his child. First and only woman he'd ever loved. He didn't need to be so skittish around her. But she messed with him in a way no one else did.

Plus, he didn't think she'd take what he had to say very well.

"I have some money set aside, and I want you to have it."

Confusion wrinkled her normally smooth complexion. She blinked. "For what?"

"For Ruby. For you. All of this time you've raised her on your own without any help. That's not right. I would have—" He clamped his jaw shut to keep from saying he would have been there for Ruby and supported her. It was true, but now that they'd both declared a truce, Luc didn't want to cause a rift in the new peace they'd found.

He might never fully understand the choice Cate had made, but he had to find a way to move beyond it. For all of their sakes.

"I want to help out. I want to be part of taking care of her. So I *am* going to give you what I have." He wished it could be more, but while he lived comfortably and contentedly, he wasn't a millionaire by any means.

They'd have to figure out better logistics going forward, but he wasn't ready to deal with the thought of Ruby and Cate leaving the ranch at the end of the month.

"I didn't find you because I was looking for money." She searched his face as if scavenging for the meaning behind his offer.

"I know."

"Ruby and I have always done okay."

"I'm not saying you haven't. But are you telling me there's not a pile of medical bills filling your mailbox? Or that there won't be shortly?"

The scuffed wood floor beneath their feet caught and held Cate's attention.

Luc gently nudged her chin up so their eyes met. "Give me this, at least. Let me do this." Then it would feel like he was doing *something*. Cate made mothering look so easy, Luc feared she really didn't need him. And the past few years had proved she didn't.

A group of guests walked by the front door, the hum of their conversation trickling into the lodge.

"Well?" he questioned when their voices faded.

Her hands momentarily rose in defeat. "I want to say no, but I don't think you're going to let me."

"I'm not."

She waited one beat. Two. Three. A faint smile sprouted. "Okay, Lucas. You win."

When she looked at him that way—with softness instead of a crisp outer shell, his full name falling from her mouth like silk—Luc couldn't help feeling like he *had* just won. It was the first time he truly had hope that a second chance—for their daughter—was an actual possibility.

Chapter Eight

"**D**addy, watch!" Ruby held on to the back of Molly, the ranch's black Lab, and squeezed for all she was worth. Thankfully, Molly had the sweetest temperament of any dog on planet Earth and barely blinked an eye. "Molly likes to give me huggles."

"That's great. Good job." Luc wasn't sure whether he was saying it to his daughter or the dog.

The Saturday afternoon sun beat down on them, and Luc removed his hat and swiped his brow before plunking it back on his head. He should probably throw some sunscreen on Ruby, though they'd only been outside the lodge for a few minutes.

Cate had trained him to apply the stuff whenever there was even the slightest chance the sun would come into contact with Ruby's fair skin. As a kid, Luc hadn't thought twice about sunscreen. And he'd spent as much of his childhood as possible outdoors. Had they even made it back then? He recalled his sister Emma using baby oil to gain a tan. That had not ended well.

"Sit, Molly." Ruby wagged a finger, and Molly's rump

hit the ground. The dog gave Luc a look as if to say, *How long do I have to do this? I'd better get a treat.*

Molly knew exactly where the dog bones were kept—in an old metal milk can on the front porch of the lodge—and if Luc wasn't mistaken, she was repeatedly stealing glances in that direction.

"I did it." Ruby's hands flew into the air in celebration, as if Molly had never performed a trick before in her life.

"See if you can get her to roll over. You can get her a treat."

Ruby clapped in excitement, and Molly's soft ears perked with interest. Fast as her little legs could go, Ruby ran onto the porch, uncovered the bin and snagged a bone. She ran back to Molly just as Joe pulled up to the front steps with a pickup full of food.

The small grocery store in town ordered some of their supplies so the money could stay local. Joe or one of the kitchen staff usually picked up a load after the guests left on Saturday mornings. What they couldn't supply was delivered by refrigerated truck.

Luc popped the tailgate down as Joe eased out of the truck slowly, nursing his bad hip. Pulling a handkerchief from his pocket, he swiped the beads of sweat from his midnight forehead.

"Thanks for the help." He nodded at Luc. "Guess I have to forgive you for stealing brownies from my pan. Just like when you were a kid." Joe punctuated the sentence with a rumbling chuckle. He might talk big, but no one actually believed his threats.

Dad had hired Joe when Luc was a boy, and he'd been a part of their extended ranch family ever since.

"Does that mean I should just ignore the fact that

you've been sneaking my daughter treats? How do you think her mother would feel about that?"

Not happy. Cate had rules about the number of desserts Ruby could have in a day. But Molly wasn't the only one who knew where to find treats. Ruby had quickly figured out the head chef had a soft spot for her, and she'd happily taken advantage.

Joe harrumphed. "Don't know what you're talking about."

Luc laughed.

The man attempted to straighten the fingers of his left hand, but arthritis had locked them into a painful-looking position. Well into his sixties, he was unwilling to give up his job. Said it kept him going. But the body didn't always agree with the mind. Joe had assistants in the kitchen for all of his chopping and food prep, but Luc wasn't sure if he actually used them or if he still did that kind of painful detail work himself. Joe had been born without an off switch.

"I'll get this." Luc nodded toward the truck. "Your arthritis will be killing you if you carry any of this."

Joe looked like he was about to argue, but finally nodded. "Thanks. Appreciate it." He ambled up the stairs and disappeared into the lodge as Mackenzie bounded down the steps.

"Need some help?"

"Sure. Thanks."

She hopped up into the truck bed and slid items toward the tailgate. She was dressed in black shorts and a bright green tank with flip-flops on her feet, and her legs had earned a tan over the summer. Cate would have to talk to her about sunscreen.

"Must be nice sitting around in the sun all day," Luc quipped.

Mackenzie did a lot more than trail rides and rafting expeditions—helping manage staff and reservations, too—but he couldn't pass up the jab.

"Must be nice sitting in an air-conditioned office all day."

She knew he liked that part of his job the least. "I don't see you offering to do the bookwork. Anytime you want to take over, you just let me know."

Her nose wrinkled with disgust as if he'd offered her a pretty pink bow to wear in her hair. "Never mind. I take it all back."

With a hand on the side of the truck bed, she hopped back down to the ground while Ruby called out, "Aunt Kenzie, watch!"

Mackenzie paused, facing Ruby while shading her eyes with her hand.

Ruby had commandeered Molly into playing dead. Or just wore her out so much that she'd dropped down for a nap.

"Nice!" Mackenzie gave Ruby a thumbs-up.

Ruby started running in wide circles, encouraging the dog to follow her.

"She sure has a lot of energy for a girl who just had heart surgery. I remember when we were kids. Before you had surgery, I could always beat you in a race. But after? You left me in the dust."

"And have ever since."

Mackenzie punched him on the arm. It stung more than Luc would ever admit. His sister was one of the toughest people he knew—male or female.

Luc watched Ruby run and giggle, creator and only

participant in her game. "Isn't it crazy to think that she just had a heart procedure? I mean look at her..."

"Yeah. She's pretty amazing." Mackenzie lifted a box into her arms. "You ever think about the fact that if she hadn't needed the hole fixed, Cate might not have been guilted into telling you about her?"

"No." His answer came out fast, and her eyes narrowed.

The two of them had always shared a strong connection. Luc knew when there was a pea under her mattress, and she knew when something was off with him.

Back when he'd escaped the ranch at nineteen, thinking he needed a different life, Mackenzie had been irate.

And when he'd returned home as the prodigal brother, she'd accepted him without question.

"Liar." Mackenzie flashed bright white teeth. "Not that it's on the same subject or anything, but where's Cate?"

Luc shook his head. "You know I asked you to work on forgiving her. For Ruby's sake. And don't you dare say anything bad about her in front of—" He nodded toward Ruby.

"I wouldn't do that." Mackenzie had the decency to look chagrined. But it only lasted a moment. "Have *you* forgiven her?"

"I'm working hard on it." And that was the truth. "In answer to your question, Cate has a deadline today for some magazine she does. She's been at it all week." Luc hadn't seen much of her at all—Cate had barely looked away from her computer for days. He'd even brought her a dinner plate last night because she'd sent Ruby with him and never come to get any food for herself.

Luc didn't know how she did it. He might very well die

if he was strapped to a screen as much as Cate was. But she did look cute in those glasses she wore while working.

Because she'd been so wrapped up in work, Luc had gotten to spend a lot of time with Ruby this week. He'd been latching on to every minute. After their talk on Monday, Cate had been much better with him taking Ruby. And he'd been better about communicating. Look at them. They were practically getting along. If you didn't count the fact that they'd hardly seen each other.

"Well, the woman's not lazy. I'll give her that." And with that generous announcement, Mackenzie headed into the lodge with a box full of supplies.

Cate's everything hurt. Sitting in a chair for five days straight had taken a toll on her body. But she was finally done and could send the magazine off.

Her deadline had approached too quickly yesterday, so she'd asked for an extension until today at five. Thankfully, they were fine with her request.

And…she glanced at the clock on her computer screen…she'd be sending it in at quarter till. Nothing like beating a deadline with time to spare.

She wasn't usually so behind with the magazine, but with the time spent not working during Ruby's procedure and then redoing Vincent's project, she'd gotten off schedule.

A knock sounded just as she hit Send on the email, and Luc's hello followed, echoing into the cabin through the walls. Cate popped up, tossed her glasses onto the desk and hurried to let him and Ruby in.

Luc had pretty much taken care of Ruby all week while Cate worked. Whether their daughter had hung out with Luc or his sisters each day, she wasn't sure. A little of both, according to the stories Ruby told when she came back to the cabin exhausted and happy at night.

A quick bath and she fell asleep faster than Cate had ever seen her do before. All of that fresh air and dirt under her fingernails must be wearing her out.

Cate yanked open the door, only thinking about her appearance when it was too late. Luc's chin dropped. And not in a *whoa-woman-you-look-good* kind of way. This was more of a *what-happened-to-you* glance.

"Hi, Mom." Ruby waltzed into the cabin while Cate's hand snaked up to gauge the hair situation she had going on. Messy bun. Heavy on the messy part. Light on the bun. More of a hair band barely holding on to its dignity.

And her clothes. Cate's gaze bounced from Luc's black T-shirt, jeans and boots to her own yoga capris and pink T-shirt. The chipped toe polish on her bare feet looked as if it had been attacked by pecking birds. What in the world? Had she gone into some kind of hibernation for the past month?

"I—" She swept a hand down her outfit. "Deadline day." As if that explained it all.

Luc was smart enough not to say anything to that. "If you need more time, I can keep Ruby longer."

"Oh, no." She motioned toward the bedroom. As if he could somehow read her mind and know she was pointing through the wall at her computer. Boy, she really was a hot mess at the moment. "I just sent it in, actually."

His face lit up. "Good. I'm glad. Maybe now you can eat and sleep again." Thankfully, he didn't add *and shower*. Though Cate did in her own mind.

Luc's head tilted, gears turning in that way-too-handsome noggin of his. "We should celebrate."

Cate planned to. With a bubble bath and sleep.

"Let's go to dinner. The three of us. You could use a night out." He glanced toward her bedroom. "Or just a night away from a screen. With other people." He pointed his thumb at himself, as if she didn't remember what the concept meant.

Dinner with Luc sounded like all sorts of trouble.

"It would be good for Ruby to see us getting along."

Low blow.

"Believe it or not, there's a Thai restaurant that opened up in town not too long ago."

Her mouth watered. How did he remember she loved Thai food? Then again, she knew he couldn't stand the texture of shredded coconut, that his skin reacted when his clothes were washed in bleach and that he liked his tea unsweetened.

"And don't give me some lame excuse about your outfit. You could wear what you have on and no one would be able to keep their eyes off you."

Like an ice cube tossed into boiling water, her disobedient body melted. "I really need to shower."

"Okay. I'll swing by with the truck and get you and Ruby. An hour?"

If only her head didn't nod in response when it really, really needed to shake in the other direction. The one that said no and kept a distance between them. But she'd promised Luc she'd work on doing the opposite of that. For Ruby's sake.

She shut the door on Luc's retreating back and turned. "Ruby, let's get ready. We're going out to dinner."

The little squeal of excitement that followed was most certainly not echoed within the walls of Cate's chest. At least not out loud.

Usually she didn't celebrate the small things in life

like a deadline that came around once a quarter. There just wasn't time. And she didn't have the energy. But it was a nice idea. And Luc was right—she did need to get out of the cabin.

It was just...she hadn't had anyone to celebrate with in a really long time. Pretty much since Luc.

And if that wasn't a dangerous thought, she didn't know what was.

Chapter Nine

Just because Luc had showered and changed into crisp jeans, camel laced boots and a short-sleeved plaid button-down didn't mean tonight equaled a date. At least that was what Cate kept telling herself.

Luc parked the truck in one of the spots in the small lot next door to Thai House. The restaurant sign was newly painted, pink letters popping against a white backdrop.

Before Cate realized what was happening, he was on her side of the vehicle, opening her door.

Still not a date.

"Mommy," Ruby piped up from the back. "Let's go."

Impatience was easy to come by with a three-year-old, and Ruby had never been a fan of being strapped into her car seat.

Cate stepped out of the truck and into the warm summer evening, tossing Luc a hopefully breezy thank-you. One that wouldn't give away the pounding and banging happening within the confines of her rib cage. She wore a sleeveless navy-and-white-striped button-down, skinny ankle jeans and brown leather flats. Casual and comfortable, but not overly…date-ish.

Tonight's dinner didn't mean anything. And neither did the door. Luc was a gentleman. That couldn't be shaken out of him.

Luc released Ruby from her car seat, and she scrambled out as if headed to a parade. Perhaps they both needed some time away from the ranch. Not that Ruby hadn't fallen in love with it. She had. The lifestyle and guests had become part of her routine, and Cate had no doubt she'd miss it all when it was time to head back to Denver in two weeks.

For dinner Ruby had changed into salmon capris and a teal shirt that boasted, *I got an A+ in talking.* A legitimate claim. From the reports that had filtered back to Cate this week, Ruby greeted anyone and everyone who stayed, worked at or so much as glanced in the direction of the ranch with her trademark, "Hi, friend."

According to Luc, anyone who came across her path was quickly smitten.

Rounding the side of the building, the three of them met up with the sidewalk. Westbend reminded Cate of a vintage postcard showcasing a small town from decades past. The kind one might find wrapped in protective plastic coating tucked into a bin in an antiques shop.

A ranch supply store anchored the corner, parking lot half-full of sale equipment. The main street was lined with small stores and restaurants, streetlights lit up in anticipation of evening.

They'd passed the quaint white church that Cate and Ruby had been attending with Luc and his sisters on their way to the restaurant. Cate had enjoyed the sermons, and Ruby had even gone to Sunday school. An easier transition than Cate had expected since they attended a mega church in Denver. So many people had welcomed her, wanting to get to know her.

Luc opened the glass restaurant door, exchanging the warm outdoors for a cool blast of garlic and lemongrass.

The bright orange sign just inside—also hand-painted—directed them to "seat yo-self." The place was tiny, with a handful of tables and one long tabletop bar in the window, four metal stools lined beneath it.

Of course, Ruby wanted to sit by the window. A bit awkward for conversation since none of the seats faced each other. "How about a table instead? You can still choose," Cate added.

After two more attempts to pick the same spot, Ruby finally skipped over to a table on the far side with a cushioned bench lining the wall. She sat there with Luc, and Cate took the chair across from him.

Each table held a flickering candle in a brightly colored glass jar.

Still not a date.

The air-conditioning came in spurts of cool and then tepid air as the waitress dropped off waters and paper menus.

Luc left his untouched. "You're going to have to order for me." His grin made her stomach shimmy. How many times did she have to remind herself he was off-limits? *They* were off-limits.

Thai wasn't Luc's favorite, but over their time together, she'd found a couple of items he enjoyed. Good memories pressed in, more vivid than she'd allowed them to be in a long time.

"Mommy, what about me?"

One minute with Luc, and Cate had already forgotten about their daughter, perched on the bench next to him. Exactly why she and the man across from her were a huge *no*. The feeling of being forgotten was something Cate had carried with her from childhood to this day. Not one she wanted her daughter to experience.

"I'll order for you, sweets."

"Okay. I want the rice soup."

"Got it."

"She knows what she wants?" Luc asked. "What three-year-old eats Thai food?"

Cate's teeth pressed into her lip, biting back amusement. "She wasn't really given a choice. She grew up on it. If we ever eat out or grab something to go, which is rare… Thai is pretty much what we get."

"The first step is admitting you have an addiction, Cate."

She laughed. Luc's teasing just might be yummier than the food they were about to eat.

When the waitress came back, Cate ordered the soup for Ruby, a mild yellow chicken curry for Luc—it had potatoes in it, so he'd at least be able to recognize those—and pad thai for herself.

A small cup of crayons was on the table, and Ruby colored on the sheet the restaurant supplied. Her small tongue slipped between her lips as she concentrated.

"So," Luc said, "what do you think about living at the ranch?"

"I like it," Ruby piped in, adding a strip of red to her rainbow.

Since he'd been looking across the table at Cate, his question had obviously been meant for her. Their curving mouths mirrored each other's at Ruby's quick answer.

"Good." Luc captured Ruby in a hug. "Because I like you."

With a smile that said she deserved every compliment headed her way, Ruby wiggled with happiness, then went back to drawing.

Luc turned back to Cate, obviously waiting for her answer.

"It's not what I expected."

"What did you expect?"

"Actually, I have no idea." She laughed, and the skin around Luc's eyes crinkled in response.

"Everybody's happy," Ruby said.

"What?" Cate caught the yellow crayon as it rolled in her direction, sending it back across the table. "What do you mean?"

Ruby just shrugged and went back to drawing.

Trying to read a three-year-old's thoughts wasn't easy, but Cate had an inkling she knew what Ruby meant. Could she tell that her parents were getting along? That Cate had done her best to give up big chunks of control this week?

"Are you thinking what I'm thinking?" Luc lowered his voice. "That she's referring to us?"

"Kind of." Amazing that at her young age, Ruby still had a finger on the pulse of their relationship. Luc had been right about that. "I guess she could tell when you were making things so difficult."

Luc gave an exaggerated snort and then laughed, and her insides warmed like molten chocolate cake. It was nice finding their friendship footing again. This dinner was making Cate think they could get along as parents without letting anything romantic bloom between them.

The door opened behind her, and Luc's face lit up with recognition. A woman? Cate resisted turning, though it was as hard as waiting for cookies to cool when they came out of the oven. Scalding jealousy closed off her throat, not boding well for the pep talk she'd just given herself about her and Luc being *just friends*.

Luc waved whoever it was over, and Cate gave a stern talking-to to her overactive ovaries, which obviously thought since they'd helped create this man's child, that they somehow still had a claim to him.

But it wasn't a young, beautiful female who appeared, like her imagination had quickly conjured, but a man instead.

Maybe late twenties? Broad build. He wore jeans and a checked button-up shirt, the sleeves rolled up at his wrists. He didn't carry the rugged air of a cowboy like Luc did. He was more…fashionable. If that made any sense. Like he was wearing all the right stuff and didn't quite fit the mold.

"Cate, this is Gage, a good friend of mine. He ranches not too far from us."

They exchanged greetings, recognition tickling Cate's senses. She'd seen Gage before. At church, if she remembered correctly.

"Sit with us." Luc motioned to the table.

"I can't. Thanks, though. I just had a meeting, and I'm picking up something to go. Have a few things I need to do at home."

Scrutiny washed over Cate. Luc was always studying her, but strangely enough, it usually made her feel protected. Known. With Gage the vibe was different. More…distrusting. Not that she could blame him. She had done a number on Luc.

"I didn't know you ate this weird stuff."

Gage laughed at Luc's jab. "Still got a little of Denver

in me." They called out that his to-go order was ready, and Gage said goodbye. He left just as their food arrived.

Cate took a tentative bite of her meal, not expecting it to be…good. Not this far from the city. But she was dead wrong. It was every bit as mouthwatering as her favorite take-out place in Denver. Maybe better.

"Have I possibly seen Gage at church?"

"Yep. He goes to the same one as us."

"I thought I remembered him talking to Mackenzie. It made me wonder if maybe they were…"

Luc paused with a forkful of chicken hovering over his plate. "What?"

Could he seriously not infer the rest of her thoughts from her statement? Men. "If they were interested in each other."

"Mackenzie?" Luc scoffed. "No way. Gage has been a mess since his wife took off on him. Now ex-wife. I don't think so. Plus, the two of them wouldn't be a fit. Gage would need someone…softer than Kenzie."

What kind of guy *could* handle a woman with so much raw power oozing from her? Perhaps another superhero? "Does Mackenzie ever date anyone?"

"She did when we were younger, but he left town and she hasn't really dated since." Luc paused. Scrunched his nose. "At least, not that I know of. I'm not even sure she'd tell me. Though I'd probably have a clue. She can't really hide anything from me. It just…doesn't work that way between us."

"Twin connection is really a thing, huh?"

"It is for us."

"So do you think she's not over this guy she dated when she was younger?"

Now Luc's face wrinkled with something close to disgust. "I don't know. I don't really spend my days wondering about or analyzing my sister's love life. Either of them."

She laughed. Despite her original misgivings about saying yes to this outing, she was enjoying herself.

"Gage is a lawyer. Not many people start ranching later in life, but his uncle left him the land, and he moved there about a year and a half ago."

"Does he still practice law?"

"When he feels like it. He's done well with the ranch. Seems to like his new life."

"It's strange. I can tell he's kind, but at the same time, something's off. Melancholy or… I don't know what." She'd only met him for a minute, but Gage carried an obvious burden on his shoulders.

"That's the Nicole-effect." Luc finished his dish in record time—so he must not have hated it too much—swiping his mouth with his napkin. "Though come to think of it, I don't remember him being real happy before his ex-wife left, either."

Ruby and Luc started talking about one of the horses she'd befriended this week, and Cate half listened, her mind stuck on Luc's statement about Gage.

What had people said about her and Luc when they were together? Had they recognized happiness? Their relationship certainly had ups and downs, but at the core, Cate had been blissfully content.

The question she didn't have an answer to was whether Luc had felt the same.

Despite Cate's protest, Luc paid for dinner. They left the restaurant, the perfect nighttime temperature sliding along his skin. The evenings always cooled off in Colorado—one of the reasons he loved this blessed state.

"Want to walk a bit?" Luc nodded toward the five-and-dime store. "There's a counter full of candy—"

Ruby didn't allow him to finish. She grabbed his hand, attempting to drag him down the sidewalk. Luc chuckled and scooped her up. "Hang on. Your parents aren't as fast as you."

Your parents. Was he allowed to lump himself and Cate together like that? Sure, they were Ruby's parents, but that didn't make them a "them."

Cate walked beside him, the faint hint of her sweet perfume teasing his senses. Had she spritzed it on for him? Not a chance. Cate wanted nothing to do with him outside of Ruby, but the schoolboy in him had to tamp down the attraction buried for far too long.

Her hair was down in loose waves. She'd worn makeup—not that she needed it—and it brought the focus to her eyes and lips. He glanced away, uncomfortableness spreading through his body. Or more like too much interest that wasn't allowed.

At the five-and-dime, Luc propped the door open, letting Ruby down to walk in with Cate. She beelined for the counter that held an assortment of candies and sucker sticks, moving back and forth in front of the options.

Cate plucked a pack of colorful, small, round chocolates from the display. "This is what I always picked out as a kid. It was my favorite."

He palmed a pack of Big League Chew. "This was mine. Thought it would make me good at baseball. Didn't work."

She laughed. "Can't be good at everything."

Kind, lovable Cate had come out to play tonight, and

she was majorly weakening his resolve. If she kept this up, Luc couldn't be held accountable for his actions. Like kissing her until their painful history was a distant memory.

When Cate let her guard down, it was too easy to remember how good it had been. Too easy to forget how quickly she'd distrusted him.

"What are you thinking, Rubes?" Cate picked up a fruit-flavored package. "What about this?"

Their daughter's head shook, and Cate's eyes met his, amusement and exasperation playing tug-of-war. "She'll never decide without a time limit. We could be here all night."

Should he be concerned he was feeling fine with that option?

"One more minute, sweets. Then you need to choose."

Ruby finally picked out a watermelon sucker stick, and Luc paid for the three items, his and Cate's choices included. He thought she might try to argue—she was good at it when she wanted to be—but Cate just accepted the chocolate with a thank-you and a youthful grin.

He opened the watermelon stick for Ruby while Cate dug in her purse and then sprayed sanitizer on Ruby's hands. They walked back outside, meandering down the sidewalk as Ruby smacked on her sucker. Cate opened her chocolate and Luc dug into his gum. Not *quite* as good as he remembered from being a kid.

They reached the park on the west side of the street, and Ruby begged to stop and play. It wasn't much. Swings, monkey bars and a couple of slides, but at their yes—and Cate's condition that Ruby couldn't have her sucker while she played—she ran off.

Luc and Cate sat on the park bench facing the equipment, the setting sun reaching for the pine trees that lined the hills. A plastic baggie appeared from the amazing depths of Cate's bag, and she tucked the open end of Ruby's sucker inside so she could eat it later.

Her shoulder nudged into his. "Thank you for tonight. I needed it but didn't realize how much."

"That's what I'm here for. All-around good guy. Saving women from working too hard."

Her laughter went down as easy as jumping into the creek on a hot summer day.

"You know what I've always liked about you?"

"My devastatingly handsome looks?"

"No."

"Ouch, woman. Take a little time before you answer."

Her lips curved. "That you were okay with who you were. Didn't care what anyone thought. You always seemed so comfortable with yourself."

"Might have looked that way to you, but I left the ranch because I thought I needed to be somebody else and didn't want my life dictated to me. When I was away, I missed it and had a hard time admitting I'd been wrong. Then I met you and didn't want to leave you."

Luc could fill in Cate's next thoughts for her, because his were the same.

"But then I did leave."

She sighed. Twisted the package of chocolates closed. "I told you to."

"Yeah. Guess we were both part of that scenario."

"Guess we were." Cate set the chocolates between them as if erecting a barrier. "Luc, while Ruby and I are at the ranch, I really want us to stay focused on her. The two of us as a team. Like we discussed."

He must be inching into Cate's space. Making her uncomfortable with their friendship. It was so *her* to want everything tied up with a neat little bow. *You stay on your side of the line. I'll stay on mine.*

She liked her house and her life compartmentalized. Defined spaces. Luc understood it. He wanted the same thing when it came to Cate. Didn't want any of the boundaries blurred between them.

For once they agreed.

Luc still didn't understand why Cate had done things the way she had. Maybe he never would. But despite his pull toward her, nothing would ever work between them if Cate couldn't trust him. And while she'd changed over time just like he hopefully had, he didn't think that area of her life had undergone a major overhaul. Plus, Luc hadn't moved past what she'd done in keeping Ruby from him. He might be praying for a forgiving spirit, but that didn't mean it had instantly happened.

"I just think Ruby needs all of our focus on her. Having you in her life is a big change, and we need to be vigilant about helping her through all of this."

In his opinion, Ruby had adjusted lightning fast. Almost overnight. Accepting him as if she'd been watching and waiting for his arrival. Maybe she had been.

Even so, Cate didn't need to keep stating her case.

"I agree with you." Luc should be thankful they both felt the same way, but his gut sank to his boots.

Surprise flashed. "Really?"

"Of course. That's what these few weeks are all about. Getting to know Ruby. Making her comfortable with both of us in her life."

"Right." Cate nodded definitively and glanced away. Did he sense disappointment swirling from her direction? Doubtful. But if she did harbor at least a hint of re-

morse, that would make him feel better. Like he wasn't
alone in fighting off the magnetized pull between them.

"Look at us. In agreement again." Luc stretched his
arm across the back of the park bench, accidentally grazing Cate's shoulder as he did. "Who would have thought,
huh?"

Her eyes danced, lips matching his grin. "Who would
have thought?"

"Mom, Dad." Ruby paused at the top of the slide.
"Watch me!" She flew down, popped up at the bottom
and ran toward them. She pushed between their legs,
happiness palpable.

"Daddy, can I go on the campout this week? I want to
go really bad. Pretty, pretty please!"

Every Wednesday the ranch offered an overnight campout. It was a popular activity. Stars like most people had
never seen before. They had tents for those who wanted
them, but most chose to sleep near the fire.

Ruby had probably heard about it at Kids' Club.

Luc might be surprised by the request, but that didn't
mean it wasn't possible. He wasn't the one running it,
but they could still go. It would be a good memory for
the two of them to have together. Growing up, he'd done
it more times than he could count with his dad.

"I suppose we could—"

"Ruby," Cate interrupted. "Why don't you go swing
for a minute while I talk to your dad about it?"

"Okay." Ruby skipped back to the equipment, her two
twisted hair buns bouncing along with her.

"I thought we were parenting together," Cate snapped.

Had a cold front rolled in during the last minute? "We
are. I was *going* to tell her that you and I could talk
about it."

"Oh." She eased back against the bench, her exhalation uneven.

"But if she wants to go, I don't see why she can't. I'm happy to take her. I'll keep her safe and bring her back if anything goes wrong or she doesn't want to stay. There's no danger in it."

"No danger?" Large eyes landed on him, sparking with the first hints of orange sunset. "Sleeping in the middle of nowhere with mountain lions and snakes and bears and who knows what else? She's not even four years old!" The last sentence came out in short, angry bursts.

Luc moved his arm back to his lap, swallowing a bark of laughter at Cate's overactive imagination. As if the animals she mentioned were prowling around the campfire while everyone slept. But then exasperation ignited, quickly burning up the remaining oxygen in his lungs. Hadn't they already had this discussion?

"I thought you were actually letting me have a say in Ruby's life. Or was that just because you had a deadline and needed help? Was that all that was going on this week? I should have known better."

"That's not true." She crossed her arms, one hand pressing so tightly into the flesh of her biceps it caused the skin to turn white beneath her fingertips.

How long could they keep dancing to this song that never ended? "Cate, I promise, it's completely safe. If it wasn't, we wouldn't be able to do it with our guests every week. Our liability insurance would shoot through the roof if anything ever went wrong. But it doesn't. I'm not saying I can promise nothing will ever happen to her. Neither of us can do that, but I will take care of her."

"Watch me!" Ruby called from the swings. She pumped her legs, sending her sandals reaching for the sky.

They cheered her on, Luc welcoming the momentary interruption. "That's pretty amazing she can pump already. Did you teach her?"

"No. She figured it out at day care this summer. Luc, I just can't imagine why she needs to sleep outside or how that's a good idea in her condition."

And they were back at it. Cate was stuck in the rut of thinking of Ruby with a hole in her heart. But she wasn't that little girl anymore. "She doesn't have a heart condition now. It's fixed."

Memories of Luc's childhood flared to life like old VHS tapes. He'd had open-heart surgery at an older age, so he remembered quite a bit about that time. People tiptoeing around him. Rules and regulations. He'd always wanted to be doing what all the other kids were doing. And after recovering from surgery, that was exactly what he'd done. One night he'd heard his mom and dad discussing it, and he knew it had been hard on her. But she'd also learned to let go. Which, in his opinion, Cate definitely needed to do. Not that he could tell her that straight-out. He did *not* see that going well.

"She doesn't have to do the campout. But she wants to. I don't think it's a big deal, but you do. So what are we going to do about that?" *Let me guess. You're going to win.* Luc had never been more thankful for words to stay in his head and not leap out of his mouth.

"I don't know." Agitation radiated in the tense lines of Cate's body. "I've never had to do this before." She motioned between them. And he finally understood at least one of her reasons for keeping Ruby from him. So she could control everything. And now he was pushing all of those buttons, making her share parenting with him. She must hate every moment. Every time he had an opinion meant she didn't get her way.

"Since we can't agree, maybe we let the doctor decide?"

An impartial mediator. He resisted rolling his eyes. Did they really have to go that route? Overkill, in his opinion. But what other choice did they have? The two of them weren't going to agree on a decision. "Fine."

A chill followed the conversation, the warmth resonating between them only minutes before dropping by the tens, and not just because the sun had slipped behind the hills. Would have been smart of Luc not to expect massive changes in one week's time.

And in case any romantic thoughts of Cate fought for air, Luc would snuff them out with the heel of his boot.

Because she definitely didn't trust him yet.

Chapter Ten

"Don't forget your toothbrush," Cate called to Ruby on Wednesday evening.

Ruby popped into the cabin bathroom, her excitement over the campout causing her to skip and gladly comply with everything Cate asked of her.

Where exactly would her three-year-old be brushing her teeth in the middle of the woods? Three! If Ruby could hear her thoughts, she would quickly call out, *Almost four!* Either way, she was far too young for this. Cate's head shook, though no one was present to witness her strife.

She'd never camped growing up. That hadn't been high on her family's priority list. She wasn't sure what to send with Ruby, so she'd asked Luc for a list. It was surprisingly short.

On Monday Cate had called the doctor's office. She'd expected them to voice concern. To ask questions. But the nurse she'd spoken to had seemed surprised Cate had called at all. She'd gotten the all clear for Ruby to go on the campout that not one part of her had been wanting.

If only they'd said no. Then Cate wouldn't have had

to tell Luc he was right. And her daughter wouldn't be about to spend the night outside in the mountains.

Cate hated being the not-cool parent. The overprotective mama bear. This whole coparenting thing had her scrambling to figure out how to fit together the puzzle pieces of their new life. And to make matters worse, when she'd told Luc, instead of rubbing it in that she'd been wrong to worry and call the doctor, he'd just thanked her for making sure it was okay for Ruby.

The old Luc had been a fighter. Not one to back down easily. But God had changed him. Made it hard for Cate to keep her eyes on the prize—Ruby—and not on the man who kept stealing her attention despite her best efforts not to let that happen.

Ruby bounded over to Cate, handing off the toothbrush. Cate added it to her pink backpack just as a knock sounded at their cabin door.

"Come in," she called out, and Luc let himself in. A snarl came from the kitchen sink—a place Prim would never occupy back in their apartment. Cate was starting to think the cat could sense when Luc might be arriving, because that was the only time she'd crouch in that particular hiding place. It was almost as if she wanted to torment Luc. Cate was trying desperately not to find it funny when Prim surprised him. So far she'd failed miserably at that attempt.

"Good to see you, too, Prim." Luc's dry tone earned a giggle and an enthusiastic hug from Ruby.

Currently, Cate sided with Prim. She was as excited to see Luc as she would be to run smack-dab into a hornet's nest. Because while he was starring as the picture of maturity, she'd taken the lead role as big ol' baby. And had learned over the past few days, unfortunately, that she excelled at the part.

"Cate?" Luc stood in front of her, too close for comfort, the questioning pucker of his brow telling her it wasn't the first time he'd said her name. She was falling to pieces—trampled wildflowers plowed over by horse hooves—and Luc smelled like a forest and looked as tall and strong as a one-hundred-year-old pine.

Jerk.

"Nothing is going to go wrong." His hands landed on her shoulders, the dueling colors of his hazel eyes leaning more toward hickory in the early evening light. "Ruby will be fine. We have emergency measures in place for the guests on a normal week. We can use them, but we won't need to. If she wants to come home, I'll bring her back no matter what time it is. The campout is simple. We'll ride up to the campsite. Tell stories, sing songs. Then we'll sleep on the hard ground and love it while you sleep in a pillow-soft bed. Ruby will be back in the morning and might even need a nap tomorrow."

Why was he being so nice to her? Cate would almost prefer feisty Luc. Then she could reach for anger instead of having to deal with her real emotions. Those were much harder to process. Concern and fear and maybe even a little dread all rolled together. With a sprinkle of loneliness on top. Ruby had never spent a night away from Cate.

Or maybe the bigger problem was that Cate had never been away from Ruby for a night.

"I'm not going to convince you about this, am I?"

Her head swung back and forth.

Luc's hands dropped to his sides. "Then I'm going to

quit trying. You can come with us, you know. The offer still stands."

Cate had considered it, but one, she really didn't want to sleep on the ground, and two, she should be able to let her daughter spend a night camping out with her father. She had to practice letting go. Had to. "Thanks, but I'm good staying here. You two have fun."

"Okay, then, off we go. Rube-i-cube, give your mom a hug."

Ruby bounded over to her, and Cate held on until she squirmed to be released. Then Ruby ran out the front door, singing a made-up song about fires and stars and sleeping bags. She didn't seem *quite* as broken up about the whole thing as Cate.

"Her sleeping bag's by the door." Cate handed him Ruby's backpack and pointed to the pink sleeping bag, which would likely come back needing a good scrub. The one that Ruby had begged to include when they'd packed for the ranch. Cate had acquiesced, thinking it silly but not wanting to battle over something so small. And yet now here she was using it.

Luc snagged the bundle, and unexpected humor surfaced at the sight of such a rugged man holding so much pink.

"What caused that smile?" Luc glanced down, then back up, a full-fledged grin igniting. "I look good, huh?" He turned his chin to the side and struck a pose with supermodel flair.

She laughed. "You look funny." And heart-stopping. She wasn't going to tell him what she really thought. That watching him be a fantastic dad to Ruby was an attractive thing. That he was so good with their daughter that sometimes it made Cate ache all over—like a what-might-have-been flu.

"I'm going to assume by 'funny' you mean incredibly handsome."

"I'm going to assume you meant it when you said you'd bring her back if she freaks out. She's so little, Lucas."

Lucas. She'd always used his full name when she meant business. Recognition of that flashed in his eyes. They held on to hers, all kinds of emotion flooding the space between them.

"I promise. I'll take good care of her."

And then he was out the door and gone.

Luc probably thought that last statement was what had her so upset. So agitated. And absolutely, Ruby's safety was her highest concern. But running a close second was the thought of someone else taking care of Ruby. And doing a good job of it. Cate not being needed.

And therein lay the true problem. From the moment Luc entered their lives, Cate had begun losing Ruby bit by bit. And tonight another chunk of their relationship was being torn away. Built into something new.

Prim jumped down to the floor and sat at Cate's feet, her look questioning. Tears formed as Cate scooped her up, rubbing a hand along her spine.

"He doesn't understand."

Prim's head angled to one side as if to say, *Then why don't you tell him?*

Not only was Cate talking to her pet, she was imagining the animal—or her conscience—answering her. A habit she didn't want to admit was commonplace.

Cate deposited Prim on the floor, and the cat immediately went to lie down in the patch of remaining sunlight by the back window.

"We have a night to ourselves. What should we do, Prim?"

Strangely enough, no answer.

Cate had just finished a big deadline, but more work awaited. Always. She could use the alone time tonight to get ahead. And if she focused on a project, then maybe she wouldn't be consumed by the image of Ruby sleeping out in the open with mountain lions prowling about, their golden-green eyes glowing in the darkness.

A knock sounded. Could something be wrong already? Cate hurried to answer, practically ripping the door off the hinges with her herculean effort.

Emma stood on the step, holding the screen door open. "Hey, what are you doing tonight? I was thinking about making a frozen pizza and watching a chick flick. And I know Luc's taking Ruby on the campout." Her free hand rested on the hip of her peach shorts that were paired with a simple gray T-shirt. When she worked with the kids and horses, Emma wore jeans and boots, but otherwise, she was often casual in cutoffs and flip-flops. "No pressure if you just want a night to yourself. I know you never get that, either."

Warmth cocooned Cate at the unexpected offer. "Can you do that? Make a pizza and not eat with the remaining guests in the dining hall?"

"Yep." Emma beamed. "Dinner is covered. I'm not in charge tonight. You in?"

Cate looked toward the bedroom as if she could see her computer through the wall, waiting for her. She was always so responsible. Had to be. But with the money she'd saved eating here and not paying for day care, and the check from Luc, things weren't as tight for once. She could breathe. And maybe that was exactly what she needed to do. For once in her young life, work could wait.

"I'm in."

A charcoal backdrop, tips of pine trees reaching for the stars, a deep, full breath filling Luc's lungs with the taste of campfire and crisp mountain air…and best of all, his daughter right beside him.

It didn't get better than this.

They'd roasted marshmallows and sang along while the talented Kohl played his guitar. The kids had run around earlier, playing tag, chasing each other with giggles and flashlights until parents had started calling for them to snuggle into their sleeping bags.

Ruby had spent all of her energy and now sat beside him, eyes glazed as she watched the flames dance.

"Tired?"

Her head shook, fast and furious, denial at its best.

"I think maybe we should just rest in our sleeping bags. You don't have to sleep yet." Though he imagined she would conk out once her head hit the small travel pillow.

A sheen of moisture joined the orange reflecting in the brown pools of her eyes. Luc snuggled her onto his lap, and she sat back against his chest, facing the fire.

"You okay?"

She glanced across the fire to where the family of kiddos she'd been playing with were settling down for the night. "My friends had to go to sleep." Her *r* sound switched into a *w*, and Luc pressed down on a grin. When she was tired, her words got groggy, too. "How come Mommy didn't come?"

A question Luc wouldn't mind the answer to. But he

could guess. "I think she might not want to sleep outside on the hard ground. Isn't she a weirdo?"

Ruby giggled. Nodded and grew serious again. "I miss Mommy."

"If you need to go home, we can do that. You don't have to stay all night. There's nothing wrong with wanting your mom."

She twisted into his shoulder. Finally, she spoke. "No. I stay."

He tucked a finger under her chin, tipping her eyes up to meet his. He had to know she meant it. Not one part of him wanted her to do this if she was frightened. It wasn't worth it. They could come back and do it a different week or month or year.

"Are you sure? Because we can go home easily. It's not a big deal."

"Are you gonna sleep right by me?" Ruby's eyes were big and beautiful. So trusting. Their message stole the air from his lungs.

"Definitely." She might be asking about their current situation, but in Luc's mind, it was a lifetime commitment to be there for her wrapped up in that answer.

"Okay, good." Ruby climbed off his lap and into her sleeping bag, and though most of the adults weren't settling in yet, Luc took off his boots and zipped into his so he was near her.

Quiet voices and guitar strings created a lullaby with the crickets. It wasn't long before Ruby's lashes rested on her cheeks, casting shadows in the flickering light.

Beautiful girl. Inside and out. Luc stared up at the bright, endless stars, his mind full.

You missed so much of her life.

Yes, but Cate didn't have to tell me about her at all. And she did.

The two camps warred, agitation stealing his immense peace from only a moment before.

I don't want to do this anymore, God. I don't want to live this way. I have to let go of the choice Cate made. Help me.

He'd been praying along those lines for weeks, but tonight he meant it. Luc could take either fork in the road in front of him, and he knew which one he didn't want: bitterness.

What would it have been like if Cate had told him about Ruby right away? He would never know the answer to that question. But he did realize things wouldn't have been perfect. His behavior and attitude at twenty years old would likely have equaled a pile of manure. Especially because he didn't have a moral compass back then to direct him. Now God was his guide.

Maybe it had all worked out for the best that he hadn't been a part of Ruby's life until this summer. Either way, there was nothing he could do about it now. And he was tired of holding on to self-righteous anger.

It was time to release all of it and move forward.

Under an expanse of sky that reminded him just how great and infinite God's love was, his prayers were finally being answered. He was shedding scars and leaving smooth skin in their place.

Luc shifted to study Ruby's sleeping silhouette. *Me and your mom...we're going to be okay. The three of us will be just fine. No need to worry your pretty little head about anything other than what horse you want to ride this week. Or if you can teach Molly a new trick.*

She smiled while still in peaceful slumber. Dreaming

of s'mores? Or something else? Luc had been surprised by how well she'd handled the evening so far. Ruby just… fit. With him. At the ranch. The campout. She was a part of the tapestry of this land.

He'd loved watching her play tonight. Her infectious joy. The sense of adventure and high spirits that permeated her life.

Cate had done a really good job raising her.

And for once he wasn't irritated at the thought.

Finally! Luc blinked back unexpected moisture and stifled the desire to give a loud, whooping cheer. The rest of the guests likely wouldn't appreciate him waking the children or understand his happy relief at how amazing this change in him felt.

In the morning Luc woke with the scent of smoke in his nostrils and he assumed hair and clothes, one particularly annoying rock biting into his lower back, one sweet girl curled up in the sleeping bag next to him. When Ruby had whimpered during the night—only once—he'd looped an arm over her bag and she'd snuggled into him. And then she'd gone right back to sleep.

Luc had stayed awake for a chunk of time to make sure she was okay, drifting off after realizing she was.

Now the smell of coffee tempted him to brave the crisp mountain air and snag a cup. One of the wranglers had brewed it and put out the pastries that would make for a simple breakfast before the ride back down. Then if the guests wanted to grab a full breakfast with some protein back at the lodge, they could. Not everyone participated in the campout, so Joe would still have a full meal set up and ready to go.

Ruby turned onto her back, eyelids still closed, and he leaned over, close to her ear. "You did it," he whispered.

Her eyes popped open, a mega grin overtaking her tiny face. "I was a big girl."

"You were a very big girl."

Luc wouldn't have minded taking Ruby home last night, but he couldn't deny he was proud of her for pulling through.

During the ride back to the ranch, Luc felt lighter than on the way up. As though he'd left something heavy and dark up on that hill. And he had, in a way. He'd finally buried the thought that he would have handled things better than Cate. That he would have done the right thing when she didn't. The truth was, he didn't have a clue what he would have done as the person he was back then.

"I'm a-cited to see Mommy." Ruby's version of *excited* was one of his favorite scrambled words she used. No one corrected her. In fact, he'd taken to using it himself at times.

Me, too. The thought shocked him, and his shoulders straightened in response.

"She'll be so happy to see you," he answered Ruby, mind jumbled.

He couldn't *want* to see Cate, could he? Couldn't have missed her like Ruby did. That had to be a misfire in his brain. One that didn't even need addressing. Besides the fact that he'd just reached the point of forgiveness with her, Cate wanted nothing to do with him outside of his role as Ruby's father. She'd made that very clear the night they'd had dinner and watched Ruby at the playground.

Their focus was to be on their daughter, not them. And Luc agreed with her then and now.

So he needed to rein in his thoughts. They had absolutely no business getting so far off track.

Chapter Eleven

Cate opened the cabin door before Luc even had a chance to knock.

She scooped Ruby up as if she hadn't seen her for weeks, squeezing her tight. Luc set her things just inside the door. No doubt clean Cate would have everything put away in a matter of minutes after he left. She ran a tight ship.

Cate looked and smelled fresh from the shower, her hair still damp. She wore white shorts and an army-green sleeveless shirt today, her feet bare. Considering he and Ruby had slept in their clothes next to a campfire, Luc shouldn't even be allowed in the same room with something as pristine as the woman in front of him.

"So how was it?" She moved to the couch and sat, Ruby snuggled against her.

"It went great. She did amazing. One small moment of homesickness, but when I asked if she wanted to come back early, she said no. So we stayed." He stretched his arms behind him, trying to work out the pesky new kinks in his back. Luc had led the campout a number of times when he'd been in high school and didn't remember having any issues. Guess those days were over.

"What did you think, sweets?"

She's questioning Ruby, not you. He gave himself a stern warning, just in case any of his rampant thoughts hadn't shaken off him on the trail.

"It was so fun, Mommy. We ate marshmallows. Lots of 'em. I think I had ten."

An accusing look swung over Ruby's head, hitting Luc square between the eyes. He raised his hands in defense. "It wasn't that many."

"And then we sang songs and somebody played the brown thingy."

"Guitar," Luc filled in.

"I'm so glad you're back." Cate ran her hand over Ruby's forehead in a comforting gesture Luc wouldn't mind experiencing himself.

"We should get you cleaned up. I'll start a bath for you."

"But I don't want a bath!" Ruby wailed at a volume too loud to come from such a small body. She'd thrown a hissy fit once or twice since she'd arrived at the ranch—mostly in attempts to get her own way—but nothing that sounded remotely like this.

"But you love baths. We'll get out all of your toys. I'll even get you some kitchen stuff to play with in the tub."

Despite Cate's soothing, the tornado-siren coming from Ruby increased in magnitude.

"Don't. Want. To." Ruby squirmed in Cate's arms, fighting to break free.

"Okay, okay, we can do a bath later. Calm down." Cate tried that forehead soothing thing again. Didn't work this time. Like trying to pet a writhing shark. "She's exhausted." Her eyes met Luc's, something close to blame residing there.

"I'm sorry."

"It's not your fault. This isn't the only time she's had a meltdown. They're more common than not when she's tired. You can go, if you need to."

And leave Cate to handle the temper tantrum on her own? No way. Luc crossed over to them. Without asking permission, he plucked Ruby from Cate's arms. Her body went stiff as a board. He held her against him anyway, her head near his shoulder. Though of course she didn't loosen a muscle to let it rest.

"We had a fun time, didn't we, Rubes? Let's not cry too much or your mom will never let you go again." He strode from one end of the small living room to the other, needing to do something. He had to prove to Cate—and himself—that she wasn't the only one who could handle a cry-fest. If Ruby would be going back and forth between them in the future, it mattered that he could take care of her if she flew off the handle. Luc kept talking, and eventually Ruby's cry quieted. He listed the fun things they'd done at the campout. He repeated himself and went in circles, likely wearing a path in the wood floor. Sometime during his verbal explosion, Ruby's head had drooped to his shoulder.

"Luc." Cate touched his arm, and the warmth stopped him in his tracks. "She's asleep." Cate motioned to Ruby's face, which Luc couldn't see because she was facing away from him. "Do you want to lay her in bed?"

He nodded. After depositing her on top of the bedspread, Luc covered her with an extra blanket. Ruby rolled over and snuggled in, her eyes remaining closed.

Only then did he allow himself a huge breath of relief.

Amazing that she could still be so stinking lovable after a fit of those proportions. He grinned, head shaking, and walked back into the living room to find that Cate had taken over his pacing.

A mixture of exhaustion and frustration eased along his spine. Was she going to lose it on him? Technically, Ruby's meltdown was his fault. He'd taken her on the campout. He was the one who hadn't thought it would be a big deal.

The idea of slipping out of the cabin tempted him. He teetered with indecisiveness near the end of the couch, then walked around the coffee table and dropped to the cushions. If he was in trouble, he might as well get it over with.

"Guess I shouldn't have taken her."

Cate's arms crossed in a protective barrier. "It's not about that."

Then what had her so agitated? Was it something with work? Or another part of her life?

"What did you do last night?" Knowing Cate, she'd been glued to her computer screen all evening.

"Emma and I shared a pizza and watched a movie." She stopped at the back cabin window, staring out as if she'd caught a pair of squirrels dancing together.

"That's good." His little sister had the best heart. It always made him concerned that she'd get taken advantage of. She was missing the edges Mackenzie had. Ones that protected. He'd have to tell Emma thank you, though he knew she'd say she liked Cate and had hung out because she wanted to, not out of any sense of responsibility.

"So if it's not about Ruby's fit, and it's not something bad that happened last night, what has you so hot and bothered?"

Her head jerked in his direction. "Me? Nothing."

He attempted to cover his bark of laughter with a cough. She didn't react. Didn't say anything at all.

Luc pushed up from the couch and crossed over to her, stopping too close for comfort, hoping invading her space might snap her out of this daze. "I smell like a campfire."

She still faced the window, arms in a protective self-hug. "You're fine. You always smell a little like the outdoors."

Huh. Interesting. Curiosity wrangled his tongue. "Is that a good thing?"

Just when he didn't think he'd get an answer, she nodded. "It is. You wouldn't be you without it." That might be one of the nicer things she'd said to him.

Her eyes were glossy. Worn. Could she be sick?

"Did you sleep at all last night?"

"Off and on. Better than I expected to, actually."

"She really didn't cry like that at the campout, Cate. She was a little sad before bed. I offered to take her home and she wanted to stay. She did great, if that's what you're worried about—"

"It's not!" Moisture escaped, cascading down her cheeks, forming a line like baby ducks following their mama.

What was he supposed to do? Leave? Stay? Was she mad at him?

She swiped the tears away quickly, but new ones kept appearing. "I'm not upset thinking that it didn't go well. I'm upset thinking that it did." Her wail was painful and oddly reminiscent of Ruby's. What in the world did that mean? He didn't have a clue, but he did hate seeing Cate like this. So he did the only thing he could think of. What he'd just done with their daughter.

He held her.

Just like Ruby, she stiffened. Not deterred, Luc tucked her against his chest and tightened his arms around her, communicating that he didn't plan to let go anytime soon. After a second of hesitation, her hands fisted his shirt, not to push him away, but more like she was holding on. She sobbed into his T-shirt while he cradled her, all the while thinking that if Cate wasn't losing half the moisture in her body in tears, this wouldn't be the worst place in the world to be.

Catherine Malory had survived being pregnant on her own and raising their daughter for three—almost four—years by herself. But all it took was a month of Luc back in her life for her to break down in a heap and use him as her crash pad.

And the worst part was she didn't want to tell him why.

Somewhere during her episode, Luc had started rubbing her back in a comforting circular motion. He felt good. All warm and strong. A tower the strongest gust of wind couldn't budge.

Only he was the problem. So how could she explain that to him?

Her tears had stopped spilling a few minutes ago. At this point Cate was just prolonging being tucked against Luc's chest. But who could blame her? It was nice in this little cocoon. Safe from the world and any troubles. From her feelings, which had bubbled up too fast for her to shove them down like she normally did.

After one deep breath—and secret inhalation of Luc's somehow still addictive scent—Cate forced herself to peel away from him. Her body complained at the rush of cool that replaced Luc's hold.

He grabbed the tissue box, offering it to her.

"Thanks." She took one, attempting to make less of a mess out of what was sure to be a red, splotchy face. "Sorry about all of that. And the souvenir." She pointed to his shirt, where she'd left a wet circle of tears behind like a drooling baby. Classy.

Luc glanced down, then shrugged. "It's okay." A grin played with his features. "If it wasn't for the crying part, I would have been just fine with the rest of it."

Heat inflamed her face at the implication of his words. Had he meant them? Would he take them back? She didn't want him to.

She'd missed being someone's person. Missed Luc and the way he'd always been such a support to her. Her biggest fan. But Cate couldn't afford to feel that way about him again. He was already taking over too much of her life in the form of Ruby. She couldn't let herself fall this time. Not when Ruby's happiness was at stake.

When her parents had attempted getting back together after the divorce and it hadn't worked, it had been even more painful than the first time for Cate. And she refused to do anything of the sort to Ruby.

"Do you want to talk about what's wrong?"

"No." Cate shook her head in double answer.

"Can you at least tell me what you meant when you said you were upset the campout went well?"

He'd heard that? How was she going to explain?

Cate wanted to send Luc home. To buy herself a few days to regroup and sort out the emotions that had tumbled so out of control today. But if she did, things would stay the same, and she'd live in constant fear of losing Ruby. She couldn't continue functioning under the weight of this dread. It was killing her slowly.

She moved to the couch and sat. Luc followed, leaving a ruler length of space between them. How could he be too far away and too close all at the same time?

"I told you about my parents' divorce when I was a little girl."

Luc nodded.

"I shared pieces of it with you, but not all of it." He remained silent, but his eyes were on her in a way that told her he was listening. "During the divorce, things got rough. They seemed to almost enjoy fighting each other. Neither wanted to give in. It didn't matter what was at stake—they both put up a fight. Even when it came to me."

Cate struggled to even out her breathing. She hated talking about this. "They couldn't agree on custody. Both of them bad-mouthed each other to me, trying to sway me to their side. It was awful. Finally, the judge asked me where I wanted to go. Who I wanted to live with." She plowed ahead, knowing if she quit talking she'd never find the courage to finish. "I was ten years old and they made me choose between them."

Luc blinked, a sheen of moisture evidence of his sympathy. "What did you do?" His voice was low, quiet and filled with pain that matched the stabbing in her chest.

"I picked both of them. How was I supposed to decide something like that? I went back and forth, and they shared custody. I didn't know what else to do. I wanted to please everybody and didn't realize until much later that I couldn't."

Luc covered the space between them, his jean-clad leg landing snug against her thigh as he snaked an arm out and tucked her into the nook of his shoulder. Despite her misgivings and the warning sirens blaring in her mind—products of all the *why she shouldn't be doing this* reasons she'd just rehashed—Cate didn't fight him. Just one more time she'd let it slide. Accept the comfort he offered. The future wouldn't be filled with moments like this, so was it so wrong to enjoy it? To let herself believe she didn't have to do life alone?

Besides, it would be easier to say this next part without looking at him.

"I don't want to fight with you over Ruby." She felt him tense and continued before she lost her nerve. "That's why I didn't tell you about her when I found out I was pregnant. Yes, it was our argument and the fact that you never contacted me again. But it was also my fear."

Cate straightened and met the questions written on Luc's face. "I didn't want to lose her, and I was petrified that we'd end up fighting. That we'd do to her what my parents did to me—focusing on each other and not on her. And now that we're here, and you two are bonding, I'm worried that when we leave to go back to Denver, you'll file for custody and we'll end up arguing over her. I *will* share her with you. I promise. We don't have to go through the court system. I know we can figure it out." Her voice dropped to a pleading whisper. "But please don't try to rip her away from me, because then we will end up like my parents. And I don't want to do that to Ruby. I don't want her to feel like I did as a kid. I was a rope in my parents' hands, constantly pulled in one direction and then the other. But I never felt loved. Noticed. If anything, their fighting made me feel completely alone."

She sat on her hands to keep from answering the call of her fingernails, which were begging for her to indulge in old habits. "Seeing that the campout went well... I mean, yes, she had a meltdown after, but she does that after any late night. It wasn't you. You handled her so well when you got back here. It's like I'm not needed. And that frightens me."

Could she leave one thought in her head instead of letting them all fall out at once? Luc was going to think she was nuts and then she really would lose Ruby.

Cate's shoulders rose and fell as she tried to calm her racing nerves. She'd just dumped a lot on Luc. Some she hadn't planned to say. What would he do with all of it?

Warm, soft empathy radiated from his handsome face, the scruff from last night a shadow against his cheeks and chin. "Cate, I'm sorry about your parents. They shouldn't have done that to you." He swallowed, Adam's apple bobbing. "I can't imagine you as such a young girl having to make a decision like that…" His head shook. "And Ruby needs you. Always. There's no doubt about that. Even I need you to parent with me. I can't do this alone. And we're not going to do what your folks did. We're not them. You're nothing like your selfish parents. And I'd like to think that I'm not, either."

"You're not. That's why I'm asking for this. I get that it's a little unorthodox, but I just—"

"This is what you need to feel safe. To know that Ruby is protected and loved."

She nodded.

"Of course I want Ruby in my life, but I wouldn't fight with you at her expense. We'll figure it out together. I would never try to take her from you."

Relief trickled through her limbs, relaxing cranky, tense muscles. "Even after what I did to you? Why not?" She wanted to slap herself for the question and the panic it ignited in her, but at the same time, she needed to know.

Needed to get all of this out now so that she could finally be free of this anxiety.

"Because that wouldn't be good or healthy for her. I don't ever want her to doubt how much we love her. Plus… I've forgiven you."

"What? When?" Cate whispered, afraid she'd heard wrong. Afraid she'd heard right and she would be missing one of the strongest walls that stood between her and Luc. She wanted that barrier between them. To know that he'd never harbor feelings for her again. That he could never love her. Because if there was a chance he could again…how would she resist?

Cate couldn't let her heart make another botched attempt at something that would break it forever.

"It was actually at the campout. I've been praying about it since I found out Ruby was mine, but last night that stronghold finally broke free. You not telling me about her is over and done, and I want to move forward."

Surprise and disbelief registered at the same time. "But I don't deserve your forgiveness." Not after what she'd done.

The skin around Luc's eyes crinkled. "That's exactly what grace is all about."

Cate had experienced mercy when she'd become a Christian and truly understood for the first time that God loved her, inside and out. The good and the bad. But never did she think that the human being who would show her that kind of forgiveness on earth would be Luc.

The idea of trusting him with Ruby and the impact he could have on all of their lives…it was still scary. But she was willing to take a step in that direction.

And that was a first for her.

Chapter Twelve

Luc was supposed to be working. Instead, he was fighting constant thoughts about Cate. Like, what was she doing right now? Was she thinking about him? And then there was his personal favorite: What would it be like to wrap her in his arms and steal a kiss?

Like he used to have permission to do. *Used to* being the key phrase Luc needed to pound through his thick skull.

Ever since their conversation last week when Cate had opened up to him about Ruby and her childhood—her reasons why she'd done what she'd done—he'd had a hard time concentrating on anything *but* her.

Cate telling him didn't have anything to do with their relationship—it had been about protecting Ruby—but it was getting harder for Luc to only focus on their daughter. He'd begun to think of himself, Cate and Ruby as a family. And of the two of them as permanent fixtures at the ranch.

Not his most brilliant idea since none of those were viable options. In two short days they would head back to Denver. Luc kept reminding himself that was a good thing. He and Cate were better as parents and friends. A large chunk of him wanted more…okay, all of him. But he still wasn't sure Cate fully trusted him—about what had happened between them in the past, or what could happen in the future.

And he wasn't going down that road if she couldn't. Because despite what she might think, he was trustworthy. And he wanted someone who knew that down to their bone marrow. Who harbored no doubts.

A knock sounded on Luc's office door, and Gage poked his head inside. "Hey."

"Hey, man." Luc leaned forward and propped elbows on the desk. "I needed an excuse to quit for the day and here you are."

"At your service." Gage dropped a wedge of papers on the desk. "Brought you something."

"What is it?"

"Info about petitioning for allocation of parental responsibilities. The woman I asked got back to me about a week ago, and I kept forgetting to drop these off for you. Sorry for the delay. Of course I'll help if you decide to file yourself."

Ice slithered through Luc's veins. He'd shelved the conversation he'd had with Gage about custody, forgetting they'd even talked about it. At the time he'd been furious and still in shock.

It would not be a good thing for Cate to know about that initial exchange or these papers. Not after what she'd told him last week.

"I spaced that we'd even discussed this." Luc pushed the papers a few inches in Gage's direction as if they were a contagious disease, wanting to scrub his hands clean after touching them. Or use some of Cate's always-ready hand sanitizer. Like she made Ruby do after handling pretty much…anything. "I'm actually not going to file for custody. Cate and I are going to work things out between us."

Luc had gone over and over the same question in his mind since Cate had opened up to him: Could he trust Cate with his daughter? His gut said yes. And after prayer, that answer hadn't changed.

Gage's jaw slacked, and he rubbed a hand across it, confusion evident.

"I'm sorry your friend did all of that work and I'm not going to use it. I can pay for it. Hate to waste anyone's time."

Dropping to a seat on the futon, Gage leaned forward, resting elbows on his knees. "I'm not worried about that. It's just…what changed your mind?"

"Cate."

"Did she tell you not to file? Because I don't think that's a good idea. You don't know what she'll do when she leaves here with Ruby, and—"

"I do know." Luc swallowed a rush of frustration. Gage was only trying to help. But sometimes the bitterness of what he'd been through with his ex-wife jaded his perception of the whole world. "We talked about it. We're going to work everything out. There's no need for paperwork or the court."

"But how can you just trust her?"

"Because I'm choosing to." And Luc wanted the same respect from her. He wished she would have trusted him when he'd denied seeing anyone else like she'd accused him of. Maybe they wouldn't be in this predicament now if she had. If there was anything he understood, it was the need to be believed.

"Does that seem like a good idea?"

"It's the one I'm sticking to." Luc didn't tell Gage about Cate's childhood. That was hers. Personal. He imagined it had been hard for her to share it with him, and he was thankful she had. Ever since their talk, he'd been much more at peace, knowing she would make sure Ruby stayed in his life, too.

"I'm sure you're silently calling me a cynic right now, but shouldn't you rethink this? As your lawyer—"

"You're not my lawyer. You're my friend."

"Okay, then, as your friend—"

Luc laughed. Shook his head. "There's no one I'd rather have in my corner than you." He picked up the papers and held them out to Gage. "But I don't need this info. And you're just going to have to be okay with that."

Gage groaned. "Fine. I'll let it go."

"Take these." Luc waved the stack.

"Keep 'em. Maybe something will change in that hard-headed noggin of yours and you'll come around to the logical side again."

Luc dropped the incriminating evidence back to his desk with amusement.

The door opened without a warning knock, and Ruby flew into his office. "Daddy!"

He moved around the desk and swept her up. "Hey, Rube-i-cube." He squeezed her in a hug, the stress of the conversation with Gage quickly taking a hike. "Do you remember Daddy's friend Mr. Gage?"

Gage stood, greeting Ruby, asking her about her time at the ranch and receiving answers about how much she liked the horses and the people and even her bedroom. Luc's chest swelled with pride. She was such a sweet girl.

Willing to talk to anyone. And the fact that she loved the ranch as much as he did didn't hurt, either.

"Ruby?" Cate's voice echoed down the hall, and Luc swallowed a flash of panic. The paperwork.

He sat on the edge of the desk, praying he covered the sheets. "We're in here."

Cate entered his office. "Sorry. I started talking to Emma, and Ruby just took off to find you." The woman was an irresistible bit of sunshine in a bright yellow shirt, navy capris and brown leather sandals.

He strangled the urge to stand up. "What are you girls up to?"

Cate's head tilted, confusion evident. "We came over to eat. It's dinnertime."

"Right." Luc glanced at the wooden clock on the wall. "Gage was here, and I lost track of time."

"Okay." Cate stretched out the *ay*, implying he wasn't doing a great job of acting normal. She greeted Gage, and the two of them chatted while he tried to figure out how to get Cate out of his office without her seeing the stack on his desk.

"Gage, you're welcome to stay for dinner," Luc offered. "It's rib night." And then the square dance would round out the evening. Though thankfully Luc wasn't in charge of that. No one wanted to see his lack of rhythm on a dance floor.

"How can I say no to that?"

"Good. Glad you're staying, Gage." Cate quirked a thin eyebrow in Luc's direction. "Should we head to the dining room?"

He fought every instinct in his body screaming for him to push off the desk. He already felt awkward being the only one in the room *not* standing.

"After you." Luc lightly patted Ruby on the behind, and she grabbed Cate's hand, pulling her toward the door.

"Come on, Mommy. I'm hungry." Good girl.

He waited for Gage to follow, then quickly turned, shoving the papers his friend had delivered to the bottom of his to-do pile. Not a permanent fix, but it would get them out of sight for the moment. He'd have to come back later and shred the evidence.

He hurried to catch up with them, thanking the good Lord above Cate hadn't spied that information. The last thing he needed was to backtrack on all the progress they'd made and how far they'd come in their relationship. He wasn't sure they'd ever recover from what he'd once considered.

A small group lingered after devouring Joe's amazing fall-off-the-bone ribs, now sipping decaf coffee and overindulging in banana pudding cupcakes. Cate had quickly gotten used to the abundance of baked goods that came from Joe's skilled hands. Good thing she didn't have much longer to stay at the ranch, or she'd have to take up running or trailing after Mackenzie in order not to pack on extra pounds.

The hum of conversation around the table caused a sense of peace in her. Tonight's dinner had been easy. Even with Gage and Mackenzie. Were they warming up to her? Gage had been rather distant with her previously, but tonight he'd made more of an effort to engage her in conversation.

Cate couldn't shake the thought that she was fitting in with this crew. And liking it. Just as she and Ruby were gearing up to move back to Denver—they planned to pack up the car on Sunday—she'd found her footing.

But it was still good news for the future, because while she might not be living here, she would be involved in Luc's life and he in hers. That was what coparenting was all about.

If only the thought of being separated from Luc didn't smart like an art critique in college. Those days in school were the worst—her hard work up for everyone to criticize. She'd agonized over her projects for days beforehand and was currently fighting that same sense of dread.

But why? This was what she'd planned for all along. What she wanted. For her and Luc to be able to function as single parents who put their daughter's needs above their own. Wasn't it?

Luc's shoulder nudged hers. "You okay?"

His quiet question was for her ears only. Intimate. Goose bumps spread along her arms. "I'm good." Perhaps too much so.

But really, she should be the one asking him that question. He'd been jumpy in his office earlier. But at dinner he'd seemed fine.

Strange.

Ruby had finished her cupcake and now scooted around the table behind Luc, throwing her arms around his neck. He latched on, lifting her off the ground and causing a squeal of delight. In a split second he'd pulled her to his lap. She perched on her knees and held his face in her hands to procure his attention.

"Daddy, I want to go to the church thingy tomorrow night. There's going to be bouncy houses and games and cotton candy."

Cate vaguely recalled the pastor talking about the kickoff party for Wednesday night church clubs happening tomorrow evening—Saturday. But how had Ruby remembered?

"Sorry." Emma winced. "My fault. I'm taking my friend's boys tomorrow night, and we were talking about it." She motioned between her, Mackenzie and Gage.

Cate waved off Emma's concern, turning back to Ruby. "Sweets, we're not going to be here for Wednesday night church in the fall. Remember? We'll be back at our apartment in Denver by then."

Ruby's lower lip protruded. "I know, Mommy, but I want to go anyway. Pastor said everyone could go!" She must have been listening in church last week, too. Ruby picked up on more than Cate gave her credit for.

"I guess I don't mind. What do you think?" Cate asked Luc. "I can take her if you can't go."

"I don't have anything going on. I'm willing."

Guests left on Saturday mornings, and Luc usually took the day off after they were gone. At least he had since she and Ruby had been here.

"Yay!" Ruby jumped down from Luc's lap, spinning in circles of excitement behind them.

A night with just the three of them? It sounded...nice. Too nice. When it made her heart dance a jig with Ruby, Cate slammed the lid on her unacceptable reaction.

Those thoughts needed to remain tucked away, right where they belonged.

Tomorrow night would be a good way to end their time at the ranch and create a bridge to the next chapter in their story. To go back to the life she had with Ruby.

Messing everything up by allowing romantic thoughts about her and Luc to surface wasn't an option. Not when things were going so well between them.

It was just...ever since she'd confessed her fears to

Luc, she'd been drawn to him like a bug to one of those
zapper lights. A choice that could ultimately end in its
demise. She kept trying to be logical and do what was
best for Ruby. But the temptation to lean into Luc, to let
herself inch in his direction, body and soul, was hard
to fight.

A whiff of Luc's pine/grass/fresh mountain air scent
spiraled her way, causing her to inhale slowly. To latch
on to the small piece of him, knowing she couldn't keep
him. But if things were different? If she could protect
Ruby and have Luc? She'd let her head rest on his strong,
capable shoulder. Slide her hand into his under the table
like a teen not wanting to get caught.

If there was a different choice, she'd hold on to him
and never let go.

It's not a date.

Once again Cate reminded herself that being out with
Luc and Ruby did not a family make.

Even if she'd created a bit of trouble by wearing a red
sundress with black wedges. It was supposed to be casual.
Fun and flirty. If Luc's smoldering eyes when he'd shown
up at the cabin door to pick them up were any indica-
tion, she'd accomplished that last one with flying colors.

Numerous times on the way into town, he'd glanced
across the front seat of the truck and opened his mouth
as if to say something, then swallowed and stared straight
ahead.

Thankfully Ruby had jabbered from the back seat the
whole way into town.

And it wasn't helping matters that Luc wore a short-
sleeved plaid button-down, jeans and square-toed boots.
The man cleaned up well. He'd shaved, the faint smell

of lotion mingling with his typical scent in the cab of the truck.

They parked in the overflow parking—pretty much a field of run-down grass, weeds and dirt. Carnival-like sounds and the sugary-sweet aroma of cotton candy drifted across the summer night air as they got out.

"Can I have a treat?" Ruby's pleading caused her and Luc to share an amused look. They hadn't even taken a step yet.

"Maybe in a little bit," Cate answered.

"I agree with your mother," Luc added before Ruby could beg him for a different outcome. "The ground is kind of muddy from the rain. Probably should have dropped you girls off."

The downpour overnight had been hard and fast, drumming against the cabin roof. Luc snatched up Ruby, holding her on his left side. "I'll carry you over the bad part." She'd worn her pink sandals with a white sundress. One Cate would surely have to bleach by the end of the night. But when Ruby had requested to wear a dress so she "looked like Mom," Cate hadn't been able to refuse.

"Here." Luc held out his right hand to her.

What was she supposed to do with it?

"The ground's uneven. I'll just steady you until we're out of the lot."

She eyed her strappy wedges that peeked out below the midcalf hem of her sundress. "Guess I should have worn more logical shoes."

Though Cate had been feeling anything but. She and Ruby had enjoyed getting ready. Cate would like to think it was just because they were getting a night out. But one greedy glance at Luc told her otherwise.

"I'm not complaining." Luc's quip held a grin and more. A message she wasn't sure she should read.

She took his hand. What was a girl supposed to do? Raising a fuss about it would only make her feelings more known.

Once they made it across the overflow lot, Luc released her hand and plunked Ruby on the ground. The absence of his touch wove through her, a foreshadowing of the week to come.

Ruby spotted the red-and-blue bounce house and took off in a run. They followed.

She got in line, and within a few minutes she was romping with her new friends from church—two little girls whom she'd hit it off with in Sunday school.

Cate spotted Emma across the churchyard and waved. She walked toward them, holding the hands of two little boys, one a few inches taller than the other.

"Hey, guys. These two are my dates for the evening." Emma introduced them just as a cry came from inside the bounce house.

Didn't sound like Ruby, but Cate should probably check.

"I'll make sure Ruby's okay." Luc read her mind and strode across the grass. She stole a glance or three at his retreating back. Was there anything more attractive than Luc being a father? Cate didn't think so.

She snapped her attention back to Emma before she got caught. "What are your friends up to tonight? You never said."

"Date night. They were in desperate need and I had nothing going on, so I offered to bring the boys down here."

"You're the best. I could have used a friend like you when I first had Ruby."

"Well, you've got me now. Anytime you need anything, even in Denver, let me know."

"Thanks." That meant a lot. It was so Emma to do for everyone else and act like nothing made her happier. "Did you at least relax a little today?"

"Yep." Emma's peaches-and-cream complexion shone with contentment. "I went out to the hot springs for a bit and read a book. It was a good day." Her eyebrows wiggled. "By the way, you look beautiful tonight."

Heat singed Cate's cheeks. "I'm overdressed, aren't I?" Especially considering Emma wore black shorts and a T-shirt that said *I was country before country was cool* in yellow letters over gray. Coupled with charcoal Converse, she had irresistible down to a science. Funny that Emma never talked about dating. Never mentioned any guys she might be interested in. Cate wanted to ask, but the opportunity to probe had never presented itself.

"Not in the least. Your dress is perfect for a night out. And I'm sure my idiot brother hasn't said a thing about how gorgeous you look." Emma punctuated the sentence with a huff.

Cate laughed, neither confirming nor denying. Though they had been with Ruby. That might have been awkward if he had said something. Or maybe he hadn't noticed her at all and she'd only imagined his interest earlier.

Luc came back to them just as the boys lost their patience and began clambering to go in the bouncy house.

"Ruby's fine. It was one of the other kids."

"You guys should leave Ruby with me for a bit," Emma offered. "Go walk around town. I'll be here anyway. No reason we all have to stay."

She and Luc most definitely did not need alone time. And Cate loved being near Ruby. Always had. Being with Luc minus the buffer of Ruby *did* sound like a date.

"I guess we could." Luc's questioning gaze landed on Cate. "What do you think?"

"Don't ask, Lucas Wilder," Emma called over her shoulder as the boys dragged her toward the wildly moving bounce house filled with screeching children. "If she's smart, she'll come up with any reason to avoid you." She beamed with little-sister victory and sass.

When Ruby slid out to let a new group in, Emma bent to speak with her. Ruby's head bobbed, and Emma waved at them. Dismissed. Just like that.

A rush of uncomfortableness and a hint of anticipation danced across Cate's nerves at the idea of time with Luc. Just the two of them.

"Okay, then. Guess we're not needed here." A grin that would cause any woman in a one-hundred-mile radius to sigh surfaced on Luc's handsome mug. "Let's walk. You okay in those shoes?"

"You okay in those boots?"

He laughed.

The sound of kids giggling and people talking faded to a quiet hum as they hit the Main Street sidewalk. A few of the stores had sale items out on tables or hanging on racks. Others had their doors propped open with welcome signs placed prominently in the windows.

Cate perused a table of clearance kids' clothing. Not a huge selection, but one pair of snow boots that might fit Ruby over the winter. Still a little out of her price range. She could probably get them for less if she shopped online or in a mom swap group. As they left that storefront, a group of teens strolled by, not noticing them and almost plowing into her. Luc grabbed her hand, nudging her behind him. Protective man.

But once the kids passed and they walked again, he didn't let go.

She wasn't sure whether to be flattered or concerned or try to run. All three sounded like good options. Luc's fingers loosened. Cate held her breath. But then he simply switched from cupping her hand to threading his fingers through hers. Her stomach dipped and rolled. Being with Luc like this felt like coming home after far too long. But those thoughts shouldn't be on her radar. She was supposed to be thinking about her daughter and not herself. The opposite of what her parents had done.

Still, she could relax about a little hand-holding, couldn't she? Even if it was making her mind flood with memories of when she and Luc had been inseparable. Back then he'd always held her hand…if he was driving. Or walking. Breathing.

Oh, man. This was exactly why she should be running from him right now.

At the local fudge shop they stopped for a free sample. The taste of salted caramel lingered on Cate's tongue as they exited the small store.

"I was thinking—" Luc nudged her shoulder with his "—since we don't have Ruby with us—and she's perfectly well taken care of by Emma—that maybe we can just be us. One night off from parenting. From only focusing on Ruby. We can allow ourselves that, can't we?"

Ever since Ruby was born, Cate hadn't let her guard down. Not once. Through all of the medical appointments. The diagnosis. The sleepless nights and long days of work. Her mind churned with the mistakes she wanted to avoid making and this precious time with Luc she so badly wanted. Maybe even needed.

"I'll take that as a yes." Luc's hand squeezed hers, and Cate opened her mouth to protest, but not even a squeak came out. So much for standing strong. She was already entangled with him, and they hadn't even been alone for ten minutes. What did that say about her? Maybe it said she was human. And a girl who'd once loved a boy with all of her broken pieces. For a few moments she wanted to not overthink.

Besides, what would be the harm in one night off?

Chapter Thirteen

Luc had set a lot of boundaries for himself regarding Cate, and tonight he'd leaped right over them without a backward glance. Stupid? Probably. But Cate's hand was currently linked with his, and after he'd touched her, his logical senses had signed off for the night.

"So I've been meaning to ask you something." Cate peeked at him through a layer of her warm brown hair. It was down tonight with a slight curl.

Yes, you and Ruby can stay at the ranch. You fit so well. I was thinking the same thing.

He barely tamped down a snort at his foolish thoughts. "What's on your mind?"

"I love your ranch slogan. 'Get out in the wild.' It's perfect."

"Thanks. That's not a question."

"Who designed your shirts and made your logo?"

Luc racked his brain. "I think some kid that worked for us a long time ago. Not sure I remember. Why?" Her teeth pressed into her upper lip. Buying time? Why did she hesitate to answer? "Whatever it is, just say it."

"Okay." Cate paused, facing him. "You could use a

new logo." Curving lips softened the statement. "It's too bad you don't know anyone who could help you out with that. Pro bono."

"That is too bad."

She whacked him on the arm, and he began walking again, keeping her with him. Not planning to let go of her anytime soon. And if he only had tonight, he'd like to add that kiss he'd been preoccupied with to their list of things to do.

"So will you let me do it? I have an idea already."

"Let you? Of course. If you really want to. Are you sure you have time?"

"I'll make time. Being at the ranch has been good for me. For Ruby. I know I wasn't keen on the idea, but it's been nice. It would be fun to do something for the ranch in return."

If only his body didn't flood with hope. She'd said the ranch, not him. He could read between the lines all he wanted, but that didn't change the truth.

They'd reached the end of most of the stores on their side of Main Street, so they crossed over at the stop sign. No traffic light yet, though there'd been talk about it in the local paper.

"Now that you've had more time here, what do you think of Westbend?"

"I like it. It's quaint. Welcoming. Even church has been good. I expected some judgment in a small town like this." She tipped her head in his direction. "For our situation. But so far I've only found kindness."

"If anyone treated you badly, I'd want to know."

Her lips pressed together as if resisting a smile. "What would you do? Beat them up?"

"No." A chuckle shook his chest. "But I'd say something. We both made decisions back then. And we've both changed."

It was true. They had. Luc believed differently now, just like Cate did. Neither of them would have the kind of physical relationship in the present that they'd had in the past. Not until his finger had a wedding band on it. Because now he understood intimacy meant so much more than what he'd believed at nineteen.

Just like his parents had tried to teach him when he hadn't been listening.

"By the way, my parents are planning a trip. They want to meet Ruby and you. Think you'd be willing to come out to the ranch for dinner when they're here?" Luc had been talking to them quite a bit. Filling them in. His mom had even commented that his tone regarding Cate had changed recently. Funny that she could tell from so many miles away.

A shaky breath came from Cate. "Wow. I guess. I'd be so nervous. Don't they hate me?"

He squeezed her hand, the answering pressure from her doing things to his insides he didn't want to acknowledge. "You don't need to be. It took them a bit to wrap their minds around having a granddaughter. But I've been sending them pictures of Ruby and they're already her biggest fans. They've come around quickly even though it was unexpected."

"Well, you forgave me." Cate squared her shoulders. "Guess I'll just have to pray they can, too."

Luc liked seeing Cate reach for faith. It was an attractive quality. Not that he needed to add any more to the many she already had.

"How are things with Mackenzie? Any better?"

Cate had confided in him that she wasn't sure Mackenzie could forgive her for what she'd done. But he'd told her that was just Kenzie's way—protective like a bear with her cubs. And that she'd come around with time. She'd better, or he'd get after her about it. Luc was trying to be patient. To give the two of them the space to work things out without his interference.

"A little bit, actually. The interesting thing about her is that I think I could trust her with Ruby's life, even if she's not sure about me."

And…that was his sister to a T. "Sounds right."

"I want her to like me, but at the same time… I don't deserve it."

"None of us deserves anything, really. We're all messes redeemed by God's grace. But I get what you're saying. You want her to believe your heart is good. You want her to see you for who you are, not what you've done."

"Yes!" She brightened. "That's exactly what I want. How I feel."

"Back when…" He paused. Swallowed. Was he really broaching this subject? Cate always skirted around their history, but Luc needed to talk about it. Might as well be now. "That's what I wanted from you, too, back when you asked if I was seeing someone else. I needed you to believe me. To know that I would never do something like that. And I couldn't imagine how you thought otherwise. That's why I lost it and left. You not trusting me just about killed me."

Her pretty face contorted with pain, which hadn't been his intent. He just wanted her to understand why it mattered so much.

Luc continued. "When I was a sophomore in high school, I was accused of vandalism with some friends.

I didn't do it, but even my parents didn't believe me. I was so frustrated by their lack of trust. Hated that feeling. And when it repeated with you…" Agitation rose up, choking him. "So much worse." Understatement of his life. Because he'd loved her with every single cell in his body.

Just like he did now.

The thought might have surprised him, but Luc instantly felt its truth. Cate had swept back into his life, conjuring a snowstorm of emotions. Anger at first. Then frustration, confusion, hurt. And now…love. Though if he had to guess, that one had been hiding in plain sight all along.

She didn't trust him as far as she could throw him, and yet he loved her. He couldn't help it. It was like he'd been born a match for her, and he refused any other options.

But what could he do about it?

There was still too much unresolved between them. Loving her wouldn't fix everything. Plus, Cate wasn't ready to hear the words tumbling around in his head. If he said them right now, she might run. And Luc was nowhere near ready to lose her all over again.

"I hate that I did that to you." Cate should have known better, but at the time, she'd been young and immature. She'd let herself be swayed against believing Luc when that was exactly what she'd wanted to do. She'd been afraid to be wrong. To be one of those girls who accepted a smooth answer only to find out later that she'd been a fool.

"When Roark first told me that he'd spotted you with some other woman, I didn't believe him. My first thought was to trust you. But he had so many details, I couldn't imagine that he'd made it all up. And then I panicked, thinking I'd missed something. That you weren't who I thought you were."

Luc stopped so fast that his hand, still entwined with hers, brought her to a screeching halt. "Roark? What does he have to do with anything?"

"He's the one who told me."

His eyelids momentarily slammed shut. "Well, no wonder. Now it all makes sense."

"What do you mean?"

"Roark had a thing for you. I knew it the first time you introduced us."

"There's no way." Her head shook vehemently.

A twitch started in Luc's jaw. "Where did he say he saw me?"

"Park Meadows Mall. Holding hands with another woman. Kissing her." The confession hissed from her lips, causing a stabbing pain all over again.

A groan/laugh combination escaped from Luc and she barely resisted a slap to his face. How could he find humor in something like that? When Roark had told her, she'd crumbled into a thousand pieces.

Luc bent so that his eyes were inches from hers. Direct. Mesmerizing. "When in your life have you ever known me to go shopping? I've never even been to that mall. He made it up, Cate. Spun a story to get to you."

"But I don't think he would—" No. Couldn't be. But at the same time, Luc was right. That wasn't something he would do—someplace he would be. Even then, the story hadn't quite fit. Hadn't made sense.

"Did he ask you out after we broke up?"

Her head bobbed. "Yes. Wouldn't take no for an answer until I found out I was pregnant with Ruby. After

I told him that, he left me alone." Her hands were both entangled with his now, fingers squeezing life and apology. What had she done? What had they done? "Luc, I'm so sorry. I didn't know. I'd grown up with Roark. Our families were friends. I didn't have any reason not to believe him."

"But you had a reason not to believe me?"

Ouch. "I wanted to, but I was scared. And the more questions I asked, the more you shut down."

This was what she'd wanted to know back when they were twenty. And finding out now, after all of this time... after she'd kept Ruby from him... Cate didn't know whether to cry or scream.

"I was too immature to answer you then." Luc cradled her face, and she pressed her cheek into his warm palm, needing the comfort he offered. "All I could think about was you not trusting me." His sigh wrenched between them. "I didn't handle any of it well. I should have listened and explained. I should have fought for you, not with you. I'm sorry, Cate."

"Me, too." So much. Why hadn't she gone with her instinct back then? Said more—something, *anything* but heightened accusations. Why hadn't he? They'd been young, but that wasn't a worthy excuse for how they'd treated each other.

They couldn't change the decisions they'd made, but they could redirect the future. She wanted them to disassemble the jail cell they'd unknowingly built together. That had trapped them under assumptions.

"Lucas, do you think it's possible for us to let go of what happened?"

Why couldn't she breathe? Had her respiratory system gone on vacation? Her vision blurred, Luc's smooth jaw waning in and out of focus. Everything in her waited for his response, time standing still. She could survive without him. She'd done it before. But she didn't want to do it again. Even if it was just friendship—and Ruby— keeping them connected, she needed him.

His hands moved farther into her hair, kneading her neck while her muscles waved a white flag of surrender.

His Adam's apple bobbed as he gave a definite nod, then gathered her against his chest as if she was made of sugar and spice and everything nice. If holding was a school subject, Luc would earn an A+ every semester. Wrapping her up tight had always been his go-to— though she wasn't sure he even realized it. He'd done the same last week just before she'd confessed her fears to him.

He had the best grip—tight enough to feel wanted. Safe. Not so constraining that she couldn't budge.

Unwinding started at the top of her head, swirling down her body until even her toes felt the change.

When he loosened, she moved back, but barely. Somewhere in the exit from his delicious embrace, her hands had slid up his arms. Currently they were wrapped around his biceps like it was her job to check their circumference.

Luc? Professional holder. For her only, of course.

Cate? Measuring each of Luc's chiseled muscles one at a time.

His gaze dropped to her lips and held, enough tension and anticipation to supply the city of Westbend with all the electrical current needed for a month.

Would he kiss her? Did she want him to? The answers to those questions came quickly: he'd better, and *yes*.

A rush of impatience gripped her like Ruby in a candy

store, wanting it all and despising the line. Cate had told herself numerous times Luc wasn't hers to have. To take home for keeps. She'd believed she was doomed to repeat her parents' mistakes. That she and Luc revisiting their relationship would only end in brokenness.

What if she'd been wrong all along?

Five seconds earlier Luc would have been able to repeat his and Cate's conversation, but the last few moments had completely erased that possibility.

When had they gone from talking to tangled up in the middle of a sidewalk? Like they could erase the hurt between them with each other's touch?

Luc was definitely willing to give that theory the old college try. He wanted nothing more than to kiss Cate, but all kinds of warning sirens blared. Would he ruin everything they'd just bandaged if he did?

Did she want the same?

She'd had ample opportunity to scoot back after he'd hugged her in answer to her question. Could they move on? Start over? Leave it all behind?

Check the yes box for him.

Luc memorized her mouth like a starved man, though the reminder wasn't necessary. The details had been singed into his brain years ago. When their eyes met, hers were brimming with… That couldn't be love, could it? No. But maybe something close. Like. Interest.

Invitation.

Hopefully, he hadn't read that last one wrong, because Luc was done waiting for a hand-addressed envelope to show up in his mailbox. He brushed her lips with his, planning to wait for her response—to see if she'd pull away. But his patience flew out the window the moment their mouths met.

Her hands slid behind his neck, and the street noises muffled as the sound of his pulse roared in his ears. It had been so long since he'd kissed Cate. He held on, praying for healing for all of the sorrow they'd caused each other. Wanting their connection to make it all disappear.

Maybe she needed the same comfort he did. But this was far more than a Band-Aid for their mistakes. This was what he wanted for the future.

Luc eased slightly from her magnetic pull.

In a matter of minutes they'd gone from digging up the past, to burying it, to creating something fresh. Luc liked that last one the best. Because this Cate was a mix of old and new woven together. The mother of his child. His first love and his second, and he never wanted to stop kissing her.

So he didn't.

He swooped in for one more taste. What if he'd been wrong earlier? What if there was a chance she could love him again? He wasn't lazy. He would work himself to the bone to make that happen. If only she could trust him.

He was definitely in love with Cate all over again. Not in a childish way this time, but in a way he'd never experienced before. He wanted a life with Ruby and Cate. Wanted to fight for that. There was no going back. With Ruby to consider, they'd have to be fully committed. And he was. But was she? Knowing her, she'd need time to process. If he pushed right now, she'd scatter like raindrops on a windshield. One swipe and gone forever.

Voices sounded, exiting from the coffee shop two doors down, cutting off their *just one more kiss* that had heated faster than metal reflecting the Colorado sun.

Cate stepped back, amusement evident. Her jaw tipped up, a sassy little move that only tempted him to head in that direction next. She was a mix of shy and sweet, embarrassed and yet refusing to give in to that last emotion. "Maybe in the middle of town isn't the best place for our second first kiss."

Second first. He liked the sound of that. A grin spread so wide it stretched the skin tight over his cheekbones. "You're probably right. Have I told you how beautiful you look tonight?"

She answered with a slowly shaking head, doubt shadowing the playfulness sparkling in her eyes. "I think I'm too dressed up for such a casual night."

"I think you're perfect." He'd wanted to tell her in the truck earlier that she looked gorgeous, but he'd been hesitant to say something like that in front of Ruby. "There aren't enough words in the dictionary to do you justice, Catherine Malory." Luc didn't allow her the time to protest. Instead, he tucked her close and held on as they began walking.

If only he could be confident the future held more of the same.

Chapter Fourteen

What had she done? What had they done? This was why Cate didn't take time off from focusing on Ruby. Because the lapse left her awake in the middle of the night, sheets twisted from her tossing and turning, heart beating out a rhythm of mingled fear and hope while she wrestled with the knowledge that if Luc walked through the door right now, she'd kiss him all over again.

Last night after their walk through town, she and Luc had gone back to the church to spend the rest of the evening with Ruby. Cate had relished their time together—all three of them. The night had been something close to perfect, at least in her mind. On their way home Ruby had conked out in the truck. Luc had carried her inside and tucked her in. Then he'd pulled Cate out to the front step to say good-night. He'd been so...careful with her. Like she was a precious gift he wanted to wait to unwrap. He'd held her for a long minute, kissed her cheek, and then he'd been gone before she could decipher the many emotions flitting across his features.

The man was more tempting than tiramisu crafted from the aged hands of an Italian grandmother.

Cate attempted to retuck the fitted sheet that had recently slipped free from the corner of the mattress. When her efforts didn't pan out, she tore out of the bed and gave it a strong tug, taking a moment to realign everything her worries had tangled during the night.

What kind of monster could sleep in disheveled sheets?

Prim gave a meow from her spot in the corner that sounded strangely like a sigh. Cate's antics had woken the princess.

After opening the bedroom window to let in cooler air, Cate plopped back into bed and glanced at the time. Five in the morning. So not exactly the middle of the night, but her exhausted body told her she hadn't gained much in the way of sleep in the hours before.

She ran her hand over Prim's back as the cat slunk along the edge of the mattress. Prim paused to accept the comfort she offered. A bit like Cate had done last night when she'd broken all of her self-imposed rules and leaned into Lucas.

"I wasn't that bad."

Prim meowed.

"Okay, so I like him." She scooped Prim onto her lap, easing back against the headboard in a sitting position. Why pretend sleep would come at all?

Cate would be lying to herself if she didn't acknowledge that Luc had always held on to a portion of her heart. They'd never been over and done. And not just because Ruby linked them together as parents. But because he was Lucas. And she needed him far more than she wanted to admit.

So much for all of the plans and stopgaps she'd set in place to keep this exact thing from happening.

Cate must have squeezed Prim a bit too hard—frustration surfacing in her grip—because the cat tossed her head with snotty annoyance and escaped from Cate's lap to curl up on the other side of the bed. Her narrowed eyes seemed to say, *Pull yourself together, girl.*

"I'm just trying to figure things out."

Prim's eyelids grew heavy, head resting on her paws.

"And you're a rotten sounding board as usual. Where's your good advice, huh?"

The cat's spine lifted and fell with each steady breath. Once again, Cate was talking to her pet and expecting answers.

She groaned. "I'm totally going to become an old cat lady who carries on conversations with her tabby. I'm already halfway there. A few more years and some gray hairs—goal met."

Cate punched the pillow into submission and slumped down on her side, staring at the alarm clock on the nightstand.

Obviously she had feelings for Luc. She didn't need anyone to listen to her—Prim included—to know that. They'd worked out the past, and she felt peace. Cate could finally allow herself to believe what she'd wanted to all along. That Luc would never have done what Roark accused him of. What a jerk Roark had been to throw fake stones like that.

And she'd been distrusting enough to listen.

Shame on her.

But what now? Luc hadn't said anything about the future. Could they actually attempt a relationship again? Did he want to? They couldn't be wishy-washy. They didn't have that liberty...not as Ruby's parents. Cate needed to know what he was thinking. For her sake and for Ruby's. Because she *would not* let a relationship between them— or even the possibility of it—hurt their daughter.

By the time six thirty rolled around, Cate had showered and dressed in a soft pink shirt and flowered pencil skirt she could wear to church. She applied makeup and did her hair, then paced back and forth in her bedroom, praying. Asking for wisdom not to make the same mistakes she had last time. Even praying that she would remain open. Cate struggled with that after watching her parents make so many blunders. It was painfully hard for her to believe there were people in the world who could love each other unconditionally.

But what if she and Luc were the exception to the rule? She had to talk to him. Should she call? Text? No. It had to be in person.

Cate checked on Ruby—still asleep.

The girl never slept in, but today she showed no signs of waking. Each second Cate waited to get answers from Luc aggravated like someone smacking gum inches from her ear.

She retreated to the living room. The house where Luc was crashing with his sisters was just a few steps down the hill. Within sight. Cate could run over, see if he was home and be back before Ruby woke.

She slid on black sandals and flew down the hill, knocking lightly on the front door.

Please let Luc answer. Please let Luc answer.

The wooden interior door unlocked, Mackenzie visible as it swung wide. She pushed the screen door open. "Cate?"

Really, God? You couldn't even give me Emma?

For a second Cate cowered. But then she pressed her shoulders back. She was on a mission, and even Luc's intimidating sister couldn't stop her.

But exactly how long had Mackenzie been awake?

Her hair flowed in waves, a yellow T-shirt and shorts spitting two of the longest, tannest legs into the universe.

"Do you just roll out of bed looking like that?" *Whoops.* Based on Mackenzie's laughter, she'd actually just said that out loud.

The skin around Mackenzie's unique gray-blue eyes crinkled with enough kindness to give Cate courage. "Everything okay?"

"Yes." *No.* "Is Luc here? I need to speak with him."

"He left a bit ago. He's an early riser, but I don't know where he's off to on a Sunday." Mackenzie had a toothbrush in her hand, and she pointed toward the lodge with it. "Might try his office."

"Thanks." Cate took a step back, then glanced at her cabin. She couldn't leave Ruby alone. She'd just have to calm down like a big girl and wait it out.

Mackenzie studied her. "Do you need me to stay with Ruby while you go talk to him?"

What? Seriously? Mackenzie might not be waving a big white truce flag, but she wasn't snarling, either. Maybe the woman was coming around.

Was accepting her help the right thing to do? Cate was desperate to calm the questions swirling inside her. "Yes. Please. She's asleep right now."

"Just like her aunt Emma." A flash of white teeth and Mackenzie disappeared inside, leaving the door open. And then she was back, toothbrush discarded, flip-flops on. The door clicked shut behind her.

Cate didn't move. Her shoes had suddenly become very attached to the ground directly beneath her.

"Go ahead." Mackenzie nodded toward the lodge. "I may not be Emma but I can handle hanging out with my niece, whether she's asleep or awake. We'll be fine."

Little did Mackenzie know that wasn't the issue tying Cate into knots.

No more overthinking. Cate would lose her resolve if she waited any longer. After a thank-you to Mackenzie, she hurried to the lodge.

When she knocked on Luc's office door, he didn't answer. "Lucas?" She twisted the knob and peeked inside. The lights weren't on.

Cate paused at the threshold. He could be over in the barn. Or somewhere else in the lodge. But if she went looking for him, she'd likely miss him.

She'd wait in his office for a few minutes and see if he showed.

Cate flipped on the light switch and then sat on the futon that faced Luc's desk. After a few minutes she jumped up, nerves making her limbs twitchy. She crossed to the far window. It showcased the sprawling ranch like a framed photograph, morning light dancing across dew-dampened grass.

Unable to stay still for more than three seconds and feeling a little like Ruby, Cate turned and strode by the desk, her hand bumping a stack of papers perched on the corner. They jostled, and she began straightening them. She couldn't handle it when the edges didn't match up in perfect symmetry.

The words *parental responsibilities* popped out from the top corner of one located at the bottom, and her body morphed into a glacier. That fancy phrase translated into custody.

"I should ignore it." She stared at the wall above the futon, begging one of the family photos there to capture her attention. "It's probably just a guest's paperwork. Nothing to do with me or Ruby."

Just like Prim, the walls didn't answer her.

Abandoning her OCD task, Cate scooted back to the futon and dropped down. But suspicion slithered in through the cracks of her broken pieces. The papers called out, mocking her.

What if she looked? Proved her concerns wrong? She could do that, couldn't she?

Cate lunged for the desk, quickly shuffling to the bottom of the stack. The paper-clipped sheets revealed more than her trembling limbs could handle. Information about how to file for custody lined the pages, a handwritten note in blue ink scrawled across the top of the first page: *Lucas, call with any questions or to set up a meeting.* The phone number beneath it blurred through her watery vision.

The room tilted, and she closed her eyes against the sensation of free-falling.

No way. She didn't believe it. Not after what they'd talked about. How close they'd gotten. After last night.

Luc might not have said how he felt, but hadn't she read his feelings loud and clear?

Had it all been a lie to get her to let down her guard? So that he had time to pursue custody? Her teeth chattered, the shaking transferring through her whole body.

And to think, she'd believed him. Trusted him with not only herself, but Ruby, too. She should have known better. Some people got second chances.

She just wasn't one of them.

Cate's looking for you. I sent her to your office.

Luc palmed his phone, the time stamp on Mackenzie's text from fifteen minutes before.

Was it a good or bad sign that Cate was up early, wanting to see him? *Please, please let it be the first.*

This morning he'd woken before the sun, finally given up on sleep and headed out for a ride. Some time to process and talk to God about the restless fears holding his head under water. He'd left his phone in his room.

Now he slid it into his back pocket and beelined for the lodge.

For weeks Luc had been capsized by the idea that Cate would never truly trust him. And even after discovering Roark's part in what had happened, he hadn't told her he loved her. He'd been afraid that she wasn't ready to hear it. That their past could still so easily repeat itself. But after venting it all out to God, he felt renewed. Luc worshipped the King of mercy and miracles and second chances. He could trust in that. In Him.

He'd been a wuss not telling Cate how he felt last night, and he refused to hide behind lame excuses any longer.

Luc still had part of today with Cate and Ruby here, and he would rectify his mistake. He needed to tell Cate he was so far gone, he couldn't stop loving her if he tried. He loved everything about her. The way she clung to control and the sweet victory when she released things from her iron grip, handing them over ever so slowly to God's keeping. Her fierce protectiveness of Ruby. And then there was the way she looked at him when she let him in…like there wasn't anywhere else in the world she'd rather be. Like he was her safety net. He craved all of her. Even the battle scars from her childhood that had shaped her into being strong and vulnerable at the same time. He was unwilling to live without her and Ruby in his life. Luc wanted the three of them to be a family, not spread out over two cities and thousands of acres of land.

And if he had to wait for her feelings to catch up with his, that was exactly what he would do.

Luc flew up the lodge steps and through the lobby. His office door was open. Inside, Cate stood next to his desk. She wore a straight flowered skirt, a light pink shirt and sandals. Her hair was down with a slight curl. The most beautiful woman in the world had not only crashed back into his life, but she'd also given him the best daughter he could ever ask for.

He blinked back emotion as he crossed the space. "Hey." His voice came out low, somehow managing to crack one syllable into two. He captured her in an embrace that scooped her off the ground. It felt *so good* to hold her. To think that she could actually be his again and he could be hers.

After he and Cate split, Luc had thought he might never feel about anyone the way he had about her. Turned out, he'd been right. She was *it* for him.

Here he was, right back in love with her all over again.

"Nine hours is way too long to be separated from you. We're going to have to figure out another system." One with a wedding ring, if he had anything to say about it. "Woman, you are not conducive to good sleep." He pressed a kiss against her neck, considering the flesh that rose in goose bumps as a good sign.

But then again, maybe he was jumping the gun… Cate's arms hadn't reciprocated. She didn't shove away, but she hung against him like a limp, lifeless baby doll of Ruby's.

Concern spread through him, and he eased her feet back to the floor.

"What's going on? You okay?"

"No." She hugged herself, hands scrubbing along her upper arms.

Maybe he'd confused her last night by not stating clearly how he felt. "Listen, Cate, about—"

"What are these?"

She lifted a stack of papers from the desk. Her eyes were cold. None of the warmth and openness from the evening before remained. Like a switch had been turned.

Invisible fists gripped his windpipe, crushing any chance for air. *No, no, no.* Luc hadn't been back in the office since Friday when Gage had dropped the papers off...when he'd been wanting to get Cate out of here so that she wouldn't see them. He'd spent Saturday with Cate and Ruby and hadn't given the custody info a second thought.

Why hadn't he come in just to throw them away? Or torch them? Dread edged along his spine. Luc needed to convince Cate that what she held wasn't the truth. He edged to block her path to the door, buying himself time.

"They're not what you think."

"Really? They're not filled with information about you filing for custody of Ruby?" She sounded hollow. Shattered.

Of course they were. Stupid, stupid move on his part. He'd like to blame Gage, but Luc was the one who'd given him the go-ahead in the first place.

"Gage offered to help me way back in the beginning. When you showed up with Ruby and I didn't know what to do. I was concerned that you could just take her and disappear, so I told him to look into it."

Luc wasn't going to make the mistake of not completely discussing everything like the last time. He and

Cate needed full disclosure. He kept his voice easy. Non-confrontational. He had nothing to hide. He should have just told Cate about the papers after Gage had dropped them off on Friday. Explained everything to her then. If he had, maybe he wouldn't be in this situation right now, panicking that this was the final nail in the coffin of their momentary second chance. But he hadn't said anything because he'd worried that she would react exactly like she was now.

"He brought them in Friday afternoon. I told him I wasn't interested anymore. That you and I were going to work things out. He left them here, and I planned to throw them away. I just haven't been in the office since then. I've been with you and Ruby, and I didn't think about those papers once over the weekend. That has to tell you something."

Luc prayed that Cate would really hear him, but she looked vacant. A listless shell that didn't register his defense.

Desperation took root. He grabbed her arms. "I love you, Cate. I wasn't going to follow through on the custody stuff. I know how much that scares you. Are you hearing me?"

No answer.

Luc didn't know what to do. Kiss her? She'd slap him. Trap her here and hold her captive until she accepted his explanation?

"Remember everything we talked about last night? You didn't believe me when we were twenty and we lost four years. Don't do that this time. You can trust me. I promise." He inched closer, celebrating a surge of victory when she didn't immediately shrink away. The hold he had around her wrists softened, thumbs tracing over her jumpy pulse. "I need you to believe me, Cate. Please."

"I can't." She retreated, stark trauma written in the bruised half-moons under her eyes.

"Why not? You said you should have last time. Why can't you now?"

"Last time I didn't have proof." The papers shook in her hand. "This time I do." She shoved them against his chest, jutted around him and ran from his office as the mess fluttered to the floor.

His rib cage exploded with pressure, the repaired organ in his chest giving signs of surrender.

All of this time he'd questioned if Cate would choose to trust him moving forward. Now he had his answer.

Chapter Fifteen

The boom of the twelve-gauge shotgun echoed from the surrounding hills as Luc caught the next clay target in his sight and pulled the trigger.

"It's about to storm. Wasn't sure if you'd noticed," Mackenzie called out from behind him, her sarcasm as thick as the charcoal clouds rolling in. Luc took one more shot before switching the trap thrower to the off position.

He perched his gun on the wooden holding rack and faced her, sliding his ear protection to the back of his neck.

"I noticed." The sky touching the pine-covered hills was dark and vicious, but so far no rain had fallen. No thunder or lightning yet.

Luc had run the afternoon skeet session for the guests. Once they finished up, he'd sent them back to the ranch, leaving the cleanup for himself. But he hadn't been able to resist a few rounds before packing everything into the back of the truck.

"You just out here sulking?"

"Shooting. Not sulking." Actually, Luc thought he'd done a pretty good job of keeping it together since Cate and Ruby had left on Sunday. He hadn't yelled at anyone. Family or staff. Hadn't lost his temper. No tantrums or outbursts. Mostly, he'd just been quietly stewing over things. Though he'd yet to come up with any answers.

The worst part had been the conversation with Cate after she'd packed up.

"Here." She'd handed him a piece of paper. "This is a possible list of times for you to have Ruby. Built around your time off. Look it over and see what you think or if you want to change anything. We can adjust when you move to the fall schedule."

No tears. No *maybe I made a mistake in not believing you.* Cate had switched off her emotions like a garden hose. One twist—done.

Luc didn't have the same ability. It had taken everything in him not to say something more to her. But what? Her response to his explanation on Sunday morning had been to storm out of his office. Had she even heard him say he loved her? She'd certainly never acknowledged his declaration.

Mackenzie braced hands on her hips, stance wide. "Have you heard from Cate?"

Only in email. She'd sent him new logo options for the ranch, of all things. Their arrival in his inbox had sent his pulse skyrocketing, making him wonder if she'd changed her mind. Until he'd realized it was all business.

Choose one. Let me know. I can tweak it.

That had been it.

The funny part was, the first logo was perfect. She'd captured the feel of the ranch, yet she didn't want to be anywhere near it or him.

Go figure.

He retrieved a box of shells that had tumbled to the

grass and tossed it into the plastic bin on the tailgate. "Why do you care? You never liked her anyway."

"Not true. I took my time getting to know her. Didn't trust her at first."

"And now?"

"She's grown on me. Probably stemming from the fact that she and Ruby make you happy. Believe it or not, I want that for you."

Luc let out a half grunt, half laugh. "Well, you're going to have to deal with a brother who's not all sunshine and rainbows, because Cate wants nothing to do with me."

"That's not what I gathered when she showed up on our step Sunday morning."

Before everything had imploded into a fiery mess. "Then your detective skills are wrong." Last time Luc had fought with Cate, he'd been young and angry. Now, in the course of four years, he felt old and worn. Sadness hung around him. Despair permeated his body. They'd done this one too many times. She'd chosen not to trust him one too many times. How could he overlook that?

"You do realize that I know you're upset, right? It's not like I can just turn off the twin connection when you're being annoying."

A sigh leaked from his chest. "Just give me some space. I'll get over her again. It just takes time." Unfortunately, he knew from experience.

"Why?"

"Why what?"

"Why get over her? You two are connected by Ruby. But I think there's more than that to what you have."

He'd thought so, too. Luc had been positive he and Cate had earned their second chance over the past month.

"The two of you will always be in each other's lives

because of your daughter. So what do you want that relationship to look like?"

Mackenzie's question strangled him. Like a family. That was what he wanted. But he couldn't just ignore the fact that Cate had once again tossed him into the gutter. How could a relationship be built on that?

"The way I see it, you can spend the rest of your life fighting with her, or for her."

Luc's jaw unhinged. "Are you seriously giving me dating advice? Love advice? You, who hasn't—"

"Lucas Wilder, we're not talking about me. We're talking about you. Don't change the subject." Mackenzie's *don't mess with me* expression told Luc he didn't stand a chance of winning this argument.

"Fine. You're right. I'm wrong. Are we done now?"

Her exaggerated groan cut into the air as Luc spotted Gage heading in their direction.

Great. Another person coming to poke and prod?

"I give up." Mackenzie whirled toward the lodge and shoved a finger at Gage as he neared them. "You handle him. I tried." And then she was off, her boots raising up dust, agitation and disapproval evident in every step.

"You come to yell at me, too?"

"Me? Never." Gage retrieved a twenty-gauge shotgun from the wooden holder and loaded it.

This was Luc's kind of conversation. He reloaded, and when both of them were ready, he flipped the trap thrower switch to On. Blasts reigned for the next few minutes as the two of them took turns demolishing orange flying targets.

Almost gave his grief a place to hold on to.

When a raindrop hit him on the forearm, Luc turned off the machine. He and Gage began packing up.

"Emma told me something went south between you and Cate, though she didn't give me details. I'm sorry, man." Gage didn't add the *I told you so* Luc half expected to hear. "At dinner on Friday night when I saw you two together, I actually started believing you might make it work. That you were getting the do-over most people never have." Gage paused from cleanup and tapped against his chest. "Almost made this stone heart of mine pump with blood again."

Humor surfaced. While Gage had shut down since Nicole left, Luc was certain the man underneath all of that still existed. But it would take someone amazing to carve him back to life again.

"Cate found the paperwork. After I promised her I wouldn't file for custody and that we'd work things out." Luc bent to the ground, unhooking the trap shooter from the battery as another raindrop nailed his ear.

"Oh." Gage scraped a hand along the back of his hair. "Can't help feeling like that's my fault."

"It's not. I should have just told her about it. Or thrown it away. I tried explaining that I didn't plan to do anything with it, but she didn't believe me."

The churning clouds held Gage's attention. "I always believed Nicole. I was naive. Never thought she'd do any of the things she did." He collected shells, tossing them into the plastic trash bin. "Not to make it about me."

"I'd rather talk about you than me."

"So what are you going to do?" Gage snagged the other side of the thrower and they hoisted it into the back of the truck.

Luc slid it forward along with the other supplies and then slammed the tailgate shut. "Do? Nothing. Be a dad to Ruby. Try to move on."

"Aren't you going to go after her? Fight for your family?"

Now he sounded like Mackenzie. "Would you? Did you?" The questions came out harsher than Luc planned. But he was curious. Gage didn't talk a lot about what had happened between him and his ex-wife.

"The difference is, I didn't have anything left to fight for. Nicole was gone long before she actually took off. I was just holding on so tight, trying so hard to keep her, that I wouldn't let myself see the truth. But you, on the other hand…you do have something worth fighting for. Ruby. And the fact that you love her mother—because I'm guessing that's the case—is the best thing you could ever give her." Gage swiped at a raindrop that landed on his forehead. "I thank God every day that Nicole and I didn't have kids who would have to deal with our split."

Luc hadn't thought about it that way. He'd only been focused on loving Cate and her not returning the sentiment. But in all of Cate's desire to protect Ruby, she'd forgotten one thing—that their daughter would benefit from the three of them being a family. Ruby would be over the moon about it. What would make her feel safer than that?

"But Cate doesn't trust me. How do I handle that?"

"Why doesn't she?"

Luc was about to fill Gage in on what had happened between them in the past when understanding hit him like a left hook.

Her parents.

Each had pitted her against the other when she was just a little girl. They should have protected her. Instead, they'd destroyed her ability to trust.

It wasn't about him. It had never been about him.

"Her parents broke her heart, I think." And then he'd come along and done the same. Twice.

Cate struggled with believing him, but it wasn't because he was untrustworthy—though that was how she'd made him feel. It was because the very people who should have adored her had done the opposite. They'd been focused on themselves.

In Cate's world, love had to be earned. It wasn't freely given. She didn't believe that anyone could love her unconditionally. But Luc wanted to be the one to prove her theory wrong.

He already loved her that way. Just because she'd moved back to Denver with Ruby didn't mean he'd stopped. It had just been laced with hurt and confusion the past few days.

But now, thanks to Gage—and maybe with slight credit to Mackenzie—he knew exactly what he wanted. He just had to figure out how to get it.

"When are we going back to the ranch, Mommy?"

Six days of the same question from Ruby. Each time Cate answered in a high-fructose corn-syrup tone. Fake. Overly sweet. Trying for patience with everything in her.

"I'm not, sweetie. We're going to live here in our apartment, remember? But your dad's going to pick you up for a sleepover in a little bit. So you'll go to the ranch sometimes, when he has you."

"Why aren't you going?" Ruby's tiny brow crinkled with the innocent question.

"Because Mommy has work to do." Her favorite fallback. Cate should do something today besides work—go somewhere, be with friends. But she didn't have the energy. "You'll have a good time with your dad."

The one friend she had been communicating with—surprisingly enough—was Emma. Cate had received a text from her on Sunday night, a few hours after she and Ruby had left the ranch.

Just wanted to make sure you got home okay. We miss you both already.

Cate wasn't sure who the "we" referred to, but she was confident it wasn't Luc. Not after how things had ended between them. But Emma had been sweet to include Cate in that second part.

She'd responded, and they'd texted every day since.

Luc, on the other hand, had only contacted Cate once this week. He'd texted to tell her that he'd pick up Ruby this morning. That had been it. He hadn't even responded to the email she'd sent with logo options for the ranch.

The whole situation was eerily similar to the last time they'd fought.

During the week, Cate had gone over and over what Luc had said in his office on Sunday. But when the desire to believe his explanation surfaced, she snuffed it out.

She just…couldn't. Not when she'd seen the proof.

It was better to nip things between her and Luc now, before they got too out of hand. Before she was crushed beyond repair.

Oh, wait. Too late for that.

Cate had hoped they could salvage things for Ruby and prevent her from getting hurt, but that ship had also sailed. Ruby had really struggled this week, whining and crying at the slightest things.

So much for Cate's plan to keep her daughter safe. Unaffected. Protected and loved.

Ruby's lower lip protruded. "I want you to come."

"You don't need me, sweets. Your dad will take great care of you." The truth of those statements pricked like a needle. Luc was fantastic with Ruby. Especially for having come into fatherhood years into her little life. Cate might not be happy about what he'd done with the custody stuff, but she could give him that.

Right before leaving the ranch, Cate had given Luc a schedule of times for keeping Ruby. He'd said they worked for him, and that had been the last of it.

So far. But he could still choose to file for custody. What reason did he have not to now?

"I don't want to go to Ms. Betty's house anymore, Mommy."

Cate swallowed the groan begging for escape. She didn't know what to do with this new Ruby. The girl had always adored day care. People. Anything new. But since they'd been back and she'd returned to Betty's on Tuesday, Ruby had been full of complaints and stomachaches. She'd tried every excuse to stay home: *My tongue feels silly. I can't find my bear. The horses at the ranch need me.*

So far Cate had been conveniently blaming Luc for Ruby's angst. If he hadn't convinced them to live at the ranch, Ruby wouldn't know that other life existed. She wouldn't have fallen in love with the freedom, the place and the people.

"Let's not think about Ms. Betty's today. You have two days off."

Luc was planning to keep Ruby until after church on Sunday. At that point they'd meet up to exchange her.

A knock sounded at the door, and Cate checked the peephole. Luc. Already? Thankfully, she'd changed out of pajamas and into a light blue T-shirt and capris this morning. She opened it. "Hey, you're—"

"Early. I know." He didn't even have the decency to look chagrined. Luc strode into the living room as Cate's mouth fell open. She hadn't even invited him in! He could go wait in his truck.

Only…he had insisted on driving all the way here to pick up Ruby. And he hadn't fussed about the schedule she'd suggested. She should probably count those as victories and not stick a broom handle into a hornet's nest.

The door slipped from her fingertips, closing just as Ruby flew into Luc's arms, their embrace reminiscent of years of separation.

"I missed you this week, Rube-i-cube."

"I miss-ded you, too, Daddy."

Cate blinked away moisture. Now was not the time to break down.

Luc lowered Ruby to the carpet. "Why don't you grab your stuff, okay?"

"Okay!" She took off for her room.

Sitting on the couch, Luc stretched long legs in front of him, acting like he owned the place. "So, Cate, how've you been?"

"Fine." The word snapped out, nowhere near the truth.

"Good for you. How have I been? So nice of you to ask. Not fine, actually." She couldn't decipher the message that radiated from his stormy eyes. "Here." He shifted to retrieve something from his back pocket. Held a white envelope toward her.

Cate's knees swirled, fear stirring her emotions into a tornado-like spin. What was in the envelope? Was he planning to file and telling her up front?

Please no. Ruby deserves better from us. God, I'm

begging. They might have to share her, but they didn't have to fight over her.

"What...what is that?"

"Something from Gage."

Gage? That didn't give her peace of mind. She took it but made no move to open it.

Luc stood and crossed over to her, stopping only when he'd invaded her personal space. Fresh-air scent clung to his clothes, and Cate resisted swaying closer to breathe him in.

She'd missed him this week. The thought came without permission. When would she get a handle on the emotions Luc had reignited in her over the past month?

"You really don't believe me, do you? Do you think that's about custody?" He pointed to the envelope.

She looked to the floor, attempting to hide the truth, but her resolve weakened. "Yes." She wanted to scream it, distress bubbling to the surface.

"It's not." Luc's hands fisted. "I said it on Sunday and I'll say it again. I love you, Cate." His voice had dropped low, probably so that Ruby wouldn't hear, but the effect registered even stronger. Her bones reverberated with the intensity. "I was never going to file for custody. I agreed to your dates. They work for me, so I'm still not going to. You asked me not to battle over Ruby, and I plan to honor that."

He edged closer, and even though Cate wanted to step back, she didn't. Part of her was drawn to him. Unable to move.

"Last time I fought with you, not for you. And I'm not going to make that mistake again." His finger bounced between them. "We're nowhere near through, just so you know."

Could a person's lungs deflate from sheer shock? Because hers were no longer functioning.

"I don't know what it's going to take to prove that I love you and that I'm never going to stop. When we were younger, I let anger win. Not this time. I want the three of us to be a family, and I'm going to keep fighting for you. For us. Until you know you can trust me. Because you can."

"I'm ready, Daddy!" Ruby bounded out into the living room, and Luc took a step back. Still wasn't enough space to calm Cate's ricocheting nerves, but she'd take it.

Ruby listed through the things in her bag, but Cate's mind was spinning too fast to manage a coherent thought. Plus, she'd already packed Ruby's stuff for her. So as long as she wasn't removing things, it should be fine.

"Sounds perfect, sweets." Her voice came out surprisingly even.

"Don't forget Boo-boo bear," Luc added, and Ruby disappeared down the hallway and into her bedroom.

"Then what's in this?" Cate held up the envelope.

"Gage's testimony. About what I said when he dropped off the papers. That I never planned to do anything with them. I thought it might help if you had someone to back my side of the story."

Cate needed time to process. To deal with everything Luc was throwing at her.

"Got him! Boo-boo was sad I almost left him, but I gave him a smooch and made it all better." Ruby's arms wrapped around Cate's legs. "I love you, Mommy." Her sadness from earlier had been replaced with excitement, and Cate wasn't going to ruin that for her. She caught her daughter in a big hug and said goodbye.

As Luc pulled the door shut behind them, his hazel

eyes held hers until the last second, saying everything she wanted to hear but fought believing.

At the click of the knob, she dropped onto the sofa, head falling into her hands, and did the only thing she knew to do.

She prayed.

Chapter Sixteen

"I'm so glad you called." Emma slid into the booth across from Cate at the small café located about halfway between the ranch and Cate's apartment.

"Really? I keep thinking you're going to cut me off because Luc and I…" Cate wasn't sure exactly how to finish that sentence. Fought? Couldn't get on the same page?

It was more that she couldn't trust him. Anyone, for that matter.

"Nah. If I had to pick between the two of you, I'd probably choose you."

Cate laughed, appreciating the sentiment even while knowing how loyal Emma was to her family.

"Now, Mackenzie, on the other hand…" Emma sprouted a cheeky grin. "Would you believe she's come around to your side?"

What? Impossible. Mackenzie was Team Luc all the way. "How did that happen?"

"She got to know you. We all did. And she's just as annoyed at our brother for doing something stupid to mess things up between you guys. Before you left, we thought you and Luc were getting back together and we were both happy for you. Well, I was ecstatic. Mackenzie was cautiously optimistic." Amusement lit her face but quickly fell. "It had felt…right."

It had felt right. Until it had gone so wrong. Again.

"Do you two even know what happened?"

"Not the details. Luc's been pretty tight-lipped."

"And you're still taking my side?"

"I'm on both of your sides. I want what's best for all three of you. You're family, too, Cate. You're my niece's mom. That counts. Plus, my friend."

Just like that, Cate's tight nerves began to ease. Emma, as usual, was good medicine.

This morning after Luc left, Cate had been a mess. She'd prayed and cried and read her Bible. Last time when she and Luc broke up, she'd barely been more than a kid, and she'd had no relationship with God. This time, no matter how confused she was, she had someone to turn to. Eventually, she'd left her apartment with peace. No answers, but confident that God would guide her. Maybe even with a kick in the pants. Cate needed those nudges more than she liked to admit.

The waitress approached and took their drink orders.

After she left, Cate leaned forward, resting her arms on the table. "It's not all his fault, you know." It was and it wasn't. Why'd Luc have to ask about custody paperwork in the first place? But then again, wouldn't she have done the same in his shoes? She had kept his daughter from him for over three and a half years.

Luc had said he wasn't going to follow through on filing. And Cate had no doubt he was upset she hadn't believed him. Again. But it was *so hard* for her to trust.

"He denies doing what I think he did." Or planned to do in the future. Cate wasn't sure how much more to tell.

Emma's soda and Cate's iced tea arrived at the table. The younger girl took a sip through her straw, face contemplative. "If there's one thing I can say about Luc, it's that he's honest. He might not always be the most patient, and he's definitely made his share of mistakes in life, but he always tells the truth. It's just part of who he is. He can't help it."

Emma opened and studied her menu as if her comments hadn't just leveled Cate to the ground.

When Luc had explained how the paperwork had ended up on his desk, Cate had thought it made sense. That the story rang true. But she'd held on to distrust instead of choosing to believe him. She'd latched on to the papers in front of her instead of the man standing inches from her.

The unopened envelope from Gage was in Cate's purse. She hadn't broken the seal…because she didn't want to read it and find out Luc was telling the truth. Where would that leave her? Ripped wide open. He'd been her first love, but now he was her second, too. Their relationship was different this time around. They did a lot less fighting. A lot more talking. Luc had coaxed so many things out of her. He made her feel loved. Safe. The month with him had brought back to life the feelings lying dormant inside her.

And that was scary stuff.

If she believed Luc, that meant she'd have to tell him how she felt. That she loved him and didn't want to live without him in her life or Ruby's. That she wanted the three of them to be a family, too.

Cate had been searching for something she'd never find—assurance that she and Luc wouldn't turn out like her parents. But life didn't work that way. She wasn't going to know what was around the next bend. Just what stood in front of her. And a few hours ago, that had been Luc.

Thinking of him, standing in his office and her living room, confessing his feelings to her while she didn't accept them…didn't even acknowledge them. Her face heated. She'd been so awful to him. What had she done?

Cate knew Emma's words were true—she could trust Luc. Not only that, for the first time, she wanted to.

God had heard her desperate prayers for wisdom and guidance earlier today, and He'd softened her, making fear dissipate while faith took its place.

And with a little unintentional nudge from Emma, Cate could finally admit she loved Luc. It was frightening to think it. Would be even harder to say it. But it was the truth.

Giddiness swam through her torso, warming her face. Good thing Emma still studied the menu, because Cate's features were surely displaying her every thought. Not that Emma would mind the change.

"Do you know what you're going to order?" Wrinkles marred Emma's usually smooth forehead—the only part of her visible behind the massive menu.

"Luc." Cate slapped a hand over her mouth and consequent burst of laughter.

The menu lowered, steel blue eyes sparkling with merriment over the top. "I think that's a good choice for you. Though I won't say that I'm going to have the same."

Luc sat on the floor next to Ruby's twin bed, his back against the small side table.

"Daddy." She shifted to face him, head creating a

small indent in her pillow. "Is Mommy going to say good-night to me?"

And there went his heart. Trampled to pieces all over again. How many times could the thing take a beating and get back up?

"She's not staying at the ranch tonight, remember? You'll see her tomorrow." Things had gone well since Luc had picked up Ruby this morning, but nighttime was proving to be tough.

He hated that this was the normal they had to adjust to. It wouldn't be if Luc had anything to say about it. But his conversation with Cate this morning had been stilted, and Luc wasn't confident that he'd gotten through to her.

All day he'd been praying. Begging God that Cate would come around. And he'd been asking for peace for Ruby. So far he wasn't sure any of his requests were making a hill of beans difference.

"I miss Mommy."

"I do, too." Oops. He hadn't meant to admit that.

Ruby giggled. "You're silly, Daddy."

He crossed his eyes and stuck out his tongue, earning another laugh.

Tonight they'd gone into town and had ice cream. Then Ruby had played at the park while Luc had sat on the bench alone. Missing Cate. Missing what he'd so recently hoped they could have.

"Will you read me one more book?"

How could he refuse that request? "Sure. Pick one out."

Ruby popped down from the bed, showing little sign of being tired, and dug through the small basket that held a few toys and books.

Emma and Mackenzie had shown up at his cabin earlier today with new pink sheets for Ruby's bed and the contents now spilling from the bin. Luc would never have thought of the small touches until too late. His sisters had saved the day. Ruby had noticed the stuffed bunny, brightly colored books and smattering of toys right away and been delighted by the finds.

"This one." She slid back under the covers.

Luc read *The Story of Ferdinand*—a bull who preferred to smell flowers over fighting. Which, pathetically, only reminded him of Cate, because: flowers.

"Your dad's a real sap, Rubes."

She patted him lightly on the cheek. "Good boy."

He closed the book and said a bedtime prayer, then pushed up from the floor, body complaining.

"I'll be right out here in the living room." He paused in her doorway. "I'll leave the door open, okay?"

She nodded, but the lurking sadness in her eyes slayed him.

Luc dropped onto the sofa, elbows on his knees, head in his hands. He hadn't realized how hard this would be—on Ruby, or on him. Though right now he was far more concerned about her.

Should he call Cate? Have her talk to Ruby? He wanted their daughter to feel safe and happy, not worried and anxious. Luc could ask Emma for help. She'd know what to do. But he didn't want to talk to his sister right now. The woman he wanted to communicate with had blocked him out of her life, and he wasn't sure how to worm his way back in.

Cate might not want to hear from him, but if it was about Ruby, he had the right to call, didn't he?

Before he could overthink anymore, he snagged his phone from the coffee table, found Cate's number and pressed Send. Just hearing her voice would be worth it. And she'd never be bothered about a phone call over Ruby. If there was one constant about Cate, it was the way she loved their daughter. If only that sentiment could be transferred over to him also.

"Luc?" His name held a multitude of questions and concern, so he answered before she could tumble down the mama-bear slope.

"Ruby's fine."

"Oh, good." Her relief practically oozed through the phone in his hand. A beat of silence stretched, and he pictured Cate refilling her lungs. Tense shoulders lowering. The woman was over-the-top protective of Ruby. Like one of those news stories about a mother lifting a car off her child—Cate could manage that with her pinkie finger if any harm came Ruby's way. "So what's up?"

"Ruby misses you. I did my best with her, but I'm just not sure it's enough. When we did the campout, I think she was comforted because you were minutes away and I could bring her home to you at any time. But now I think she's just overwhelmed by the changes." Luc could sympathize with that. He didn't like them, either. He would much rather be back to sleeping in the spare bedroom at the house and have Cate here. Or, even better, be able to call Cate his wife and all live in the same place.

"My reception isn't perfect, but I caught most of that. Do you need me to come?"

How should he answer? If it was up to him, yes. He wanted her here—for him and for Ruby. But he didn't want to disrupt her night alone, either. Maybe she had plans.

"I don't know," he answered honestly.

"Lucas." The sound of his full name warmed him. "I

prayed a ton this week about Ruby staying at the ranch with you." He pieced her words together through the spotty reception. Where was she? Not at her apartment, if he had to guess. "And I really think God is going to work it out. Ruby's going to be just fine, whether I come or not."

Tension fled his body with Cate's encouragement. She was right. Ruby would be okay either way.

"Is it just Ruby who needs me?" Cate's question was so quiet, he almost missed it. And then Luc was certain he'd misheard. How could she even ask something like that?

He needed Cate like oxygen. Or land under his boots. *Catherine Malory, if I tell you I love you one more time and you don't accept it as the truth, I'm going to lose my ever-loving mind.*

A knock sounded on his door. Faint, but noticeable.

"Hang on a sec." Luc was thankful for the interruption. The time to know how to answer her if he had heard right. Because he didn't think yelling his thoughts from a moment ago would be the best option.

He swung the front door open to find Cate on the step. His hand—the phone still in it—slid down to his hip.

"What are you doing here? How did you get here so fast?"

She wore jeans that hugged her legs and brown leather sandals. A white shirt with dainty polka dots. Her hair framed her face and bright, vulnerable eyes that shone in the outside cabin light. The sight of her stole the moisture from Luc's mouth.

One shoulder lifted. "I was already on the way."

Bird wings fought for release from the confines of his chest. "To see Ruby?"

"No." A timid smile claimed her lips. "To see you."

Shock gripped him. He stood there silent, a thousand thoughts flying through his mind at once.

"Can I come in?"

A nod would have to suffice since his voice had gone missing.

Cate walked to Ruby's bedroom as Luc latched the door. She disappeared inside for a few seconds, then returned to the couch and sat. "Ruby's asleep." She looked at him expectantly.

Again mute, he followed, sinking onto the sofa.

"Lucas, I'm so sorry I didn't believe you about the custody papers. That I didn't trust you right away. I do now."

The calmly said statements detonated, creating a roaring in his head. What did that mean? She wasn't exactly confessing her love for him. Was it just about Ruby for her? About them getting along for their daughter's sake?

"What changed your mind? Did you read Gage's note?" His friend had been factual but convincing, backing up Luc's story.

"No." She dug into her purse, handing him the still-sealed envelope. "I didn't need to. I already knew the truth. I'd just been denying it. I had lunch with Emma today." Luc hadn't known they were planning to meet. "And she said some things I needed to hear. But mostly confirmed what I didn't want to admit. Because then I'd have to confess that I love you, and I could get hurt. So could Ruby."

Cate kept going as if she hadn't just said three words that rocked his whole world.

"Choosing us...it's messy. Our relationship doesn't come with guarantees. And that's scary for me. Especially with what I grew up witnessing. But I don't want to let my parents' decisions control me anymore. So I'm letting faith win. I choose to believe you for—" she swallowed "—the rest of our lives, if you'll have me." She leaned forward, earnest. "Because, for Ruby's sake, we're either committed forever or nothing at all. I won't do that to her. And if you're not ready for that, that's okay. But those are my terms."

If he'd have her? *If?*

Those big, beautiful eyes of hers stared into his as her fingers squeezed his arm. "Lucas, can you forgive me for not believing you?"

"Do you think you can trust me in the future?"

Strength and peace radiated from her. "Yes."

"There's your answer."

Luc tugged Cate closer. He couldn't find the words he wanted—they'd all fled the moment he'd opened the door to find her standing there—so he kissed her. For all of the moments that had gone before and for the future. One he already impatiently couldn't wait for.

Cate's arms wound around his neck. Hearing she loved him back drowned Luc in contentment. In bliss. It was a tie with finding out about Ruby. And in a month and a half, he'd gone from not having either of them to having both.

Thank You, God.

Luc made himself pull away from her captivating lips, knowing that if he had his way, kissing Cate would be a full-time job. He didn't go far—their arms were still tangled up like a jumbled pile of extra electrical cords. Considering Luc never wanted to let go, the next few years could get awkward.

Cate's eyebrows shot up. "So? You never responded to everything I said."

That kiss wasn't enough of an answer for her? Luc

grinned, fighting the desire to meet her adorable, questioning mouth again. She'd offered him forever—all or nothing—and he definitely had an answer for that.

"If that was a proposal, I accept."

Epilogue

Catherine Wilder needed to find her husband. Pronto. She'd scoured the cabin and lodge for him when she returned from town twenty minutes ago but had yet to catch sight of his maple cropped hair and strong shoulders.

Ones that would need to stay sturdy for the news she was about to share with him.

The red barn loomed up, reaching for the clear, crisp Colorado sky. Last place she knew to check.

She stepped inside, letting her eyes adjust to less light and cinching her red winter jacket with a fur hood tight around her to battle the biting air.

A crash sounded, and she followed it through the barn to the storage area behind.

Luc wrestled a stack of sleds into submission, hanging them on hooks that had been ignored by whoever had used the plastic saucers last.

His movements were quick. Precise. Of course, Luc was overqualified to be organizing sleds, but she imagined he'd come by, seen the mess and gotten to work.

She liked that about him. She liked a lot of things about her husband.

Cate and Luc had married a month after she'd shown up at the ranch for the second time in a small ceremony at the little white church they attended. Ruby had switched to a local preschool, where she only attended mornings and spent the rest of her day tagging along with Luc, Cate or one of her aunts. Their girl was delighted by her new life, as was her mama.

Approaching behind Luc, Cate wrapped her arms around his middle. Taut stomach muscles greeted her when she squeezed.

"Hey." His hands covered hers, returning the hug as he glanced over his shoulder, eyes alight. Luc turned, switching so that she was wrapped up in his arms. Pretty much the best place to be in the whole wide world.

He kissed her hello. It was likely meant to be short and sweet. A greeting. But it quickly morphed into something more. Cate lost herself for a minute, just because she could, then inched back while remaining in his embrace.

"Stop distracting me. I have something to tell you."

Luc's nose wrinkled with disgust. "I don't like that command."

She laughed. Held his face in her hands. "Focus."

"That I can do, Mrs. Wilder."

Whenever he called her that—and it was a lot—her stomach leaped and danced and threw a party. If Cate had known she could be this happy, she would never have wasted all of those years without Luc in her life.

He wasn't the answer to all life's problems, and they still had off moments, but they always came back to each other with love and figured out whatever tried to mess with them. And it wasn't much. Mostly, the transition from single parenting to a family of three had gone better than she'd ever imagined.

A good thing, considering what she had to tell him.

"I had my doctor's appointment this morning."

Cate had been feeling off. More tired than normal. So she'd gone to the doctor, just to make sure everything was okay.

"How was it? What did Dr. Sanderson say?"

"He said I do have something going on." She was toying with him a bit, but she couldn't help having a little fun. After all, she'd been reeling from the news for the last hour.

"What's wrong?" Luc tucked her hair back, eyes full of concern. "Is it something we can fix? Is he giving you something to help?"

"He is. Prenatal vitamins." Cate still couldn't believe she was pregnant when they'd taken precautions to make sure that didn't happen immediately. She and Luc definitely wanted more kids, but they'd planned to wait a bit. Give everyone time to adjust.

So much for that.

She'd asked the doctor, *"Are there ever people precautions just don't work for?"* Because if that was anyone's story, it was hers and Luc's. She should have known better. Expected it even.

He'd replied, *"Sometimes. Mostly, I think God just laughs at us, thinking we're so in control down here. He likes to remind us that, ultimately, we're not."*

Cate was gathering that message loud and clear.

Luc had morphed into a statue. He blinked slowly, numerous times. "What did you say?"

"I said he wants me to take a specific kind of prenatal vitamin for the babies."

Cate tamped down on her still-in-shock smile begging for release. She'd walked around town in a daze after her appointment, coming to terms with Dr. Sanderson's revelation that they were having twins.

The doctor had tried to determine how far along Cate was based on her cycle, but she'd been quite distracted lately and unable to fill in the dates he'd requested. Next thing she knew, he'd had her prepped for an ultrasound. Turned out, Dr. Sanderson did all of the health care in this town, from pregnant mama to the elderly. And lo and behold, two sacs had been visible. Cate totally wanted to blame Luc and Mackenzie for the development, but Dr. Sanderson had pointed out that an increased likelihood for fraternal twins was only hereditary on the mother's side, and identical twins were purely from chance.

"But I thought we weren't...that couldn't... Did you say *babies*?" Luc put emphasis on the *s*.

"That's what I thought, too. And yes, as in plural. Twins."

His head shook, eyes crinkling and shining with moisture. And then he laughed, elation spilling from him. Cate had known it would be okay—that Luc would be supportive, possibly even excited. But she hadn't expected this reaction.

Suddenly, her feet flew off the ground. Luc had swept her up in a hug and now swung her around in a circle. "You are amazing." He let her down slowly, her lined winter boots meeting solid ground.

She wasn't sure why she deserved the credit for getting pregnant whenever Luc so much as glanced in her direction, but she chuckled at his boy-like delight. As if suddenly realizing the babies were already there with them, Luc reverently touched her stomach. He knelt and began talking to them.

He told them how much he loved their mother. Moisture filled her eyes. How much he loved their sister. One tear slipped free, quickly followed by more. And then he told them they were all going to be together. Forever.

A small hiccup escaped.

Luc rose to his full height, tenderness in his touch as he thumbed moisture from her cheeks. "What's wrong? Why are you crying?"

"I don't know." But she knew pieces of it. "How are we going to handle two babies at once? And where will we live? And—"

"My sisters already offered us the house and we refused. Now we accept. They'll take the cabin and be perfectly fine. And there's two of us. Plus Emma and Mackenzie. You'll have a village of help this time. You won't be on your own."

His words should have induced guilt, but they didn't anymore. Luc had forgiven her so completely for not telling him about Ruby that there wasn't even a hint of malice in his statement. Cate had never experienced such a deep, abiding, freely given love from another human before. Not dependent on her behavior. Because if it was, she wouldn't be standing here face-to-face with the man she loved.

"You're right." She motioned to her cheeks and the flash of tears that had now ceased. "When I found out, I may have panicked. Just a touch."

His grin eased into play. "I think that's understandable. I'm sorry I didn't go with you to the appointment. I should have." He drew her close, holding her snug against his chest. "We're going to be just fine, Mrs. Wilder."

"I love you, Lucas." The declaration was muffled by his jacket, but she knew he'd heard by the tight squeeze that followed.

He pulled back enough for their gazes to meet. "I love you, too." A gentle kiss landed on her forehead. "So much that I'm not sure how I ever survived without you." The emotion of his statement coupled with what was to come, the wide-open future, the unexpected gift of more *babies*, all with this man...it crashed into her, almost making her sway.

Thankfully, Luc held her steady. Just like he always did.

* * * * *